OUTSTANDI[NG]
SEAN McF[ATE AND] TH[E]
TOM LOCKE SERIES

HIGH TREASON

"McFate just might be the next Tom Clancy, only I think he's even better. . . . The action is nonstop and shuttles back and forth between scary-believable and rollicking good fun. I read *High Treason* during a six-hour plane ride and the trip went by like the snap of my fingers."

—James Patterson

"*High Treason* has brutal assassinations, shocking betrayals, even heated gun battles in the shadow of the White House. It had me breathless—from the sheer audacity of its storytelling to its breakneck pacing. It's not to be missed!"

—James Rollins, author of *The Last Odyssey*

"A pulse-pounding, suspense-filled ride. . . . Fans of Tom Clancy or Brad Thor will certainly find the world that Sean McFate has created to be an exciting and familiar one. . . . Like the escapism of a great action movie. . . . Exceptional sense of pacing . . ."

—TheNerdDaily.com

"Plenty of political intrigue and is action packed. . . . Tom Locke is a hero people can get behind. . . . He and Lin make a good team and will remind readers of Brad Taylor's Pike Logan and Jennifer Cahill."

—*Crimespree Magazine*

"A realistic tour through political intrigue mixed with plenty of excitement from the frontline operators."

—*Kirkus Reviews*

"A firestorm of action scenes. . . . It's all done with such energy and skill."

—*Booklist*

"McFate knows his way around bold, riveting stories, fascinating characters, and ground-level combat that are sure to please fans of Brad Thor, Tom Clancy, and Daniel Silva."

—Mark Greaney, author of *One Minute Out*

DEEP BLACK

"Locke is another strong hero in the growing subgenre of black-ops thrillers, and *Deep Black* is a maze of treachery and intrigue to the very end."

—Booklist Online

"Has an enjoyable, realistic feeling . . . will appeal to action junkies and armchair diplomats alike."

—*Kirkus Reviews*

SHADOW WAR

"*Shadow War* has pace like a catapult, sudden and fierce, and it will hit readers straight between the eyes."

—Ted Bell, author of *Dragon Fire*

"Wars produce warriors. Some, like special-operator-turned-mercenary Tom Locke, find it a curious calling that pulls them into the darkest of nights and most dangerous of places. *Shadow War* brings all of it to life in fascinating detail."

—General Stanley A. McChrystal

"For Black Ops and lots of military action, join Tom Locke for an exciting, wild ride."

—Catherine Coulter, author of *Deadlock*

"Intelligent, funny, gritty, Ferrari-paced—at times even electric."

—Ben Coes, author of *The Russian*

"An American James Bond meets the twists and turns of *Homeland*."

—Admiral James Stavridis (Ret.),
Supreme Allied Commander at NATO

"A gripping journey inside the world of modern warfare and espionage, and those who enjoy a good military thriller will be hoping that more Tom Locke adventures will follow quickly."

—*Booklist*

"With experience inside the elite 82nd Airborne Division and work as a private contractor, McFate knows the world of his first thriller intimately. . . . The novel provides plenty of drama and a realistic view of political intrigue, and McFate really shines with lines that ring with authenticity. . . . A promising debut from an author who clearly knows the realities of the mercenary's trade."

—*Kirkus Reviews*

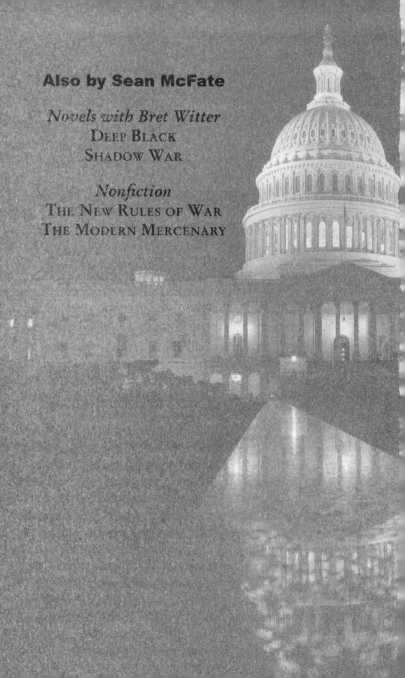

Also by Sean McFate

Novels with Bret Witter
DEEP BLACK
SHADOW WAR

Nonfiction
THE NEW RULES OF WAR
THE MODERN MERCENARY

HIGH TREASON

A Novel

SEAN McFATE

WILLIAM MORROW

An Imprint of HarperCollinsPublishers

This is a work of fiction. Names, characters, places, and incidents are products of the author's imagination or are used fictitiously and are not to be construed as real. Any resemblance to actual events, locales, organizations, or persons, living or dead, is entirely coincidental.

HIGH TREASON. Copyright © 2020 by Sean McFate. All rights reserved. Printed in the United States of America. No part of this book may be used or reproduced in any manner whatsoever without written permission except in the case of brief quotations embodied in critical articles and reviews. For information, address HarperCollins Publishers, 195 Broadway, New York, NY 10007.

First William Morrow mass market printing: May 2021
First William Morrow hardcover printing: June 2020

Print Edition ISBN: 978-0-06-284366-1
Digital Edition ISBN: 978-0-06-284367-8

Title page photo © Shutterstock, Orhan Cam
Cover design by Pete Garceau
Cover photographs © ninjaMonkeyStudio/iStock/Getty Images (Capitol);
© Tim Robinson/Trevillion Images (man)

William Morrow and HarperCollins are registered trademarks of HarperCollins Publishers in the United States of America and other countries.

21 22 23 24 25   CPI   10 9 8 7 6 5 4 3 2 1

If you purchased this book without a cover, you should be aware that this book is stolen property. It was reported as "unsold and destroyed" to the publisher, and neither the author nor the publisher has received any payment for this "stripped book."

To those who defend our democracy
against Potomac fever.

"Plan your enterprises cautiously . . .
carry them out boldly."

Sir Geoffroy de Charny
From *A Knight's Own Book of Chivalry* (c. 1350)

CHAPTER 1

"Goddammit!" said the vice president, hanging up the phone and sinking back into bed.

"What is it, love?" asked his wife, still wearing pink eye shades.

"That was the White House. They want me to attend the prayer breakfast."

Silence.

"Apparently," he continued, "the president is 'sick.'"

"Again?"

"Yeah."

"God help him," she said, rolling over to check the time. "We only have an hour."

"Actually, less. The Secret Service said we need to leave in twenty minutes."

She pulled the covers over her head. "Well, I'm sick, too! You're going to have to pray solo, mister."

Henry Strickland smiled. They had been playing this game for forty years, she trying to lure him back into bed to play. He trying not to be late for work. He was late a lot.

"Martha, you know you have to join me, and we can't be late," he said, lumbering out of bed.

"Not on your life," said a voice under the covers.

"Duty before pleasure, and country before politics."

"Oh God, you're serious. You're really going to make me go."

"Amen," he said, walking into a closet of monochromatic blue suits and white shirts. "Now, what should I wear?"

The motorcade left the vice president's front door precisely twenty minutes later. The 1890s white-brick mansion sat in the middle of the U.S. Naval Observatory, ten acres of premium land in the middle of Washington, DC, but you would never know it. Somehow the designers had hidden it among a thistle of buildings, trees, and asphalt that constituted the nation's capital.

"Honey, you're crowding me," said Martha, as she applied makeup with one hand while holding a compact mirror in the other. Across from the vice president sat an attractive woman, half their age.

"Sir, your speech," said the young aide, handing him a folder. "I've taken the liberty of modifying the president's speech to fit your style."

"Thank you," he said, flipping open the file. His lips moved as he read, and he scribbled in the margins. Every year the National Prayer Breakfast was held at the Washington Hilton Hotel on Connecticut Avenue. The Secret Service nicknamed it the "Hinckley Hilton" because it was where a mentally disturbed John Hinckley shot Ronald Reagan in 1981. His reason? To impress actress Jodie Foster, with whom he had an obsession. Threats lurk everywhere.

Martha sat next to him, brushing rouge on her cheeks. Both ignored the sirens and flashing blue lights surrounding them. A logistical symphony, the thirty vehicles wound through the grounds of the U.S. Naval Observatory.

"Mongoose, this is Pilot," a voice crackled over the motorcade's radio network. "Mongoose" was the convoy commander and "Pilot" was the lead vehicle, each in an armored Chevy Suburban.

"Copy," replied Mongoose.

"Linking up with the Route car." A Washington, DC, police cruiser awaited the motorcade at the front gate, its lights blazing. Once it spotted the black SUVs, it flipped on its siren and sped up Thirty-Fourth Street, toward the National Cathedral, clearing rush hour traffic for the motorcade.

"Approaching Cleveland Avenue, now," said Pilot over the radio. Other black SUVs followed, while four Harley-Davidson police motorcycles, or "sweepers," zoomed ahead to block intersections and get cars out of the way. Normally the police would have closed the streets, but today's motorcade was last-minute and the morning rush hour particularly stubborn. The motorcade slithered through the traffic like a black snake.

The man called Mongoose looked like a college wrestler who had abandoned his weight class long ago but still moved like a champion. He checked his watch: 0736. On time.

"Mongoose, Stagecoach has cleared the gate," radioed the driver of the vice president's limousine, code-named Stagecoach. If a Cadillac STS and an up-armored Hummer mated, they would produce a presidential limo. The Secret Service dubbed it "the Beast," and it was battle proof. The windows could withstand armor-piercing bullets, and the body was made of a steel and titanium composite, like a tank. Each door was eight inches thick and weighed more than the fuselage door of a Boeing 757 jet. A reinforced five-inch steel plate ran under the car, shielding it from roadside bombs. The tires were a specially woven Kevlar, allowing the Beast to drive over spikes. If the tires were blasted away, it could escape at speed on steel rims. The fuel tank was encased in foam that prevented it from exploding, even if it suffered a direct hit. The limo was equipped with night vision cameras so it could drive in the dark, and the cabin was sealed with its own air supply in the event of a gas attack or the vehicle plunged into water. It even had a supply of the vice president's blood type on board. The Beast was a mobile bunker with a leather interior and a shiny black paint job.

The Beast wasn't alone. The convoy had three of them, and they weaved in and out of traffic together, playing a game of three-car monte to conceal the vice president.

"Jesus!" said Martha as the limo hit a pothole, causing a mascara smudge.

"Honey, you look fine," said Henry, without lifting his eyes from the speech.

The motorcade sped through red lights and intersections without stopping, the sweepers keeping traffic at bay.

"Mongoose, this is Pilot. We're approaching the Calvert Street bridge, but there's heavy congestion."

"Where, exactly?" asked Mongoose.

"A block before the bridge, at the intersection of Calvert and Connecticut Avenue."

"How heavy?"

"We're rolling to a stop."

Not good, thought Mongoose. Seconds later, the entire convoy eased to a standstill in a narrow two-lane street. The first law of motorcade operations: Never Stop. He picked up the radio handset, "Sweepers, clear the traffic."

Police motorcycles sped around them, their riders waving furiously at stopped cars. Cars nosed closer to the curb, but not enough to let the motorcade pass. It was no use. Traffic was backed up for blocks, and the motorcade was engulfed. Behind Mongoose sat the three presidential limos, wedged in between more black SUVs and civilian cars. Cars honked, being late for work.

"We've stopped. Is something wrong?" asked Martha.

"It's just a little traffic," said Henry, still fixated on his speech. The aide sat attentively across from him, an open laptop on her knees.

Unconvinced, Martha looked out the window. Upscale apartments lined the streets, sandwiched between big hotels, the kind that hold enormous conventions.

Mongoose furled his brow.

"There's gridlock in every direction," said Pilot.

"What's going on?" asked Mongoose.

"There's a three-car accident in the intersection, and it's obstructing traffic in all travel lanes." One car's trunk was crumpled, another car's right front smashed in, and a third was squashed in between them. Crushed glass and liquid covered the road; deflated air bags stuck out of car doors. The occupants sat on opposite curbs, glowering at each other as an angry fire truck, also stuck in the traffic, blasted its horn in the distance.

"Are emergency vehicles on-site? Tow trucks?"

"Negative. It looks like it just happened, but no one is seriously hurt."

"Shit," Mongoose muttered, startling the driver next to him.

"Everything OK, boss?" asked his driver, a former Marine still sporting a military high-and-tight haircut.

No, Mongoose thought. *Something isn't right.* He knew the area well, having driven these blocks and this bridge more times than he cared to admit while serving three presidents in twenty years. Gridlock was common during Washington rush hour, as were accidents. But they didn't happen on this stretch of road. Not at this time of day, and not just as a motorcade was passing through. There were no coincidences in this line of work.

It could be an ambush, thought Mongoose, scanning the tree-lined sidewalks. The last time his instincts pinged this hard was just before his platoon was attacked by the Taliban in Wanat, an armpit of a place in far eastern Afghanistan. He lost two friends that day. His thinking was the same then as now: *Get out of the kill zone! Get off the X!*

"Can we take the Connecticut Avenue bridge?" he asked.

"Negative. Accident traffic has backed it up, too," said Pilot.

Mongoose turned to his driver. "Can we make a U-turn here?"

"*We* could, sir, but the Beast would never clear it."

Mongoose leaned forward on the dashboard, gauging the lane to their left. The accident had blocked opposing traffic, so it was clear, but his driver was right. The limo's length was longer than the lane's width, making a U-turn difficult but not impossible.

"Stagecoach, can you execute a U-turn?" he asked over the radio.

There was a pause. "It would take a twenty-point turn. Maybe a few minutes."

Too long, Mongoose thought, *and too exposed.* The only thing worse than being stuck in traffic was having the limo perpendicular to it, with no easy escape. It would make a perfect target for a broadside, something a clever ambush team could engineer using a fake traffic accident. There was only one way out—forward.

"Pilot, Sweepers," Mongoose said. "We need to get the Package moving. Make a hole." The "Package" was the vice president.

"Copy," voices crackled over the network. Two black SUVs darted into the left lane and sped toward the accident. The sweepers directed surrounding traffic to inch away from the travel lane. A fire truck, an ambulance, and a tow truck arrived simultaneously.

"Tow truck on-site," said Pilot.

"Clear the intersection!" said Mongoose. Firemen helped connect the tow truck cable to one of the wrecked vehicles.

"Clear!" yelled one of the firemen, and the tow truck driver pulled a lever. The tow cable went instantly taught, and dragged one of the wrecks out of the intersection. Metal screeched on pavement, adding to the din of distant sirens and honks.

"Sir, ten o'clock," said Mongoose's driver, still sitting in front of the stationary limos. Two burly men moved briskly down the sidewalk opposite them. Each man was wearing a bulky overcoat and carrying a briefcase. It was February, so outerwear was normal. However, they walked like soldiers, not lawyers.

"Eyes on ten o'clock," said Mongoose over the radio, alerting the convoy to the possible threat.

"Seven o'clock," someone said on the radio. Behind them, walking in the opposite direction, were two women in running clothes and pushing baby strollers. Each stroller's bassinet was covered to keep the baby warm. Or conceal enough Semtex explosives to breach the Beast. The limo's top was its least armored area. The blast could kill the occupants, and maybe that was their mission.

"All vehicles, cover down on the Package," said Mongoose. Multiple black SUVs lurched through the traffic and surrounded the three limos, encasing them behind a wall of armored Chevies.

"Finished!" Martha exclaimed. "At least the traffic gave me a chance to look good."

"You look spectacular, dear," said Henry without looking up.

"Sir, perhaps this would be a good opportunity to mention the trade tariffs the president is pushing," said the young aide.

"At a prayer breakfast? Don't you think that's a little inappropriate?"

"No."

"OK, let's see if I can work it in."

The two men with briefcases continued to walk toward the baby strollers. Mongoose zoomed his binoculars on the men's overcoats. Did they have bulges under the armpits, concealing weapons? What was in those briefcases? Did they look heavy?

"Sir, above," said the driver, nodding in the direction of a second-story open window directly across from them. "It just opened."

"Unusual to open windows in winter," said Mongoose, training his binoculars on the windows, but saw nothing inside. "It's a perfect overwatch position for heavy weapons."

"Affirmative," said the driver, tenseness in his voice.

"Honey, how long are we going to sit here?" asked Martha. "We should be there by now. We're going to be late."

Henry looked up, as if lifted from a spell. "Tony, what's the matter? Why can't we get around this traffic?" Secret Service Agent Tony Russo sat in the front seat and was a combat vet, like Mongoose.

"There's an accident ahead, sir. Traffic is blocked in every direction, but we should be moving shortly," he said unpersuasively.

Mongoose saw a shadow move behind the open window. Below, the businessmen were approaching the women pushing baby strollers, about to converge across from the Beast. The timing was too perfect.

The life of a Secret Service agent is like a cop's. Duty is years of routine boredom, interspersed by seconds of absolute terror, when everything can go wrong. Poor judgment or slow reaction time is the difference between the quick and the dead. Now was such a moment for Mongoose.

"Dismount, but do not draw," Mongoose ordered. SUV doors opened, and Secret Service agents exited and stood behind their vehicle for cover, hands on holsters.

Martha leaned forward with concern. "Tony, what's going on?"

"It's probably nothing, ma'am," he said. "Just doing our job."

"I hate being late. How long will we be stuck here?"

"I'm sure we'll be moving soon. Once we cross the bridge, it's just five minutes to the Hilton."

Martha sat back and unconsciously chewed on a knuckle while looking out the window at the agents, hunched behind the SUVs. The doors facing the limo were open and she could see stacks of M4 carbines and smoke grenades lying on the passenger seats. She had never seen this before.

"Henry, take a look," she whispered to her husband, gesturing at the weapons.

"It's a good time for prayer," mused Henry. "Maybe I can work this into my speech, too."

She thwacked him with her hand. "This is no time for jokes!"

Mongoose sat in the vehicle in front of them, binoculars shifting between the men, the strollers, and the open window. *Steady,* he thought. *Just keep walking, everyone.*

"Sir, should we apprehend them?" asked the driver.

"Negative. Just let them pass," Mongoose said. He had to be sure. This wasn't Afghanistan; it was Washington, DC.

"Sweepers, status?" asked Mongoose.

"We've almost cleared a hole," said Pilot. The tow truck was dragging the carcass of the last vehicle out of the travel lane, leaving a trail of green shattered glass and radiator fluid.

"ETA, Pilot?"

"One minute."

Too long, thought Mongoose. The two men slowed slightly as they approached the women. If there was an ambush, it would happen now.

"Get ready," said Mongoose over the radio. The agents tensed up, hands still on weapons and ready for a quick draw.

One man nodded to the women, who ignored him. All kept walking. No movement in the window.

Mongoose exhaled loudly. "Stand down. Stand down. All teams, stand down."

"Sir, look," said his driver. Traffic was creeping forward.

"Mongoose, we've cleared a hole," said Pilot.

"Move out!" Mongoose ordered. Agents scurried back into vehicles, and the motorcade accelerated around the traffic, sirens blaring.

Thank God, thought Mongoose, heart still pounding inside his rib cage. *Now to cross the bridge and get to the Hinckley Hilton. Five minutes, tops.*

"See, honey, I told you it was nothing to worry about," said Henry.

"We're going to be late."

"No, we're not. They're just early," he said with a grin, handing the speech back to the aide.

Henry felt the blast wave through the Beast and saw the traffic ahead of them geyser upward, toward the heavens. A millisecond later, the *BOOM* of a colossal explosion threw him backward as the monstrous limo lifted off the ground and pointed into the blue sky. All the bulletproof windows spider-cracked as debris flailed the vehicle. Then the sickening fall. Henry felt weightless as they descended through the hole where the road should have been. Dozens of vehicles and pedestrians fell 130 feet to the gorge floor, crushing everyone below. The massive 1930s bridge imploded on top of them. Several tons of stone and steel buried the survivors alive.

CHAPTER 2

Halfway around the world, I was finishing my daily run on the white beach of Tel Aviv.

Maximum effort! I thought, breaking into a mad sprint. *One hundred meters to go!* Seagulls flew out of my way as I splashed down the sand.

Warp speed! I commanded, lungs burning. I shot past my personal finish line: a cartoonish nine-foot statue of David Ben-Gurion doing a headstand on the sand. Slowing to a trot, I checked my time. Five miles in thirty-five minutes. Not bad. I walked for another ten minutes, cooling down. Tel Aviv has one of the nicest beaches in the world, if you don't mind the Apache helicopters buzzing overhead.

"Shalom," I said, ambling into Lala Land, my favorite beachside bar. I was a regular, and my tahini-fruit shake awaited me.

"Shalom, Tom," said the bartender.

I had been on the run for a year now, ever since I got sucked into a Saudi palace coup d'etat and ten stolen nukes. The coup was foiled, but the nukes were never found. Since then, the Kingdom had placed a million-dollar bounty on me, and no place was safe. Except maybe Israel. Doomed to spend the rest of my life on the run made me angry, and it was all because of one man.

Brad Winters, I thought, and shivered despite the Mediterranean heat. He was my former mentor at Apollo Outcomes, a powerful private military corporation. Apollo was a covert world power unto itself, and Winters was its sovereign. He betrayed me and left my team for dead, so I returned the courtesy. Last I knew, he was beheaded in Riyadh for his role in the failed coup. I wish I could have been there. He was dead, but somehow I wasn't free of what he'd done.

"Can you turn on the news?" I asked the bartender. Everyone spoke English in Tel Aviv. They also spoke Russian, French, Arabic, and, of course, Hebrew. The place made me feel like an underachiever.

"Sure thing," he said, and flicked on the TV above the bar. The news was in Hebrew and showed Palestinians throwing Molotov cocktails at Israeli troops, who fired back tear gas and then live ammunition. People died. It looked like a foreign warzone, but it was only forty-five miles away.

"English, please," I said, slurping my smoothie, and he found an American cable news channel.

"Another?" asked the bartender, pointing to my empty mug.

"Sure," I said. "Throw in more tahini and mint this time."

"Tom!" said a voice behind me. "I thought I'd find you here."

"Ari!" I replied.

"Goldstar, please," he said, and the bartender slid him a beer.

Colonel Ari Roth was a gaunt man of average height. Drinking while in uniform was normal in Israel, but Roth's uniform was not. He wore a standard infantry of-

ficer's insignia with lackluster ribbons. In reality, he was
a commando in the Sayeret Matkal, the Israel Defense
Forces' most elite unit. It was comparable to the U.S.'s
Delta Force or SEAL Team Six. Like Israel's nuclear
weapons program, Sayeret Matkal didn't officially exist
(hence Ari's misleading uniform) but everyone knew
about it, and called it "the Unit."

"You're off early," I joked. "What's the matter? Run
out of terrorists to kill in Syria?"

"I wish," he said, taking a long swig from the bottle.
"It's shabbat and even we sometimes get time off."
Shabbat was the weekly holy day, or sabbath, and Israel
shuts down.

"If they're giving you time off, it means they've got
a nasty suicide mission waiting for you," I said with a
smirk. "Bartender, get this man drunk. He dines in hell
tomorrow!"

Ari waved off the bartender with a smile. "No, seriously. It's just time off."

Members of the Unit don't get time off, I thought.

"Yeah, we get time off," he said, as if reading my
mind. "You have a horrible poker face, Locke."

"Dammit! Bartender, give me a double scotch, no ice.
Enough of the fruit shakes. They're making me soft."

"To time off," he said, grinning and holding up his
beer.

"To being on the run," I said, clinking my tumbler.

"Not the same thing."

I had been sleeping on Ari's couch for the past year.
We met as captains in early 1998, when the U.S. Army
deployed my Green Beret team to Haifa. Saddam Hus-
sein was threatening to attack Israel with SCUD missiles, and the U.S. secretly sent a Patriot missile unit to

blow the SCUDs out of the sky. My mission was to keep the Patriots safe, and so was Ari's.

Now I was a mercenary on the lam, and he was a colonel behind a desk. We had both seen finer days. He spent most of his waking hours at Mossad's headquarters, which was nicknamed the "cinema complex" because it was oddly adjacent to a mega-movie theater in north Tel Aviv. Not exactly a secret location.

The TV cut to breaking news. A bridge had collapsed in central Washington, DC, and black smoke plumed into the sky. Vehicles lay lifeless on a valley floor, surrounded by dozens of fire trucks. Rescue workers were pulling bodies out of the rubble, and sniffer dogs worked the site.

"Hey, bartender, can you please turn it up?"

". . . bigger than just a terrorist attack. It's also the most significant political assassination since JFK," said a TV talking head wearing a bow tie.

The beach bar went silent and all heads turned to the multiple TV displays. Many Israelis had family in the United States. The news helicopter zoomed in on several black SUVs, burning in the wreckage. The rear end of a black limo stuck out of the debris upright, like a sinking ship frozen in its descent. Firemen were struggling to cut it open but couldn't because of its armored skin.

"That's a presidential motorcade," I said to Ari.

"Was," he corrected me. "That *was* a presidential motorcade."

". . . it's the work of radical Islamic terrorists," said another pundit, who looked too young to shave. The screen showed people chanting "DEATH TO AMERICA!" outside U.S. embassies across the Middle East and Pakistan.

"Looks like Washington is undergoing its own intifada," said Ari.

"Now joining us is our all-star panel of experts," said the woman news anchor. Three pundits appeared on-screen looking a mixture of despondent and pompous. One was a retired general with a stone face, another a professor wearing a bow tie, and the third was a think tank expert who looked twelve. They began bickering immediately.

". . . it seems that the terrorists had been planning this for a long time," said the bow tie. The news showed more live shots of the destroyed bridge.

"Terrorists didn't do that," I whispered.

"What?" said Ari.

"Terrorists didn't blow that bridge."

"Then who did?"

"Apollo Outcomes. They blew it, and made it look like terrorists did it."

"Mercenaries? You must be joking." He chuckled, then went silent in thought. "A false flag operation. It's possible, if they are very, *very* good. Why do you think so?"

"Because I conducted these same ops for Apollo for years. In other countries, of course. I would recognize their operational signature anywhere. We would blow bridges, crash planes, stage deadly car accidents, and arrange heart attacks. We made it look natural or framed another party, otherwise it wouldn't be covert."

Ari paused, then downed his beer with a shrug. When he was done, he let out a belch. "I'm always shocked how much that stuff is outsourced now."

"More than you know."

Ari screwed up his face in puzzlement. "I thought

Apollo Outcomes was an American company that carried out the U.S. government's dirty work. I thought it was an exclusive relationship. Why would Apollo assassinate the vice president of the United States?"

I stared at the bridge carcass and the crushed cars, and was angry. "I don't know, but I intend to find out."

CHAPTER 3

Jennifer Lin stared at the TV screen, hand over her gaping mouth, and watched the live news coverage. The daughter of poor Chinese immigrants, she broke her father's heart when she insisted on joining the FBI instead of going to law school. That was five years ago, and the last time they spoke.

Lin was not alone. Other FBI special agents crowded around the large-screen TV in the break room, coffee breath close. Their collective shock was thick in the air.

LIVE BREAKING NEWS, read a glitzy graphic before it swooshed offscreen, replaced by a young, blond anchorwoman.

"Authorities are calling it the worst terrorist attack on U.S. soil since 9/11. At approximately eight o'clock this morning, the vice president's motorcade was on its way to the National Prayer Breakfast at the Washington Hilton. As it crossed a bridge, the bridge exploded and the entire motorcade fell to the ravine floor, hundreds of feet below. The vice president was pronounced dead at the scene, as was his wife."

"This can't be happening," muttered someone.

"Because it was rush hour, the bridge was crowded," continued the anchorwoman. "Other victims include multiple commuter cars, two crowded buses, and families with children on their way to school."

"Radical Islamic terrorists," said an agent behind Lin, almost spitting. "Gotta be."

"So far, there are around one hundred estimated casualties," continued the news anchor, "but authorities expect the death toll to rise into the hundreds. Let's go live to the bridge."

The screen faded to an aerial view of the carnage, taken from a news helicopter.

"That's the Duke Ellington Bridge over Rock Creek," exclaimed one of the agents. "I took it to work this morning," he added, but no one was listening.

The scene was grisly. Below the chopper lay the remnants of a massive neoclassical bridge, a sickening gap between its two ends. Fire billowed from its ruins, and flashing lights of emergency vehicles lit up the bridge carcass, its graceful aqueduct-like arches broken on the valley floor below. Dozens of cars lay entwined with the bridge wreckage. Trucks were flattened under armored Secret Service SUVs, themselves crushed by massive slabs of concrete and limestone. A DC street bus was shorn in half as rescue workers searched for survivors, carrying the "jaws of life" rescue tool. Worse, the 750-foot bridge collapsed atop another crowded commuter road on the ravine floor below, pulverizing twenty more cars. Then there were the bodies shrouded in plastic sheets.

The news switched to a reporter on the ground, who was sneaking around the fire trucks and moving toward the bridge. The camera jiggled as it followed him. Sirens wailed in the background. He was clearly not supposed to be there.

"Police have cordoned off all traffic around the area, so I am going to try to approach on foot," wheezed the TV reporter, probably thinking of an Emmy Award. Three survivors sat on the ground, wrapped in Red Cross blankets. One woman gently swayed back and forth, holding herself while crying. Perhaps she had lost a loved one. Maybe a child.

"Hello, we're from News Channel Eight," said the journalist while the bright camera light shone in the woman's face. "Could you tell us what you're feeling right now?"

The camera zoomed in. Her eyes were red, and her anguish turned into bafflement, then rage, as the reporter violated her grief.

"Hey you! You're not supposed to be here. Get outta here!" someone yelled offscreen. The camera pivoted to show a policeman moving toward the lens. His meaty hand reached out and violently jerked the camera down. The pavement and the cameraman's foot were the last image shown before the picture went black. The TV control room quickly switched back to the anchor-woman, who looked shaken.

"Now joining us is our all-star panel of experts," she said after a moment, turning to the pundits: a young think tank expert, a professor wearing a bow tie, and a retired general. All were men.

What bullshit, Lin thought. In her five years as an FBI agent, including a year working on an interagency task force, she had learned one thing: national security was a man's game, all the way around.

Last summer she blew a big case in Brooklyn by "accidentally" pummeling a Russian mob boss who had groped her during a sting operation. To be fair, she was posing as a high-end escort, and she had the body for it. But he didn't have permission to touch her. So she broke his arm, a tooth, and two ribs, then put him in an anaconda chokehold before the FBI assault team crashed through the hotel room door and pulled her off. However, they never caught the mobster committing crimes on tape, and they blamed Lin for screwing up the operation. It started her slippery slope to a desk job in Washington.

"This is bigger than just a terrorist attack. It's also the most significant political assassination since JFK," said the academic, leaping in before the news anchor could even ask a question.

"Who's behind it?" asked the news anchor.

"Clearly it's the work of radical Islamic terrorists," said the young think tanker, then rattled off a list of possible terrorist groups that few had ever heard of.

"Concur," interrupted the retired general, gruffly. "We've been picking up chatter for the last few years about plans for a big attack on U.S. soil. ISIS and cousin groups have expressed a desire for a 9/11-type attack to rally the extremist world. This was it."

"Told ya," said one FBI agent. Others nodded. A few had done tours in the Middle East, where the FBI had offices in U.S. embassies.

"Do you think there will be more attacks?" asked the news anchor.

"We must assume so," replied the general.

The pundits sat in silence for a second, as did the break room, absorbing the gravity of the statement. All knew it to be true, but somehow hearing it aloud made it real.

"What is scarier," said the academic pundit, hijack-

ing the conversation again, "is this was an attempted
presidential assassination. The president was sched-
uled to speak at today's prayer breakfast, not the vice
president. The only reason it failed was because the
president canceled at the last minute, sending his VP
instead."

"Indeed," said the think tanker, as if it was his idea.
"Think of the propaganda victory it would have been
for the terrorists, if they had actually assassinated the
president."

The news anchor kept trying to get a word in but
was edged out by the dueling pundits.

"In the nation's capital! It would have been a rallying cry for every terrorist organization in the world.
It shows the world that we are vulnerable," said the
academic.

"It already *is* a rally cry," concluded the think tanker,
a little smug. "We should expect more attacks."

"I would not jump to any conclusions. Nothing followed the 9/11 attacks. Plus, our law enforcement has
been training for this moment for years and is on high
alert. If there is another planned attack, I have high confidence our law enforcement will foil it."

The think tanker frowned, checkmated by the academic. He disagreed but didn't want to declare U.S.
law enforcement incapable on national news during a
moment of crisis. Few would welcome such a line, and,
like all pundits, he lived for applause.

"General, this seemed like a fairly sophisticated
attack," said the anchorwoman, finally breaking into
the conversation. "Are terrorists really capable of such
things? Could it not be a foreign power like Russia,
China, or Iran?"

"Certainly, those powers could have done so, but I doubt it," answered the retired general.

"Why is that?" asked the anchorwoman.

"Because they know we'd eventually figure it out and there would be reprisals. But terrorists don't care about such things," said the retired general.

"Yes, but—" interrupted the bow tie.

"That may be—" added the think tanker, leaning in. Both were ignored.

"Still, are terrorists really capable of this level of attack?" the anchorwoman asked. "It's far more sophisticated than anything we have seen before, at least in this country."

"Yes, it is possible and even likely," said the general, also ignoring the academic and think tanker. "Terrorist groups have been growing in sophistication ever since 9/11. They no longer need to weaponize commercial airliners, as their capabilities and organizations mature despite our best efforts. For every leader we kill or network we disrupt, three more pop up to replace them. We can't kill our way out of the problem."

"It's definitely al Qaeda or one of their franchise groups," said one of the FBI agents. Others nodded in agreement, but Jen Lin knew better. While her colleagues spent most of their careers chasing terrorists, she had spent her time hunting other things in the complicated shadows. Bad things.

"Wrong. Terrorists didn't do this," she said. "Russia did."

Two men laughed under their breath while another scoffed, "That's crazy, Lin. Russia would never do it because it would be an act of war. Even they're not that stupid. Besides, it profiles as terrorism."

Lin stood her ground. "Don't be so sure. Strategic deception is the Russian way of war. They even have a name for it: *maskirovka*."

The man chuckled as the group dissipated, leaving her alone in the room. *Idiots,* she thought.

CHAPTER 4

National Security Advisor George Jackson sat at the head of the table, hands clasped together under his nose, concealing a frown. Jackson was a gaunt man of average height, with wisps of white hair and wire-rimmed glasses. He looked more like a history professor than a history maker, and he dressed the part, too, eschewing power suits in favor of tweed sport coats with elbow patches and a bow tie. Jackson could think in whole paragraphs, and he spoke with a slight Boston Brahmin accent that revealed an Ivy League pedigree. Yet he was tough, and those who mistook his genteel mannerisms for weakness were soon checkmated. White House staff nicknamed him Yoda.

The White House Situation Room was standing room only. Movies depict it as a space of nobility and decision, but actually it looks like a townhouse basement converted into a recreation room, complete with low-hung ceiling and big-screen TVs. At the back of the room, staring directly at Jackson, was a wall-size monitor showing the head of the president of the United States.

President Hugh Anderson had double bags under his eyes and a scowl that would intimidate a drug lord. His temper was legendary, even by Washington standards. A full head of gray hair and incremental plastic surgery over the years made him look early fifties rather than seventy-three. The man was obsessed with winning a second term. In school, he was the kid who always ran for class president because he craved the approval of strangers. Six decades later, he was no different. Some thought him the Captain Ahab of polls, chasing good numbers and throwing tirades when they were low. They were down a lot in recent weeks, and now this. He was pissed.

"George, why don't you know who's behind this yet?" he demanded. "It's been an hour and you still don't have any answers."

"Sir, we're doing the best we can," Jackson said, frustrated.

"Your best is disappointing. Men are made or broken in a crisis, and I refuse to be broken. This is my legacy moment. You, on the other hand, are disappointing."

Jackson sat motionless, while other people in the room looked away in nervousness.

"Find me some facts, George," said President Anderson. "I've gotten more answers out of congressional hearings compared to this farce. Twelve years a senator, only to be bamboozled by my own National Security Council!"

"Sir, if I can explain—"

"Call me when you know more," said President Anderson, cutting Jackson off. "And it better be in ten minutes. I have a call with Moscow now. Proof of life. No telling what those maniacs might do if they thought I was dead."

Jackson's shoulders slumped.

"Answers, people. Answers!" scolded President Anderson as he reached for a button and killed the connection. His mammoth face was replaced by the presidential seal, the White House's screen saver. The room sat frozen, still absorbing the barrage. Then everyone turned to Jackson and waited for him to say something.

What am I going to say? thought Jackson. The president wanted to be on the news networks giving Churchillian speeches, but instead he was cooped up at a secret bunker in West Virginia. There could be no legacy speech until he had something to say, such as who killed the vice president. And that was Jackson's job.

Except Jackson had no idea who was behind the bridge bombing. They had no leads and were in the dark.

"All right team, let's start over," he said, and the room sighed. People were angry and tempers were rising. "Homeland, you go first."

"Here's what we know so far," said the secretary of Homeland Security. "The bridge was blown from inside. The bridge is hollow, built in 1935 with interior space for a trolley car propulsion system. The terrorists packed it with explosives and waited for a motorcade to cross."

"How much explosives?"

"About five thousand pounds of dynamite," she said, and someone whistled in amazement. "The suspects placed it at critical structural connections in the old trolley car workings, crawlspaces, and cross girders, and triggered it as the VP's—" she paused "—uh, Henry's limo approached the median point of the bridge. The explosion induced a progressive collapse by weakening critical supports, allowing gravity to bring the bridge down."

"Whoever did this sure knew what they were doing," added the secretary of defense, almost in admiration.

"So the terrorists—or whoever did this," corrected

Jackson, "wired the bridge and simply waited for a presidential convoy?"

"We believe so. It was inevitable that a convoy would travel this bridge, owing to its centrality, whether the convoy departed from the White House or the VP's residence. All the perpetrators had to do was wait."

"Are the other bridges wired too?" asked Jackson.

"No. We've inspected all other major bridges and tunnels in the metropolitan area and they're clean."

The others in the room sat in silence, pondering it. How many other U.S. bridges and tunnels were vulnerable to this kind of planned attack? Too many.

"We're tracking down leads on the explosive material," said FBI director Carlos Romero, a broad-shouldered man with the bearing of a boxer rather than a bureaucrat. He built a fearsome reputation locking away MS-13 gang members as the United States attorney for the Central District of California.

"And?" asked Jackson impatiently.

"And initial forensic analysis tells us it's a commercial dynamite with a high percentage of nitroglycerin and traces of RDX, a military explosive. Not easy to procure, but procurable. Whoever did this covered their tracks well, and took their time doing it."

"How much time?" asked Jackson.

"Hard to say. Probably up to a year because that's the shelf life of commercial dynamite."

"How the hell does someone buy two and a half tons of dynamite in a year, and no one knows?" interjected the secretary of state in an undiplomatic tone. Jan Novak was a known hothead and a difficult choice for America's lead diplomat. They had reviewed the same stale facts five times already and he was losing patience. So were others. "I mean, don't you need a license or something? Isn't that what you law enforcement people do?"

"Yes, you need a license," replied Romero slowly as if speaking to a child. "They probably sourced small quantities from multiple vendors and/or smuggled it in from abroad. The U.S. has lots of enemies abroad. Isn't that what the State Department does?"

Novak glared at Romero, who didn't back down.

"Gentlemen, please," said Jackson, holding up both hands as if stopping a truck. "Henry was a friend to all of us, and we're upset. Let's keep it civil."

The temperature was hot, in every way. The National Security Council's principals crowded around the oblong table in executive office chairs. Behind them stood or sat their deputies, shoulder to shoulder. It was a bit undignified, given their professional station. White House staffers wriggled around them delivering messages on small scraps of yellow paper as new intelligence arrived. The small windowless room was not intended for this many, and they had a long day ahead of them.

Jackson leaned forward, cradling his head in his hands and his elbows on the table. "DNI, do you have anything new for us?"

"Not since ten minutes ago, George," answered Michael Taylor, tossing his pen on the legal pad in front of him. He was the DNI, or director of national intelligence. Behind him sat Nancy Holt, director of the CIA. In her midfifties, she had a runner's physique and silver hair that draped around her shoulders. Her sun-weathered face revealed that she spent most of her career outside the wire, and her eyes scanned the room like an operator rather than a politico.

"Tell us again anyway."

A staffer handed the DNI a folded piece of paper. He opened and read it, eyebrows raised, before passing it to Holt. Both had inscrutable faces, which irritated Jackson.

"What's it say?" asked General Jim Butler in an annoyed Southern drawl. A third generation West Pointer, he hailed from Georgia. Now he was the chairman of the Joint Chiefs of Staff, the highest-ranking soldier in the nation.

"Sir, we just learned that a body pulled from the wreckage is a known radical Islamic terrorist," said Holt, steel in her voice. "An autopsy will be performed within the hour."

"Finally, a lead!" said Jackson, smacking the table with his right hand and smiling. The room exhaled. Holt walked to the front of the room and stuck her CAC identification card into the Situation Room's laptop. A few keystrokes later, terrorist mug shots adorned the main screen for all to see. She scrolled through several pages with lightning dexterity and then singled out one man. A fulsome beard and receding hairline did not mask a bullet hole in the forehead. The picture was dark and grainy, as if taken at night.

"No, that's not him. We killed him months ago," she said, scrolling further. "Ah, here he is." Another young man with a heavy black beard. He was smiling and carrying an RPG but looked like he was going to prayers. The photo was rasterized, having been overmagnified.

"So this is the bastard who killed the VP," hissed the secretary of state. Everyone around the table leaned in for a better look.

"Who is he?" asked Jackson.

"Facial recognition software estimates he is Abu Muhammad al-Masri, with a 90 percent confidence interval," said Holt. "He was a member of the Emni, a secretive branch of ISIS that built a global network of killers. They staged the Paris attacks and others across Europe. They tried to hit the World Cup in 2018, but we foiled it. A real nasty lot, with skills. Think of them as ISIS special forces."

"ISIS special forces, huh?" said Butler cynically. "Never seemed that 'special' to me. Just thugs."

"It's conceivable they executed today's terrorist attack, if they were resourced by a wealthy patron," said Romero.

"FinCENs has been picking up a surge of hawala activity out of Riyadh over the past six months," said Declan Hill, the treasury secretary, referring to FinCENs, or the Financial Crimes Enforcement Network. It is Treasury's lead task force for tracking illicit money around the globe.

"And we're just now connecting the dots?" asked Jackson.

"You retasked us to focus on Russia and China," responded the treasury secretary protectively.

Jackson ignored it and turned back to Holt. "Is Saudi Arabia involved?"

"We don't know enough yet," said Holt.

"Best guess then," said Jackson, but Holt shook her head.

"We're looking into it right now, George," answered the DNI. "I doubt their government has anything to do with it, but we can't rule it out. Their king is erratic."

"We also know there are several elite families in the Kingdom who secretly support the Islamic State," added the treasury secretary.

Holt stepped away from the laptop podium. "Here's a theory. A wealthy ISIS patron extracted the remnants of the Emni during the last days of the Islamic State and reconstituted the unit somewhere in the Kingdom. Then they deployed it here. Its mission: stage a spectacular terrorist attack, like 9/11, to rally the extremist world and take back the caliphate."

Jackson paused, considering Holt's scenario. The more he thought about it, the more it made sense. Still, he had to be careful. "Any other theories?"

"We're also working a Russia angle," said the DNI. "They have the capability and will to accomplish this, but we have nothing solid to report."

"How about China?" asked the general. "They're the rising threat."

"We're looking into Beijing too," added the DNI. "Same with Iran and North Korea."

"But here's what I don't understand," said the secretary of defense. "Why would any of those countries undertake such extreme measures? They know we would eventually discover who was behind today's attack, and it would be an act of war."

"Concur. It could lead to nuclear war, and all these adversaries have safer ways to disrupt us," said Jackson. "But terrorists don't give a damn."

Heads nodded.

"Anything else?" asked Jackson. "Our ten minutes are up, and I need to call back the president."

Heads shook.

"It's settled then. We're going with the terrorist theory until we find contrary evidence," said Jackson as he reached for the phone.

Holt smiled.

CHAPTER 5

What a miserable day, I thought as I cleaned my 7.62 mm SCAR assault rifle in the dark. Sometimes repetitive tasks like cleaning weapons helped me think, and I needed to think. It was past midnight and I could not sleep, angry over Apollo Outcomes' assassination of the vice president and the world's failure to see it. After reassembling the SCAR, I sat back in my bed, which also doubled as Ari's couch.

"Think!" I whispered to myself, and plugged my phone into the stereo, selected Mahler's Seventh Symphony, and blasted the volume. Its dark, menacing opening echoed around my mind at high decibel, and I inhaled deeply.

"Hey, everything OK in there?" yelled Ari from down the hall. "I know your country is under attack and all, but some of us have to sleep so we can deal with the terrorist threats to our own country."

"Sorry, Ari!" I said, turning down the music. *Sorry, Ari* had become my household refrain over the past six months.

"Bravo to Mahler, though!" said Ari, padding out in a bathrobe. "Could you spin the Ninth? Last movement?"

"Sure thing," I said, switching to Mahler's Ninth

Symphony. I carried an entire classical music library on my phone; it was my lifeline to sanity. Ari and I shared a passion for classical music, scotch, cigars, and war. Coincidentally, we were both single.

"Today's terrorist attack in Washington still on your mind?" said Ari as he sat down on the couch.

"I'm telling you, Ari, that was no terrorist attack. It was committed by Apollo Outcomes and made to look like a terrorist attack."

Ari shook his head in skepticism as he turned on the TV and muted the sound.

I'm the only one who sees what's really happening and no one believes me, I thought bitterly as I watched the news blame radical Islamic terrorists. The day's headlines were a nonstop drumbeat: AMERICAN VICE PRESIDENT ASSASSINATED BY TERRORISTS. AMERICAN PRESIDENT ACTUAL TARGET. 230 KILLED. The world was rocked. Several terrorist groups claimed responsibility, some I had never heard of, and I've heard of most. TV pundits ranted all day, and all were wrong.

"Well, what did you expect?" said Ari, as if reading my mind.

"Fools!" I said. "I spent the day on my satellite phone calling every friend I have left in the U.S. national security establishment. Most of them didn't take my call."

"And who could blame them? Tom, you're an internationally wanted man."

I nodded. What I didn't tell Ari was those who picked up the phone laughed and hung up, saying never call again.

"Did you try the American embassy here?" asked Ari, pouring a midnight scotch.

"Of course I did, using a fake identity. I got a meeting with the DAT"—the defense attaché—"and told him the facts, but he yelled at me for wasting his time, then ordered the marines to throw me out."

Ari let out an involuntary chuckle. "Well, I got similar treatment from higher."

"You ran this up the Mossad flagpole?" I said, surprised. You don't go to the Mossad with half-baked speculations; they are a no-bullshit organization.

"Yeah. No joy."

"As a last-ditch effort, I met with James. You know, MI6. He laughed for five minutes then demanded another pint for wasting his time. Wanker."

"Sounds like the day was a total shutout."

I closed my eyes and shook my head in frustration. "I have to stop this before it gets worse, Ari. And it *will* get worse."

"O-o-o-o-r," began Ari with caution, "maybe they are right, and Apollo was not involved." I turned to him in anger, but the thought had nagged at me all day. The more I puzzled it, the less I liked it.

"Ari, the operation was signature Apollo Outcomes. I know because I used to do these things for them overseas."

"But was it really Apollo? Think about it, Tom. Blowing a bridge and framing terrorists is classic Apollo, but assassinating the vice president? Targeting the president? Killing Americans? Operating in the middle of Washington, DC? No. They would not do that. Admit it."

I sat back and pondered it. "No, you're right. It's not Apollo's style."

"Nor is it in their business interest," added Ari.

I cradled my head in my hand as I thought. "Then who did it?"

We sat in silence because no answer made sense. Finally, Ari spoke: "What is Apollo's motto, again?"

"Its unofficial motto is 'Figure It Out.'"

"Then figure it out, Tom Locke. If what you say is true, then the U.S. and the world is in graver danger than everyone realizes. I'll take on a terrorist group any day before going muzzle to muzzle with Apollo Outcomes. Hell, I'd sooner go to war against Iran than Apollo. They fight dirty compared to Tehran."

The comment jarred me upright, owing to my many years working for the company, but Ari was probably correct. Apollo was a mercenary corporation, and that was no metaphor. They did Washington's dirty work: political assassinations, illegal renditions, experimental interrogations, black-on-black hits, covert coups d'etat, color revolutions, and domestic military operations. They recruited from SEALs, Delta, British SAS, Israeli special forces, Polish GROM, others. But they were more than for-profit warriors; they also hired MIT hackers, Harvard MBA savants, and criminal geniuses. Apollo was a cross between Delta Force, the NSA, and Goldman Sachs, and they executed the missions the CIA and military wouldn't or couldn't. Apollo Outcomes was lethality without the red tape.

God, I miss it, I thought. Now Apollo and I stood apart. My sin? I was associated with Brad Winters, its ex-CEO gone rogue and my old mentor. Winters even tried to kill me, twice. For that, I sent the man to his doom, damned to a Riyadh torture cell and then beheaded. However, none of that mattered to Apollo and its primary customer, the U.S. government. They just saw me as a threat.

It's why I can never go home, I thought wistfully, sipping my scotch. *And why no one will believe me now.*

"Could Apollo assassinate the VP in the middle of Washington, DC?" asked Ari.

"Of course, but why? They would never betray their primary customer. Winters always told me that money imbues its own honesty, and that profit motive is the most reliable motivation of all."

"It's a conundrum. Yet the facts all point to one thing: Apollo blew that bridge. But it makes no sense."

"Indeed," I whispered as I swished my scotch unconsciously. *Why would Apollo take such extreme measures?*

Then I understood.

"It's all about the money," I muttered. Apollo worked for Washington the way the old British East India Company serviced the Crown—it was difficult to know who served whom. "Perhaps Washington finally grew savvy to Apollo's game and threatened to pull significant contracts."

"It would threaten Apollo's existence," said Ari, crossing his arms and legs with unease.

"A desperate Apollo would take radical steps to ensure solvency."

Ari nodded deep in thought. "But here's what I don't get: Why doesn't Apollo just get a new ten-digit retainer from Moscow, Beijing, the Fortune 500, or the global 0.1 percent? That's what mercenaries do: auction their loyalty."

It hurt to hear him say it, but it was often the truth. I knew ex-SEALs who once draped themselves in the

American flag and now work for China in Africa. However, I only took missions that were in the U.S.'s interest and not the company's bottom line. Or at least so I thought; Winters lied to me about that, too, in Ukraine.

"I don't think so because Apollo needs the U.S. as its super-client. Think about it. No other rich country has more security needs than the U.S., and that's what Apollo sells: security in an insecure world. Apollo must keep America as a client, at all costs."

"Even if it means holding the government hostage to terrorism?" said Ari, again shaking his head in disbelief. "How does that work, exactly?"

"Isn't it obvious? Apollo assassinates POTUS or the VP, frames terrorists, the nation panics, and it guarantees another quarter century of lucrative counterterrorism contracts for Apollo. More attacks will follow until the company gets what it wants."

"Disgusting but plausible. Even likely. Washington created a real Frankenstein in Apollo, the result of outsourcing too much wet work to the private sector," said Ari, nose upturned as if he had just smelled something disgusting. "What are you going to do now?"

"I don't know," I said, slumping into the couch. The more I thought about it, the less I liked.

"Locke, let it go. You did your best, but everyone thinks you're crazy. You're like Noah and the flood. It's not your fight anymore, and Apollo will not get away with it. The CIA, FBI—everyone—will figure it out, and when they do, they will end Apollo." Ari leaned in and whispered: "Trust me."

But Ari was wrong. He didn't know Apollo like I

did. Few did, and especially not the CIA or FBI. Apollo easily manipulates them for more contracts.

"Let it go," coaxed Ari.

No, I can't, I thought. I knew that I should not have cared, but I did. Both the U.S. and Apollo had left me for dead. If I wasn't a corpse, they would both finish the job because I knew too much and was deemed a renegade.

"You've done all you can do," said Ari in a gentle voice. But I knew that was wrong, too. There was still one more thing I could do, but I shuddered at the idea. *Still, I am a patriot,* I thought, *and I always was.* Perhaps I got lost along the way, but I never forfeited my soul. I never worked for an enemy of America. My grandfather, who was shot and left for dead at the Battle of the Bulge, always told me as a young boy: "Tom, you will serve. No matter what you do in life, you will serve your country in uniform." And so I did. I found other ways to serve too, leading me to Apollo. Not everyone there was a mercenary.

"Let it go," soothed Ari, sensing my mounting rage. The American people had no idea what was about to slam them. Worse, the government did not comprehend the insider threat. Eventually they would, as Ari insisted, but too late. By then, the nation would be panicked, and Apollo could dictate terms to make the "terrorist attacks" stop. It was racketeering. Extortion. A shakedown.

"You've done everything you can," continued Ari.

"No, I have not."

"Tom . . ."

"There is *exactly* one more thing I can do."

Ari's tone switched from calming to commanding. "Locke, don't do anything stupid."

"Only I can stop Apollo. I'm the only one who could get to the bottom of this quickly and put the fire out before it got worse. And it *will* get worse."

Ari let out a loud sigh of anxiety.

"We must all take a side, Ari. You know that most of all." It is the one rule that binds all warriors, no matter what allegiance, and affords honor in the killing of enemies. Ari nodded grimly.

"Then you're going to need this," he said after a moment and walked to the closet. After rummaging around the top shelf, he pulled down a black ballistic case. "I was saving it for your birthday."

"I didn't think you knew my birthday," I joked.

"I don't," he said with a smile, handing me the case. It was heavy. I popped open the two latches and lifted the lid.

"They're beautiful," I said, and they were. Nestled in gray sponge-foam were two Heckler & Koch Mark 23 handguns with screw-on sound suppressors, laser aiming modules, and four extra magazines, fully loaded. The Mark 23 was the pistol of choice for U.S. Special Operations Forces, which listed it officially as: Offensive Handgun Weapons System—Special Operations Peculiar. *Peculiar* was a euphemism for "assassin's tool." But what made it particularly lethal was its stopping power. It shot a .45-caliber slug that blew holes in targets that dinky nine-millimeter rounds would only dent.

"I was saving them to mark your six-month anniversary with my couch," said Ari with a smirk.

"So thoughtful," I said deadpan while pulling out the Mark 23s. I held one in each hand. They felt good.

"You're going to need them."

"Screw Apollo," I uttered in agreement.

"Find evidence. Then people will listen to you," counseled Ari. "And then the government will shut down Apollo for good."

"Apollo must be stopped," I agreed. *And only I can stop it.* If not me, then who? The world was blind, and no one knew Apollo's moves better than me, given my background. More important, I had surprise. They thought me dead or, worse, drunk in some shithole country.

Fuck them all, I thought as I downed the last of my scotch and reached for my satellite phone.

CHAPTER 6

That night a black Chevy Suburban sat alone near the edge of a runway. Commercial airliners flew less than fifty feet overhead as they touched down at Washington National Airport, but they took no notice of the Suburban, camouflaged in the moonless night. A narrow channel of water separated the airport's main landing strip from the small parking lot on Gravelly Point. A few disused picnic tables and rows of approach lights were the only things on this spit of land, which was invisible from nearby roads despite its centrality.

Across the river was Washington, a small city surrounded by heaps of suburbs and traffic. However, the heart of the city was beautiful, especially at night. The Capitol Dome shimmered in the distance, and the obelisk of the Washington Monument was lit up in glory. Lights from surrounding monuments, bridges, and highways reflected off the Potomac River, giving a Monet-esque impression of the nation's capital.

Another black Suburban crept down the single access road with its lights off. The driver was careful not to tap the brakes and give away their position. The Suburban glided into a spot ten feet from the first Suburban and bounced gently off the parking bumper.

Men in dark suits leapt out of both vehicles and

opened opposing passenger doors. At first nothing happened. Then an older man stepped out of the first SUV, his loafered foot gingerly making contact with the asphalt. The darkness obscured his features as he walked the few paces to the other vehicle and climbed inside. All doors shut.

Five minutes passed. Multiple jets roared overhead. The river continued to twinkle with city lights. Then the dark-suited men jumped out of the vehicles and opened up the opposing passenger doors again. The older man gently returned to his vehicle. Doors closed. Both black Suburbans drove into the night, traveling in opposite directions.

CHAPTER 7

The next morning, the FBI headquarters was buzzing. The J. Edgar Hoover Building was a brutalist concoction of office building meets underpass. Today, the place was angry. The terrorist attack had occurred two miles from headquarters, a galling fact.

Lin had shared her theory about Russia's responsibility for the terrorist attack with a few senior colleagues. Their response was universal. First, it was laughter. Then it was: "The Russians wouldn't dare." Followed by: "You're a junior analyst. Watch and learn." Ending with: "Stay out of trouble."

She wanted to strangle them.

Maybe they're right, she thought, leaning back in her desk chair and closing her eyes. She had learned to be humble about most things since her demotion to the desk.

"Tough day at work?" joked Jason, at the desk next to her. He was her age, and had been that kid in high school who was All-American everything. Unlike Lin, he saw working at FBI headquarters as an opportunity, and he had ambition. Working a desk did not bother him. Only the boss had his own office; the rest of her division worked in an open bay. Management claimed it was for improved "situational awareness" during collaborative investigations, but Lin was convinced it was to ruin everyone's personal life. Open offices are an eaves-dropper's paradise.

"Jason, not now," she said, eyes shut and rubbing her temples. Jason had been hitting on her for six months, and it was getting old. He was a nice guy, but it would never happen. She often wondered how such a talented detective could be so oblivious.

"They got me chasing smugglers," he whispered, followed by a pirate "*Yaaaaargh!!*"

"Great, Jason," she said flatly.

"What do you call a terrorist who swallowed dyna-mite? Abominable," he chuckled.

"Jason. Shut up."

"I'm following a hot lead right now," he continued. "I might even get out of the office on this one."

The room's air smelled stale, and the windows were sealed. It was like working in a submarine with natu-ral light. Lin got up and stretched. Her long, black hair spilled onto the floor as she touched her toes. Stretching always helped clear her mind. People in the office were used to it and took no notice of her occasional tai chi movements.

". . . turns out you can still smuggle just about any-thing in a container ship . . ."

Lin dialed him out and let her thoughts find her happy place. She learned the technique in army survival train-ing as a way of withstanding torture. Occasionally, the FBI got slots in the Survival, Evasion, Resistance, and Escape, or SERE, School at Fort Bragg. It was three days of hell, but she fought for the opportunity to prove to the boys that she was tough.

". . . did you know there's a whole community of

implosion watchers? There are hundreds of videos on the internet. I'm surprised no one got the bridge on video . . ."

Concentrate, she thought, and Jason's voice faded away. She was back at her father's second-story martial arts studio on Geary Boulevard in San Francisco. It smelled of sweat and rubber mats. The steady drone of large standing fans was punctuated by someone yelling "Aye!" followed by the slam of another's body on the mats.

She was nine but already the equivalent of a black belt, and she trained with kids twice her age and weight. She won because she was faster and more clever, taking down opponents with grace rather than brutality. Those who underestimated her because of her size and sex lay at her feet, rubbing aching body parts.

"Those too stupid to learn are made to feel!" she would declare to her victims. It was something her father told his students. Her mother died young and she had no siblings. The rest of the family remained in China, making her father the only family she had. In between practice sets, they would study the *Tao Te Ching* and consult the *I Ching* together. He taught her that power without judgment is tyranny, and that was why she joined the FBI: to stop tyrants. Why couldn't he see that?

". . . Antwerp . . . Newark . . ."

One night, when she was twelve, a homeless man in the Tenderloin jumped her, demanding her money and virginity. With a rapid-knife hand strike, she crushed his larynx and then threw him hard into a wall. Lin still remembered the distinctive *smack* of his skull hitting the brick. The creep lay motionless in the alley as she walked away. Maybe he was dead; she didn't care. *One less scumbag,* she thought then and now.

". . . Russian mob . . ."

Lin's happy place was sucked back into the Hoover Building.

"Wait, what?" she said.

"Haven't you been listening, Jen? Sometimes I think your mind wanders when we talk," said Jason.

So-o-o-o oblivious, she thought. "Just repeat what you said."

"The Newark field office got an anonymous tip last night from a dock worker. Said he felt it his patriotic duty after the bridge attack."

"What was the tip?"

"Something about a container ship last week from Antwerp with an unregistered container being offloaded before the ship went through Customs."

"How is that possible?" she asked.

"Dunno. Also, most people smuggle things *inside* containers, and not the whole container itself."

"Weird. Why would anyone do that? It seems a lot harder."

"It is, and that's the big mystery. It's why they called HQ this morning for backup."

Lin sat down and thought about the anonymous tip. New York City was her old hunting ground, but the quarry didn't leave much of a trail. "A ghost container isn't a lot to go on."

"If it was easy, it wouldn't be an FBI case," said Jason absentmindedly as he worked.

"What about the Russian mob?"

"The informant said the *bratva* did it." *Bratva* meant "brotherhood" in Russian and referred to mobsters.

"Anything else?" said Lin, sitting upright.

"He said it happened once before, sometime last year, but didn't say more. That's all we have, and now the Russian Organized Crime Task Force is working the case."

Lin looked sullen. It was her old unit.

"Don't worry, Jen. If there's a Russia angle, they will find it. But so far, they're rolling snake eyes."

"They must be desperate if they're turning to you," she joked, but her humor failed and Jason grimaced at the swipe. "No offense. But seriously, Jason, you don't even speak Russian. I spent two years on that task force. I know the players, the lay of the land, the threat. I should be doing this, not you." Her expression turned to anger. "Why didn't Mr. Prick assign me to the case?"

"Mr. Prick" was what she called their boss, a spasmatic jerk and one of the biggest in the building. She was sentenced to his division as punishment for blowing the New York sting operation. At least that was what he told her, with a disturbing measure of pride. Things went downhill from there, mostly because he was a bully and she always stood up to them.

"You know why," said Jason, turning back to his computer screen. "Anyway, I think Newark is a dead end."

"Why do you say that?" she said, surprised.

"Because they can't find the mystery container, and don't even know if it exists. All they have is an anonymous guy's tip. Even if true, there's probably no link to radical Islamic terrorists. It's not the mafia's style." Jason sighed and looked up. "Also, Manhattan is being deluged with new counterterrorism leads by the hour and there's a shortage of agents. I think the ADIC will shut down the ghost container investigation before lunch." The assistant director in charge, whose acronym was pronounced "ay-dick," ran the show.

Lin frowned, but it made sense. Yet something gnawed at her. Tips like this were not random and the FBI knew it, which was why they were investigating. The informant was probably from a rival mafia with credible knowledge, or was trying to set up their competitor. Either way, smuggling in an entire container was new and alarming.

Who would do that? Why? Lin twirled a pen between her fingers. *Because the sender did not want the mafia knowing what was inside the container.* Only a few "senders" had that kind of power over the Russian mafia. It didn't smell like organized crime; it stank of the Federal Security Service, or FSB, the KGB's successor. It would explain how five tons of extremely regulated explosives were sourced. The container would also be an expedient way to smuggle in the expertise needed to conduct the assassination plot.

Lin smiled. It was starting to make sense, except for one glaring fact: the FSB did not work with radical Islamic terrorists. If the anonymous tip was accurate, then there were only two conclusions. First, the mystery container was simply crime related: drugs, weapons, or women. This was the prevailing theory, according to Jason.

Or, thought Lin, *the container is linked to the bridge attack, as the informant implies.* If true, it led to dark places. The Russian mob worked only for itself and occasionally the Kremlin. The mob has no reason to kill the American president or VP because it would rain down agents upon them, putting them out of business. *But Moscow has reasons,* she thought. *Many.*

She looked around and saw everyone was hustling: working the phones, tapping away at keyboards, waiting over a printer, or huddled in impromptu meetings. *No one is thinking. They're just working,* thought Lin. An hour ago, her boss stood on a desk and told the team it was an "all hands on deck" moment, and "we need to catch these terrorists before they strike again."

Maybe they're wrong? she mused. What if it wasn't terrorists but someone framing them? Terrorists were too crude to orchestrate such a sophisticated attack, but not the Kremlin. Making it look like a terrorist attack would be the perfect decoy to dodge America's law enforcement and divert the FBI's attention, as the true bad guys staged their next attack. The FBI was like a bull to the cape when it came to counterterrorism, and all the bad guys had to do was act the matador. *And the FBI is falling for it,* she thought, involuntarily crossing her arms and legs. *We're charging the cape.*

"Jason," she said, leaning closer. "Where did you say that ship originated?"

"Antwerp," he said absently while typing.

"That doesn't make sense," she said.

Jason stopped typing. "What do you mean?"

"I learned a thing or two about international smuggling while working the Russian mob." She explained that Antwerp and Rotterdam had some of the best port security in the world. "Only an inside job could get an unregistered container on a ship at Antwerp, and terrorists aren't that good. But the Kremlin is."

"Look, Jen. Drop the Russia thing. Please," he said in

a whisper. "The boss already warned you, and you're on unofficial probation as it is."

"He may be too dim to get it, but it doesn't make me wrong. I have to try," she said, standing up.

"No Lin, don't even think about it!"

She ignored him and walked into the boss's office, shutting the door behind her.

CHAPTER 8

"We have a problem," said Holt.

No one ever likes hearing the head of the CIA utter those four words. Jackson frowned and waved her into his office. He was midconversation with the secretary of state, Jan Novak, who turned around in his chair to greet her with a fake smile. "Please have a seat, Nancy. Jan just left the Oval and is back-briefing me on his conversation with POTUS. We're in a tough dialogue with Saudi Arabia over the terrorist attack. They're being especially recalcitrant, even refusing to support our investigation." Jackson sighed. "Anyway, I hope you don't mind if Jan sits in."

"No, I don't mind," she said, clearly minding.

"It must be serious if you came from Langley to deliver the bad news in person," said Novak.

Holt winced. The man had a gift for the velvet putdown. It was how he got ahead.

"It . . . is," she said, chagrined. She carried a briefcase and set it down beside her chair. They waited for an aide to shut the office door before talking.

"What kind of problem?" asked Jackson in a measured tone. He was paid to be a problem solver and not a blame shifter.

"The terrorist theory. It's falling apart."

"Falling apart?" responded Jackson, startled.

"What do you mean, 'falling apart'?" added Novak. "I just spent the last twelve hours on the phone yelling at Riyadh, and now you are telling me I was wrong? It was *you* who put forward the terrorist theory to begin with, and the FBI keeps finding corroborating evidence pointing to the Islamic State, or whatever they call themselves now. The FBI even found a dead terrorist on-site. Foreign terrorists are clearly responsible. It's a slam dunk!"

"Yes, but there are problems."

Novak was about to reply when Jackson held up a hand for silence. Jan Novak got to his station in life by sucking up and spitting down. By contrast, Holt was no pole-climbing political appointee. She had spent a career in the CIA's Directorate of Operations, mostly as a targeter. Some thought her methods extreme, but Jackson liked her because she got stuff done, bureaucracy be damned. That was why he'd urged the president to appoint her the CIA director, even though she initially turned down the honor.

"Explain," said Jackson.

"It's TS/SCI. It can't leave the room," she said, meaning the intelligence was highly classified, and if leaked, it could compromise sources and methods.

"Go ahead, Nancy. We're all cleared here. You know that."

"The terrorist we found in the bridge wreckage—" said Nancy.

"Abu . . . something or other," interrupted Jackson.

"Abu Muhammad al-Masri. I don't think he was involved."

"What?!" said Novak in disbelief.

"I knew when I first saw his body something was off," she said.

"How so?" asked Jackson.

"I've been hunting jihadis most of my career and I ran the targeted assassination program that decimated Emni. I know them the way a magician knows a deck of cards."

"But wasn't al-Masri a part of Emni? I think you said so earlier," asked Jackson.

"Correct, he was. When we identified his body, my gut told me something was wrong. At first, I dismissed it. Then it hit me," she said, reaching into her briefcase and pulling out a thick red folder marked TOP SECRET in bold, followed by code letters. She handed it to Jackson.

"What's this?" asked Jackson as he opened the folder.

"The problem," she said.

Jackson carefully removed files from the folder and laid them out on his desk. Each was about thirty pages thick and clipped together, with a photo and cover sheet on top. Novak stood up and walked around Jackson's chair to get a better view. There were five files in all.

"Who are they?" asked Jackson as Novak fumbled for his reading glasses.

"This is al-Masri's terrorist cell in Emni. He wasn't the leader but a member," she said. "They were tight, and always worked as a unit. Always."

"That's unusual. They not trust other jihadis?" said Jackson.

"Hard to say. Perhaps that's what made them so effective. They staged the Istanbul airport attack in 2016 that killed forty-eight and injured 230. They also acted as enforcers inside the caliphate and liked to crucify non-Sunni men and gang-rape unwilling women."

"A combination of cunning and cruel," said Jackson softly as he flipped through a file.

"Sounds like pure evil to me," muttered Novak, hovering over Jackson's shoulder so he could read the CIA action reports.

"They are," said Holt, and let them riffle through the files. Jackson's face betrayed no emotion, but Novak's was a picture book of horror. He let out a low whistle at one point.

"So, what's the problem?" asked Jackson, looking up and putting down a file. "They seem to fit the threat profile perfectly."

"True. But here's the problem," she said, stabbing one of the files with an index finger. "That's the leader. He's dead." The two men looked surprised and Jackson picked up the file.

"When?" asked Jackson.

"Ten months ago. An Agency direct action team from Ground Division took him out vicinity Raqqa, Syria. Bullet in the chest and head." She gently grabbed the file from the National Security Advisor's hands and flipped to a page showing his corpse. The photo was dark and grainy, as if taken through night-vision goggles.

"What did they do with the body?" asked Novak.

"They left it. The CIA doesn't offer hearse services." Novak scowled at Holt's jab.

"Go on," said Jackson.

Holt pointed to another file. "This guy is dead too. We hired a contract kill team to assassinate him, under Title 50 authorities. That was five months ago, in September."

"Where did you find him?" asked Jackson.

"FATA region, Pakistan, under ISI protection," she said, referring to Pakistan's notorious Inter-Services Intelligence, which also sheltered Osama bin Laden. "That's why we used Apollo Outcomes rather than our own guys, to avoid escalating tensions between our countries should they become compromised. Contractors offer good plausible deniability."

"Makes sense," said Jackson.

"Wait a minute. You hired a private-sector hit team? Mercenaries?" asked Novak in a pitched tone. He had been a high-paid Washington lawyer before being appointed as the secretary of state. He had scant background in international affairs but rendered legal services to the president during the campaign, and many thought the appointment was a quid pro quo. No one knew what those services entailed. "Is that even legal?"

"Sir, with all due respect," she said in a tone suggesting none, "there's a lot you don't understand about modern war."

Novak was about to retort, when Jackson cut him off again. "Continue, Nancy."

"These next two guys were killed by the Wagner Group in North Syria in October. Our sources inside the GRU confirmed it."

"You mean Russian mercenaries killed them," said Novak.

"Not just any mercenaries, but elite ones. The Wagner Group is Russia's version of Apollo Outcomes," said Holt.

"Just not as good," added Jackson.

"Not by a long shot," said Holt, grinning.

"Tell me about the last guy. Is he dead too?" said Jackson with unease on his face.

"Yes. He's the guy we pulled from the rubble, but a different photo of him."

Both men leaned in and stared at the picture. The terrorist looked ten years younger than the body they found in the wreckage, even though the photo was less than a year old. However, it was clearly the same individual.

"And it gets worse," said Holt. Both men's mouths hung open.

"Worse?" said Novak.

"What does that mean?" said Jackson, sitting upright.

"He didn't die here. The first autopsy was done in the field and didn't show much. However, the second one revealed he died weeks ago, and his body was preserved through refrigeration, around forty below Celsius. We found cold damage and slight body decay. Apparently, he was not immediately frozen after death but ripened along the way."

"Where did he die?" asked Novak, sitting back down and stowing his reading glasses in his breast pocket.

"We don't know, but it wasn't two days ago and it wasn't here. Someone placed his body inside the bridge, probably in a crawlspace to protect him from the initial blast and collapse."

"You mean somebody wanted us to find his body," said Novak.

"Correct. And make erroneous deductions about who was behind the terrorist attack."

"A false flag operation. I don't like where this is heading," said Jackson in a dark tone. "Nancy, do you have a new theory? Be careful and be precise."

"Yes. These men did not do it," she said, gesturing to the files on the desk. "This terrorist cell was dead

months before the bridge attack, making it impossible
for them to be behind the VP's assassination. Rather, the
actual perpetrator is framing them. Meanwhile, we're
burning precious time and resources chasing down fake
leads and alienating allies like Saudi Arabia."

"You're saying this whole thing is a setup?" said
Novak, sinking deeper into his chair. "The political
fallout with Riyadh could be significant."

"Affirmative," said Holt.

"Well, shit," said Novak.

Jackson sat in thought, and finally asked, "Then who
did it?"

"We don't know," replied Holt.

"No theories?" asked Novak.

"None," she said in a grave manner. "No country
would do it because it risks war, and they know we
would eventually figure it out and retaliate. No terrorist
group could do it, other than the Islamic State, and we
just ruled them out. I doubt organized crime could pull
it off. Even if they could, why would they? It would
risk much yet gain little. I'm not sure who is left." She
tapped a foot as she thought. "I don't know who did
this, or why."

They sat motionless in information shell shock as
they pondered the implications. Jackson broke the silence. "Whoever did this is very, very good."

"And very, very dangerous," added Novak.

"Now you understand why I came to you in person,"
she said, and he nodded.

"But surely someone this good would know that
we'd eventually connect the dots and realize the dead
guy was a setup. It doesn't buy them much time," said
Novak.

"Jan, the deception wasn't for us," replied Holt. "It was for the press. 'Fool the media and fool America' is what the terrorists say. But it's what the Russians do."

"Nancy, who else knows about this?" asked Jackson.

"Some of my staff, but it's code-word classified and the information won't go anywhere. Among the principals, no one knows. Just us three."

"Good," he said, staring at the files on the desk. Holt and Novak sat quietly, awaiting Jackson's decision. After a few minutes, he leaned forward and picked up the phone. "Convene a principals meeting of the National Security Council. Immediately."

CHAPTER 9

Deep in the bowels of the Hoover Building, Lin sat across from her boss. The conversation was not going well.

"Radical Islamic terrorists are not behind the bridge attack because they're simply not that good. Everyone knows it but no one wants to say it," said Lin.

"Say what exactly?" asked her boss, exasperated. He had slept in his office last night and the lack of rest was showing. His eyes were beset within dark circles and what little hair remained on his head stuck out as if attacked by static electricity.

"That it's not terrorists! It's a false flag operation. It's Russia. Moscow killed all those people and framed terrorists to get us off their scent. Deceit is their way of war. They manufacture the fog of war and then step through it. It's how they stole the Crimea, interfered with our elections, and now assassinated the VP—who they thought was POTUS. The Kremlin is framing terrorists to get away with murder. Literally."

He sighed, wanting to scream at her but too exhausted to do so. It was the third time she had pushed her Russia conspiracy theory, and he was determined it would be the last. The FBI had terrorists to catch and had no time to waste on unsubstantiated hunches by a junior analyst.

Correction. Failing junior analyst, he thought. His own boss had formally counseled him about anger management issues and told him to become a better mentor to young agents. *But they're so stupid these days,* he thought. Still, he had to make the effort, something his boss had made excruciatingly clear. *Lordy, give me patience,* he thought.

"Lin, listen to me. Carefully. The entire interagency is throwing its full weight into finding these terrorists. People with clearances and pay grades way above yours know things you do not. For example, the terrorists have grown more sophisticated in the past year, and they have the means, motive, and opportunity to execute the bridge attack. We are confirming leads everywhere. We even found a dead terrorist at the scene of the crime—"

"The Russian's could have arranged it," interrupted Lin. "Easily."

Her boss grimaced and looked up at the ceiling while clenching fists. *Perhaps he's looking for divine patience,* she thought, and could see a vein pulsating on his right temple. He was about to blow.

"No. The Russians could not," he said finally, combating his temper. "Anyway, why would they? Why risk World War III? They have better ways to attack us than assassinating the vice president. Admit it."

Lin folded her arms, trying to think of a good response. None came.

"There is *no* Russia angle. Got it? No more bullshit about Moscow out of you."

"But—"

"There is no 'but'!" he interrupted, pounding the desk with a hammy fist. "We have fourteen thousand agents looking for terrorists, everyone except you. Fall in line, Lin, or forfeit your badge and gun. Final warning!" he said, thinking, *Screw my boss.*

Lin left his office fuming and sank back into her desk chair. Jason gave her the I-told-you-so look, but she held up a hand in protest. "I don't want to hear it, Jason. Not now."

"So-o-o-o-o, how'd it go?" he asked with a sardonic smile.

"Not well."

Jason shot the I-told-you-so look again and she turned away. "Lin, everyone is pretty convinced it's terrorists. Especially the director. So are the CIA and the other fifteen intelligence agencies. Maybe you should think so too."

"A bad idea embraced by millions of people is still a bad idea."

"Lin, there was a terrorist's body on-site. It's conclusive."

"No, it's deceptive. The Kremlin staged it."

"You've got to be kidding me."

"Think about it, Jason," she said, swiveling her chair to face him. "Russia has been killing terrorists in Syria for years. Putting a dead one on ice and then planting him inside the bridge would be easy for the FSB," she said.

"It would be damned hard for the FSB or GRU or anyone to import a frozen terrorist," he said, laughing at the idea.

"Don't underestimate the Russians."

Jason groaned, equal parts pity and incredulity. "You know you would be a rising star in the Bureau if you just had patience for the rules."

"Jason, don't give me that bureaucratic bullshit. We

have a country to save, and we're losing precious time. We should be tracking leads on Russia, before they evaporate." Lin's voice turned angry, tired of being ignored.

"Jen . . ." said Jason in a soothing tone, trying to calm her.

"The Kremlin sometimes uses Russian organized crime as a fifth column. I know because I worked on the Russian Organized Crime Task Force before I was exiled here. The *bratva* can procure tons of dynamite, no problem. Import a dead terrorist?" She let out a "Ha!" that startled a nearby agent. "Too easy. They can smuggle in anything from anywhere and bribe anyone. Terrorists can't do that."

Jason leaned back, closing his eyes. "Jen, do one for the team and stop thinking. Last time you did, we *both* got in big trouble. The boss reamed you for . . . how did he put it? . . . 'Girl gone rogue!' Then *I* got chewed out for letting you go. As if I was your babysitter!"

Silence.

"Jen. Jen?"

More silence. He cautiously opened one eye.

She was gone.

CHAPTER 10

I was entranced by the mystical chords of Hovhaness's symphony "Mysterious Mountain" when my spell was broken by turbulence. The Gulfstream IV jet bucked through the wind shear as we initiated our descent. I looked out the large oval window but saw little. The moonlight only revealed light and dark splotches below us, indicating trees and farmland. Small clusters of amber lights indicated the occasional human settlement.

I had spent the last twelve hours in the air, and all my money, too. The charter jet business was run by air pirates, as far as I was concerned, but discretion is expensive. Plus, my itinerary involved heaps of "transaction fees" or bribes to bypass normal formalities. I had to empty out my black bank account in Cyprus, a holdover from my days at Apollo Outcomes. Program managers like myself received dark money for random operational expenses, and I had squirreled some away in several offshore accounts.

Now we were on final approach to a small country airstrip somewhere in Shenandoah Valley, Virginia. The rural airport closed at dusk, making it an ideal point of entry for anyone wishing to avoid customs. Dulles was not possible for me, at least not now. We flew over the

polar cap and down through Canada, avoiding Homeland Security's gazing eyes. They looked southward, at
the Latin American smuggler routes. Not many smugglers came from Canada, especially by air.

"Pilot, what's our ETA?" I asked over the intercom.

"Twenty minutes," said a voice in a thick Bulgarian
accent.

I picked up the phone and made a call, then switched
back to the intercom. "The runway lights will be on in
fifteen minutes."

"Affirmative," replied the pilot.

One-fifty grand bought me a fixer on the ground,
local transportation, and a temporary safe house in
Washington. It also got me an amnesiac airport em-
ployee to throw the light switch and flee.

The plane's cabin attendant fumed quietly in a forward
seat, eyeing me. It had been this way for nine hours. Over
the course of the flight, I had turned the corporate jet's
posh interior into a *Guns and Ammo* centerfold. Black
duffel bags were seat belted to leather seats, and the polished wooden tables were overloaded with tactical gear
and things that go boom. Now it was all packed into a
small ballistic chest, two duffel bags, and a weapons case.
Only the M32 revolver–type grenade launcher lay on
the couch, snug in its tactical bag. It was too big to pack.
We made a quick stop in Beirut to pick up some choice
items from an arms dealer who owed me a solid. Then we
stopped in Cyprus, a hub for oligarchs and people like me.

The flaps extended with a whir of hydraulics, and the
landing gear released with a clunk. I could feel the plane
slow down in my gut, and I peered out the window.
Farmland, patches of trees, some houses, a ridgeline in

the distance. It looked lush compared to my two years in the Middle East. I never thought I would come home again, especially this way.

The plane nosed up as the ground drew closer. Power lines passed uncomfortably close to our landing gear, and the dark horizon and sky merged into one color. The plane wobbled in midair as the pilots brought it to near stall speed before there was any runway beneath our wheels. The turbines throttled up and down in rapid succession, and the ground came up fast. The attendant was gripping the ends of his armrests, staring straight ahead.

"Short runway," said the flight attendant, fear in his voice. "Not made for this size aircraft."

"I know."

We touched down hard at 2250 and the pilots slammed the brakes, causing spare ammo magazines, loose rounds, and cocktail napkins to hurtle forward. The reverse thrusters kicked in, and I felt my body weight strain against my seat belt. Things behind me crashed to the floor and one of the galley cabinet doors flung open with a crack. The plane edged left and right as we rapidly decelerated. Out the window, I saw the small terminal building zoom by; it marked the halfway point on the runway.

"Too fast," said the flight attendant, shouting over the blast of the reverse thrusters. "We're running out of runway!"

The brakes squealed, and the plane shimmied until we skidded to an unnatural stop on the grass, just past the runway's edge. The pilots throttled the starboard reverse thruster and port engine simultaneously, causing a violent U-turn back onto the runway.

"I hope we didn't wake up the entire countryside," I said.

"If the police show up, you're doing the talking," said the attendant. I had asked our fixer about this contingency, and he said it's the one thing he could not fix. Getting caught in an unregistered jet flying from the Middle East full of smuggled weapons and cash and landing in the dark of night in rural America is hard to explain to local juries.

"I need to ghost in ten minutes," I said, and the flight attendant nodded in vigorous agreement.

The Gulfstream taxied back up the runway to the small terminal, where the pilots cut the engines. I opened the fuselage door and aluminum stairs unfolded gracefully to the tarmac. The air smelled sweet and cold.

"It's good to be home," I said, walking down the stairs in a tailored suit and carrying a SCAR assault rifle with sound suppressor at the ready. I would have preferred nonlethal weapons, but they had no range. Plus, Middle East smugglers rarely stock such items. Turning around, I saw the Gulfstream dwarfed the small, single-engine planes near it. The small airport's frequent flyers were recreational pilots, and I wondered if a jet had ever landed here before.

No time for a security sweep. I need to find my ride, I thought. There were a few small hangars, some Cessna 150s, and a glorified snack bar that passed as the terminal. No one was here but us.

I saw the black BMW M5 competition sedan tucked in between hangars, waiting for me, right where the fixer promised. I felt under one of the wheel wells and peeled off the keys taped inside. Seconds later I was in the driver's seat, and the twin-turbo V-8 came to life with a throaty roar.

"Magic," I said, a phrase I had picked up in South Africa. The Beemer looked like a standard Washington lobbyist's ride but had the soul of a track car. The fixer had it enhanced, too, adding horsepower and removing the antitheft tracking device. There was no GPS or anything else that could talk to the internet. A road atlas and street maps of Washington, DC, sat in the front seat. Perfect for my needs.

I spun around to the G-IV and backed up to the plane's stairs. The attendant stood at the top, arms crossed, glowering down at me. It took us a few minutes to unload the aircraft.

"That's it," I said, walking down the stairs with the M32 grenade launcher and throwing it in the trunk. The BMW sagged slightly in the back under the weight of the weapons and ammo. It would affect evasive maneuvering at speed, causing the car to fishtail around corners. Once I reached Washington, I would make a weapons cache separate from my safe house.

I checked my watch again. Nine minutes. *Pretty good.*

"Time to pop smoke," I said, nodding to the attendant who grinned and waved as he retracted the stairs and sealed the door. The jet engines whirred to life.

I got behind the wheel and strapped in. The Gulfstream's turbines crescendoed, and the plane began rolling forward. I accelerated out of the way and toward the airport's exit, a chain-link gate conveniently left wide open by the fixer. The Gulfstream took off and thundered over my head, its landing gear retracting, as I sped down the country road.

It's good to be home, I thought.

CHAPTER 11

Of all the prestigious private-member clubs in Washington, DC, the Cosmos Club was the most elite. Like all clubs of its genus and species, it was unassuming to the casual eye. No sign announced its existence. Only those who "mattered" in vanity-obsessed Washington recognized the belle époque mansion on Embassy Row, flying its own flag.

A black Mercedes sedan sat in a line of luxury cars waiting to be valet parked. Membership was highly curated, and an invitation to dine at the Club was rarely refused.

"Good afternoon, sir," said one of the valets as he opened the Benz's passenger door. An antique cane stuck out, followed by a leg. The man grunted as he maneuvered a second, stiffer leg onto the brick pavement. With focus, he rose to his feet.

"Welcome back to the Cosmos Club, sir," said another staff member with a smile. The tall man ignored him and hobbled into the mansion. Despite his age and limp, he bore an impressive physique, like a retired linebacker. People moved out of his way as he lumbered forward and made his way through the club. The ballroom looked like Versailles and the library like Oxford.

He passed through a corridor covered in pictures of

members who had won a Nobel, Pulitzer, Presidential Medal of Freedom, or other prestigious recognition, including the Cosmos Club Award. There were hundreds. Then there was an alcove of framed postage stamps with members' faces on them. The tall man ignored it all.

"Sir, your guest is already seated," said the maître d' as the man shuffled past him and into the dining room. White tablecloths with complex settings lined the room, but none too close together. The scent of grilled steak and truffle potatoes filled the air, as did the *glug-glug* of wine being poured into glasses. The Cosmos Club's seal was subtly ubiquitous: a winged earth flying over clouds but under stars, with a Masonic-looking eye beaming light down upon the cosmos.

"Please follow me."

They passed senators, diplomats, generals, judges, clergy, CEOs, lawyers, foreign dignitaries, and others locked in quiet conversation. The Club was a safe haven for privacy and a neutral ground for meetings, away from the hoi polloi of the press and public. The Club prohibited electronics, business cards, and notetaking. It was a back room where deals were cut in the DC swamp.

"Here you are, sir," said the maître d', opening the door to a private dining room lined with bottles of wine behind glass and a crystal chandelier that filled the small space. Inside sat a man wearing a bespoke suit who was only slightly younger. The average age of Club members was seventy. The man with the cane moved forward without acknowledging the maître d', who rushed to seat his guest and then slipped out. Once they were alone, the two men regarded each other.

"Good to see you, old friend," said the man with the cane.

"And you too."

"What shall we talk about?"

"You know exactly why I called you here. We have a problem."

The other man nodded.

CHAPTER 12

My safe house near Capitol Hill was underwhelming. A real estate agent would describe it as: "lots of living space," "great potential," "unique design," and "lots of possibilities." Translation: a dump. The place was a dilapidated taxi warehouse abandoned to pigeons in the industrial part of the city. Neighborhood features included an eight-lane highway overpass, railroad tracks, a coal power plant, abandoned cars, and trash. Lots of trash.

But it was home. For now.

A garage door opener was clipped to the BMW's sun visor, and now I knew why. After pressing it, the mammoth garage door opened and I drove in, headlights on. The interior was a concrete cave, and the dank air assaulted my nostrils. It smelled of axle grease and rotting rubber. I donned my night vision and SCAR and conducted my security sweeps. Ten minutes later, I discovered the biggest threat was tetanus.

At the center of the warehouse sat an RV trailer, arranged by the fixer, that would serve as my tactical operations center. The front door creaked open, and I flipped on the interior lights. HOME SWEET HOME, read a sign on the fridge in fake needlepoint. I opened the fridge door and found a six-pack of cheap beer and a cold pizza.

"Thoughtful," I said, grabbing a slice of pie. I hadn't realized how hungry I was. Four laptops sat on the table, across from a large monitor on the wall. These laptops were special because they could probe the internet anonymously. I opened one. A few clicks later, the wall monitor came alive with feeds of low-light cameras around the warehouse. Rats were the only thing moving outside.

"Now to find some friends," I said, working the keyboard.

Hours later, I sat in the corner of a coffee shop, sipping a triple espresso. Morning commuters were rotating through, when two men walked through the door. They were not like the others. The first was colossal. He wore sideburns and dressed like a lumberjack; all he needed was an ax. The second was wiry and shopped out of mountain-climbing catalogs. Sun had engraved lines into his face, making him look older than he was. Both moved like athletes.

"Tom!" said the lumberjack in a gravelly baritone.

"Lava, Tye!" I said, standing up. We shook hands, firm grips all around, and took seats around the café table.

"I couldn't believe it when you said you were back," the big guy said, smiling. No one knows where he got the nickname Lava. He was a West Point quarterback turned special forces legend, eventually commanding the U.S. Army's most elite unit: the Combat Applications Group, aka Delta Force. After retirement, he was scooped up by Apollo Outcomes, taking a lot of guys with him, including Tye. When I first joined Apollo, I was lucky enough to be an operator on Lava's team.

"Hi Tom," the wiry guy said, in a faint Southern accent. He grew up in the green hills of Tennessee and enlisted in the army at seventeen. A few years later, he was selected for Delta and spent a career fighting America's secret wars. Tye was a patriot to a fault; he only saw the good versus evil in his missions, and never the ocean of in-betweens. I never understood why a guy like him joined Apollo, and owing to this, I didn't fully trust him. But Lava did.

"Heard you was dead," said Tye.

"Turns out I'm hard to kill. It takes more than Russians and ISIS to eliminate me," I said, and gave them a quick update of my missions involving Ukraine and the Islamic State.

"Sounds like you've been in some sticky places," said Lava, not fully convinced that I was relaying everything.

"Lost my team, Lava. Outside of Donetsk. We were ghosts, and there's no way the Russians could have tracked us. No way."

"Sorry about your team, Tom. What do you think happened?"

"Someone inside gave away our position."

"Inside Apollo?" asked Tye.

"Possibly," I said with caution. *The CEO, Brad Winters, sold us out, the double-dealing opportunist!* I wanted to scream but couldn't. Up to this point, I had left Winters's name out of it. Winters and Lava got along, and I needed to know where Lava's loyalties stood. If I wanted help, I needed to win over Lava. Tye and others would follow.

Lava looked away, and Tye to the ground. *That's weird*, I thought.

"You been flying nap of the earth for a year now?" asked Lava, referring to when military aircraft fly under the radar. It was a soldier metaphor for operating undetected. "You landed five hours ago, and no one knows you're here? You're sure about that?"

"Yes," I said, puzzled by his suspicions.

"Well, your timing's shit," said Tye.

"What do you mean?"

"Follow me," said Lava, and we got up and left the coffee shop. Outside was a black up-armored Chevy Suburban. They were ubiquitous in Washington.

"Get in," said Tye, holding open a backseat door. I clambered in and reached for a seat belt. I didn't like where this was going. Tye got behind the wheel and Lava in the front passenger seat. Seconds later we swerved into traffic, and Lava turned to face me.

"Who else knows you are back?" asked Lava.

"No one, I swear. I called you first. You told me long ago that if I was ever in trouble, call you first."

Lava starred at me. Judging me. I took it.

"No one?" repeated Tye, looking at me in the rearview mirror.

"No. One."

Lava turned around, facing forward as we crossed the National Mall and turned onto Constitution Avenue. Patches of frozen snow lay on the ground and there were a few geese.

"The situation is worse than you realize, Tom," said Lava. "Do you know what we were doing last night? Hunting. For the past six months we've been hunting splinter cells across the metro area."

"Terrorists? Foreign nationals? Russians? The Chinese?"

"Worse."

"Worse? Who's worse?"

"Apollo Outcomes," said Lava, turning to me. Tye eyed me through the rearview mirror, gauging my reaction. My head exploded. *Did I just walk into a trap?*

"I don't understand," I stuttered. "I thought you still worked for Apollo."

"We do," said Tye.

"Then who is Apollo working—"

"Apollo is secretly at war with itself," interrupted Lava. Silence followed as I absorbed the implications.

"You're telling me an Apollo team has gone rogue? Here, in DC?" I said, not believing it. I just couldn't see how this was possible.

"Not just a team," said Tye. "A whole squadron."

"And they're working for a foreign client. No one knows who," said Lava.

"And Tom, you are listed as one of the rogue operatives," said Tye. "KIA last year, along with two others."

"Boon and Wildman," I said quietly. I hadn't heard from them in months and assumed they were in hiding. Perhaps they were dead.

"Affirmative," said Tye, then added sympathetically, "Wildman was a friend."

I slumped in my seat, daring to trust them. Lava had never lied to me before, why would he now? He was no Brad Winters.

"There's a kill list," said Lava. "You're still on it, even though you're listed as KIA. I never understood why, but now I know. It's because someone got sloppy. They thought you were dead but had no confirmation."

"It's why we were shocked to get your call," said Tye, "and why it's good you haven't contacted anyone else."

I sat stunned.

"You really didn't know, Tom?" asked Tye, in amazement.

"No."

We turned around at the gate of Arlington Cemetery and headed back toward the Lincoln Memorial and the Mall.

"Well, I guess I should not be surprised," I said. The time had come for the whole truth. "After all, it was Brad Winters who sold out my position to the Russians in Ukraine. He also issued a kill contract on me, when I was in Syria and Iraq. But he got what he deserved."

"What do you mean?" asked Lava.

"Winters backed a failed coup d'etat in Saudi Arabia, and I exposed him to the Kingdom's security services. They captured, tortured, and beheaded him. Wish I was there to see it," I said with satisfaction.

Tye started laughing, and so did Lava. Their laughing grew louder.

"What's so funny?" I asked.

"Winters is alive," said Tye, once he caught his breath.

"And he's leading the renegade squadron," said Lava.

CHAPTER 13

Rush hour on K Street was normally a throng of angry cars, double-parked trucks, rude bike messengers, and rushing pedestrians in suits. People outside the beltway think Capitol Hill is the epicenter of American power, but DC denizens know better: it's K Street. The intersection of K and Connecticut, and the blocks surrounding it, are home to crisis communication companies that manipulate the news cycle, law firms that have partners without law degrees, and boutique political-risk consultancies that practice the dark arts of subterfuge. Together, they formed the troika of Washington's seedy underbelly.

Today K Street was empty, even though it was a weekday morning. The threat of another terrorist attack kept even the soulless home, leaving Lin the wide boulevard to herself. She took her time walking and thinking.

Be a good soldier and just do it, she thought grimly. She knew she had to return to the Hoover Building and play the game. But it wasn't her style.

If you don't, you are just a civilian, she thought. When she left the building an hour ago, she wanted to solve the case on her own. However, going AWOL during a national crisis was guaranteed job termination. Now she just wanted to save her career.

I need to make repair, before it's too late. The FBI had given her third, fourth, and even fifth chances. She was a born badass but was marooned to a desk for her sins. However, the desk was her last chance.

How did it all go sideways? Lin stopped and felt her eyes tear up. *It wasn't supposed to be this way. Not for me!*

A year ago, she was taking down Russian mobsters as part of a FBI assault team, its only woman. In a single night, the FBI's Joint Eurasian Organized Crime Task Force arrested more than two dozen members of the Shulaya gang in Brooklyn, although the word "gang" didn't go far enough. This bloody group trafficked drugs, women, weapons, and even children—anything to turn a profit, they didn't care.

Lin cared, though. She still remembered the moment. The raid was like any other, and something they trained for in the shoot house for hours. But training cannot prepare you for everything.

"Breach!" the team leader had shouted, and she heard the battering ram crash through the shabby apartment's door. She was third in the stack and shuffled in, covering her sector with her Colt M4 carbine. No movement, no threats.

"Clear!" she shouted. They snaked through the living room, pizza crusts on the floor. Lin moved smoothly, despite being turtled up in black body armor. The room was empty.

"Clear!" they each shouted, and the four-person stack moved on. Somewhere, a young woman was sobbing. A closed door ahead. The stack advanced.

Automatic gunfire tore through the wood door, splintering it, and caught the team leader in the chest. He went down, saved by body armor, but he struggled to breathe, as if someone had taken a sledgehammer to his solar plexus.

"Man down! Man down!" someone shouted.

"Laying down suppressive fire," said Lin, taking a knee, flipping to full auto, and firing back through the shredded door. The other two members of the stack reached for the team leader's equipment vest and pulled him back through the living room and out the front door.

Click. Lin's magazine ran dry. Time slowed as her heart rate spiked and adrenaline panicked through her veins. She rolled right as automatic gunfire from the other side of the door blew it apart and exploded the cheap chandelier overhead. Her Kevlar helmet took a bullet and fell off, while her weapon slipped from her grip as she rolled. She was alone in the room.

A mammoth, shirtless man emerged through the door frame, sweeping the room with his AK-47 and screaming in Russian like the possessed. His torso was covered in tattoos: a large Eastern Orthodox crucifix over his heart surrounded by winged skulls and Cyrillic encircling it all. Saints in chains were on his shoulders and upper arms.

The man stopped and smiled at her. Russian mobsters are all men, the worst kind.

"Get out of there!" shouted one of the FBI agents from the hallway, but Lin knew better. The gangster would mow her down the moment she sprinted. Instead, she stood up, chin high and facing him, unarmed. He smiled, not because she was a sexy woman but because she was a challenge.

"You are mine, bitch," hissed the man in Russian.

"I'm nobody's bitch, bitch," replied Lin in Russian.

"What are you doing?! Get out of there!" yelled her partners from the outside hallway. One peeked around the corner with his M4 but the Russian was quick and shot the door frame around the agent's head. The man slunk back around the corner.

Simultaneously, Lin kicked the kitchen table toward the Russian. As he spun around to block it, she bounded toward him: the first step on the floor, the second step off the sliding table, the third step her legs around his neck. She twisted her hips and they both crashed to the floor. The man pointed his Kalashnikov at her head as he gasped for breath and flailed. Lin's legs tightened around his throat while she yanked the AK-47 barrel upward, causing it to fire on automatic into the wall. She ignored the pain of the hot barrel.

Click. The AK-47 was dry.

The FBI agents ran forward but not before the mobster flipped Lin on her back and put a knife to her throat, its point under her chin. She could feel warm blood trickle down her neck. One thrust and the knife would go through her nasal cavity and into her brain.

"Stop or I kill her!" shouted the Russian in a heavy accent. The two agents froze, weapons trained at his head. One called for backup.

"You do that, we blow you away," said the other FBI agent.

"I do not fear death. I am death."

Fuck this, she thought. In a rapid motion, her hands swept inward and caught the Russian's knife hand; her right connected at his inside wrist while her left walloped the back of his hand. The knife went flying across the room. She incapacitated him with a knuckle strike to his throat, leaving him grasping his Adam's apple as she rolled him off.

"Are you all right?" asked one of the agents as the other handcuffed the Russian, who was still straining to breathe.

"Yeah, no problem," she replied. Her father had taught her well in Chinese martial arts, and the most important lesson was no fear. Fear is hesitation, and hesitation is death.

As Lin stood up, she heard crying from the next room. She entered and felt the air get sucked from her lungs. Two naked thirteen-year-old girls were tied to the bed. One was crying and the other was unconscious or dead. The Russian had had his fun, for days. It was a mess.

Lin spun around and drew on the Russian. The man's eyes bulged out in comprehension. The other agents screamed at her, but too late. The top half of the Russian's head exploded as she pulled the Glock's trigger. Bits of brain and skull splattered the rear wall.

There was an internal investigation, but her teammates covered for her. They reported it as self-defense, and she was exonerated. But people knew. No one wanted to work with her after that, and her corridor reputation was set: loose cannon. It is a curse inside the Bureau. No assault team leader wanted her after that, despite her abilities, and the task force director saw her as a public relations catastrophe in the making. He exiled her to the Hoover Building for "your own safety," he had told her.

That was a year ago. She had been a top agent whom others envied, and now she just wanted to remain in the Bureau.

"They will fire you," she whispered aloud, anxiety in her voice. She could not imagine life outside the Bureau. It's all she ever wanted to do. But the notion of appeasing her boss and working a dumb desk to find nonexistent terrorists was odious. Especially when the real bad guys—the Russians—were getting away. She could almost hear them laughing inside the Kremlin, toasting vodka and slamming down shots at America's expense.

I hate the Russians, thought Lin as she stared at the black smoke in the sky a mile to the north. It was the remnants of the blown-up bridge, an act of war invisible to the government.

Morons, she thought, and picked up her pace. *I need to get back on the task force. I'll make the Russians pay. Maybe not now, but later, when I'm a senior agent. I shall not forget!* "I SWEAR IT!" she shouted at the plume of smoke. A lone passerby eyed her nervously and crossed to the other side of the street.

Lin made her plan. She would march back into headquarters, make up with the boss, become the model desk agent, get transferred back to her old task force, and then kick ass. It would take time, but she was committed.

Bzzzzz. Bzzzzz. Lin pulled out her work phone and read the text. It was from her boss.

"RETURN TO BUILDING ASAP. SURRENDER BADGE AND GUN AT SECURITY OFFICE. YOU ARE ON ADMINISTRATIVE LEAVE W/O PAY PENDING MISCONDUCT INVESTIGATION."

"Crap," uttered Lin as her hands trembled. She had just been fired, by text.

Lin stood still for minutes, lost in cognitive dissonance. Then walked aimlessly. She paused at a metro subway station, its escalators running but with no people. Downtown looked like the zombie apocalypse had ravaged the city of its population, yet all the escalators, traffic lights, and other automated machines toiled on without purpose. She felt like the escalator.

Then Lin smiled with a glint in her eye. She bounded down the escalator to the subway below. She discovered her purpose after all.

CHAPTER 14

Banging on my front door.

I was lost in a dreamless sleep.

More banging.

My hand reflexively reached for my SCAR assault rifle before my brain registered the fact that someone was inside my ultra-secret safehouse and standing at my trailer's front door. And knocking. Banging, actually.

"Locke, get your ass up!"

It was Lava. I lowered my weapon and sat up in my cot, checking my watch. Almost midnight.

"Let yourself in!" I shouted back.

"It's locked."

I shuffled to the door and opened it. Lava's burly frame and stern expression awaited me. I felt like a scrub at Ranger School again.

"Daylight's burning, Locke. You need to suit up," he said, brushing past me and entering the trailer. "Real shithole of a place you got here. Know that?"

"What are you doing here? How did you know where I was, and get past my defenses?"

"Don't insult me. Here, drink this," he said, pulling out a small metal thermos.

"What is it?"

"Energy drink. Special stuff. You're going to need

it," said Lava. Before I could protest, he opened it and shoved it into my hand. "Drink it." Normally I wouldn't, but Lava was my last, best commander. He took care of his people, and I wanted to be his people again, so I drank it against my better judgment.

"Tastes like fruit punch," I said, handing back the empty thermos.

"And take this," he said, handing me a kit bag. I opened it; inside was exotic Apollo tech and weapons. During my exile, I would have killed for such equipment, but not today. Not under these enigmatic circumstances.

"What's this?" I asked.

"We don't got all day, cupcake," said Lava, tossing me a tactical cuff. It was among Apollo's most coveted proprietary tech items, and far more advanced than anything governments issue. Looks were deceiving; it was a black Velcro cuff that attached to one's inner forearm. Simple enough. But opening the inner flap revealed a touch screen that was beyond next-generation technology. It connected with the wearer's tactical suit and linkable weapons; monitored vitals; interconnected with all Apollo team members and command nodes; and delivered ultrasecure global communications, limited artificial intelligence assistance, collective targeting, and near-perfect situational awareness in a firefight. It was the envy-lust of every special operator in the world, for those who knew of it, but only Apollo had them.

"Why are you giving me this?" I said, cradling it in my hand. It was unlocked and in setup mode, awaiting my biometric confirmation.

"Because I need to know if I can trust you."

"And so you give me Apollo tech? I'm flattered but don't understand."

Lava shook his sideburned head. "If you're gonna be on my team again, Locke, then I need to trust you. And it's been a long time, Locke. You went rogue, remember?"

"It's more complicated—"

Lava cut me off. "You don't know someone until you fight with them, or against them. I need to know if I can trust you again. Suit up. We're going on a mission."

"Mission?" I stammered. "What, now?"

"Now."

Lava's missions were usually infamously impossible but never impromptu. Like SEALs, Delta, and other elites, they were meticulously planned by Tier One operators who worked exclusively on a team for months, even years. They never took along war tourists.

Unless I was the mission, I realized. Was Lava trying to eliminate me? Yes, if he didn't trust me. But would he? I doubted it, but times change. I was caught up in a secret civil war, and I had gone rogue with Winters, the enemy. Lava had reason to doubt me.

"Where are we going? What's the mission?" I said as I suited up. The body armor was exquisite. It looked like black carbon-fiber plate mail, but it could flex with the body and it was light. I felt I could pole-vault in the stuff.

"Need-to-know only," said Lava, thumping me on the chest as he passed me and disappeared into the dark warehouse. "And you don't need to know."

I still held my SCAR. If I was going to end this, now would be my best chance. The sooner you make a break from your captors, the better your chance of survival. Those who wait for later opportunities usually find themselves in a hopeless prison cell, or dead. Sooner is always better. It's basic escape and evasion.

"Locke?"

But would Lava really kill me? Somehow I doubted it. He was my former commander, and we had endured things together that bond men. Or perhaps that was just hope for an old friend. Who was a survivor. And a killer.

You must decide, I thought. *Either you kill him, or he kills you. Or he saves you. Or I kill my only friend and ally.* Or perhaps his rifle was already aimed at my head. Whatever I did, it would be consequential, and I had only seconds to decide.

"Hey, how did you get in here anyway?" I yelled into the darkness, buying time as I weighed my options. They all sucked.

"Stop stalling, Locke," came Lava's voice from the shadowy recesses. "Hurry up. Let's bounce."

OK, let's see where this goes, I thought as I strapped on the cuff and exited the safehouse.

"Good man," whispered Lava.

Half an hour later, around 0030, we pulled into a corporate airfield in Maryland, just outside the Capital Beltway. Lava drove the black Suburban down the tarmac, past rows of private jets, and into the last hangar. Inside was a lone plane. It looked like a military transport, with twin turbo-props on a high wing and a T-tail. Its back ramp was down, and men in combat gear were hauling weapon cases and parachutes from a van. I counted ten men, and they were preparing for a high-altitude low-opening, or HALO, jump mission.

"Your new team?" I asked Lava as we parked in the hangar.

"Old team," Lava said. "You're the FNG." Fucking New Guy. Also, bottom of the food chain.

It's gonna be a long night, I thought.

"Hey guys, I brought a new recruit," said Lava.

"Locke, good of you to join us!" said Tye with sarcasm and a smirk. He introduced me to the rest of the team. They were all ex–Tier One special operators: six Americans, one Aussie, a Brit, a Canadian, a German, and an Israeli. All looked combat weathered, and none seemed pleased to see me. But I was the FNG, and I knew the deal. I used to be one of them. Hell, I led my own team under Lava's command in the early days.

"Body armor, grenades, and ammo in the van," said Tye. "Grab your pleasure and get on the iron bird. Wheels up in five."

"Thanks. Where are we—" I began before Tye cut me off.

"Just get your shit, Locke."

I stared at him and he stared back, giving no quarter. In the van, I grabbed the armor, a few boxes of 7.62 mm for my SCAR, .45 rounds for my twin HK Mark 23 handguns, and four frag grenades.

"Where's my parachute?" I asked.

"We already got one waiting for you," said Tye, his smirk disappearing. "On the plane."

I didn't like it.

"Thanks, Tye, but I see one here, toward the front of the van." I clambered over the ammo crates, and felt Tye's firm grip on my calf, stopping me.

"Stop wasting time. Like I said, your chute is already on the plane," he said. We locked gazes.

"Locke, move your ass! We're moving out," yelled Lava from the plane's tailgate, his assault rifle dangling at his side. A tug began pulling the aircraft from the hangar while the ground team got in the vehicles and started the engines.

"Leave it, Locke. Let's go," said Tye.

If I were to bail now, Lava could have capped me: one in the back and the other in the skull. He had a gift with bullets. So I followed Tye and leapt onto the plane's back ramp as it began to lift. The turboprops whirred to life once we cleared the hangar, and the van and Chevy Suburban drove away into the darkness. Lava's team sat on benches facing each other, looking slightly like cyborgs in their battle suits. Meanwhile, I was struggling to put mine on as we taxied to the runway. Seat belts were ignored as we took off.

"Are you going to tell me where we're going now?" I shouted over the din of the turboprops.

"You will know it when you see it," said Lava.

"What's the mission?"

"Need to know."

"I *need* to know," I said, gesturing at the aircraft and heavily armed team of strangers. We were about to parachute into a fight, and I had the right to know why I was risking my life.

"Need to know," repeated Lava as he leaned back and closed his eyes for a nap. So did the rest of the team.

Holy hell, I thought. But being an old soldier, so did I. Pulling a weapon would be suicide because I had nowhere to run. Better to get some shut-eye. Rest was the only preparation for an imminent fight, for those strong enough to sleep before battle.

I awoke to Tye shaking me.

"Wake up. It's time," he said. The rest of the team was donning parachutes and doing function checks on weapons. I checked the time: 0146.

"Here, for you," said Tye, pushing a parachute into my chest. I stared at it. Was this Lava's weapon of choice? If he wanted me gone, a malfunctioning chute at thirty thousand feet would be a clean erase.

"Who packed it?" I said involuntarily.

"I did," said Tye with his smirk. "Put it on."

I yanked it from him and inspected it. I was a former HALO jumpmaster with 221 jumps and a static line jumpmaster with 144 jumps. However, there's only so much you can tell about a packed chute. You only know if it works when it opens, or doesn't.

"Hey, soldier," said Lava, witnessing my doubt. "Take mine." He took my chute and shoved his into my hands.

"No, it's fine, Lava. I'm good to go with that chute."

"No, take it. I insist," he said with faux politeness as he strapped on my chute. I stared at my new parachute.

"No time, Locke. We're over the DZ in four mikes. Chute up!" cried Tye, referring to the drop zone.

Everyone was ready to go, except me. Whatever was about to happen, I knew the aircraft's tailgate would soon open and we would all tumble out, with or without a parachute. I quickly strapped it on and adjusted my combat load. My oxygen bottle pressure and flow were good, and I could breathe.

"Omega, this is Valhalla. Radio check, over," said Lava over the command net. Apollo's tactical command in northern Virginia was call sign "Omega" and Lava was "Valhalla."

"Valhalla, this is Omega. Lima charlie. Warno: possible two bogies and hot DZ," came a voice over my earpiece. Translation: We read you loud and clear, but there may be two enemy aircraft and ground enemy on the drop zone.

"Roger," replied Lava, and turned to face us. "Sound off."

"One OK," said the first guy.

"Two OK," said the second.

"Three OK."

When it got to me, I said, "Twelve OK."

"All OK," said Lava. The interior lights switched from white to red, and my night vision adjusted instantly. Through my heads-up display, or HUD, I could see the identities of each team member in green, as well as their vitals, and what was behind me. Tye.

"Get ready!" said Lava. The aircraft's tailgate lowered, and we felt the blast of freezing air rip through us. Below, the terrain was unmistakable.

Manhattan! I thought. What the hell were we doing thirty-five thousand feet over New York City? Probably imitating the flight path of a commercial airliner as cover for action.

A long minute passed as we stood ready. The jump light was still red. Should I jump or not? Lava and Tye could have given me a dud parachute deliberately. I had worked for Brad Winters too long and mysteriously showed up in the middle of Apollo's civil war, and that was reason enough.

"Five, four, three," counted the pilot through our ear pieces.

I can't risk it, I thought. *I can't jump.*

"Two."

Do not budge! I grabbed a strap dangling from the ceiling and planted my feet.

"One."

The light above the tailgate went from red to green.

"Go! Go! Go!" shouted Lava. The twelve-man team pushed forward as a unit. I held on to the strap, but Tye plowed into me, rugby style, and knocked me off my feet. We all rolled off the tailgate as a scrum, and dropped into the sky.

CHAPTER 15

Lin sat on her bar stool wearing a slinky black dress and tried to look interested in what he was saying. It was difficult. The big man on the stool next to her looked like a washed-up boxer who drank too much beer. Or, in his case, vodka.

"You know what Stalin once said during a speech?" said the man, in drunken Russian. He went by Dmitri, which was undoubtedly not his real name.

"No, what?" Lin replied in fluent Russian.

The man feigned seriousness, waving his fists as if he were Stalin. "'I am prepared to give my blood for the cause of the working class, drop by drop.'"

She made herself chuckle. He continued.

"Then someone passed a note up to the podium, and do you know what it said?"

"No," she said.

"'Dear Comrade Stalin, why drag things out? Give it all now.'" He let out a huge snort-laugh, smacking the bar with a hairy hand.

"Oh, that's funny!" she lied, as he ordered more shots of rail vodka.

The Baltimore dive bar's dim lighting and few patrons made it an ideal place to meet an informant.

Actually, she had never met Dmitri before, but he came highly recommended from one of her old FBI informants in Brooklyn. Dmitri helped manage Russian mob transactions at the Port of Baltimore and was networked into the *bratva,* even though he wasn't a mobster himself. She also learned Dmitri was her Brooklyn informant's cousin.

"How is your cousin doing?" she asked, sipping her shot as he downed his.

"Vasily? He's a cocksucker, but you already knew that!" he said, laughing hard. "Vasily told me you were luscious, and he was right." Dmitri placed his hand on her inner thigh and slid it upward. She swatted it away and crossed her legs. They had been at this for half an hour: her asking questions, and him laying his paws on her.

"Vasily said you knew of a ship that came from Europe to Newark about a week or two ago. He said it was registered in Liberia and had a Russian crew. True owner unknown," she said nonchalantly, and then looked up at him with an inviting gaze. "Vasily said you could help me."

"Did he, now?" Dmitri laughed and downed another vodka. "Ships like that show up every day in Newark."

"Yes, but this one is special."

"How so?" asked Dmitri, flagging the bartender for another round.

What Lin said next wasn't strictly true. "Vasily told me it was hauling contraband. People, drugs, or . . ." She stopped midsentence and hoped he would finish it. She learned this technique in the FBI's interrogation course. People abhor silence in friendly conversations and will fill it, sometimes with the truth. But all Dmitri did was belch.

"Vasily said you were a connected man. I'm disappointed," she continued, with firmness in her voice. *You know something. If I can't trick it out of you, then I'll shame it out. Or worse.*

"Vasily is an asshole," he said, laughing and gulping another vodka.

"So, you're not a man in the know?" she said in a silkier tone. "Not a man worth *knowing*?"

He smiled, and gave her a refilled shot glass, which she downed. "I am a man worth knowing."

"I thought so, and I look forward to knowing you. For a long time. Tell me what I want to know."

"Maybe."

"Maybe what?"

"Maybe I know something, maybe I don't."

"Maybe you tell me?" she said, leaning forward with a coy smile.

He eyed her chest and then her face, gauging her smile. "Maybe I do know a little something about that ship."

"Like what, Dmitri?" she coaxed, her index finger slowly tracing the rim of his empty shot glass. He watched her finger and swallowed.

"Something about a container ship that came into Newark, not long ago," he said in a low voice.

"What made the container ship so special?"

"How about I tell you at my place? It's close."

"How about you tell me now?"

"Nothing is free," he said.

"Tell me first. And then we go to your place."

They stared at each other, a standoff of sorts. Finally, he looked away. "I have to take a piss," he said, sliding off the bar stool. "Don't go anywhere, little lady."

She watched him lumber off to find the men's room. He was heavy but moved like a man who could handle himself.

He knows something and I'm running out of time, she thought. Over the past two days, she had called in every favor, reached out to every contact, and broken almost every FBI rule to find out how the Russians killed the vice president—if they had—and what their next move would be. Drunk Dmitri was her last lead.

Frustrated, she checked the time. It was almost midnight. *Crap,* she thought. The bar shut down in minutes, and then she would have to go to his place to continue the conversation. Lin frowned at the thought. *Better to get it over with now.*

Her phone buzzed with yet another text message from Jason, still at FBI headquarters despite the late hour. "WHERE R U?!" it read. There were dozens more like it. "BOSS ASKING 4 U"; "CAN'T COVER YOU MUCH LONGER"; "GET IN HERE!!!!"; "CALL ME!!!!!!" She ignored them all.

Lin sighed and put the phone away in her purse, nestling it beside her Glock 19M. She hated her desk job, and it wasn't why she joined the Bureau. Jason was the only one who took her seriously, and that was only because he had a crush on her. But tonight wasn't proving any better. She didn't relish the idea of more cheap vodka, Dmitri's terrible jokes, and his hands ambushing places they ought not go. Especially on his couch. Yet her only hope of walking into the Hoover Building again, without being fired, was showing up with a tangible lead. And Dmitri was her last chance.

She was getting desperate.

"It's for a good cause," Lin reassured herself, kicking off her stilettos and slipping on flats from her purse.

Then she bent over so that her long black hair touched the floor, and then wrangled it into a ponytail. She hated it when hair got in the way.

"Want anything, miss?" asked the bartender. "Last call."

"No. I'll be back in a jiffy," she said, walking toward the men's room, clutching her purse. The bathrooms were down narrow stairs, in the basement, which smelled of bleach. She tried not to touch the walls. The basement corridor was even dimmer than the bar—the management wouldn't splurge for a few light bulbs. The only sounds were the steady thump of eighties rock music above and the flushing of toilets. An old pay phone was at the end of the hallway, its handset torn off long ago. Vintage rock concert posters behind Plexiglas were drilled into the walls.

Lin cracked the door to the men's room and peered inside. It was small and disgusting. Two urinals, two stalls, sinks. Another man was rinsing his hands and wiped them on his jeans. She closed the door and stood in front of the lady's room, as if she were waiting in line to enter. The guy with wet pants exited and brushed past her, taking no notice.

Dmitri is alone, she thought. *I'll surprise him.* She opened the men's room door again and slipped in, bolting it behind her. Dmitri was in a stall. *Perfect,* she thought, putting her purse down on a sink and straightening out her short cocktail dress, adjusting its spaghetti straps in the mirror. The toilet flushed. Moments later he emerged, and Lin stood before him. Her sleek body and long legs startled him as he took her in. She smiled, and he smiled back.

"I agree," he said, undoing his belt buckle and then his fly. "Let's fuck right here. Why waste time?"

"Yes. Why waste time?" She delivered a perfect side kick to his solar plexus, sending the 240-pound man through the bathroom stall and onto the toilet seat. Dmitri sputtered on the grimy floor, gasping for air. His face was red and eyes bulged out; her strike paralyzed his diaphragm, starving his body of oxygen. Lin waited for him to recover, arms crossed.

"Tell me what I want to know!" yelled Lin. "What's the name of that ship?"

"You bitch!" he growled, lunging for her.

Using an aikido move, she sidestepped out of his path, grabbed his wrist and nape of the neck, and aimed him for a sink. His head connected with enameled steel, producing a sickening thud, and Dmitri ricocheted onto the floor, dazed.

"What's the name of the ship?"

Dmitri lay motionless, as if dead.

Crap, Lin thought. *Not again.*

Then he began writhing around on the floor, holding his concussed head and gasping for air again.

"When was it in Newark?" she continued. "Who in the mob handled it? Tell me what I want to know!" She grabbed his wrist and twisted it backward and up, causing him to scream.

"Enough! Enough!" he pleaded, holding up the other hand in surrender.

"Then tell me what I need to know," commanded Lin. In her experience, informants always broke under pressure. They were the weakest animals in the criminal jungle, and that was what made them squeal. The trick was knowing how to apply pressure, and Lin preferred joint locks. Unfortunately for her, the FBI disagreed.

"A sh-sh-ship called *Lena*," he said, stuttering from the concussion and rubbing his head. "A container ship. It did two trips from Novorossiysk to Newark."

"Wait, what? Novorossiysk?" said Lin in disbelief and struggling to roll the name off her tongue. It sounded like *novo-roh-SEEEESK*. "You mean Antwerp, right? Antwerp."

"Antwerp?!" Now Dmitri looked surprised. "No! I thought you were talking about the *Lena* out of Novorossiysk."

"Where the crap is that?"

Dmitri looked like a kid who had accidentally told burglars where the family safe was. The *bratva* would kill him if they found out.

Lin looked sympathetic. "Don't worry, Dmitri. Just tell me about the ship and no one has to know my source. I won't even tell the FBI." A promise she would try to keep. Try.

"Novorossiysk is a Black Sea port, and where *Lena* originated."

"When?"

"Nine days ago. Six months ago."

"And what did the *Lena* deliver?"

Dmitri shook his head and looked down. "I don't know."

"You're lying. Don't piss me off!" she said, and Dmitri looked up at her in terror.

"A container in August," he blurted out, "and another last week. They were unregistered and no one knows what was inside."

"Who handled them?"

Dmitri paused. He wasn't prepared for this level of confession.

"Who offloaded the containers, Dmitri? You either tell me now or I tell the *bratva* you're hitting on an FBI woman. What's the punishment for that, I wonder? Probably involves a razor blade."

Dmitri cringed and closed his legs.

"Dmitri, last chance. Who smuggled in those containers in Newark?"

"The Shulaya," he said, head down.

Lin looked astonished. "The Shulaya? Impossible. We busted them a year ago. They're gone."

"Apparently not all of them," he said, sitting up and holding his head. "Word is they secretly offloaded each container and moved them to a distribution warehouse in Secaucus. From there, no one knows what happened. Presumably the containers were unpacked and loaded onto trucks, but no one knows for sure. Not even the Shulaya."

"What does that mean, not even the Shulaya knows?"

"That's all I know, I swear! It's supersecret mafia shit. Only the bosses know, not people like me. We get paid to mind our business and ask nothing."

"Don't give me that bullshit," she said, grabbing his wrist and twisting backward, causing him to yelp. "I'm an FBI agent and I know when you're lying. What else have you heard?"

Someone was knocking on the bathroom door. Lin ignored it.

"Only rumors," Dmitri said in a whimper, his free hand clutching his skull in pain. The door knocking turned into pounding.

"Go away!" Lin shouted at the locked door.

"Is that a chick in there?" shouted a man on the other side. "Open up!"

"Hold it or use the women's room!" she yelled, then turned back to Dmitri. "What else have you heard?"

"Are you speaking Russian in there?!" asked the man outside the door. "Look you stupid Slavic whore, turn tricks in your home. Or, better for you, the dumpster. I gotta pee!" Lin's fists clenched at *whore,* and Dmitri reflexively put his hands over his head.

"What did you call me?" asked Lin in a calm voice.

"Whore," said the man, with satisfaction. "Stupid. Russian. *Whore.*"

Lin walked to the door, unbolted it, palm-heeled the guy's nose, and bolted the door again while the man gripped his nose in pain. Dmitri winced as he heard the man's body thump to the ground through the door, followed by screams of pain.

"You bwoke my nose! You bwoke my nose!" the man yelled in a nasally voice, but the bar's loud music up-stairs drowned out his cries. Or no one cared.

Lin turned back to Dmitri. "I know the Russian mafia occasionally works for the Kremlin here. Don't lie to me. Why did the ship come from the Black Sea? What was it carrying?"

"Just ru-ru-rumors," stuttered Dmitri, still staring at the bathroom door. "Russian intelligence has been run-ning a major operation in the capital region for months. Double agents, hackers, a tech team—"

"Why?"

"I don't know," he said.

Her hand formed a palm heel.

"I don't know!! I swear I don't know!"

Lin relaxed, and Dmitri sat back up, rubbing his nose

unconsciously. "Also, I heard a heavy team arrived in town last week."

"What kind of team?" she asked.

"A black-on-black hit team. Spetsnaz, I think."

Russian special forces. Lin paused.

This is my big lead, she thought, masking her elation from Dmitri. It was possible they came in on the container, along with a whole lot of Spetsnaz firepower. More urgent, they represented a clear and present danger. If she could verify their presence, it could reorient the FBI toward the true threat: Russia. But obtaining proof would be difficult; she would have to survive.

"I don't suppose you know where I could find them?" she asked casually, pulling out a lipstick from her purse and applying it in the bathroom mirror. She mashed her lips together so it spread evenly, and then looked down at the big man, still sitting in a fetal position at her feet.

"No," he gulped for air. "But the FSB has safe houses in suburban Virginia."

"Where?" she asked in a matter-of-fact tone while putting the lipstick away.

"McLean, near the CIA. That's all I heard. Rumors. You have to believe me!" he pleaded.

She shook out her ponytail, combing her hair with her fingers. "I do, for now. Anything else I should know?"

Dmitri shook his head. Satisfied, Lin grabbed her purse, unbolted the door, stepped over the other man's squirming body, and turned back to Dmitri.

"And one more thing. Don't leave town. We might need to talk again," she said, and proceeded upstairs.

Dmitri looked horrified.

CHAPTER 16

Hell's bells! I screamed in my head. I was in a flat spin thirty-four thousand feet above Manhattan and out of control. The city lights, the plane, and the moon spun ever faster around me, and I was getting dizzy. Soon I would black out.

The whole team was out of control. We bounced off the tailgate like tokens spilling from a slot machine, falling everywhere, rather than a coordinated group exit. Now we were in trouble, hurtling to the earth at 120 mph.

"Locke, control your descent!" I heard Lava shout over my earpiece. "It will get worse unless you correct now."

The spin accelerated, and soon the moon and Manhattan were one. My altimeter read thirty-two thousand feet on my HUD, giving me two minutes to rectify the situation. I arched my back and stuck out my leg wing to regain control, but little happened. If this were a training exercise, I would pull my rip cord now and deploy the parachute. But it was a combat jump and I had to assume there were hostile drones in the air. Also, I wasn't sure if Lava sabotaged my parachute.

"Ball up!" said an Aussie accent. The lateral Gs were pushing blood to my brain, and I felt the blackout coming.

Focus! I commanded, and breathed deeply to calm my pulse.

"Dive out of it!" shouted Tye.

Diving won't work, I knew. I was spinning too fast. Instead, I dug my right knee into my elbow, catching air against the direction of the spin with my arm wing. The spin began to slow, and Manhattan and the moon were once more recognizable.

"Keep it up," said Lava.

The spin stopped and I spread my arms and legs, deploying my wingsuit like a flying squirrel. Wingsuits gave jumpers range and control, for those who could master them. The dizziness lingered and I felt I might throw up in my oxygen mask.

"Super-duper paratrooper," said Lava. "Your vitals were spiking. You're rusty."

"I blame the equipment," I joked, and scanned for the team, but all I saw were moonlight clouds below.

"AI, find the team," I commanded my onboard artificial intelligence, embedded in the tactical cuff.

"Team located 1,200 feet below tracking 245 degrees. Shall I plot a course?" said my AI in a tranquil woman's voice.

"Affirmative," I replied. A pale blue trajectory line lit up in my HUD, pointing me toward the team, far below. Zooming in my optics, I could see they were traveling in a V formation westward, toward Manhattan. The pilot green-lighted us well past the city to match the flight profile of a commercial airliner, and now we had to "fly" back via wingsuit several miles to downtown. The Atlantic was directly below us.

Gotta catch up or get left behind, I thought. I assumed a flat track position, tucking my arms tight to my sides, palms down, legs together, and toes out. My body became an arrow, descending rapidly until I caught up with the V and changed into a delta position.

"Good of you to join the flock," said Tye.

"Silence," said Lava. In the distance, I could see the grid lights of the city and the dark rectangle in the middle—Central Park.

"Switching to tactical," said Lava, and my HUD transformed into a polychromatic dazzle of friends, foes, and obstacles. Beneath us, a 747 was on approach to JFK airport, illuminated in yellow, as was an Airbus taking off. The new trajectory line led to a red blinking dot on the west side of Midtown, off the Hudson.

"That's our objective," said Lava.

"Where's our DZ?" I asked, seeing only a concrete rain forest of skyscrapers.

"You're looking at it."

I saw nothing. Just tall buildings. Maybe there was something wrong with my system. Or it was sabotaged. "I'm not seeing it. The flight path leads downtown, and there's no place to land."

"We're not landing in downtown. We're landing *above* it," said Lava, and my heart jumped with alarm. I zoomed in my optics for a closer look at the DZ. It was one of the tallest and newest skyscrapers in the city, rivaling the Empire State Building. And it shimmered. It looked like it was made of mirrored glass that reflected the darkness around it, making it hard to see. Then I spotted the DZ, marked in pale blue by my HUD.

Holy shit, I thought. The DZ was a narrow sixty-five-foot triangular observation deck 101 stories up, almost at the very top of the building. Successfully landing there would be like hitting a hole in one, if the hole were on top of a flagpole and you were teeing off a flying Lear Jet.

"That's impossible," I muttered, and heard Tye snickering over the comms.

"Don't blow my mission, Locke," said Lava. "We don't want your body splattered in the middle of Thirtieth Street. It might tip off security."

I zoomed in more, although it was difficult given the bumpy ride. The observation deck faced us, and above it were several stories of superstructure. But it was no roof; it was a huge pinnacle in the sky with enormous triangular holes that artfully concealed machinery and water tanks. If we touched down there, we would either slip through one of the holes and crush our bodies on the machinery below, or bounce off the forty-five-degree incline and fall to the asphalt 120 stories down. There would be no recovery time, just certain death.

"Lava, that's no DZ!"

"Ten thousand feet," said Lava, ignoring me. We were zooming over Brooklyn and would be at the DZ in seconds. Quickly, I glanced around for alternative DZs. Better to piss off Lava and walk away than risk gory death, but there were no good DZs because it was New York City.

"Nine thousand."

Hell, I didn't even know if my chute would open.

"Eight thousand."

We all banked slightly right to line up the approach to the skyscraper's small observation deck.

"Seven thousand."

This is insane! I thought.

"Valhalla, this is Omega. Building is hacked. DZ is secure," said Apollo command.

"Six thousand. Copy, Omega."

I could see the small balcony clearly now. It looked like a shelf at the top of a Saturn rocket.

"Five thousand. Pull at two."

EEEEEEEE! An alarm screeched in my earpiece. "Tango," shouted Lava. My HUD illuminated a rotary wing drone in red, flying random patterns around the building in stealth mode, although I could not see it with my naked eye. My AI listed it as potentially heavily armed, an extreme measure for Manhattan. Whatever was inside the building was important enough to risk an aerial firefight above New York City.

Who would take such a risk, and what's in that building? I thought, realizing I might soon find out.

"Four thousand. Watch the crosswind."

We whooshed by the Empire State Building's antenna tower.

"Three thousand."

My AI had me pulling my rip cord high and right of the building, compensating for the crosswinds. Would the parachute deploy when I pulled the rip cord? Almost reading my mind, Tye asked: "Locke, do you trust us?"

"Do you trust me?" I retorted. He did not respond.

"Three, two, one, deploy!" shouted Lava, and I pulled the rip cord. The opening G shock tore through my body, knocking my breath out, as the canopy deployed. My boots kicked up in the air, and the crosswind caught my wingsuit, sending me away from the observation deck, three hundred feet away. Lava and three other team members touched down. Four more were on approach. However, I was off azimuth and would miss the DZ.

"Locke, you're wide," yelled Lava. I yanked on my right riser, which steered the parachute, and I swung hard right toward the sixty-five-foot isosceles triangle in the sky. Under my boots was 1,500 feet of air then traffic then asphalt.

Three others touched down on the roof deck, and Lava was already at the glass doors, working the security system. Meanwhile, I was still flapping in the wind.

EEEEEEEEEEE! The alarm sounded off. "*Warning. Enemy drone detected seven hundred thirty feet below and rising,*" said my AI in her unnervingly calm voice. I looked down through my boots and could see the armed drone's blades slice the air. It looked like a quarter-size black helicopter with no lights, probably used only at night to avoid day gawkers.

"Locke, evade!" said Tye. I yanked the toggles on both risers and swung up. The drone remained motionless, but didn't spot me. Drones often have a blind spot: they cannot see above them, which might have been a reason Lava chose this crazy ingress route.

"Locke, you're about to be blown off DZ!" said Tye, meaning I would soon cross a line of no return and have to land somewhere on the street below. Although, I doubted I would get that far. The drone would spot me and shoot up my canopy, if it was armed. I would fall to my death.

"*Warning. Enemy drone rising,*" said the AI. I had only seconds. Far down, I could see the Thirty-Fourth Street subway yard. I could try to make it.

"Locke, the drone!" said Tye, strain in his voice. Lava and the rest of the team already disappeared inside the building. Apparently, Tye was my assigned battle buddy after all.

Just get back over the balcony, I thought as I strained on the risers and did a sharp 180-degree turn, catching

an updraft. Fifty feet beneath me was the tip of the triangle, and two hundred feet below that was the ascend-
ing drone.

"Locke!" cried Tye as I drifted away from the balcony and over the street. In one second, I would be
below the DZ.

Now or never, I thought, I pulled hard on the left
riser, and violently swung toward the balcony, twenty-
five feet away. At the same time, I yanked the quick-
release on both risers and hurtled weightless through
the air, with 1,100 feet of space between me and the
ground. Glancing down, I saw the drone's blades rising
as I bicycle-kicked to maximize my forward momentum. But I came up short. I bounced off the outside of
the observation deck's glass wall, just managing to grab
the top with my left hand.

"Locke, hang on!" said Tye, rushing over to help me,
but the glass walls surrounding the observation deck
were fifteen feet high. I was dangling in space.

"Locke, the drone!" said Tye, as the *chop chop chop*
got louder. With a grunt, I did a pull up in full combat
gear and threw a leg over the glass wall. I rolled over
the rim and slid down the safe side, hitting hard. Meaty
hands pulled me to my feet.

"Move! Move!" cried Tye, and we sprinted for the
observation deck's door. Apollo command had already
hacked the building's security as we HALOed in, but it
could not control the armed drone.

"Inside!" he said as we dove behind large planters.
We could hear the thing hover above the observation
deck, scanning, but the planters concealed our body
heat from the drone's thermal cameras. Off a side-
window reflection, I could see the machine's silhouette.

It had weapons pods on its flanks. No guns or missiles protruded, but their purpose was unmistakable. After a moment, it buzzed away.

"Gutsy move, Locke, jumping like that. I thought you were a goner."

"Victory to the bold," I said, still catching my breath. "Is that thing actually armed?"

"Yeah, but don't worry. Apollo shut down the internal defenses, so we should be good to go now."

I paused, digesting what he just said. "Defenses? Like, *armed* defenses?"

"Roger."

"What kind of skyscraper is this?" I whispered.

"A fortress. The first ninety floors are normal. The top ten are the enemy's North American headquarters. They own the whole block too, through a front company, of course."

"Who is the enemy? Who flies armed drones in New York?"

"I'll let Lava fill you in. But they're like us. Dangerous. Watch your six."

"Tye, sitrep?" said Lava in his command voice.

"Operative recovered, area secure. Moving to your location now," said Tye, standing up. He looked like a black cyborg in his head-to-toe armor but moved like a gymnast. "Stay quick, Locke. Follow me close. Trust nothing in here. Nothing."

I nodded as I removed my wingsuit and oxygen bottle, but was alarmed by Tye's cryptic warning. I had no idea what we were walking into, other than it was lethal. Tye ran into the darkness and I followed, weapon at the ready.

CHAPTER 17

Rock Creek Parkway is a secret highway that runs through Washington that only locals know. There are few, if any, signs that note the entrances in order to keep the tourists out. Trucks are illegal, and those who sneak on get their tops chopped off by the low stone bridges.

The winding road snakes up the center of the city, but it looks like a bucolic valley in Connecticut rather than the urban hubbub surrounding it. During rush hour, parts of Rock Creek convert to one-way, terrifying lost tourists who mistakenly wander into its corridor.

Picnic tables with stone grills line Rock Creek for Washingtonians to have family outings. Some even have weddings there. More than a few picnic areas are set back from the road, and a few are hidden. After midnight, it was a place for teens to hook up or conspirators to meet.

The two black convoys arrived almost simultaneously. Three armored Chevy Suburbans from the south and three more from the north pulled into a parking lot side by side but facing opposite directions.

After a moment, armed men from the middle vehicles stepped out and opened the passenger doors. A tall man with a cane stepped from one backseat to the other, the door shutting behind him.

"Thank you for meeting me at this hour."

"We are allies, if not friends," said the man with the cane in a raspy voice.

"We have a new problem."

"Oh?"

"More of a complication than a problem. But left to fester, it will become a problem."

"What is it?" said the hobbled man with displeasure.

"The president. He's not following along with the script."

Silence. Finally, the man with the cane broke it. "But isn't that your job?"

More silence. "It's *our* job."

The man with the cane squeezed the ivory handle in rage but his weathered face revealed no emotion. "And what do you want me to do about it?"

"The CIA. They're the source of the problem. You can reach them in ways I cannot. Can I count on your—" the man paused, choosing his words carefully "—oblique approach to steer their analysis?"

The man with the cane could not help but chuckle. "It's the oldest joke in Washington: research agenda. You want me to provide the agenda and they perform the research? Seems like something you could easily manage yourself."

"Not this time. It has to come from outside government. It has to come from your organization. Understand that I'm not asking you to alter the plan; just throw them off the scent."

The man with the cane pondered the task with displeasure, but finally acquiesced. "Fine. I will see what we can do, but I make no promises." He looked the other man in the eyes. "We go back a long way, you and I. But do not take our friendship for granted. If you continue to modify our original agreement, there will be consequences."

The other man stiffened, not expecting such a riposte, then nodded. The man with the cane rapped on the window, and a stocky bodyguard opened the bulletproof door.

Two minutes later, the convoys sped off into the darkness, going in opposite directions.

CHAPTER 18

Tye ran like a heavily armed gazelle, bounding over desks, couches, and whatever else stood in his way. My parkour skills were respectable, but Tye leapt before he looked. It was suicide.

"Tye, hold up!" I panted.

"Keep pace," he commanded, speeding around a corner. I rounded it and saw the open elevator shaft.

"Tye!!" I shouted, skidding to a stop at the edge of the 1,100-foot drop. Peering over, I glimpsed only darkness, and listened for the crash of his body, 101 stories down. I would need to find a different route down.

"You think I'm that easy to kill?" said Tye over the headset.

"Where are you?"

"Floor ninety-seven. Beat feet!"

This is going to be sparky, I thought, as I backed up and then ran for the shaft. I timed it so my left foot pushed off the edge of the open elevator shaft while I spread my arms wide. My inner right arm caught the high-tension cables midflight, spinning me hard clockwise. I locked my legs around the cables, but I was not prepared for the speedy descent. My body zipped down the slick cables, and my stomach rose to my throat. Floor 97's door was propped open and I had only one chance, so I leapt. My body was weightless once more as I plunged through the darkness. My left hand caught the elevator's threshold while the rest of me dangled down the shaft. With a grunt, I heaved myself up and faced Tye, who was waiting for me.

"You have a thing for hurtling through space?" he asked. I could almost see the smirk through his black visor.

"Yeah, it makes me feel all tingly inside," I joked, but he simply turned and kept moving. So did I. The place looked like a high-end hedge fund office: ultra-modern glass and steel design, exotic wood flooring, and whacko modern art. It smelled of cappuccino and rug cleaner, even though there were no rugs.

The hallway emptied into a two-story atrium, with a glass balcony and near-360-degree view of the city, as seen through the floor's glass walls and floor-to-ceiling windows. It was magnificent. Overlooking us from the balcony was artistic stupidity: an eight-foot marble statue of a man that looked like Michelangelo's *David* except his head was a gigantic chrome cloud. No doubt it was "priceless."

The team had moved all the furniture out of one corner and were now measuring distances from the walls with laser range finders. Another was taking the measurements and drawing a perfect circle on the Brazilian hardwood floor with indelible marker.

"Lava, we're here," said Tye.

"Roger. Tye, on me. Locke, on demo."

Demolitions. I liked demo. One of Lava's team was

pulling out thick plastic tubes from his rucksack and screwing them together. As I approached, he didn't look up; he only held out a roll of 100 mph tape.

"Take it, rook," he said.

"Ain't no rookie," I responded, snatching the black duct tape from his hand. "I was leading an Apollo team when you were still a Bat Boy." It was a term for an army ranger. Rangers were my friends and I had gone through ranger school, but they were not known for subtlety, just like this guy.

"You watch yourself down there," he said coolly.

"Placement area ready," said the guy holding the marker in a deep bass. The ex-ranger and I carried over the tube, which was surprisingly heavy. On the floor, the trooper had drawn a four-foot diameter circle, noting distances and angles to various side walls.

"Ready the tape," said the ex-ranger, laying down the tube on the circle while I taped it to the floor. It fit perfectly. The tube looked like thick det cord, but it was something else.

"What is this stuff?" I asked.

"Been a while, eh, rook?" he said smugly while fastening the blasting caps. "It's Apollo proprietary: two parts CL-20 and one part HMX. Make big boom."

"Omega, we are preparing to breach," said Lava, and we scurried for cover.

"You are green," responded Omega.

"Fire in the hole!" cried the ex-ranger, and I muted my helmet's enhanced hearing. The explosion's shock wave walloped me in the chest, and shook the floor and windows. The marble man statue tottered and crashed to the floor with another loud boom, decapitating him. I sidestepped the chrome cloud head as it rolled by, adding a sense of surrealism. No alarms sounded, due to Apollo's building hack. But some security measures cannot be hacked, and my HUD indicated fire teams a few floors below us moving up the stairs.

"Valhalla, you are red. Security mobilized," said Omega. "Engaging countermeasures. You have sixty seconds before contact."

"Roger, Omega," said Lava, not surprised, as the team vanished down the newly made hole. In the background, I could hear automatic gunfire on the floors below, but not from small arms. They sounded heavier, like crew-served machine guns. But here? It could only mean one thing.

"Are those automated turrets?" I asked Tye.

"Affirmative. Retractable ceiling turrets on the floors above and below. They're controlled by the building's automated defense system, but Omega hacked them when we were in freefall. Now Omega is using the turrets against the enemy's quick reaction force, but it won't take long for the QRF to take them out."

"Fifty-five seconds," said Lava as he disappeared down the hole. Tye dropped down and I followed, tucking my arms and weapon to my chest. The room below was dark and warm.

"Don't touch nothing," said Tye as he moved forward. It was a computer room. Actually, it was a computer floor. Rows of black computer racks the size of refrigerators lined a raised floor, presumably for cabling. The only entrance was a twenty-ton, circular bank vault door—sealed and locked—explaining why Lava chose to breach through the ceiling. The ex-ranger was already placing C4 charges in its guts.

"Find Alpha three-one-three-five," commanded Lava, and the team fanned out and searched the server rows.

I flipped on my point-to-point comms with Tye. "What are we looking for?"

"A specific node board, in a specific rack, in a specific server, in a specific quadrant. Alpha three-one-three-five," he said as I followed.

"This has gotta be the most expensive server farm on the planet, given the real estate prices around here," I quipped.

"Ain't no server farm, it's a supercomputer. And it ain't no ordinary supercomputer; it's a Frontier Super-AI, the fastest in the world. Even faster than its twin at Oak Ridge National Laboratory, and smarter too. It runs our enemy's everything."

Impressed, I asked: "And we're hacking it?"

"No," said Tye, stopping to face me. Multicolor computer lights reflected off his black visor, giving him a robotic look. "No one hacks Elektra, and she would fight back if they tried."

"Wait, it has a name?"

"Just watch your six in here," he said with impatience, and continued down the row. Looking, I noticed every other rack had an enormous but subdued letter on it in an ultramodern font spelling E-L-E-K-T-R-A across the entire row, with a silver lightning bolt through the A. I wondered if bullets would do any good against a foe like Elektra.

"Thirty seconds," said Lava. Tye and I were zigzagging, looking for the magic number.

"Valhalla, enemy on your floor," said Omega.

"Copy. Come on people, find me that rack!" yelled Lava.

My head was a volcano of questions, as I scanned for Alpha 3135. "Tye, if Elektra can't be hacked, then how did Apollo hack the building?"

"Because the building is not Elektra, and the enemy is not the only one with a Super AI."

"Wait, Apollo has an AI too?" I asked, flabbergasted. Apollo was many things, but not that.

Tye turned to me. "Who says it's ours? It's our client's. Now shut your pie hole and search."

Who was the client? Who was the enemy? What were we doing here? It reminded me why I left Apollo: ask a question and get two more in return.

"Omega, status?" asked Lava.

"Helicopter extraction on standby. Ground recovery team ready," replied Omega.

Lava paced. I had never seen him pace before. Perhaps he was nervous because he knew how Elektra would fight back. "Any new breach points?"

"Negative. Just the main entrance."

Lava turned to face that direction. "Is the vault door prepped and demoed?"

"Affirmative," said the ex-ranger over the comms. "Once the tangos touch it, the internal stanchions will blow and render it an unmovable hunk of junk. It will be impassable."

No sooner had he said that when a muffled explosion came from the enormous vault door, followed by a dull thud. We were sealed in, but not for long. The enemy would somehow find another way in; we sure would.

"Omega, update!" said Lava.

"Main entrance sabotaged. Tangos moving to points here and here," said Omega, and my HUD showed red dots massing at opposite ends of the floor. "They must be secret breach points, where the walls are thin, for contingencies like this. We estimate you have one minute before they breach, maybe less."

Silence as Lava weighed his options. Abort was one of them, but I've never known him to give up. Ever. Finally, he spoke: "Tye, Locke on breach point one. Hernandez, Kim on breach point two. The rest find me our node board!"

Tye and I sprinted to the other side of the floor and took up fighting positions, pointing our weapons at the breach point. At present, it was a wall. Soon it would be a hole with tangos swarming out. We each took cover behind a computer rack, lying in the prone position. By my side were two grenades, ready to throw, while Tye's weapon had an integrated 40 mm launcher. I could hear Tye controlling his breathing, readying for what came next.

"Found it. Cover down on me," said one of the commandos. Peering behind me, I saw two commandos far down the row pulling out a tray from the rack; inside were vertical rows of circuit boards, about twenty in all. Another unpacked a flat ballistic case he parachuted in with him.

"Omega, confirming node board Alpha three-one-three-five," said Lava.

"Good copy. You are green to proceed," said Omega.

"Careful now, we get only one shot at this," said the Israeli operator. One of the commandos inspected the contents of Alpha 3135, pulling out five large circuit boards and dumping them on the floor.

"Now hand me the replacements," he said. The other commando opened the ballistic case and took out five nearly identical boards.

"The swaps must be flawless," said the Israeli, "or Elektra will know."

"Preparing to insert new cards," said Lava.

"Copy, Valhalla. We are standing by for network penetration," replied Omega.

As I listened to the radio chatter, I grew confused. "Tye, you said it was impossible to hack Elektra. But it sounds like we're hacking her. What's going on?"

A pause. "Locke, you're a real burr in my ass, you know that?"

"I'm risking my life for this. You can at least tell me why."

Another pause. "It's true, you can't hack Elektra. We've tried. But there is another way, and it took months to figure out. People died."

"New compute cards inserted. Performing electrical tests on the PCBs," said the Israeli. Somewhere beyond the wall, I heard a loud clang. They were getting closer.

"Tye, what's the other way? What are we doing here?" I asked.

"Elektra can only be hacked from the *inside*. Someone has to physically swap out good circuit boards with bad ones inside the artificial neural network. But it can't be any circuit board; it has to be five specific boards within a critical control node."

"Alpha three-one-three-five," I said.

"Correct. We corrupted Alpha three-one-three-five with vulnerabilities our AI can exploit—"

"A back door," I interrupted again.

"Yeah, if you want to call it that. If all goes well, our AI will hack their AI and we win. If not . . . improvise."

Improvise. It was the Apollo way, and not my favorite

strategy for dealing with mortality, even though I was good at it.

"Omega, swap complete. We are ready to integrate node board back into the system. Proceed?" said Lava. I saw the team's collective heart rates spike on my HUD.

"Proceed."

Sirens blared and floodlights lit the entire floor.

"*Emergency.* Oxygen levels dropping," warned my onboard AI, although "AI" seemed a misnomer in the presence of Elektra. The comms channels went static. Even the polite female AI voice began distorting into a grotesque baritone as a massive electronic tidal wave jammed our systems. My head pounded, too.

"Guess it didn't go well," I shouted to Tye over the shriek of the sirens.

"Mission fail," confirmed Tye.

The wall in front of us blew inward, spraying our armor with concrete and steel. Elite mercenaries wearing advanced body armor and oxygen masks assaulted through the breach, shooting. Tye and I threw grenades into the hole, and the concussive blast threw them against the wall. But one got up, his body armor unbelievably strong. Then a second.

You gotta be kidding me, I thought, as a third sat upright. I had never seen grenade-proof armor, unless it was those turtled-up Explosive Ordnance Disposal guys who looked like a Kevlar Michelin Man.

Let's see how good your armor is, I thought. My SCAR fired high-velocity 7.62 mm cartridges with tungsten-carbide bullets, specifically designed to penetrate body armor. In rapid succession, I shot the three in the face, where body armor is weakest. They dropped instantly, but others swarmed in.

"There are too many. Let's go!" screamed Tye, but I knew he was wrong.

I have to thin the herd, or we won't make it five steps, I thought. Switching tactics, I shot three in the leg. They crumbled on impact, and their buddies swooped in and pulled them to safety, ridding me of nine enemies with three bullets in two seconds. The enemy had temporarily ceded the battlefield.

Tye yanked my boot. "E and E!" he shouted through his face mask, telling me to escape and evade. The enemy mercs were gathering on the other side of the breach, readying for another assault.

"Let's go-o-o!" yelled Tye. I pulled a grenade from my vest and threw it into the breach. The enemy mercs scattered instantly, but were too late. The explosion caught two in the chest, blowing them into the wall, killing them. The rest recovered, but they would not throw grenades back as we were in the guts of Elektra.

"Triple time!!" he shouted. I ran but grew dizzy from the depleted oxygen. We ditched our HALO oxygen bottles with the wingsuits on the 101st floor, but kept our reserve chutes and harnesses.

Tye staggered then collapsed, succumbing to the lack of oxygen. I grabbed him by the arms and lifted up, doing the fireman's carry, and stumbled toward the ceiling hole.

"We're surrounded," yelled Lava, as he grabbed Tye and lifted him up like a rag doll. Four hands reached down and pulled him up. I followed, then Lava. We were the last.

"Fire in the hole!" shouted Lava, pulling out a shiny steel cannister from his pack. He flipped open the control pad and armed it, then stuck his head down the hole and chucked the bomb into Elektra and the other mercs.

"Away! Away!" he screamed, as he stumbled backward from the hole. I turned to run and felt my ears compress like a skydive, then the shock wave blew me sideways through a glass wall. I heard and felt nothing, just blackness.

"Get up!"

Gunfire.

"Get up!!"

Explosions.

"Wake up!" It was Tye, crouching above me and firing, empty cartridges bouncing off my visor. I rolled over, disoriented from being knocked out by the blast. Flames licked up from the hole in the ground and black smoke filled the atrium. So much for Elektra.

Tye bolted away, but I felt too woozy to move. The rest of the team moved out, firing in short controlled bursts as they retrograded. Glass flew everywhere, as the firefight exploded the crystal office and modern art. Simultaneously, the sprinkler system rained on us, creating a surreal battlespace.

"Watch the left flank!" shouted Lava, followed by the buzz of a mini-Gatling gun and a waterfall of glass shards.

Get in the fight! I willed my legs to move, but they were kryptonite. As I lay sideways, I could see boots advancing along the floor, and they were not Apollo's.

Get. In. The. Fight. Shaking, my hands reached into my med-pack and extracted an ampule. Opening my visor, I bit off the cap and stuck the ampule up a nostril, squeezed, and inhaled. Starbursts lit up behind my eyes as I felt my body power up. My heart turboed and each breath felt like a scuba tank of air. My senses buzzed and my limbs were itching to pounce. My brain turned predator.

The boots were approaching, but in slow motion now. I rolled to the prone position, SCAR up, and fired four shots. Three men tumbled to the ground, screaming as they clutched their blown-out ankles. Three more shots ended them.

I got up and saw I was alone, except for the enemy mercs twenty feet away. For a millisecond, we all paused, equally surprised. Then the gunfire erupted. I drew like lightning, capping one in the head as I dove sideways and slammed into the floor. A small, octagonal grenade bounced off a cubicle desk and rolled to a stop in front of me, and I sprint-rolled behind a steel filing cabinet. The explosion was deafening, even through my enclosed Apollo helmet, and propelled me into the next cubicle. But I felt nothing, other than the urge to kill. The chemical I snorted unlocked the primitive brain, and it was why everyone at Apollo called it "Mr. Hyde Dust."

Taking a grenade from my vest, I pulled the pin, cooked it for three seconds, and lobbed it for an airburst. The shock wave blew shrapnel through the cubicles like paper. The enemy screamed, and I liked the sound.

Brrrrrrrrrrrr. I ducked and the cubicles around me exploded in splinters as a mini-gun shredded the area with six thousand rounds per minute. I could hear the multiple barrels spin to a stop, and a merc shouting at me in Russian. Poking my SCAR rifle around the corner, I could see the shooter from my muzzle camera. He was huge with a dense beard, and was so cocky that he stood straight up on a desk for all to see, like death itself.

Screw him, I thought. I knew I should keep moving and find Lava, but I wanted to rectify this faux grim reaper. Low-crawling, I slipped under two cubicles and peeked over the rim with my muzzle-cam. Fake reaper still there, like a statue in the sprinkler rain.

Good, I thought. With adrenaline-crazed fury, I popped up, obtained a perfect sight picture of his skull, and squeezed. One shot, one kill. A hailstorm of lead responded to my surprise attack, and I rushed ahead. The enemy ran down a parallel hallway, and we fired at each other through the glass walls on full automatic. Glass blew everywhere.

Find Lava and Tye, I thought. Through multiple glass walls, on the other side of the floor, I could see muzzle flashes and explosions. *Has to be them.*

As I sprinted, two mercs followed. Like Tye, I used parkour to leap over furniture, and shot my way through glass doors. A bullet clipped my left scapula, ricocheting off my armor and making me stumble.

Enough! I sprint-leapt onto the thirty-foot mahogany table and flipped so I was skidding backward on my stomach with my weapon up and aimed at the door. The merc charged in and I shot him in the chest. A second merc dove in as I skidded off the table. We unloaded at each other under the table, but hit only chairs and table legs, sending splinters everywhere.

Keep moving or die! screamed my intuition. I ran out a different exit, toward Lava and the skyscraper's windows.

"You are red," said Omega, the signal improving as I got closer to the windows.

Not helpful! I thought as I emptied a magazine and swapped it out for a new one.

Ahead of me, I could see the team pinned down in a swank corner office. They turned a massive brazilwood desk on its side for cover as a ring of mercs fired into the office space. The glass windows were shot out, and the enemy was trying to drive Lava's team over the edge. This was not a prisoners-of-war kind of war.

One of Lava's team was frantically waving me off.

Why the wave-off? I was trying to rescue them, I thought, then the glass walls around me exploded with the *brrrrrrrrrrrr* of another mini-gun. Bits of ceiling were still collapsing on me as I snuck my muzzle-cam above the remnants of a desk. To my right was the gunner, tucked behind a weightbearing wall, its dry wall shot away to reveal steel and concrete. To my left was the drone in a perfect hover ten meters outside the windows. Its weapons pods were retracted, showing an M134 Mini-gun and two missiles, in case I made a jump for it. As if that were even an option.

Well, that sucks, I thought, as I was thoroughly pinned down. I didn't do surrender, and they didn't do POWs. Life just got simpler.

"Locke, is that you? Sitrep, over," said Lava over my earpiece. Being near the window restored some communications. The drone buzzed back and forth between us. It dared not open fire above Manhattan, unless we did something stupid.

"Affirmative. I'm pinned, over," I said.

"Roger. Keep your head down. We're about to exit, just be ready."

About to exit? Maybe shell shock had finally warped

Lava's mind. I didn't blame the man; he was a battlefield legend. But there was no way out this time.

"Locke, pull out your reserve's pilot chute," instructed Tye.

"Say again?" I asked with incredulity.

"Ready your pilot chute!" yelled Lava.

No, no, no, no! my mind screamed as my hands snaked out my reserve parachute's pilot chute. Lava intended to BASE jump out the window, which was crazy. But I remember Lava once told me: it's not crazy if it works.

"Locke, on my command, shoot out the windows," said Lava.

"Copy," I said, leveling my weapon at one of the huge window panes.

Lava began the countdown as the enemy mercs crept forward. "Three, two, one, fire."

I unloaded half my magazine and the thick glass blew away, but not all at once. It was thick stuff. The rest of the team blew out their corner office, and the drone zoomed toward Lava's position. But he was ready.

"Fire in the hole!" cried Lava, as one of his commandos popped up with a stubby antitank missile on his shoulder and fired at the drone. It exploded, and the weapon's backblast knocked down the enemy mercs.

"Jump!" cried Lava, and the whole team leapt out the shattered windows, ninety-eight stories above the street. Without hesitating, I sprinted for the broken window in front of me, holding my pilot chute in my hand. I heard automatic gunfire behind me, and felt the zing of bullets around my head as I leapt into space and dropped like a stone. Far below, I could see a ball of fire falling, the dead drone. Seconds later it crashed through the roof of a nearby building in a flash of orange.

One thousand, I counted as I plummeted headfirst. I could see my dark silhouette against the skyline reflected in the mirror-like building. If I deployed my parachute too soon, I would be in range of the enemy. Too late and I would be splat.

Two thousand. The skyscraper was getting closer the farther I fell, as the wall tapered outward. If I didn't pull soon, I would smear the mirrored glass like a bug on a windshield.

Three thousand. I let go of the pilot chute and it caught wind, dragging the reserve parachute out of the pack. The opening G shock never felt better, but the crosswind blew me back toward the building, a dangerous situation.

"Damn you, riser," I said, pulling on my risers, but the parachute barely responded. Reserve parachutes are like doughnut spare tires; they get you where you need to go, but not with performance.

Uh-oh, I thought, as I drifted toward my reflection. The parachute would collapse if I collided with the building, and then I would fall. Looking up, I saw eleven other dark parachutes, all heading south. Somehow, they escaped the crosswind.

"Think!" I said, as I watched my reflection about to collide with me. I had maybe twenty feet before impact. Then I began rocking back and forth, like a kid on a swing set, a trick I learned as a paratrooper in the U.S. Army's Eighty-Second Airborne Division. I got higher. On my third swing, my boot tips nearly scraped the skyscraper's windows.

"Almost there," I said, swinging backward and then forward again. This time, I planted both feet on the window and pushed off. The next swing landed me on the window, and I was parallel to the ground. I pulled in my risers slightly, the parachute canopy partially collapsed, and my body begin to fall. At the same time, I twisted around so I faced straight down toward the street.

No fear, I commanded myself. I ran sideways along the windows at a forty-five-degree angle, the half-inflated canopy following me like a balloon. As I gained speed, air filled the parachute and yanked me off my feet. I swung out hard and felt the g-force against my harness, but now momentum was moving me away from the building. Working the risers, I sped away from the mirrored tower.

"Omega, this is Valhalla. Need immediate extraction. Lighting up LZ now," said Lava as we floated down. A light blue rectangle lit up in my HUD a few hundred feet in front of me. Our landing zone, or LZ, was a large warehouse roof. Two parachutes touched down in complete silence.

"Copy Valhalla. Choppers inbound, three mikes," replied Apollo command. As I floated down, I could see the warehouse was the length of the entire block and was actually a U.S. Post Office processing plant.

Four more chutes landed. Several stories down were late-night garbage trucks and street noise. But there were no sirens. No police. It seemed that I had stumbled into a secret war.

As I drifted in, I readied my body for a parachute landing fall. The ground came up faster than expected, and I landed on my feet, ass, and head, in that order. Not my best. But I was in grass! I looked around, and the top of the building was a converted meadow, almost custom made for renegade parachutists.

"Outstanding!" I cried, and heard others laughing and joking, too.

"Omega, this is Valhalla. We have twelve chutes, no injuries or casualties," said Lava, as I heard choppers approaching.

"Good copy, Valhalla."

Two black helicopters flying nap of the earth with no lights suddenly appeared above us. I flopped on my chute to prevent it from being sucked into the rotors, as they descended in perfect synchronization and hovered a foot above the roof.

"Get in! Get in!" yelled Lava. Abandoning my chute, I sprinted for the closest chopper and jumped in, next to the door gunner. Four Apollo drones hovered nearby, acting the armed sentry. As we pulled pitch, I saw black parachutes swirl beneath us before disappearing into the night.

A big paw clasped my shoulder. Turning around, I saw Tye with his helmet off. "Thanks for saving my ass back there. I would have suffocated for sure, and they would have capped me."

Lava removed his helmet, too, a big smile on his face. "You did good, Locke. You did good."

CHAPTER 19

The next morning Lin walked down Connecticut Avenue with her scarf up over her face. The FBI would be after her by now, but she knew they were too preoccupied to care. At least for now. A cold drizzle had blanketed the city, and people walked with their heads down. An umbrella almost poked her in the eye, and she swatted it away unconsciously. Her mind was elsewhere.

What cargo was the Lena *delivering?* she thought, assuming Dmitri could be trusted. As far as informants were concerned, he ranked toward the bottom. Lowest of the low. However, he was the only lead she had, and her future hung on it. *I need to deliver a big clue to get back into the FBI,* she thought grimly.

She'd spent the previous night lying in bed, trying to put the pieces together, but they didn't fit. The *Lena's* mystery cargo and the defunct Shulaya mob running it. The FBI was so distracted chasing terrorists that it was missing the Russia angle. *Or,* she thought with alarm, *perhaps there is no Russia angle.*

"Keep it together, girl," she told herself as she marched on. "Trust your gut."

When she got home from the bar last night, she texted Jason to call her, but he was already asleep. Then he texted her this morning saying he would call her as soon as he got into the office. That was about now.

She stopped at the Mayflower Hotel to get out of the weather. The place had a marble foyer and establishment Washington ambiance. The lobby had large TV monitors for a news-obsessed city, and they all showed the same thing: a partially burned roof of a Manhattan building where a drone crashed. According to reporters, it malfunctioned and the owner retrieved the wreckage before police could investigate, raising important issues about drone safety and regulations. Jen ignored the news as she took a seat in the foyer bistro and removed her wet jacket. A waiter promptly appeared.

"Green tea, please," she said, and the waiter nodded and left. Lin looked around the lobby but saw nothing suspicious. Just the usual: foreign diplomats, well-heeled lobbyists, and Midwestern tourists. She checked her personal phone again but still nothing from Jason.

Come on, Jason, she thought. Jason was her only inside contact, and the only person who could feed her FBI updates. It was times like this that she wished she could talk to her dad. He always knew what to do in a crisis of confidence. It seemed he had a Chinese saying for every contingency.

For a second, Lin thought about throwing the *I Ching,* asking the ancient oracle what she should do. She had three coins and could look up the *I Ching*'s text on her phone. All she needed was a hexagram or two. Then her tea arrived.

"Thank you," she said to the waiter, and inhaled the warm vapors with a smile. A crew of Chinese businessmen sat nearby, and she couldn't help overhearing their conversation. Sometimes the Chinese got lazy, assuming no one understood them in DC, so they could speak freely. Their mistake. However, in this case they were simply talking about the attractive young waitress from the previous night's steak dinner, albeit in colorful language.

Ugh. Men. They are all the same, Lin thought in Mandarin.

Then she felt it. A buzzing in her purse. She dug around her Glock and pulled out her personal phone. It was Jason.

"Jason!" she said, a bit too loudly. The Chinese men stopped talking and spotted her. They began ogling her while assessing her physical features in Mandarin, like a risqué beauty contest. She turned away and cupped her hand over her phone, so no one could hear her. "Jason, I need your help."

"Lin, where the hell are you?" said Jason. There was a brief silence, then he spoke in a low tone so others wouldn't hear him in the open-bay office. "Our boss went ballistic and said he fired you. Is that true?"

"Jason, be quiet and listen. This is important. Do you have a pen?"

"But Jen—"

"Jason," she interrupted again. "It doesn't matter. Here's what matters: the ship. Are you still working the Newark ship case?"

"No, the ADIC shut down the investigation shortly after you disappeared. Yesterday they had me tracking down hazmat licenses in New Mexico. Now I'm researching demolition vendors in Oakland. Super boring. Seems I'm just a computer monkey, backstopping whatever field office is most overwhelmed. I didn't join the FBI for this crap."

She ignored his rant. "The ship's name is *Lena*. It sailed from Novorossiysk in the Black Sea, and not Antwerp."

"Wait. Are you still chasing the ship—"

"Jason!" she yelled and the Chinese men froze and stared at her, then continued their conversation. Lin resumed her low voice. "Take notes. We don't have much time."

"OK, OK, fine." She heard him rummage around his desk for a pen. "How do you spell Novo-whatever it was?"

She spelled it. "The *Lena* made two trips, one in August and another nine days ago. It flew a Liberian flag and had a Russian crew. Owner is unknown. You can pull up the arrival manifests and port logs for details." She could hear him scribbling. "Each trip had one unregistered container, and the Shulaya secretly offloaded it before the *Lena* went through CBP," she said, referring to Customs and Border Protection.

"What's a Shulaya?"

"Not what, but who. They are a particularly nasty branch of the Russian mafia in New York. We busted them over a year ago, and the FBI thinks they are defunct, but they're not. That gives them perfect cover for action, since the Shulaya are no longer on the FBI's radar."

"How do you know all this?" said Jason when he finished writing.

"Don't ask. It's better if you don't know."

Jason paused, comprehending the gravity of his situation. He could get fired, too, but he knew Jen wasn't bullshitting. "All right, go on."

"The Shulaya delivered each container to a transit warehouse in Secaucus, New Jersey."

"Do you know the address?"

"No, but it should be easy to find. They are probably linked to a warehouse. Check the databases."

"Will do. What was in the containers?"

Lin sighed. "No one knows. The Shulaya never opened them. Weren't allowed."

"Seems unusual."

"It is," said Lin. "Listen, Jason. You need to get a team to investigate the warehouse in Secaucus ASAP. That's where the trail goes cold."

She heard him guffaw on the other end. "Who do you think I am, the director?"

"Seriously, Jason, you need to find a way. Do whatever it takes." She could sense Jason's apprehension. It was a big ask. Higher-ups would question him and there were no good answers. It could end badly for him.

"Why don't you call your old task force?" he said. "I'm a nobody to them, and they would remember you. Even if you did—" He was about to say *screw up their major bust* but obviously thought better of it.

"Because I'm toxic right now," she said reflexively, but then reconsidered it. *No, they would invite me in for an interview, then nab me.* She had to remain on the street where she could investigate the Russia angle and feed Jason information, who could work the inside. It was their only chance.

"Wait! Hold on," said Jason. Their boss was talking in the background, then his voice got muffled, replaced by a steady *thump-thump-thump* that quickened. Lin realized Jason was holding the phone to his chest and she could hear his heartbeat. Whatever her boss was saying was stressing Jason out.

A minute later, Jason returned.

"You OK?" she asked.

"No, not really. That was you-know-who, and he's asking about you again and now threatening my career. He wants your gun and badge." Jason paused. "I don't think I can cover for you much longer, Jen. He senses I'm holding out on him during a national emergency. This is career suicide." His voice was stressed.

Lin felt awful, but only for an instant. "Jason, this is bigger than either of us, or the boss. The terrorist attack was not done by terrorists, do you understand? It's a smoke screen, and the FBI is lost in it. We need to shift the Bureau's focus toward the real perpetrators before it's too late."

She waited for him to say something. Silence.

"Jason, I need you. I'll work the outside, and you work the inside. Together we can find enough evidence to reorient the Bureau. We have a duty, remember? We swore an oath. It's not to our boss, it's to our country. Can I count on you?"

Silence.

"Jason, can I count on you?" she said with a tinge of desperation. Everything would be for naught without someone on the inside she could trust, and that left only one person.

"Jason?" she asked softly.

"Count me in."

CHAPTER 20

A caravan of black vans and an armored SWAT truck that looked like it came straight out of Afghanistan sped over a bridge and took a right on Seaview Drive, which had no view at all. Secaucus was an industrial park masquerading as a town. Vast warehouses lined the street and the traffic was mostly trucks. A trainyard was a central feature, surrounded by brownish water and interstates. In the distance was its client, the Manhattan skyline. The town was part of the logistical warren in north New Jersey that fed the great city and much of America's northeast.

The SWAT convoy traveled at speed, passing trucks with ease, but it did not use sirens or flashing blue lights. The element of surprise was essential.

"Approaching objective," said Sergeant Corelli, the SWAT commander, over the radio. He wore two sergeant's hats: one with the police and another with Army Special Forces in the reserves. He had completed three combat tours in Afghanistan and one in Iraq before seeking the quiet life of a New Jersey SWAT commando. Things had never been busier.

"Get ready," said Corelli as they took a left turn and snaked around a back street, crossing railroad tracks. Ahead of them was a warehouse, small by Secaucus standards. It was merely a gigantic building rather than a city block with a roof. It looked decrepit and unused. The parking lot was empty and weeds sprouted out of cracks in the asphalt. Beyond the building were marshes and the Hackensack River, a simmering toxic stew. A chain-link fence topped with concertina wire surrounded the facility, and the entry was locked by a heavy chain and meaty padlock.

"Breach team," said Corelli as they rolled to a stop. Two men in black fatigues jumped out of a van and popped the chain with bolt cutters. The armored vehicle rammed open the gate and the two men hopped back in the van.

"There," said Corelli, pointing to a front door made of steel with an iron outer gate. One van drove around the back, covering the rear exits. The other dropped off its team in front of the warehouse and then zoomed back to the main entrance, blocking the only vehicular escape route. The armored truck pulled up to the front door.

"Out, out, out!" yelled team leaders as SWAT ran out of the vehicles, all dressed in black. They had helmets with built-in radios, ballistic goggles, combat vests, Glock .40s strapped to their thighs, and M4 automatic assault rifles. Four-man teams ran stealthily with muzzles down to the warehouse exits. The lock on the front door was high-end, and not something any locksmith could pick. Small, high-tech cameras were tucked away in every corner of the lot. The place looked abandoned yet had impressive security. A red flag.

I don't like it, thought Corelli. He gestured to the armored truck and it backed up to the iron gate. A SWAT operator opened the back and yanked out a tow strap, attaching one end to the front door's iron gate and the other to the vehicle's tow hitch. Another team member took up position near the door with a shotgun, and two more had their M4s up and aimed at the door.

"Red in position," said the red team leader. Blue, green, and gold followed. From front gate to positions took less than twenty seconds.

"Copy all," replied Corelli. *Go time.* He walked up to the steel door and banged with his fist. "Police! Open up!" He nodded, not waiting for a response. The armored truck accelerated, ripping the iron gate off its hinges and dragging it across the parking lot.

The man with the shotgun chambered a shell and moved in, pointing its muzzle at the door lock. He aimed forty-five degrees in and forty-five degrees down, and squeezed the trigger. *Bang.* The cylinder lock blew inside. The breach man spun around, back-kicked the door open, and stepped out of the way so the stack could enter, Corelli in the lead.

"Go! Go! Go! Go!" he yelled as they entered. The building's alarm screeched in the background, but they ignored it as they worked the dark building.

The SWAT teams made their way through the warehouse, room by room and area by area. Each team had four individuals and shuffled like a centipede: the leader at the head followed by a man who kept his left hand on the shoulder of the guy in front of him and right hand clutching his weapon. When they entered a room, they fanned out, covering their assigned sectors and corners, until the room was clear. The golden rule of SWAT operations: Never enter a room alone. There is one right way and a hundred wrong ways to clear a room. Wrong means death.

"One clear!"

"Two clear!"

"Three clear!"

"Four clear!"

Corelli both loved and feared these missions most. It was a Russian mafia drug bust. You can always count on the Russians to be armed like the Taliban, think like the KGB, and fight like the devil. A tough foe.

"Stay tight, people!" said Corelli as they moved. *Hug the wall, spot the corners, scan your sector.* Corelli was known as a hard-ass, but the type of hard-ass you wanted next to you during a firefight. He had a simple philosophy: train, train, and train some more. They did this at Fort Dix, where they had access to a live shoot house. It's where his Afghanistan experience shown though, and where he earned the respect of the SWAT unit. Now he was its commander.

Where were all the Russians? thought Corelli. They were supposed to be armed, dangerous, and everywhere. The anonymous tip came in last night, and the command center thought it credible enough to wake his ass up at 2 A.M. By 6 A.M., his team was rolling down Seaview Drive.

One more room to clear, he thought as they shuffled down a lightless hall. Beams from their weapon-mounted tactical flashlights danced around the dark corridor, and the shadows were slightly disorienting. *Focus,* he thought. At the end of the hallway was a wooden door surrounded by unpainted cinderblock. It was locked.

"Shotgun on me," whispered Corelli.

"Shotgun up," muttered another SWAT. The back guy moved forward with a Mossberg and took up his position in front of the door. Corelli stood off at an angle, his M4 pointed at the door. Everyone awaited his nod.

Machine-gun fire ripped through the wooden door, and the guy with the shotgun collapsed, dead. The two other SWAT members returned fire, shielded from the bullet storm by their dead teammate. Corelli wasn't so lucky. He fell backward as if someone had taken a sledge hammer to his chest. He couldn't breathe.

Roll! Roll! he commanded himself, but his body was not taking orders. The gunfire continued through the door, splinters flying everywhere, and he saw another team member fall. *When in doubt, empty the magazine,* he thought and willed his M4 up. He switched to full-auto and emptied his magazine through the door and the enemy gunfire withered. He heard Russians shouting on the other side.

"Go! Get him out of here," Corelli shouted hoarsely. The last standing SWAT member dragged his injured comrade around the corner to safety.

More Russian shouting, and Corelli could hear them chambering fresh clips. It sounded like they were also handling ammo belts. *Shit,* he thought.

Another SWAT squad was running down the hall to support him, and Corelli furiously waved them back. Too late. A barrage of lead shot through the door and two SWAT members fell, catching it in the vest like him. *They'll be fine,* he reassured himself as he locked and loaded another magazine. The wood door disintegrated, having absorbed a few hundred rounds too many.

Corelli yanked a flashbang grenade from his tactical vest and tossed it into the room. It was a nonlethal grenade but could kill you by heart attack. *Or one can hope,* thought Corelli as he threw it. SWAT was not issued fragmentary grenades.

BOOOOM!! The sound was deafening and the gunfire stopped. Corelli staggered to his feet, breathing heavily. Two other SWAT threw flashbangs into the room. *BOOOOM!! BOOOOM!!* Corelli smiled.

"On me," he commanded, and the three standing SWAT shooters followed him into the dark room. Close-quarter automatic gunfire perforated the air, and muzzle flashes created a strobe-light firefight. People shouted and some screamed. A minute later, only two men stumbled out.

"Clear," said Corelli, blood seeping from his vest, and collapsed.

CHAPTER 21

The sun was rising as Lava and Tye dropped me off at my safe house. Being on Lava's team again was a personal victory, and an important one, too. When I came back to the U.S., I assumed I would be operating alone. Now Lava had my back, and he was the cavalry.

Or so I hoped. Maybe I was Lava's pawn? I still needed to be cautious.

"Yow," I muttered as I removed my body armor and rubbed tender spots. My right flank was bruised purple and throbbed, now that the adrenaline had worn off. Worse, the Mr. Hyde Dust had left me with a pulsing migraine, making me sympathize with Dr. Jekyll. I gulped down three ibuprofens and a liter of water to help the Hyde hangover, but I doubted it would do much good.

"I need rack," I said as I lay down on my cot and zipped up the sleeping bag. Drained, I stared at the ceiling. Five minutes passed. Then ten. My mind and body were a combination of exhausted and exhilarated, and I knew I would never sleep. Twenty more minutes passed.

"Ah, screw it," I said, getting up and grabbing civvies. I had to walk it off, despite the risks. Minutes later I was on the street, not a smart move owing to street cameras, but I needed space to puzzle things out. I bundled up in a hooded parka, hat, jeans, and sunglasses to conceal my face. I looked like an everybody.

No one walked these empty streets but me. Still, I pulled up my scarf over my nose, and avoided cameras. My only companion was a long coal train lumbering toward the city power plant. In my younger days, I would have scaled the chain-link fence and hopped a ride.

Winters is alive. The news haunted me, despite the night's battle and many questions it produced. Winters was all that mattered. How was it possible? True, the guy could talk himself out of a sunburn, but could he talk himself out of a Saudi beheading? I shook my head. Somehow, he had.

I'm not safe, I realized with reflexive dread. If Winters was alive and knew I was here, he would come after me with everything he had. In other words, half of Apollo would try to kill me. I had better chances fighting the Eighty-Second Airborne Division.

In the ride back, Lava told me to stay hidden while he ran the traps. "I'll quietly ask around Apollo's headquarters. If they still think you are dead, then you're safe."

"If Apollo HQ doesn't know you are back, then the government surely wouldn't," added Tye. "And probably not Winters either."

Only if I'm lucky, I thought. The next hours would be like waiting for a verdict in a death penalty trial.

CHAPTER 22

Corelli sat upright in the parked ambulance, wrapped in a wool blanket. His top was stripped down to a black T-shirt, and his left arm hung in a sling with a heavily bandaged shoulder. The bullet went through a seam of his ballistic vest, in between the chest and shoulder Kevlar plates. Thankfully the bullet exited but he would still need surgery, plus months of physical therapy. It might even mean the end of his shooting days, depending on how it healed. Shoulders were tricky. But that wasn't what bothered him.

Three dead. Five wounded. Fuck, he thought. In all his combat missions and SWAT raids, he never lost a single person. It was a source of pride, and why people volunteered to join his team. Now three KIAs in one day, and five hurt. Six, if he included himself.

"You OK, champ?" asked a street cop. The parking lot was teeming with first responders. Police, fire trucks, ambulances, and unmarked FBI vehicles. There was even a van from a government agency he had never heard of before. Who knew what they'd found in the warehouse? He didn't care anymore.

"Yeah, fine," he lied.

"You guys did pretty well. Killed nine Russian mobsters. Wounded three," said the cop. Corelli eyed the three stretchers across the parking lot with police around them. The wounded were handcuffed to the stretchers. Two were smoking while the third lay unconscious. Corelli fantasized about taking the cop's 9 mm, walking over, and capping all three. They deserved it.

"Yeah, guess we did," he lied again.

The FBI had locked down the site for national security reasons but didn't explain what they were. Only those in critical condition were rushed to the hospital, and the rest were stabilized. They kept the dead in the warehouse, out of sight from the nosy news helicopter that buzzed overhead.

"When can I get out of here?" asked Corelli. The paramedics gave him painkillers and an icepack, but he could feel the ache in his shoulder.

"Dunno. The Bureau sealed the building, and I saw three guys in white hazmat suits enter."

"No shit?"

"No shit."

Corelli secretly worried that his team had been exposed to some toxic nerve agent or radiation. One more thing to stress about. *Purge it from your mind,* he thought. *It's too late now.*

Across the parking lot, an FBI agent who spoke Russian was interviewing the prisoners and getting impatient with their responses. One blew smoke in the Fed's face, and the agent took a thumb and gently pressed a bandage. The Russian screamed. Corelli smiled.

Two Feds exited a side door carrying an oddly shaped metal suitcase and deposited it in the mystery van. Some FBI gathered around the van door, watching whatever was going on, then looked upset. One agent, presumably the guy in charge, stepped away and made a call. At first he was placid, then began gesticulating wildly, and finally put his phone away with a worried expression. Both Corelli and the cop stared. They had never seen anything like it.

"What do you think they found in there?" asked Corelli. His team evacuated him after he was shot and then went back inside, where they remained. No one had back-briefed him since then.

"A whole lot of weapons but no drugs," said the cop.

"Then why all the hubbub?"

"I don't know," said the cop, also puzzled. "I spoke to a buddy who came out of the building. He said something about two empty containers."

"*Empty* containers?" said Corelli with a laugh.

"Yeah, can you believe it? All this fuss over empty containers."

Both men shook their heads as more FBI agents piled into the warehouse.

CHAPTER 23

Lin sat on a park bench cradling a green tea for warmth. Squirrels danced around her, expecting food, but she shook her head at them. The park across from the World Bank was historically a hotbed for protests against Third World debt. Now it was a small copse of trees among asphalt and cars. It also lacked people, which is why Lin liked it. She was done with people.

Her phone buzzed but she ignored it, focusing on the beautiful clear morning. It was her last moment of freedom. Dmitri was ultimately a bust. Now it was time to return to the FBI and surrender her badge and gun. Staying out longer would only make things worse. They might even charge her with something.

No, she thought, *they will* definitely *charge you with something.* Her boss's appetite for schadenfreude was limitless, the sign of a bitter old man with a dead-end career. Regardless of what he tried, she was done as an FBI agent, a truth she wasn't ready to admit. The pain, her disappointed father, her failed life—it was easier to ignore it. The birds chirped happily above her, over the din of the city.

The phone buzzed again, ruining her reverie with nature. *When my tea is done, I'll walk to the Hoover Building and turn myself in,* she thought, sipping very slowly. Maybe things weren't so bad. Perhaps they would give her a third chance, she rationalized. After all, they were short agents in a time of national crisis and her intentions were good. Mostly.

Bzzzzzz. Bzzzzzz. Bzzzzzz.

Holy crap, she thought and reached for her phone. It was Jason.

"Jason, what is it?" she said, annoyed.

"You'll never believe it," he said with pride.

"Believe what?"

"Just take a guess."

"Just tell me. I'm not in the mood," sighed Lin, watching the birds fly away.

"We found the mystery containers!" he said triumphantly. She could hear him doing a victory dance at his desk and struggled to push the image out of her mind.

"What?!"

"Yeah! Your source was right. We found both containers this morning in a Secaucus warehouse."

Lin felt dizzy. Seconds ago, she was prepared to turn herself in, and maybe face arrest. Now, everything had flipped. "But . . . but, how?"

"I called it in last night, using the anonymous tip line on the internet. Said there was a huge drug and weapons shipment. I knew what key words would set off police alarm bells. It worked. They sent a SWAT team in this morning and found both mystery containers, sitting right there in the middle of the warehouse. It was glorious!"

Wow, Dmitri told the truth. She didn't see that coming.

"And there's more."

"More?"

"Yeah. Way more. The containers were empty, but they did a radiological sweep. One tested positive for traces of uranium."

"A nuclear bomb?"

"Even better: nuclear terrorism!" he said, genuinely gleeful. "The WMD Directorate is standing up a task force, and I've just been assigned to it. I'm graduating from dynamite to fissile material. It's like a promotion!"

"You must be so proud."

"This can launch my career," he said seriously, unaware of her sarcasm.

"What else did they find?"

"Not much. We're still trying to figure out who sent them, what was in them, and where the contents are now. All the essentials. Look, don't tell anyone because it's all hush-hush." He paused. "Uh-oh. The boss is on the prowl. Gotta run!" The phone went dead.

Lin sat astonished. This was a stay of career execution. She was still in play. Of all the disturbing things in the conversation, the worst was nuclear terrorism. *What the hell is going on?* The Russian mob didn't smuggle nukes because the Kremlin would never entrust them with WMD. Nor would the *bratva* work for radical Islamic terrorists; it wasn't their business model.

Yet what explained the trace uranium they found? It probably wasn't medical equipment. Also, the FBI must have found something linking it to the bridge or else Jason would not have used the term "nuclear terrorism."

She gulped the last of her green tea and stood up. Across the street was Washington's most empty tourist attraction: the World Bank gift shop, full of economic textbooks and cheap cuff links. Lin paused in the window, staring at the world map. Where would the mob obtain a nuke? Not from the Russian military. Not from anywhere.

"Impossible," she said softly. As a kid, she went

through a Sherlock Holmes phase, reading every story. It was a reason she became an FBI agent. There was one line that always stuck with her: "When you have eliminated the impossible, whatever remains, however improbable, must be the truth."

If the mob has a nuclear weapon, it must have come from Moscow with orders. Lin reached into her purse and found her phone.

"Jason here," answered the voice.

"You know 'nuclear terrorism' is a dud, right, Jason? If terrorists had a nuke, they would have used it in the bridge attack, and we'd already be incinerated."

"Jen, I'm super busy. Can we discuss later?"

Lin ignored him. "Nukes are way out of the terrorists' league. Think about it, Jason: Where would they source a nuclear weapon? The world was petrified of loose nukes after 9/11, but it turned out to be a boogeyman. Why would Iran, Russia, Pakistan, North Korea, or anyone else trust a nuke to a terrorist group? If they wanted to detonate a WMD in the United States, they would use their own people."

Jason sighed and spoke. "Or-r-r-r, the terrorists are keeping the nuke in reserve to instill maximum fear, using it when the nation is most vulnerable. It could be in a van in Times Square or buried in the pits of the Daytona 500. It could be a nuclear car bomb near Arlington Cemetery, waiting to detonate at the vice president's funeral. Think of it. All the cabinet secretaries, generals, foreign dignitaries . . . everyone will be there, and the world will be watching. It'll create waves of panic globally and fill the terrorist ranks with new recruits. A terrorist army."

Lin didn't like what she heard, not because it was wrong but because it could be true.

CHAPTER 24

Jackson sat back in his chair, foot braced against the edge of his desk, and unconsciously twirled the phone cord in his hand.

"Um-hum . . . OK . . . That's disturbing," he said, then listened. A young woman knocked gently on the door and stuck her head in. He held up a finger, telling her to wait a minute, but she shook her head and pointed to her wrist, indicating he was late.

"OK, I'll pass that along to the president . . . Yes, I understand the urgency," he said into the phone. The young intern glared at him, reminding him of his mother. He reflexively spun his chair around so he couldn't see her.

"Got it . . . Keep me apprised," he said, and hung up.

"Sir, everyone is in the Oval Office and waiting on you. Including the president."

"Thank you, uh . . ."

"Anne."

"Anne," he said, putting on his suit jacket. Normally he wouldn't address an intern by name, but she was the daughter of one of their biggest campaign donors, and the president was going to press her parents to swipe another seven-figure check during reelection season. "Lead away," he said.

He followed her down the corridor. They turned left and walked past the Roosevelt Room. Then she motioned him into the Oval Office as if she were ground-guiding a 747. *I hate millennials,* he thought, entering the yellow room. It smelled slightly of linseed oil and flowers. The National Security Council's principals were arrayed in chairs around the president, who was sitting behind the Resolute Desk.

"George, glad you could join us," said the president with a tinge of bite. A few of the others looked away in awkwardness. "Start us off, will you?"

Jackson took a seat and heard the door close behind him. Next to him sat the secretaries of defense, state, and homeland security. There were also the director of national intelligence and the chairman of the Joint Chiefs of Staff, the highest-ranking general in the military. The only person absent was the vice president.

"I just got off the phone with the FBI director," said Jackson in a smooth voice. "There's been a new development. A troubling one."

The director of national intelligence shifted uncomfortably in his seat, probably because he already knew somehow.

"There's a possibility that a nuclear weapon was smuggled into the U.S. through Newark, New Jersey." He briefed what they knew so far. "The radiological test results could prove a false positive. But until we know for sure, the WMD is our new main effort."

The room sat stunned. President Anderson finally broke the silence. "Are the two connected? Is there evidence linking this to the bridge attack?"

"No, but we have to assume they are linked," said the

director of national intelligence. "Expect the worst and you'll never be disappointed."

"It's been nine days since the ship docked in Newark. The WMD could be anywhere by now," said the head of homeland security, her voice quavering. "Mr. President, we may have to consider evacuating key cities, like New York, Washington, Los Angeles, Houston, Chicago—"

"There will be no evacuations," interrupted the president.

"We have credible evidence of a clear and present danger," she said. "We must act."

"The evidence is not credible until I say it is, and it's not. We don't want to start a panic. Period."

Her eyes narrowed, the only tell of her outrage.

"There will be no evacuations," repeated the president, sensing the tension. "We don't want to start something we can't control. That's how the terrorists win."

"We've already got the Bureau, Agency, and Department of Energy working the problem," said Jackson, turning to the secretary of homeland security. "We'll know more soon."

"Good, Jackson," said the president. "Keep me informed the second you learn something. I'm writing my speech for tonight, and a nuclear bomb changes everything. Let's have our next meeting in an hour by phone."

"Yes, sir," said everyone in chorus.

"And one more thing. Absolutely, positively, and under no circumstances can this leak to the press. The media cannot learn of this."

CHAPTER 25

NEWS ALERT: NUCLEAR TERROR flashed on televisions and in headlines around the world. Jackson watched the TV in disgust. Outside his window he could hear protestors chanting in Lafayette Square.

"Cities across the country are emptying out amid rumors of a terrorist nuclear bomb," said the news anchorwoman. The screen showed standstill traffic jams in major cities around the world.

"And who is responsible for spreading the rumor?" yelled Jackson to the TV. "Goddamn news cycle: create rumor, report rumor, repeat."

"Let's go live to New York City," said the anchorwoman.

"Thanks Cindy," said a reporter standing in the middle of the street amid an ocean of red taillights. "We're at Varick and Houston Streets, blocks away from the Holland Tunnel entrance, and as you can see, nothing is moving."

The reporter bent down next to a man who was leaning out of his car window.

"This is Donnie, from Bensonhurst," introduced the reporter. "How long have you been stuck here?"

"Six hours going on to eternity," he said in dense Brooklynese, dropping his Rs.

"How did the day start for you?" asked the reporter, yelling over the din of honking horns and expletives.

"When the news came over the TV, I grabbed the kids from school and drove into the city to pick up my wife. She works on Fulton. I thought we'd beat traffic, but will you look at this!" The man held out his hand, indicating the hoard of stationary vehicles.

"Have you considered another way out? The George Washington Bridge?"

"Yougottabekiddingme! It's backed up in every direction. The whole island is a mess! I can't even move," he said, throwing up a hand for effect. His kids were screaming behind him.

"It looks like we're all going to be here for a while. Back to you, Cindy."

"Stay safe," she said nonsensically. "There's been another attack on a mosque, this one in Houston." The news showed fire trucks around a large burning building. "Muslims and mosques are being targeted throughout the country, and police are asking people to remain calm."

The camera showed police trying to contain a crowd of people outside the White House, many holding signs with anti-Muslim slogans and images. Jackson heard the protest chants from outside his window and from the TV a millisecond later.

"Hey, hey! Ho, ho! Those Muslims got to go! Hey, hey! Ho, ho! Those Muslims got to go!" people yelled in unison.

The TV changed to live protests of people burning American flags in Cairo, Bagdad, Tehran, and Kabul.

"Anti-American protests are also occurring throughout the Middle East. It seems some people are celebrating the terrorist attack," said the anchorwoman. "Let's go live to Islamabad."

The scene cut to a reporter on the ground, where a sea of men draped in white-and-green Pakistani flags were yelling. One held up an effigy that looked like a scarecrow made of American flags, and lit it. Flames burst skyward followed by a plume of black smoke. The reporter looked terrified.

"Cindy, as you can see, demonstrators are chanting slogans against the United States and burning American flags. There are protests just like this one across northwest Pakistan. The government here says—" A bottle flew through the air and hit the camera, and the screen went dark.

The camera went back to the news anchor, who sat frozen and pale. After a brief silence, she said, "We're having technical difficulties."

"Savages," said Jackson.

The screen changed to an empty White House press briefing room, showing an empty podium.

"We are still awaiting news from the White House," said the anchorwoman in a grave tone.

"Aw, come o-o-on!" Jackson yelled. "You bastards know the president will make an address within the hour. Stop rushing us!"

The camera zoomed in on the podium, jiggling slightly and somehow making it look ominous.

"Savages!" he said, turning off the TV.

CHAPTER 26

It was midday and I had still not heard from Lava or Tye, worrying me. Lava said he would be back in a few hours, and that was more than a few hours ago. Could I trust him? I didn't know.

Lava instructed me not to leave the warehouse or turn on any electronics that emitted a signal, regardless of what my fixer promised. To make the point, Tye grabbed my four laptops while whistling the "Heigh-Ho" song from *Snow White and the Seven Dwarfs*, then proceeded to smash them to bits with a fire ax. He took great pleasure in it. In exchange, Lava handed me a crappy burner phone.

"Take good care of this," said Lava. "Only call me in an emergency."

Since then, I had slept, cleaned my weapons twice, double-checked my surviving tech, and did a round of physical training. Now I was down to playing solitaire, and losing. A mouse scurried across the floor.

"Scram, mouse! I don't have food here," I said, and heard a small squeak as if in reply. *Defiant rodent,* I thought.

Tye left me the emergency weather radio. "Thing don't emit enough radio frequency to matter," he said. Luckily, it also pulled in FM radio, so I tuned in the news. NUCLEAR TERROR. TERRORIST NUKES. NUCLEAR BOMB OF ISLAM.

"No, no, no, no, no," I whispered as I listened to live coverage that interrupted normal programming. The radio announcer described a warehouse in northern New Jersey, its parking lot filled with fire trucks and police. Gridlock had frozen all major highways exiting New York City. People were panicked.

Next came the pundit brigade. Talking heads filled the airwaves with their yapping. One claimed the terrorists could have stashed multiple warheads in cities around the country. Another brushed it off as hokum. A third, a retired CIA director, said Iran was behind it but didn't explain why. Meanwhile, the U.S. government remained silent, confirming everyone's worst fears. I continued listening for ten minutes, absorbing the horror. New experts took to the airwaves but not with new facts. Ultimately it was just more palaver.

"What idiots," I said, turning them off. I scrolled to the classical music channel, which was playing a Chopin waltz called "L'Adieu." "How appropriate," I mumbled with a smirk, as I listened to the piano weep. Yet it was comforting.

My mind drifted back to Winters, now a nuclear threat. If the news reports were true, then he was surely behind it. A shiver took hold of me, and questions came fast. What was Winters's game? Where would Apollo obtain a nuclear warhead? A rebellion inside the company? It wasn't the Apollo I knew. Winters was capable of ghastly things, but half of Apollo joining him to kill the vice president and 230 Americans? Now a nuke? No. Something was off.

It can't be Winters, I thought, although it did not

make me feel better. I opened up a can of tuna, my lunch. The mouse squeaked joy from somewhere beneath the kitchen cabinets, no doubt smelling the tuna. I tossed the empty can in the trash under the sink and heard mouse feet scamper around the cabinet. I felt like the mouse, except the trailer was my cabinet.

"OK, mouse, you win." I sighed and reached into a cabinet, unwrapped a cracker, and threw it under the sink. Happy scurrying. We were both pleased.

But the question that nagged me most: It seemed unlikely that Apollo would leave a clue for the FBI to find. That was the work of amateurs, not Apollo. Was somebody else behind the nuke? Definitely not terrorists; they weren't that sophisticated. Iran still didn't have the bomb and Pakistan wouldn't give one to a terrorist group, fearing their plan would literally backfire. China and North Korea didn't export WMD.

Maybe Russia did it, I thought. Russian mafia smuggled it in, so it made sense that Moscow could be involved. I had spent months in Ukraine dealing with Russia's shadow war there, which Russia won. The Kremlin could have used Russian mercenaries and mafia to facilitate the risky infiltration. They'd done it in other places, although not with a nuke.

Yeah, Russia could do it. But would they? Hard to know. If true, it would be a huge coup for the Kremlin, especially since Washington was convinced terrorists were behind it. Who knows how many warheads they had been secretly importing? Enough to worry.

Then it hit me like Hiroshima.

Winters does *have nukes!* I thought. A year ago, I was ensnared in Winters's scheme to steal ten nuclear bombs from Pakistan. I barely got out alive. I thought Winters was dead and the nukes lost, but I was wrong. *Winters lives, and now nukes are in play.* It was no coincidence.

Winters must have recovered some of the missing warheads, I realized in horror. The Chopin swelled into a crescendo, turning tragedy into triumph. *Not helpful, Chopin,* I thought. I opened the sink cabinet, but the mouse had vanished. I wish I could have, too. There were enemy nuclear weapons somewhere in America, and I prayed they were in the hands of the Kremlin and not Winters.

CHAPTER 27

Lin received Jason's text while in the mixed martial arts cage. She found that working out helped with stress, but pummeling strangers relieved it. Her sparring partner was a five-foot-five Hispanic man who was a flurry of hands and feet. The guy never stopped moving, making it hard to land a punch as well as see one coming. She stalled as long as she could, hoping his incessant acrobatics would wear him out, but he kept going.

Smack! He kicked her face hard, and she felt the sting through her protective headgear. Her opponent was a master of capoeira, an Afro-Brazilian martial art that is literally dance and death. It was developed by African slaves in Brazil in the sixteenth century, and—done well—was hard to beat. But Lin was a master, too.

Smack, smack, smack, oof! He landed two more punches, but she blocked the third and counterstruck with a punch that knocked him backward and sideways. In the millisecond of space, she delivered a perfect roundhouse kick to his chest like a baseball bat, sweeping him off his feet with 480 pounds of force. He lay on the floor, crunched over and sucking air, and she lurked over him like Muhammad Ali above the fallen George Foreman in Zaire. When he caught his breath, she extended a hand and helped him to his feet.

"Not bad, Little Sparrow," he said, using her gym nickname. She didn't care for it but couldn't stop it, so she'd finally accepted it.

"Not bad yourself. You almost got me with your disco moves," she said, rubbing her head with a padded glove. Lin had never met the guy before but had seen him practicing and challenged him to a match.

"Ow, that hurt," he said, still shaking off the round-house kick.

"Training should hurt. If there is no pain, there is no fear, and if there is no fear, then you are not training."

He gave a mock look of terror, and then smiled. "Another round?"

"Nah, gotta run. I just came in to loosen up. I got a lot going on right now."

"Ok, Sparrow. Maybe next time?"

"Yeah. Next time." She grabbed her towel and went to the locker room. Few women trained in mixed martial arts, so she had the showers mostly to herself. As she peeled off her clothes, she felt a little self-conscious that she was the only woman without tattoos. MMA fighters wore body art for the same reason soldiers displayed ribbons: to be admired. Their judging eyes on her ink-less body always made her feel naked, even though she knew it was silly. More than a few times cage friends suggested she get an intricate Chinese dragon tattoo with flying sparrows on her back and ass. Her answer was always no, yet they would mention it again.

Lin loved long showers. She stood under the high-pressure nozzle for ten minutes, letting the heat and pressure work magic on her aching muscles. Stress was the culprit, not cage fighting. She moved side to side, getting her entire back and then her front.

Ahhhhhh, she thought, trying not to think about the FBI, Russia, nukes, and Armageddon. She was in a holding pattern until Jason got back to her with a follow-up lead, and she was growing impatient. It was why she'd come to the gym.

Where the hell is he? she thought, irritated. She performed deep breathing exercises to slow her heart rate, sucking in steam and exhaling loudly. Ten more minutes later, she reluctantly stepped out and dried off. After blow-drying her hair, she made her way to her locker, carrying only the lock key. Reflexively she grabbed her phone as soon as she opened the locker.

"Crap!" she said, seeing all of Jason's texts over the past thirty minutes. "CALL ME. NEW LEAD!" Immediately she dialed his number and paced nervously around the locker room in the nude.

"Jason here."

"Jason, it's me."

There was a pause, and she imagined Jason scanning the office for eavesdroppers before speaking. "Well, you're not going to believe it," he said in a hushed voice. "Actually, you probably will. *I* just don't believe it."

"Jason, just tell me."

"First, you're in big trouble. You've practically made the FBI's most wanted list, and you need to come in."

"If they want me, they can come get me," she said, equally defiant.

She heard Jason sigh. "I checked with Dan in counterintelligence," he whispered. "You remember him? A class ahead of us, my height, brown hair."

"Yes, I remember Dan. What did he say?"

"He said they've been tracking an uptick of Russian spooks in Northern Virginia, and not the ordinary kind."

"What kind then?"

"He got all cagey on me, not like him. He said they were close to moving in, when they got called off. Didn't say why. Now he's chasing bridge terrorists with the rest of us."

"That's too bad. Did he say anything else?"

"Yeah. I pressed him. Literally. We were in the gym. Three-two-oh-two Rockland Terrace in McLean," he said.

"What?" she said. A young woman with a scorpion-and-roses tattoo on her hip was drying off and looking at her curiously. Lin moved away. "Say again?"

"Three-two-oh-two Rockland Terrace, McLean, Virginia. That's the safe house they were monitoring."

Lin grabbed a pen from her locker, bit off the cap, and spit it out. *Crap, where's a piece of paper?* she thought, looking around, but they were in a locker room. She was naked and couldn't run out to the front desk for a sticky note. *Screw it.* "Repeat the address." Jason did and she wrote it on her left inner forearm. "Thanks, Jason. Are they still running surveillance?"

"Remote sensors only, but actually it sounds like no one is paying attention. The assistant director pulled them all for the bridge case. Everyone is working it, except me. I'm probably going to get fired, right along with you."

"Jason, you're a good man. A patriot," she said. "Did Dan say anything else? Like who was operating out of the safe house?"

"No, and he wouldn't give me anything more. It sounds heavy duty though, and not your typical Russian Federation bullshit."

She sat down on a changing bench, twirling the pen

in her fingers as she thought. "But why aren't they investigating it? After Secaucus I assumed the Bureau would widen the scope of inquiry to include suspicious Russian activity in the Capital region."

"Yeah, they did *except* for this safe house. I asked around and the Bureau is looking into all the usual suspects, but this one address is getting a hard pass."

"Why?"

Jason was uncomfortable. "I don't know, and that's why I approached Dan when I learned he was on the team surveilling it. In fact, he specifically warned me not to ask about it. Didn't say why."

Lin sat quietly, puzzling over it but only one word came to mind. "Weird."

"I know. That's why I texted you."

She had deep knowledge of Russia, but it was mafia focused. This was different. *A Russian government safe house that's being protected by the FBI?* she thought. Could it be a double agent? Unlikely. The FBI wouldn't harbor any safe house during a national emergency, especially one involving WMD. There was only one way to find out.

"I know that silence," said Jason. "It's the patented Lin-Thinking-Something-Stupid. Whatever you're thinking, stop it."

"What am I thinking?"

"You are thinking about taking down a certain Russian safe house all by yourself. That would be galactically stupid. And certain death."

"I'm not going to take it down. I just want to see if it's there. That's all," she protested, crossing her arms and legs. It was disturbing how well Jason knew her.

"Don't. Come in while you still can," he pleaded.

"The Bureau is now looking into Russia, thanks to the Secaucus bust. Mission accomplished, Lin. You can come in now. We're shorthanded, so they may overlook everything if you pitch in and work hard."

"You know it might be too late for me, even with the big bust. That's why I need this. I can't show up empty-handed. I need more than a lead; I need a victory."

A long silence followed. Lin could hear the dull chatter of their office in the background and felt his patience fraying. Yet he did not hang up.

"One more thing, Lin," said Jason reluctantly. "And I shouldn't even be telling you this."

"What?"

"You may be more right than you know about the bridge," he said, lowering his voice. "They found traces of some new, exotic military explosive. Real state-of-the-art stuff."

"What is it?"

"Wait one second," he said, and she heard papers rustling around his forever messy desk. "Here it is. I don't understand it," he said, reading the report. "Something about the cocrystallization of two parts HMX to one part CL-20, both high-end military explosives. The new material, which they imaginatively labeled Explosive X, can produce a blast wave 225 miles per hour faster than pure HMX." He whistled in admiration, as if he knew what he was taking about. "And it's as stable and resistant to accidental detonation as HMX. Good safety tip."

"Custom-made?"

"Yup. This stuff was not cooked up in some terrorist's basement. There are only a few labs in the world capable of producing it at scale, and ATF and DIA monitor most of them. This development took the building completely by surprise. It's got everyone here on edge because no terrorist group in the world has it—"

"But Russia does," she said, finishing his sentence while doing a silent victory dance in the middle of the locker room.

"Just be careful," he said.

"Of course I will," said Lin, and hung up.

CHAPTER 28

Around 11 P.M., George Jackson snuck out the White House pedestrian gate and walked briskly across Lafayette Square, his two-man secret service detail following. He didn't want to be late. A winter gust assaulted his face, and he pulled up his scarf so that only his eyes showed. More important, he didn't want to be recognized. Even at this late hour, protestors stood on Pennsylvania Avenue, waving signs opposing police brutality, terrorism, and nuclear war. Forty people clustered together holding candle lanterns in an all-night vigil, despite the zero-degree weather.

"Hey, hey! Ho, ho! Police brutality has got to go!" chanted a smaller group weakly. The freezing temperature had taken a toll on their numbers, and only the most committed rallied on.

A twenty-foot banner read: WAR NEVER SOLVES ANYTHING. *Except for ending slavery, the Holocaust, fascism, and communism,* thought Jackson, rolling his eyes. The protestors were none too bright, yet he was sympathetic to their sentiment. They would accomplish nothing, of course. The president wasn't even in the White House tonight. Demonstrators were an irritant to men like Jackson, but he knew they were also nec-

essary. America embraced dissent, and that was what
separated it from the savage nations of the world.

Two protestors huddled together on a park bench
with a large cardboard sign leaning against their knees.
END FASCISM NOW! it read, scrawled with a Sharpie.
Two portraits bookended the message, each with a
Hitler moustache. It was expertly drawn, and Jackson
slowed to admire it. Then stopped. One of the portraits
was of him.

Bastards! he thought, and quickened his step. Week-
old ice and refrozen slush encrusted the sidewalks, and
salt crunched under his shoes. They strode past the giant
statue of Gen. Andrew Jackson atop his horse, doffing
his hat at the White House. Sirens wailed in the background. If Washington had a soundtrack, it would be
sirens, honks, and helicopters.

Jackson checked his watch again. "Let's pick up the
pace," he whispered to the secret service agents flanking him.

"Yes, sir," replied one. Jackson knew these agents
well, and he always requested them. Good men were
hard to find. In battle this meant bravery, but in Washington it referred to discretion. There are acts of cour-
age greater than taking a bullet for someone else, such
as keeping another's dangerous secrets. And Jackson
had many secrets.

They crossed H Street and walked up the stairs of
St. John's Episcopal Church. The pastel yellow exterior
and white colonnade stood in sharp opposition to the
concrete landscape surrounding it. It was nicknamed
"church of the presidents" because every sitting president had attended the church since it was built in 1816,
starting with James Madison.

The agents pulled open the huge oak doors and Jackson glided through, stomping his feet in the narthex to get warm.

"Please wait here," he said, after they followed him inside. "I need to be alone."

Jackson walked down the nave toward the altar. St. John's was small by modern standards, with a wraparound balcony on three sides consistent with the eighteenth century. The floorboards creaked beneath his feet, and the smell of incense and wood polish lingered in the air. Somehow, it reminded him of boarding school in New England, a horrible period many lifetimes ago.

Fifty-eight, fifty-seven, fifty-six, fifty-five . . . ah, here we go, he thought, and slid into pew 54. A brass plaque on the armrest read THE PRESIDENT'S PEW in modest lettering. Jackson sat down, exhaling with relief.

God help us all, he thought, gazing at the cross on the altar. Even in the dim light, the empty church cast a glow of consolation. The United States was the world's superpower, but it was not omnipotent. During times of crisis, he needed succor.

No, he thought. *I need reassurance.*

The oak doors squeaked open behind him and clanked shut a moment later. Jackson smiled. Reassurance had arrived. Without turning around, he heard the *click-click* of a cane tapping its way up the nave, until a tall man stood beside him. The gentleman carefully leaned his antique cane against the pew's back, its ivory handle an exquisitely carved monkey's head. Then, with effort, he eased his large frame into the seat next to Jackson. Finally, he grabbed his left leg and stretched it out, wincing slightly.

"Good evening, George," he said in a raspy voice.

His hoarseness came not from old age or too many cigarettes, but from injury.

"Thank you for coming on such short notice."

"Of course. Anything for a friend."

Jackson fidgeted with his glove, hesitating.

"What's on your mind, George?"

"The nuclear bomb. I need to know if it's real."

This time the tall man hesitated.

"I need to know if it's true or just rumor," repeated Jackson, both men staring straight ahead. Moments passed.

"I thought we agreed not to do this," said the older man.

"Do what?"

"Ask each other about details."

"WMD on American soil is not a 'detail,'" said Jackson in an unyielding whisper.

"You understand that it changes nothing," said the man.

Jackson stiffened, astonished by this response. Then spoke cautiously. "You *will* tell me, and I will judge what changes."

The man sighed, but Jackson didn't care.

"Very well, George. It's true. Nuclear weapons were smuggled into the country last Friday. They are in transit now."

Jackson paused, absorbing the barrage of implications. This was not what he expected. He thought the man would saunter into the church and laugh at the rumor, not confirm it. Jackson's mind felt adrift. Hundreds of questions exploded in his head, but he could only spit out three: "*Weapons*, plural? You brought nuclear weapons into the country?! Where are they now?"

"I cannot say."

"You can't? Or you won't?" asked Jackson, raising his voice in alarm.

"No more questions, George. We cooperate when we can, but do what we must. You have your duties, and I have mine. That was our arrangement, and nothing more," said the man.

"Give me the location of the nuclear weapons so my teams can intercept them."

"I cannot."

Jackson's face turned crimson and eyes bulged. His lips curled back, showing his teeth, and he whispered viciously: "So help me God, I will bring the full weight and might of the United States of America crashing down upon your head until you don't know your toes from your tonsils."

"You do that, we both burn."

"I don't care. You brought WMD into my country, on my watch. I will see us burn before I let a single American perish by your hand."

Both men hard-stared each other. Finally, the tall man broke the gaze.

"Fine, George. You win this round. I will give you something."

"What?"

"A name. A location. Something."

"Something?!"

"In time, George. In time," said the man, reaching for his cane.

"In time? Time is the one thing neither of us has. I need 'something' now. Immediately."

With a grunt, the tall man pulled himself upright and maneuvered into the nave with measured care. George sat perplexed by the man's indifference. Nuclear weapons changed the equation, and the law of unintended consequences could produce a mushroom cloud. This was never part of their deal. Never.

"I will get you actionable intelligence on the WMD soon. Very soon. I promise," said the man.

"But—"

"Have a good night, George," he interrupted, and hobbled out of the church with the *clickity-clack* of his cane. Jackson considered having his agents seize him, but that would only complicate matters, not solve them. Besides, he knew where to find the man and could grab him at any hour of any day. He was going nowhere. The heavy oak doors shut after the man exited, and Jackson slumped back into the president's pew.

God help us all, he thought.

CHAPTER 29

The next morning, Jackson sat in a corner of the press secretary's office, which was crammed with lesser staffers. Like every room in the West Wing, it was entirely too small for its purpose. Jackson's weekend cabin on the Chesapeake had larger rooms. Actually, it was a Georgian brick mansion named "Ridgely's Retreat," and it came with its own peninsula and former slave quarters. Still, it had larger rooms.

How can anyone run a superpower out of the dinky West Wing? Jackson often wondered. The press secretary, Kelsey Broderick, stood behind her L-shaped desk and shuffled through papers manically in preparation for her press briefing, which was in ten minutes. The White House press pool was hostile most days, but today was worse. Last night's televised presidential address was not the speech of destiny everyone had hoped for. In fact, it was a disaster, raising more questions than it answered, and now the media was frenzied. Hence the 10 A.M. press conference to lower the media fever.

"George, anything new?" she asked nervously.

"Not since yesterday. At least, nothing unclassified," he said. Jackson's only role during the meeting was to answer her national security questions before she faced the cameras.

"Good. Don't tell me anything classified. I might accidently repeat it," she said. "It's been that kind of morning." She turned to other staffers in the room for last-minute updates: homeland, FBI, intelligence, others.

Jackson tuned them out and watched the bank of TV monitors that lined her wall, each set to a different 24/7 news channel. He focused on one of the biggies, reading its closed captions.

NATIONWIDE MANHUNT CONTINUES FOR TERRORISTS, said the chyron. The screen showed militarized police going door-to-door in a wealthy suburb of Northern Virginia. An older man in a bathrobe was shown yelling at police, barring them from entering his home, and the police plowed by him. The man grabbed an urn and smashed it over a policeman's Kevlar helmet. Seconds later, he was on the ground in flex-cuffs, then two policemen in black fatigues dragged him across his lawn to a cruiser. An angry policeman yelled at the camera, which was then pointed down at the ground.

No, no, no! Jackson thought. *Dumb police.*

Kelsey saw it too. "What are they doing?!" she said, knowing the press pool would hold her accountable for the policemen's actions. They already looked more like soldiers than police, and now this. Civil rights groups were howling. The news anchor looked visibly shocked by the elderly bathrobed man's fate.

What a humiliating way to go, thought Jackson with a silent chuckle. *Hauled off across your lawn in nothing but a bathrobe and flex-cuffs as they dump you in a police car, and all broadcast live on international TV. The legacy of saps.* He thanked God that would never be him.

"Someone turn that off," said Kelsey. "I can't look at

the news right now." A staffer diligently switched off all the monitors. "Good. Where were we?"

As others gave her last-minute updates, Jackson pulled out his phone and checked his social media feeds. He followed all the journalists who mattered in the national security space, and they were on fire with the government's door-to-door manhunt for the terrorists. "Gestapo," "desperate," "insane." Their descriptions got worse from there.

"Time to go," said one of the staffers.

"I'm not ready," protested Kelsey, still leafing through her binder.

"Ma'am, it's time. Being late only makes them worse," said the aide. "It eggs on conspiracy theory."

Really? Conspiracy theory?! read the expression on Kelsey's face, but she nodded. "Fine. I'm ready. Let's go."

They all stood up and followed the press secretary out of her office and into the overcrowded briefing room. It was slightly bigger than a double-wide trailer's living room. The chatter quieted as she took the podium.

"Good morning," she began, and then gave an elegant ten-minute statement that said absolutely nothing. When she was done, hands shot up. One by one, she took questions, and her answers sounded convincing yet revealed nothing.

God, she's good, Jackson thought as he stood on the side with her staffers.

The volley of questions and answers continued, while Jackson contemplated his conversation last night with the tall man. It infuriated him. How dare he bring WMD onto American soil? He promised actionable intelligence, but when? He needed it now.

"I have a question for the national security advisor,"

said one journalist, seeing Jackson, who looked up in alarm.

"Oh, he's not available for questions," said Kelsey, caught off guard.

"But he's right there!" protested the journalist, pointing to Jackson. All cameras swiveled toward him and zoomed in; he looked up at the monitor and saw himself, standing in the shadows and watching the monitor in shock. Not a good look.

Busted, Jackson thought, and instantly regretted following the press secretary into the vultures' lair. A dumb mistake, but it was too late now.

"Uh," said Kelsey, feeling herself losing control. "Dr. Jackson isn't available for comments."

"Dr. Jackson," said the journalist, ignoring the press secretary. "Is it true there's an American sleeper cell?"

"Where will the terrorists strike next?"

"Is there just one nuclear bomb or are there many?"

"Could they already be planted in cities across the nation?"

"What are you doing to stop it? The American people deserve to know."

"Can you stop it?"

The barrage continued as the chorus of camera shutters crescendoed and all eyes focused on him. Then the room fell silent, expecting an answer. Live TV abhors silence.

A pack of vultures! he thought and glanced at the press secretary, but her look offered no respite. He straightened up awkwardly, knowing he was in a no-win situation.

"The FBI and CIA are still working to ascertain any and all leads. Progress is being made. We are cautiously optimistic," assured Kelsey, but it was no use.

"Dr. Jackson," asked another journalist. "Is Russia behind this, making it look like terrorists? Is this an act of war?"

Silence hung in the air, making Jackson uncomfortable. The entire world was watching the press briefing live, and refusing to answer or walking out would only validate the conspiracy theorists. However, he had no gift for evading questions like the press secretary, and lying would make things worse later. It always did. There was only one thing to do.

Jackson approached the dais slowly, and Kelsey's eyes silently pleaded with him to stop.

You lie for a living, he thought, meeting her gaze. *I cannot. I'm the national security advisor.* She stepped aside as he took the podium.

"Are enemy nukes in the U.S. right now?" asked a journalist in the back.

Damn you, thought Jackson about the tall man as he stared down at the microphone. Then he spoke.

"There are some people who think they can get away with anything. They threaten our country and our homes. They think they are smarter than us, and they will never be caught. But I say to them"—Jackson leaned forward—"we will hunt you, find you, and finish you."

CHAPTER 30

The tall man shook his head in disdain as he watched the press conference unfold. He sat behind a large mahogany desk in a dark room that looked like a palatial Victorian study. It had dark oak paneling, Empire-style couches, and a palatial Persian carpet. An antique cane leaned against the desk. The monkey's face was a mixture of tortured grimace and laughing insanity. On TV, Jackson took to the podium and the cameras zoomed in; the tall man frowned.

"Fool," the tall man said when Jackson had finished. An aide turned off the TV, while another rushed into the room looking distressed. "What?" barked the man in a raspy voice.

"Sir, he's back."

"Who?"

"*Him*," said the aide, handing a computer tablet across the desk. The tall man examined it, and his scowl turned into a grin. The aide stood by nervously, having never seen the tall man smile.

Brad Winters had not smiled in a year. Months in a Saudi torture prison had twisted him, like the carved monkey on his cane. It took all of his negotiating skills to buy back his life, and now the only evidence of his incarceration was a limp, a crushed larynx, and a massive vendetta. Tom Locke had put him in that torture cell, and he swore his vengeance daily the way other people said prayers. Now justice was at hand.

"Tom Locke," hissed Winters. "Alive."

"Yes sir."

Winters enlarged the picture. It showed Locke and two Apollo agents getting into a black Chevy Suburban near Eastern Market. He recognized one of the men as Lava, a reliable team leader who had chosen the wrong side in Winters's hostile takeover bid for Apollo Outcomes. The board had fired Winters as CEO because of unauthorized private military activity in Ukraine. Now he was back to reclaim what was rightfully his: the company he founded twenty years ago and the influence it wielded in Washington. It was to be his year of justice.

"When was this picture taken?" asked Winters, leaning back in his chesterfield leather desk chair.

"A little over forty-eight hours ago."

"Two days?! And I'm just seeing it now? Why did you take so long?"

The aide shuffled his feet, absorbing the tall man's ire. "Because we just figured out it was Locke."

"Explain."

"Locke wasn't the mark. We've been tracking one of the Apollo hunter-killer teams for the past four days. Our signals intelligence unit was able to place a transponder on their vehicle, and we've been two steps ahead of them ever since. Three nights ago, they were running agents in Langley and Meade, although the other night they went dark—"

"Get to the point," interrupted Winters.

The aide tensely cleared his throat. "Around nine A.M., they made a beeline for a coffee shop on Capitol Hill.

It's an indicator because it's completely outside their normal operational profile, triggering us to slew and cue surveillance. We assigned a drone to get eyes on, and it captured this picture. At first, we had no idea who they were meeting. The facial recognition algorithms came up blank, as if someone had erased the individual's profile from the databases. It turns out someone did."

"Fascinating," said Winters, knowingly. "Who?"

"We did. A few years back, we won the IDIQ contract to manage the IC's persons of interest databases," said the aide. *IC* referred to the intelligence community: CIA, FBI, and fourteen other agencies.

"Ah, yes. I remember now. A handy little contract," Winters said of the billion-dollar deal. "We erased the identities of all our operatives without anyone knowing."

The aide gave a pro forma chortle, and then continued. "We got lucky, sir. One of our older techs recognized Locke. They used to work together."

Winters sighed and his frown returned as he placed the tablet on the desk. The aide stiffened reflexively, but Winters sat motionless.

"Help me understand something," said Winters. The aide swallowed hard. "I was led to believe that Locke was dead. Yet here is a picture of him alive, yesterday, in this city. Help me understand."

"We thought so too," said the aide with fear in his voice. Winters did not suffer bad news lightly. "He was reported killed in Syria by Jase Campbell's team."

The aide waited for a response, but none came.

"Campbell is the—" the aide began, but Winters held up a hand.

"Locke has more lives than an Afghan warlord," said

Winters, eyeing Locke's photo on the tablet. "I'll deal with Campbell later. What concerns me is why Locke has returned. Why would he risk everything by coming out of hiding? And coming back here, my home turf? Help me understand. Why would a rogue like Locke do it?"

The aide remained silent, hoping it was a rhetorical question. It wasn't. Finally, he offered weakly: "We don't know, sir."

Winters glared. "How long has Locke been here?"

"We don't know."

"Where is Locke now?"

"We don't know."

"Dammit, what *do* you know?!" shouted Winters, who winced with pain and massaged his throat as he coughed. When he finished, his eyes turned to the aide, who was pale. "Why did you lose him?"

"We just fingered him five minutes ago. Had we known at the time, we would have abducted him. Now he's gone dark. But we're working up his digital signature. If Locke is working the Capitol region, we will find him."

Winters leaned back again, thinking. He was framed by floor-to-ceiling red velvet drapes and valanced windows that overlooked a private garden. A wrought-iron balcony and elaborate cut stonework around the windows could have passed for a Haussmann apartment in Paris. After a few minutes, he sat forward.

"Could he have been involved in last night?" asked Winters.

The aide shifted uncomfortably. The destruction of Elektra was an unmitigated catastrophe for their contract, and Winters spent the morning on the phone sweet-talking the client and screaming at staff. Heads were rolling. "Possibly. We are still conducting the post-op."

Winters stared at the picture of Locke. The aide's forehead glistened with sweat despite the room's cool temperature.

"Well, no matter. He's not our problem anymore," said Winters. He almost sounded happy.

"Yes sir," said the aide in astonished relief, not comprehending yet thankful.

"Get me a secure line to the national security advisor," Winters said. A moment later he was connected to the White House.

"Jackson speaking."

"Good morning, George. It's me. Nice performance today."

"Good morning, Brad. Thank you, I had someone specific in mind."

"Let's hope they were watching."

"Oh, don't worry. I have it on good authority he was," said Jackson with satisfaction. "Now, you are calling because you have a little something for me?"

"Indeed I do, as promised. I'm a man of my word," cooed Winters as if the world were unicorns and rainbows. He thought he deserved an Oscar.

"Thank you," said Jackson, and then paused. "I have to confess, Brad, this morning I expected you would sandbag me."

"George, we are both patriots," said Winters coaxingly. "We may have different methods, but we both want the same thing. We must trust each other, if we are to succeed."

"Agreed."

Winters picked up the tablet and stared at the picture on the screen.

"The man you're after is named Thomas Locke. He used to be one of mine, but he's gone rogue and taken a few colleagues with him. He's the one behind the WMD. I've committed every asset at my disposal to stopping them—"

"Wait, Winters!" interrupted Jackson, raising his voice in alarm. "Did you just say parts of Apollo Outcomes have gone rogue, and they have nuclear weapons *inside* the U.S.? Are you telling me you lost positive control of Apollo Outcomes?" Jackson's voice trailed off as he contemplated the horror. It was like a T-rex running loose on Noah's ark.

Winters had hoped the conversation would not veer in this direction, but perhaps it was for the best. "No George, I'm in control of Apollo. Locke is leading a splinter cell and we needed to know how large, which is why I couldn't speak about it last night. I had to be sure, and now I am. Locke is the man with the nukes. He is maniacal and has images of self-grandeur."

"Too much time in the field doing your dirty work, and now he's lost his ethical compass," said Jackson in a condescending tone.

"Doing *our* dirty work," corrected Winters. "I don't know what he wants, despite several overtures to talk reason to him. But Locke is not a reasonable man."

"How could you let this happen?" scolded Jackson. "This was never part of our deal. You were supposed to be better than this."

The words stung but Winters pushed ahead, feeling

his trap closing around his prey. "What matters now is Locke has a nuclear weapon in the continental United States and the man is unhinged. He is a Tier One threat, George. Do you understand me? Tier One."

Jackson paused. "Where the hell did Locke obtain weapons of mass destruction?"

"Pakistan. Two years ago, Locke posed as Saudi secret service and bought a bomb, leaving Saudi a big bill and bigger embarrassment. They kept it a secret for obvious reasons, and now the Kingdom is after him too. We all thought he was dead, and the nukes lost somewhere in Yemen. Saudi launched a war in Yemen partly to recover the nukes before the Iranians could find them. But no one found them. It turns out Locke was hiding with the nukes, waiting for his opportunity to strike. The VP's death was Santa Claus for him."

"If what you're saying is true, Brad, then why didn't the CIA or NSA know about it?"

Winters chuckled. "There's much the CIA and NSA don't know, George." *Especially since they outsource much of their critical work to me,* he thought with a smug grin. Cooking intelligence to land more contracts was something of a specialty for him.

Winters could feel the tension over the phone. *Come on, Jackson, you old sentimental fool. Bite!* Winters had known him for thirty years, since Jackson was just a budding lobbyist for Boeing selling jet fighters to Congress. But the man was a true patriot, and that was what Winters was counting on. Perhaps he needed a sweetener to push him in the correct direction.

Winters cleared his throat. "George, I need your help. I can't stop Locke on my own," he said in a vulnerable tone. Now for the coup de grace. "And the country needs you too, George." Winters paused for effect. "The hour is desperate."

More silence. *Come on, Jackson!* thought Winters.

Jackson sighed. "Fine, I will clean up your mess. We cannot let this stand, and we are partners in this project until the end. *Alea iacta est*," he said, quoting Caesar. He had a bevy of historical lines memorized for such occasions.

"'The die is cast,'" replied Winters without hesitation. "You are quite right, old friend. We crossed the Rubicon together months ago, and we are committed now. Let's work together and do what's best for America."

"Agreed. Where are the nukes now? Where's Locke?"

"No one knows. Find Locke and find the nukes," said Winters, eyeing Locke's photo on the computer tablet as he talked. *I got you,* he thought with satisfaction. *Checkmate Locke.*

"All I need is a description. We'll take it from there."

"Good. I'm sending over a man right now with Locke's file," said Winters, nodding to the aide, who left the room. "And George, one more thing. This Locke guy; don't underestimate him. You won't find him in any database because he's invisible. Worse, he's cunning. We originally recruited him for infiltration and assassination, but he proved"—Winters paused, searching for the right word—"artful. If you spot him, don't get creative, just take the shot."

"Understood, Brad, and don't worry. I have a Special Mission Unit at Bragg who will have Locke bagged and tagged by sundown, if the intel you give me is any good."

"Oh, it is," said Winters, beaming. "Happy hunting."

CHAPTER 31

It was the next day and I still had not heard from Lava or Tye. Even the tiny mouse had gone on sabbatical, free to roam the greater trash heaps of the I-695 underpass. *Lucky rodent,* I thought, nearly nodding off. Jet lag and solitaire do not mix.

Where are Tye and Lava? I thought about using the burner phone to call them, but opted against it. Boredom was not an emergency. Also, maybe they were setting me up. They could have been stalling, and it might be hours before they arrived. Even a day or two. Time was precious, and I was wasting it. Every hour in my safehouse was an hour lost finding evidence implicating Apollo in the terrorist attack. *This is bullshit,* I thought, grabbing my Mark 23s and holstering them.

"Who knows what side Lava is really on?" I said aloud, wanting to trust him but knowing Apollo was in the middle of a civil war. It was difficult to know where people's true loyalties lay in such circumstances.

Trust no one, and develop a contingency plan, I thought, *starting with my own intelligence sources.* Without good information, I was grounded.

"What I need is the ability to find people quickly, and track them. But how?" I said, pacing around the trailer. A good hacker could do it by scraping the web for mobile ad data. Who needs the NSA when you have large corporations spying on your every move, click, and preference through your smartphone? If I could recruit my own cyberagent, he or she could tap the online ad exchanges and track individuals for me in real time. *Bingo!* But it left a harder question.

"Now, where to find a talented hacker?" I mumbled as I absentmindedly twirled a 7.62 mm cartridge between my fingers. The University of Maryland was just outside the Capital Beltway and had one of the best computer science departments in the country. Not exactly the NSA but good enough.

"Should be easy. All I need is an underpaid and overtalented grad student who can code," I said, rummaging through one of my duffels and pulling out a cash roll. "A free meal and a thousand dollars will do the trick."

Wait! Is it worth the risk? screamed my intuition. Getting NSA-like surveillance was the vital next step. However, I had come all this way, spent all my money, and risked my life. Driving through DC in broad daylight was a rookie blunder. Or was it a rookie blunder to sit on my ass?

"'Who Dares Wins,'" I said, repeating the British SAS's motto as I grabbed the car keys.

The BMW purred as I drove it out of the garage and down the street, the sunlight blinding me for a moment. I took the side streets, away from the traffic cameras, congestion, and cops. Decades ago, during DC's crack epidemic, this area was gangster land, but now it was forgotten. One abandoned brick town house lay boarded up, with a gang of feral cats on the stoop. Progress.

My fixer had equipped the BMW with an illegal police scanner, and it chirped routine calls. Still, one had to be careful. DC is the most policed city in the country. I remembered an instructor at the Ranch, Apollo's training facility in Texas, tell us there are fifty-seven cops for every ten thousand Washingtonians—almost twice the average for big cities and about four times the national average. And that's not even counting all the special police, like Capitol, Park, and Metro. The nation's capital was a nightmare for guys like me.

Apollo at war with itself. Winters alive and leading the rebellion. What are the stakes? I mused as I drove. It seemed inconceivable. The local classical radio station, WETA, was playing Gershwin's "Lullaby," an orchestral lollipop that transported me into the Great Gatsby's parlor before dawn.

I took a right, down a back street that would eventually dump onto the Beltway, and then it was a straight shot to the campus. A faint *wump-wump* of a chopper flew nearby. The music beckoned to me, and I felt my jet lag weighing heavy upon my brain. The chopper returned, getting in the way of the sweet tempos. DC probably had the highest ratio of helicopters to people, too.

Then it struck me. I was in a deserted part of the city, and no choppers should be circling above. They should not even be transiting through this airspace; they used the rivers as highways. I slowed and scanned the sky in a zigzag pattern but saw nothing. The police scanner was quiet, too.

I must be getting tired, I thought, turning off the "Lullaby." The *wump-wump* returned, but I could see nothing. Then no chopper sound.

Am I going crazy? I rolled down the windows, cut the engine, and coasted so I could hear better. At first nothing. Then the ambient sounds of the city, a garbage truck emptying a dumpster, a fire truck racing toward an emergency, a jackhammer. A helicopter.

The chopper was due east of my position, probably two klicks out, and growing louder. I started the engine and raced forward. When things don't make sense, move! Figure it out later.

Blue flashes flooded my peripheral vision, then I heard the banshee of sirens. In every direction. Before my mind registered the threat, adrenaline shot through my arteries and rocked my brain. *Ambush!* I floored the accelerator, and seven hundred horses stampeded under the hood, pressing me hard into my seat. A police car nosed out a hundred meters ahead; I swerved and clipped his bumper, nearly spinning out. I counted three cruisers and two black SUVs behind me. No doubt there were more vehicles flanking me on the parallel roads, blocking my escape. But my real worry was the spotter helicopter. No car was faster than eyeballs in the sky with a radio.

My intuition was pinging: something was awry. All these vehicles behind me, but none in front? It was a trap. They were flushing me forward, into an ambush zone with tire spikes and SWAT. I had to find a way out.

I dropped to 30 mph, allowing the chase vehicles to catch up, then found my impossible corner: an alley that ran behind rotting row houses. I jerked the wheel one quarter to the right and slammed the brakes. The car drifted right, into the alley, with the piercing squeal of tires and smell of rubber. The left rims hit the alley's curb so hard that the BMW lifted up on two wheels, then bounced down, jerking my head. I warped from 0 to 60 mph in 2.9 seconds, which sucked the breath out of me, and I heard the crash behind me. The lead cruiser had attempted the tight turn but smashed into a row house instead, blocking the alley for follow-on police.

Now to get out of here, I thought. Too late. A police Harley turned into the alley two blocks ahead and sped for me. *Gutsy sucker,* I thought, then I saw his play. All he had to do was close the gap between me and the next street exit. If he could seal it off, I would be trapped in the alley between him and the crashed cruiser. I floored it.

"Come on!" I shouted, as I raced for the next street and the cop for me, in a twisted game of chicken. We made the street simultaneously. I pitched left, skidded, and felt the lateral g-force pull my body against the seat belt. The tires clung to the pavement, but what I would have given for thirty minutes on a skid pad a day ago. The motorcycle went down and smashed through a derelict storefront, its rider expertly rolling across the pavement.

The police chopper was waiting for me, flying fifteen feet above my head, its blades just clearing rooftops. The rotor wash kicked up dust and trash, so I couldn't see, but I punched through and emerged onto a main thoroughfare. The BMW swayed violently as I slalomed through traffic at speed.

I could hear the sirens now. A battalion of them. I flashed my lights and honked, trying to get people out of my way. RFK Stadium was ahead, then the freeway. *Avoid the highway.* It's the first rule of motorized escape and evasion because the police box you in and cut you down.

"Find an exit," I commanded myself, as I sped around the stadium at 90 mph. I veered through the traffic but could not lose the nimble police Harleys.

"Bollocks!" I shouted as a black SUV appeared in front of me, its blue lights flashing through its grill. It was headed for me, as if to ram me off the road. I swung right so violently that the car nearly flipped, and I shot three lanes over and launched onto the highway. The motorcycles and SUV were jammed in the maelstrom of traffic I left in my wake.

"*Bollocks!*" I yelled again, as I accelerated up the highway. It was the one place I didn't want to be. Hugging the left shoulder to avoid congestion and oncoming cars, the BMW vibrated unnaturally as I ran through a debris field. A flat at this speed was lethal.

Another police car and the black SUV materialized behind me, and the chopper's shadow crossed overhead. Then a second. I glanced up and saw the police helicopter had picked up a pal, a news chopper. *There goes my cover,* I thought. *I should have listened to Lava.*

Ahead was a large iron bridge that spanned the Anacostia River, and I topped 120 mph going across it. I felt the car shimmy beneath me. The police helicopter flew at eye level, and the pilot and I regarded one another, each wearing sunglasses despite the cloudy day.

A police car was waiting for me as soon as I got off the bridge. I slammed the brakes and heard the screech of tires as I decelerated from 120 to 60 mph. I thought I would rear-end the police cruiser but it sped up, then slowed down to block me. The second cruiser rode my tail, boxing me in. I skewed left, then right, but the police matched my every move. Our bumpers mashed as they slowed down, taking me with them. I was trapped.

Grrr, I grunted, as I slammed on the brakes and knocked the cruiser behind me. More important, it cleared a few precious inches between me and the lead

S E A N   M c F A T E

vehicle. Enough to get free. In that space I swerved
right, escaping the cruisers, then rammed the lead car's
rear right panel. The impact was visceral, as I lifted
the cruiser's back tires off the pavement. When they
reengaged the road, the police car turned violently
sideways at 40 mph. I tapped my brake, allowing the
cruiser to spin around my nose in a graceful arc before
smashing into the Jersey barriers. I dodged the wreckage, but the trail vehicle hit it head on.

I veered across the lanes and took the first exit too
fast, heading back into DC. The black SUV followed
me with unexpected grace. Once I hit the city streets, I
blew through lights and snaked around traffic, hoping
to lose the heavier SUV. It wasn't working. A turning
dump truck caused me to nearly skid out, and the SUV
almost rear-ended me. I could see the woman driving it,
wearing a dark suit and sunglasses, too. I accelerated,
taking a series of sharp lefts through intersections, hoping the oncoming traffic would ensnarl her. It didn't.

She's good, I thought. Maybe she was one of Winters's people. Two miles ahead was the Capitol dome.
I needed to disappear before I hit that warren of cops.
First, I had to ditch the SUV, and then outsmart the
choppers. I reached for my Mark 23 and rolled down
the windows. I could tell the SUV was up-armored by
the way it listed heavily around turns. The driver's skill
was the only thing keeping it upright. But armored vehicles have a weakness. They can't roll down their windows, which meant they couldn't shoot back. I readied
one of my HK Mark 23 handguns.

I took a side street with thin traffic, allowing me
space. She followed. I timed an upcoming four-way intersection and jerked the wheel a quarter turn right then

hit the brakes, sending the car's back end skidding. The BMW careened into a J-turn and stopped, so that I sat perpendicular to the oncoming SUV. The driver gave a toothy smile and accelerated, intent on ramming me.

I lifted my Mark 23 and unloaded the clip through my open window and into the SUV's front tires, then accelerated before the beast could T-bone me. The SUV tried to make the turn but flipped on its shredded tires. Run flats don't perform high speed turns, regardless of what manufacturers promise.

Both choppers climbed after witnessing the gunshots. Fine by me. I lurched around cars, both my bumpers half dragging on the ground from the collision with the police cruisers. I headed toward the bridges and tunnels of I-395 and the train tracks near the waterfront. Maybe I could lose the chopper in that scrum of concrete and steel. It was my only chance before the next wave of police arrived.

The police helicopter anticipated my plan and zoomed ahead to keep an eye on me as I approached. I heard sirens approaching. A lot. *Change of plan,* I thought. I skidded right, taking advantage of ten-story buildings to break the chopper's line of sight with me. DC has few tall buildings owing to a law prohibiting anything taller than the Capitol building. This gave the helicopter an advantage, but not always. I glanced at my mirrors, but I didn't see the chopper. Still, that didn't mean it couldn't see me.

Must find an underground garage or get to a safe house before being spotted again, or I'm finished, I thought grimly as I wound through traffic, drove on empty sidewalks, and fishtailed through a small park. It was all drivable terrain. Minutes later, I rolled into the empty part of Southeast, home to feral cats and my safe house. In the distance I could see the police helicopter circling around the spot where it lost me, the ten-story buildings. The news chopper hovered above it. No doubt an army of police were sealing the buildings' underground garages and exits.

Satisfied, I crept toward my safe house using trash alleys to avoid other vehicles until I pulled into my dilapidated ex-taxi home. Once inside, the warehouse doors shut automatically behind me, and I killed the engine. The roofing was thick enough to conceal the hot engine from a police chopper's thermal imaging lens, but I was taking no chances.

I rested my forehead on the BMW's steering wheel, breathing deeply in the dark. Only one question remained: *How did they find me so fast?*

CHAPTER 32

Jackson stared in disbelief at the TV, his mouth agape. The high-speed car chase was being covered live on international news, showing smashed police vehicles and the black BMW driving like a maniac through the streets of Washington, with the Washington Monument as backdrop. Pillars of black smoke beset the landscape as if it were Yemen and fire engines screamed throughout the city.

In the nation's capital! he thought, as if it were a personal affront. *The gall!*

The news reported the terrorist escaped, which his sources confirmed minutes earlier. But the damage was done. The city began panicking like New York and people started evacuating en masse. Highways grew into parking lots and gas stations went dry. The president was not a patient man and would demand answers. So would Jackson.

It was supposed to be a simple snatch and grab, he thought. *What went wrong?* Winters warned him about Locke, but his intuition screamed there was more to Tom Locke than Winters was divulging. In fact, there was more to everything than Winters was revealing, a pattern he could now see clearly from the start.

Winters has been playing me the entire time. The

realization made him woozy. Jackson did not esteem himself a fool, yet it was embarrassingly obvious that their secret partnership was a sham. It was a one-way street, and he was facing the wrong way. But what game was Winters playing, and what did it mean for national security? Nothing good. *No more games,* he thought.

"Get me Winters," yelled Jackson to his executive assistant. "*Now!*"

Ten minutes later, Jackson and Winters met at the lowest level of a downtown garage, their respective black SUV convoys filling up much of the space. All the exits were sealed, and the depth of the garage guaranteed no electronic eavesdropping. The wall-to-wall concrete and dim fluorescent lighting were a stark contrast to the Cosmos Club. The two men faced off in the middle of a circle of bodyguards wearing dark suits, earpieces, and shoulder holsters. It looked like a geriatric fight club.

"Get them out of here!" yelled Jackson, and Winters waved his bodyguard away. Jackson followed suit, and both security details returned to their vehicles, waiting out the confrontation. Only Jackson and Winters remained.

"Who the hell is Locke?! He's no ordinary operator, but a worst-case scenario. Just like everything else you've been feeding me, it's all bullshit!" Jackson fumed. "You've been a huckster from the start, Winters, getting me to clean up your myriad in-house problems while you fall short on your end of the deal. I am no longer your corporate janitor. This ends here! Now!"

"Balderdash," Winters croaked. "I've been holding up my end of our agreement, but you keep manifestly failing and then blame me for your ineptitudes. You can't even eliminate a single man! If anything, I warned you: Locke is crafty. Worse, he's lucky. The only failure here is yours, because *you* let him get away."

"Me?!" yelled Jackson, eyes bulging. "This is not about Locke."

"It is *all* about Locke!" snarled Winters, jabbing his cane in the air at the national security advisor. "You came to me for a favor; you wanted a lead on the nuclear bomb. I didn't have to, but I gave you one. In fact, I gave you more. I lined up the man responsible for the headshot and you missed. Now he's gone to ground, and you won't get another shot. You're an imbecile!"

"This isn't about Locke, you fossilized moron, it's about you!" shouted Jackson, stabbing his index finger at Winters. "Locke is part of a wider pattern of your vast incompetence. Remember, Locke is *your* guy. How did he get loose in the bullpen in the first place? Because *you* lost control of him. Then *you* called me in to clean up your fiasco. Don't fuck with me, Winters. I've been at this longer than you, and I will put you down."

Winters laughed. "Don't threaten me. We've both been at this a long time. You wish to discuss patterns of incompetence? The mark was the president and not the vice president. How could you screw *that* up? I upheld my end of the deal, now uphold yours! All the residual problems are yours to rectify."

"It's not my fault POTUS got sick that day and the VP took his place," said Jackson defensively. "They don't announce last-second changes like that for security reasons."

"POTUS was *your* responsibility. And if the president wants your scalp for the Locke debacle, so be it. I'll find a new partner."

Jackson took a step back, aghast at the concept.

"Ridiculous! I could shut you down in hours, Winters. *Remember that.*"

"You perfidious swindler," rasped Winters, his face contorting with rage. He knew it was true, but somehow he expected Jackson would never stoop so low. It was a bullet in the corporate head.

"One phone call. That's all it would take, Winters. That's all you're worth to me."

Winters's anger gave way to a hoarse belly chuckle, surprising Jackson. "You're just a swamp creature. *Remember that.* You came to *me.* You asked for *my* help eliminating a spineless president, rallying the nation around the flag, and galvanizing a complacent country against foreign enemies. You said . . . how did you put it? 'Killing three birds with one stone.' You told me a massive terrorist attack at home was the only way to unite a bitterly divided nation. We even negotiated the acceptable casualty rate for collaterals," he said. "I said six thousand minimum to make it look plausible, but you insisted on less than five hundred. I said you were squeamish and you told me my estimate was overkill. Remember that?"

"Yes. That was the plan, and it is in jeopardy now thanks to your rogue agent, Locke. You were supposed to stage a fake terrorist attack to scare people, but instead you produced an actual nuclear terrorist who might blow up a city. Locke is your guy, Winters, and he's off the leash. That's on you, Winters. Your stupidity created this nuclear Frankenstein!"

Winters ignored him. "The plan was I take out POTUS, you blame terrorists, and then you give me big contracts to go after them in faraway lands. Forever wars are my business model, something you accepted.

You would play the hero, I would get rich, and America would come together against common enemies. That was our arrangement, Jackson."

"Then why is my interagency spun up about Russia?" asked Jackson in anger. "I blame you, Winters. Your guy Locke smuggled in a nuke through New Jersey using the Russian mob. Half the intelligence community is implicating the Kremlin, and Moscow is getting twitchy. Once again, your incompetence has become my emergency. Now I have to avert World War Three in addition to cleaning up your mess."

Winters grinned wide, showing scraggly teeth. "And who says the Russians are not a part of *my* plan?"

Jackson stammered but no words came out. He felt woozy again.

"Don't fuck with me, George. You're out of your depth," warned Winters.

Jackson recovered. "You commit high treason, and then seek to dictate terms to me, the national security advisor? You are soft in the head, Brad. I can pin *everything* on you. I can connect you to the bridge, Locke, and the nuke. It will be done before the morning news cycle is over, and there are no favors or tricks you can pull that will save you this time. I'll have your ass in manacles and finish what the Saudis started. Consider it a promise, and you know I'm a man of my word."

"The only person here who will hang for high treason is you! Because that's where the evidence will lead. I can dust my tracks and disappear, but you leave a paper trail."

"You really believe that?" sneered Jackson. "I can manipulate the government, you cannot. I can direct investigators, influence findings, and steer presidential decisions. What do you have, Winters? A board meeting?" Jackson laughed. "You will burn, and I will light the fire."

Winters's bad leg nearly buckled, and he wavered on his cane. *Damn Locke!* he thought. Locke's ill-timed resurrection made him susceptible to Jackson, putting his grand plan at risk. As long as Jackson could plausibly frame him for everything, the man had leverage. There was only one way to rebalance the equation. *I must remove Locke*, he thought.

Jackson sensed Winters's vulnerability and went for the kill. "You fix Locke, or I fix you! He's your man and that makes him your nuclear terrorist. You think eliminating one man is nothing? Good, then Locke should be easy for you to kill. I want proof of death. And get me that nuke!"

"Fine, I will kill Locke. I will clean up your mess," said Winters with a smile. He couldn't resist adding the last bit.

"*Your* mess, Winters! Your man, your mess," corrected Jackson as he moved in close. "And don't *ever* threaten me again. Remember that I feed you and remain your master, not the other way around." Jackson was pointing to the floor in front of him, as if commanding a dog to sit. "I have dealt with detritus like you my entire career. Never forget that I have the power to send you to hell and keep you there."

Winters chuckled, which was not the reaction Jackson expected. "You are a swamp creature, and that makes you predictable. It's why I took out an insurance policy. Three, to be precise."

Jackson's expression changed from wrath to bewilderment.

"Locke doesn't have the nukes. *I do*."

"Bullshit," said Jackson, but Winters stood motionless like a tripod, waiting for him to think it through. "Impossible. I don't believe it," muttered Jackson, but his apprehensive tone betrayed his strong words.

"Three," taunted Winters, with the joy of a cat playing with its prey. "Not one. *Three*."

"Three?" replied Jackson weakly. He expected Winters was lying again, but could he really take chances if it were remotely true?

"Correct. The nukes are already hidden in America's largest cities. You will never locate them, so don't try. I will not hesitate to pull the trigger if I feel threatened. If anything should happen to me, three American cities will evaporate—and on your watch, Mr. National Security Advisor." Then Winters bayoneted Jackson's weak spot. "Think of your legacy. How will American history remember you?"

Jackson turned noticeably paler, even under the garage's dim fluorescent light. His mouth moved but nothing came out. Finally, just a whisper: "You wouldn't dare. Is this another bluff?"

"And you thought the president was your biggest problem. What a fool!" cackled Winters.

"This better not be more lies, Winters, or so help me God I will string you up in Lafayette Square like Mussolini. Do not gamble with American cities!" bellowed Jackson, spittle flying from his mouth. "WMD was deliberately precluded from our arrangement."

"The arrangement has changed."

Jackson clenched his fists, and Winters feared the man would strike him.

"There is no place you can run, hide, or slither, Winters, that I cannot find you. Nukes or no nukes. And if not me, then someone like me. You can't outrun the government."

"The people I work for are far less forgiving than me," said Winters in a severe tone. "They will destroy you, someone like you, or the entire government, if they must."

"People? What people?" retorted Jackson, doubt on his face. "You're a bottom feeder, Winters. All you crave is power, but there are things more important, like country."

"'Country'?! Listen to yourself, old man. You are stuck in the twentieth century, while the rest of the world has moved on. Today's superpowers are no longer countries but something else. They operate in the shadows and manipulate the rest."

"That torture cell warped your brain worse than I thought."

Winters squeezed the ivory monkey head but held his temper. "There's a war going on, Jackson, an invisible one, and it's not being fought by nations. Its weapons are not militaries, but deception and manipulation. Its pawns are countries and corporations. Nothing else matters. Don't you see it? The U.S. invades faraway places that pose no existential threat, like Iraq and Afghanistan, and stays there forever regardless of who sits in the Oval Office. It makes no sense, yet Americans wave their flags and support the troops, and for what? It's all for naught. The U.S. is no longer a superpower— it's a tool. We've been manipulated into fighting other people's wars. Sometimes the more obvious a thing is, the harder it is to see."

"When did you become a conspiracy theorist?" mocked Jackson, and Winters's face darkened.

"Talent is hitting targets no one else can hit, but genius is hitting targets no one else can see. I made a choice, George, and so should you. You're a pawn in a global war you don't see or comprehend. If you care about your country, then you should choose not to become a tool."

Winters started walking away.

"Hey, where are you going? I'm not done," yelled Jackson.

"But I am," rasped Winters without stopping. "You've been warned. I'm just the messenger."

"What does that mean?"

Winters spun around. "It means you're expendable."

CHAPTER 33

Lin waited until nightfall before driving to the mystery safe house in McLean, Virginia. Dan's counterintelligence team monitored Russian agents from this house and saw them meeting with Apollo Outcomes teams covertly. No one knew why. When his boss ran it up the chain, he was ordered to shut down his operation. When he refused, he was exiled to Omaha and his team dispersed with prejudice.

Someone high up is protecting this safe house, and I want to know why, thought Lin as she drove a little too fast. Even if she wasn't fired by the FBI, she would always choose her own car, a zippy Mini Cooper, over the FBI's joke of an unmarked car, the conspicuous Ford Crown Vic. Twenty minutes later, she found Dan's mystery safe house in a cul-de-sac of McMansions deep in suburban Virginia, ironically not far from CIA headquarters.

"There you are," she whispered as she cut the engine. Parking well up the street, she observed the surreptitious safe house. Nothing stood out. Trees surrounded the property and swayed in the winter gusts. Lights were on but she saw no movement. Nearby homes were equally quiet, but she saw people inside.

It's go time, Lin thought as she zipped up her black

jacket and pulled her wool cap low. Casually, she walked down Rockland Terrace, as if she were there visiting relatives. The houses were spaced well apart, marking it as an affluent suburb, and no one looked out their windows at this late hour. Somewhere in the distance, a dog barked.

Lin's heart beat faster as she approached the Mc-Mansion. Its front double doors were framed by a two-story colonnade and unpruned shrubbery. Sheer curtains hung in the windows, obscuring the house's interior. However, she could see the outline of a humongous but cheap chandelier hanging in the atrium; several of its bulbs were dead. Up close, the place looked inert and run down. Then she saw silhouettes in a second-story window.

Someone's definitely home, she thought, and unconsciously felt her Glock beneath her coat. Lin moved into the tree line, and the frozen snow crunched beneath her sneakers. The driveway was shoveled and salted, another clue that people lived here. She crept to the backyard and found a wooden deck and rusty barbeque. The backyard was even more unkept than the front.

An outside light flicked on. *Crap!* she thought, then realized it was a motion sensor light, the kind you can get at any hardware store. She froze, blending into the night's shadows. Seconds later, the light turned off and she moved.

Calm. Be calm, she told herself, gliding furtively up the deck stairs. Kneeling in front of the back door, she pulled out a screwdriver and a ring of bump keys, each with a small O-ring around its base. Working rapidly, she tried each key until she found one that fit the lock. She turned it slightly to the right and tapped on the back of the key with the screwdriver's handle. Two taps later, the lock turned, and she was inside.

Eeeeeeee. The house alarm buzzed, but it was not the siren that called in reinforcements. She had about thirty seconds to find the alarm panel and disable it before the real alarm blared. Alarms give owners a grace period to deactivate the alarm, even safe houses, and she was operating within that grace period.

Thirty, twenty-nine, twenty-eight, she counted as she entered the house, Glock drawn. Alarm panels were usually in a basement utility closet. Bounding across the supersized kitchen, she started opening closets. Pantry. Coats. Junk. It was the utility closet, and up near the ceiling was the alarm panel, an unassuming gray steel box. Too high for a circuit breaker.

That's it, she thought as she closed the door behind her and turned on her Maglite. Upstairs, footsteps were moving down a hallway and then down the stairs. *Fifteen, fourteen, thirteen.*

Slow is smooth, and smooth is fast, she told herself. Climbing up on a washing machine, Lin bump-keyed the steel box open. *Ten, nine, eight.* Inside lay a tangle of wires, lights, and circuit boards. Holding the Maglite in her mouth, she located the power supply and yanked it lose. *Five, four, three.* Then she found the battery backup and pried it out with the screwdriver. The alarm died.

Lin didn't move and just listened over the pounding of her heart. Someone—a man, by the weight of the footsteps—sped past the closet door and into the kitchen. Slowly, she slid off the washing machine and aimed her weapon at the utility closet's door. No sound. The man stopped in the kitchen, or did he? She wasn't sure. She could feel her pulse throbbing in her head.

Click, click. She heard him unlock and lock the back door's deadbolt. Then silence again. *Keep moving. Nothing to see here,* she thought. Finally, the footsteps crossed the kitchen and opened the refrigerator door. She heard a plate clink on the stone countertop, and she thought he was probably loading up some snacks. Then he headed back upstairs at a leisurely pace. Lin lowered her weapon and breathed deeply to tame her heart rate.

Let's see who you are, she thought as she slipped out the closet door. *If you're nobody, I'll leave and you'll never know I was here.*

Lin padded through the dining room and living room, each with a vaulted ceiling. The place was sparsely furnished in the anodyne style of a hotel lobby. There were no magazines, personal pictures on the walls, or any other artifacts of life. The McMansion had a home office/library, but the shelves were vacant and the desk drawers empty. There was not even pen and paper.

I've seen motel rooms with more soul, she thought and continued her security sweep. Stealthily, she crept up the large double staircase in the atrium, Glock pointing forward, until she reached the top floor. Bedrooms with male clothing, mostly active sportswear. A grand bathroom with no female accoutrements. Closets, mostly empty.

She heard voices. Humans. Lin stopped. Someone was watching a movie behind a closed door, an action thriller by the sound of it.

OK, time to leave, she told herself, turning around and feeling awkward. *Jason was right, I should never have come here.*

Two young men laughed in unison, then spoke in Russian. Lin froze and felt adrenaline shoot through her veins. She strained to hear them but couldn't make out the conversation, only the language. It was definitely Russian. She had to get closer.

This could be my big break, but I need to be sure, she thought, inching toward the door. Her heart thumped against her rib cage, making her Glock shake. *Steady,* she commanded as she got closer. They were talking about the movie.

"She is a sexy chick but has miserable tits," judged a young man in Russian.

Pigs! she thought, and her Glock went steady.

"Yeah, I've seen ironing boards more fuckable," said the other, laughing.

So rude, she thought as she carefully extended a hand for the doorknob while the other held the Glock. Slowly she turned it and cracked open the door so she could peak inside.

Two young men leaned back in desk chairs with their feet on makeshift desks. An array of large computer monitors hung off a steel frame, and one showed the movie. Old boxes of microwaved junk food littered their desks, and the place reeked of sweat socks and pizza. It could have been a frat house, save the multiple computer screens with high-end spy programs in Cyrillic.

Russian hackers, all right, she thought. Probably on loan from the Troll Factory in St. Petersburg, the nickname for the Russian government's notorious hacker unit. Normally they operated from the motherland. *What are they doing here?*

"I bet he screws like a squirrel," said one of the

Russians about the movie star, who was busy shooting bad guys.

"And she's his nut," said the other and laughed.

"Women need to be crushed like nuts in sex. A man must show her who is fucking who."

"As in sex, so too in life. The woman is under the man, as it's meant to be." Both young men nodded in their perceived wisdom.

"Then what does that make me?" said Lin in Russian. The men jerked upright in shock and spun around to face her, only to see her gun pointing at them. "On the ground, boys!"

"Who are . . ." stammered one, unable to finish his sentence.

"I'll tell you what. Since you're the weaker sex, I'll put my gun away." Carefully she slid the Glock back into her holster and both men eyed their own 9 mm pistols sitting on the computer console. She saw the weapons, too. "There, now it's a fair fight. Two dicks versus one woman. Let's see how it ends."

The two men reached for their pistols, but the hackers were no match for Lin. Seconds later they were flex-cuffed to furniture, each breathing heavily through the pain. One man's nose was smashed and bled all over his T-shirt and the floor. He instinctively held his nose up in the air, as if that would slow the bleeding, but it made no difference. The other was balled up in a fetal position, clutching broken ribs and taking shallow sips of air. Each breath caused sharp pain to shoot up his side. Lin stood over them, dominant.

"Looks like you're the bitches now," she said, then dug her toe gently into the second man's injured side. He shrieked and she smiled. "That's on behalf of the other fifty percent of the human race."

Lin wheeled up one of the office chairs and sat down, legs crossed and arms on the armrests, like a queen in judgment. "Now that introductions are over, I wish to have a friendly conversation. If you refuse to reciprocate, our discussion will become progressively unfriendly."

"Piss off," said the one with the broken nose, in bad English. "You have no idea who you're dealing with, bitch. We will fuck you up!"

"Not friendly," replied Lin calmly in Russian. "And do not worry. I will fuck you hard, but not in the way you think. I will crush you like a nut. I may even pulverize all four nuts," she said, holding the Glock by its barrel and swinging it like a hammer. Both men closed their legs unconsciously and turned away from her glare. "Last chance, and try to use your brains before you answer this time. Who are you? Who do you work for? What are you doing here? When did you arrive?"

Neither man spoke.

"Talk to me!" shouted Lin, and both men jumped in alarm. But they remained silent, and the man with the broken nose spat blood at her. Lin walked over to him and hammered his nose again with the butt of her weapon. His scream was horrific, and the other man grimaced with fear.

"I don't have all goddamned night," she said, and it was true. They could have tripped a silent alarm, and heavies could be on the way.

"Go to hell," wheezed the man with broken ribs, each word a stabbing pain. "You're a dead woman. Dead!" He started coughing in agony.

Lin knelt beside the man huddled on the floor and nuzzled her gun gently into his broken ribs. He screeched. "Talk to me, Ribs, or I will blow Nosebleed's head off. Talk to me or I kill your friend. Five seconds, you decide." She stood up and aimed the gun at Nosebleed's head, cocking the hammer; the man looked away. "Five, four . . ."

"Do it Yuri! Tell her!" shouted the man with the broken nose. Yuri didn't speak.

". . . three . . ."

"Stop! Stop!" screamed the man with the broken nose. Lin steadied her aim.

". . . two . . ."

"I will tell you! I will tell you!!"

Lin lowered her weapon. "Tell me what, Nosebleed?"

"The room," said the man with the broken nose.

"You traitor!" yelled the man on the floor, and contorted in pain.

"Screw you, Yuri! I'm not dying for this. Besides, she's dead anyway."

"Do I look dead to you?" asked Lin, amused.

"You will be. Now untie me, and I will show you."

"Show me what?"

"Untie me." No one moved. Growing impatient, Lin raised her Glock to his head. "Stop, stop, stop!" he said, blood still trickling down his mouth and chin. "What you want is in the basement. I promise. Untie me, and I will show you."

It could be a ploy, she thought. *But I can take him, especially in his beat-ass state.* "OK, Nosebleed," she said, drawing a small boot knife and holding it to his jugular. "But fuck with me and I will gut you." With that she sliced the flex-cuff, and he fell away, rubbing his wrists. "Up! Show me."

"Andrei. My name is Andrei."

"Whatever, Nosebleed. Walk." They moved down the hall, and she kept her gun at his back. They walked downstairs and into the basement. It was empty, save a laundry area.

"Are you lying to me, Nosebleed?" asked Lin in disbelief, holding her Glock to his head.

"No, no! Please. Secret room," he said, pointing to a dark corner. She followed at a distance and aimed her pistol at his torso as he opened up a large fuse box. Then he opened the front panel, a fake. Behind it was a handprint scanner. Andrei pressed his right hand on the scanner, and she heard a heavy bolt inside the wall release. With a grunt, he pushed and the entire wall rotated inward and to the right, revealing a spacious hidden room.

"Impressive," Lin heard herself say out loud.

"They will come for me," said the hacker, smiling. "They will kill you. After their fun."

"Who? FSB? Spetsnaz? Who?"

He smiled, blood dribbling down his chin. "Worse."

Worse? she thought. *Who's worse than Russian special forces? You have to be a qualified psychopath to make their ranks.* What the civilized world considered human rights abuse, they considered training. New recruits had to survive *dedovshchina,* or the "Rule of the Grandfathers," that left many maimed or dead. Those that made it were ethically unhinged. Even the Russian mob feared them.

"Don't bluff me, asshole," said Lin, and flex-cuffed him to a pipe in the safe room. He continued smiling, feeding off her fear. She found the light switch and flipped it. The place was an armory: racks of assault rifles, pistols with silencers, .50-cal snipers with Forward Looking InfraRed (FLIR) thermal imaging scopes, munitions crates, high-end surveillance kits, communications gear, laptops, and a large street map of Washington, DC, taped to the wall. Everything needed to start a world war, except . . .

"Where's the demo?" demanded Lin.

"I do not understand," he said with a puzzled expression.

"The demolitions! How did you blow the bridge, Nosebleed?" she repeated, but the man was perplexed. Then she heard the garage door open above, and a large vehicle drive in and park.

"They're here!" said Andrei with bloody glee.

CHAPTER 34

Tye stood with his arms folded and Lava gave a low whistle as they inspected my wrecked BMW. Both its front and rear ends were smashed in, with a lake of neon-green radiator fluid under the chassis. I wondered how I made it back to my safe house at all. As soon as I did, I called Lava on the burner phone. What else could I do? I was ambushed and he was my only lifeline. He said he would come as soon as possible; that was hours ago and now it was midnight.

"Not exactly the 'quiet professional,' are you, Locke?" teased Tye, referring to a maxim of special operators everywhere. "Every cop in the city is looking for you."

"The country," corrected Lava. "Every cop in the country. And Interpol, too. Your name, picture, and physical description are on every blotter and news website in the world. They're saying you're the terrorist that assassinated the vice president." Lava gave a mock expression of admiration.

"Me?!" I exclaimed, breathless.

"Correct. Also, Winters probably knows you are here, in the city. He will be coming for you," said Lava, and I felt the blood drain from my face. Lava nodded, as if reading my mind and affirming my dread.

"Pretty impressive for a guy who's only been on the

ground for seventy-two hours," said Tye with a smirk. "That's gotta be a record. We should create a new category for you called the FUMTU Awards."

"FUMTU?" I asked.

"Fucked Up More Than Usual."

I ignored his grin and turned to Lava. "How did they find me so fast? How could they possibly get my file? Know where I would be? I've gone over it a million times in my mind, Lava, and I don't get it."

"You should have stayed put, Tom, and let me run the traps at Apollo first," said Lava, kicking my dead bumper. It fell off.

"Yeah, I know. But I—"

Lava held up a hand to silence my excuses. Tye rolled his eyes. I felt like a butter bar again.

"Let's go inside," said Lava, and we followed him into the trailer.

"Real shithole of a place you got here, Locke," said Tye as he entered.

"Yeah, Lava said the same exact thing two nights ago."

"The man ain't wrong."

"Suit up, Locke. We need to get you out of here," said Lava.

I was already packed to go, hoping he would say that. Nonetheless, I went over my equipment one last time. Old habit.

"Learn anything at Apollo?" I asked, as I put on my Apollo armor.

"Nada. They think you're off the board."

"KIA," added Tye. "In Syria, a year ago by Jase Campbell's team. Curiously, he's MIA as of today. Go figure."

Winters had sent Campbell's team after me in Iraq. He was good, too. "If Apollo didn't ambush me, then maybe it was Winters," I said.

"Negative," said Tye. "You'd be dead if it was Winters's guys."

"Agreed," said Lava. "Unless they're framing terrorists, they don't operate in daylight. Neither do we, for that matter. You were definitely hit by govvies." *Govvies* referred to government actors such as the military, intelligence, and law enforcement. It was a term of derision at Apollo.

"How is that possible?" I asked, slipping my Mark 23s into thigh holsters. Now wasn't the time for subtlety. "I just landed and no one knows I'm here but you. The CIA is good, but not that good. I have no digital signature, so the NSA can't track me. Anyway, they're not even looking for me. Everyone thinks I'm dead." I assumed Lava and Tye didn't give up my position to the govvies, although I was beginning to wonder. Trust no one.

"I don't understand it either, Tom. Until I do, we're all at risk," said Lava in an unsettling voice, looking at Tye, who nodded. His smirk had vanished. "I got a place in Virginia, in the Shenandoah. It's real primitive but you'll get used to it. I'm taking you there until I figure this out." Lava turned to me, holding up an index finger in my face. "And *stay put* this time!"

"Yes sir," I said automatically. We began loading my equipment into the back of Lava's armored SUV. "How goes the war with Winters?"

"It's a draw at the moment. It seems the turncoats are always one step ahead of us," said Tye as we carried a ballistic chest to the vehicle. "For now."

"Maybe you have a leak in your organization. Someone with divided loyalties," I said as we heaved the chest into the vehicle's back.

"A few months back, we launched a mole hunt and it almost tore the organization apart," said Lava, tossing the grenade launcher on the backseat. "It led nowhere. I believe our opsec is tight." Opsec, or operational security, is a religion at Apollo. It meant keeping a secret.

"I don't know how they're tailing us, but they are," said Tye.

The time had come to ask the most important question. If I couldn't trust Lava now, then I was already a dead man. "Do you think Winters blew the bridge?"

Both stopped what they were doing and turned to me. Before Lava could answer, he received a text. "We need to leave now! A renegade Apollo assault team is inbound."

Tye sprinted to the driver's seat and cranked the engine.

"Leave the rest!" commanded Lava, and I dove into the back, SCAR in hand.

"Go, go, go!" shouted Lava as we crashed down the garage door and fishtailed around the corner, accelerating down the abandoned street. In seconds, we cleared six blocks.

"Wait! Slow down," said Lava, and Tye looked at him quizzically. "We need to observe this. Maybe it will tell us how they're tracking us."

"That's suicide," warned Tye. "They'll nab us for sure."

Lava didn't speak but shot him a command glance. I knew that look, and it always made me feel lower than whale shit.

"Wilco," responded Tye, soldier speak for *I under-*

stand and will comply. We donned our full-face Apollo helmets with night vision, and Tye switched to blackout drive. The street became day in the vehicle's infrared headlights. Lava pointed two fingers to the left, and we drove down a side alley.

"This should be good," he said over the earpiece. "Pull in here."

Tye took a right and we bumbled over rotting train tracks to a decrepit brick warehouse, much bigger than my safe house. It looked 1890s, with smashed-out windowpanes and a multistory coal smokestack. A rusty corrugated-steel sheet covered an antiquated truck entrance.

"Hold on," said Tye. He put the SUV in reverse and rammed through the corrugated-steel sheet. Tye was about to turn off the engine when Lava's hand blocked him.

"Leave it running," said Lava. "Grab your shit."

Tye grabbed his sniper rifle, a highly modified Finnish SAKO TRG 42. "They can run, but they'll just die tired," he joked, sort of.

I flipped on my night vision gunsight and could see everything my barrel saw, plus what was behind and ahead of me. Apollo fabricated custom equipment for its operatives, no expense spared, and it was always better than what the SEALs or Delta had. Always. It was a great recruitment tool, too.

We climbed up flights of broken stairs and then a rusty iron ladder to the roof. The place smelled like rotting machines. Once on the roof, I could see the Washington Monument, the Capitol building, and the National Airport across the Potomac River. A chilling winter breeze cut across us.

"Hear them?" asked Lava. Tye nodded, but I heard nothing.

"There," said Tye, pointing down the river. I strained my eyes and then saw them. Four black helicopters flew in perfect formation and stealth, skimming the Potomac. They were unlike any aircraft I had seen before: double rotors on top and a pusher propeller in the back. There were weapons pods on each flank and a 20 mm chain gun.

"Here they come," said Lava. "Move!" We slid down the rusty ladder, evading the choppers' thermal cameras. They flew directly over us, as quiet as golf carts and no *thwop-thwop-thwop* sound. I always thought "stealth helicopter" was an oxymoron, but apparently not.

"Follow me," commanded Lava, and we walked to the edge of the roof. Through my night vision, I saw the four helicopters hovering above my safe house. Ropes dropped from their sides and men fast-roped down. Sixteen in all. The choppers disappeared into the night while the men breached the roof and dropped into the warehouse, followed by flashes and loud explosions from within the building. The attack was withering, even from our distance, and took less than a minute.

There was no way I could have survived that, I realized.

"Show's over, let's go," said Lava. A powerful spotlight shown down on us, and then another and another and another. Rotor downdraft beat the air around us, but all I could hear was a steady whine, like a high-speed train engine, and not chopper blades. The stealth helicopters' 20 mm antitank cannons were leveled at our chests.

"Move and die," came a voice over a loudspeaker.

We were surrounded. Lava and Tye slowly put their weapons down and raised their hands. I followed their lead; we had no options beyond death. Armed men wearing the same body armor as those in the skyscraper streamed up the ladder and pushed us hard to the ground. In seconds, we were flex-cuffed and searched, all weapons removed. They even found my handcuff keys, both handcuff shims (belt buckle and rear beltloop), and the ceramic razor blade sewn into my tactical pants. In the distance, I saw the sixteen commandos evacuate my former safe house, now ablaze with a fire plume fifty feet high. Fire trucks wailed in the distance.

They yanked us to our knees and the leader removed our helmets one by one. Lava stared straight ahead, face revealing nothing. However, Tye's faced revealed everything: rage, murder, death. When they got to me, I heard the leader snort in contempt, then look up and wave.

A cable lowered from one of the black helicopters, and two men wound it around my chest and under the armpits. The leader looked up at the pilot and gave him a thumbs-up. The helicopter shot straight up, yanking me off my feet and sucking the air out of my lungs. I began rotating clockwise in midair but could see men putting hoods over Lava and Tye. They were not nice about it, either.

"Lava! Tye!" I shouted, but my voice was drowned out by distance. Ten-story buildings passed beneath my boots as we zoomed over the waterfront and then descended to the river, where they dunked me at high speed, which was like being waterboarded by a hydrofoil. My body skimmed the surface, each body blow knocking the wind out of me.

Dicks, I thought, knowing the pilots were having

fun. I was still coughing water out of my lungs when we climbed sharply, and the Potomac looked black in the moonless night. I spun in wild arcs as the chopper banked, all the while attempting to loosen my wrists behind my back, but it was no use. We crossed the far bank, passing over Route 50, and I could see the lights of the Pentagon.

The helicopter slowed to a hover above six black Chevy Suburbans, arranged in a circle with their headlights on and facing inward, making a perfect LZ. The pilots lowered me down into the middle of the circle, lined with more commandos in black, all guns on me. The towline went slack, and I hit the ground hard. The chopper accelerated back into the night. The commandos slowly walked toward me in unison as I struggled to stand up, my hands tied behind my back.

"Go ahead, assholes! It's the only chance you'll get!" I shouted, but they came to a halt, weapons trained on my head. A vehicle door opened, and an ornate cane emerged, followed by a tall man with a limp.

I couldn't believe what I was seeing.

"Winters," I hissed as he hobbled toward me. He looked different. Meaner, ghastlier, more evil.

"Did you really think I would let you get away a second time, Locke?" he rasped.

"I'm going to strangle you with my own hands!" I screamed, and two commandos rushed to restrain me, forcing me to my knees before him. "I'll beat you to death with that cane!"

Winters laughed as they placed the hood over my head.

Lin was trapped. She heard men speaking Russian on the floor above her, but the accents were strange. A few spoke like it was their second language. It sounded like there were six of them, and they were definitely military, and not FSB. *I need backup,* she thought, and tried her mobile phone, but her signal was dead inside the hidden bunker. The hacker smiled despite his broken nose. He knew she was trapped, too.

She looked around, desperately. The secret room took up half the McMansion's basement and was part armory and part electronics workbench. It had its own filtrated ventilation system and was lined with paneling that blocked electronic signals. Ballistic chests were stacked against the walls, alongside homemade weapons racks and shelves full of spy equipment. Everything except a landline.

"Do you have a phone down here?" she whispered in Russian to her prisoner, but he laughed through his duct tape gag. Furiously she scoured the armory for a way to communicate to the outside world. There were satellite phones and military-grade radios, but nothing usable. Then she found a stack of laptops under a ballistic jacket, flipped one open. It whirred to life but had a lock screen. *Maybe I can make a call using the laptop,* she thought. Although it was electronically locked, it did have a camera and fingerprint reader.

"Can you unlock this?" she asked the imprisoned hacker. He looked blank, as if he had never seen a computer before. She grabbed his right hand and he fought her, yelping through his gag. Both his hands were flex-cuffed around a vertical pipe, giving him little room to resist.

"Mmmmmm!! Mmmmmm!!!!!" he grunted in protest as she pried open his right index finger with pliers and pressed it against the finger pad. The screen went blue with acceptance and then prompted a face shot. She held up the computer camera up to his face, hoping it would see him and unlock itself. The hacker dodged and looked away, as she chased him around the pipe.

Screw this, she thought, and gut-punched him. The hacker slumped over, facing the floor, coughing through the gag. She grabbed the back of his head and yanked up while holding the computer in the other hand, so it could see him. The screen came alive. *Bingo!* she thought, and he groaned with defeat.

"How do I make a call out with this thing?" she said, working the keyboard. Everything was in Cyrillic, slowing her down. Upstairs, the Russians started shouting and running around. *They must have discovered the other hacker,* she thought. *I don't have much time.*

A metallic crash hit the floor next to her, causing her to jump in alarm. A utility shelf full of loaded magazines and equipment lay on the floor, with a smiling hacker lying next to it. He had kicked it over, so his comrades above would hear it. Then he started screaming through his gag.

"Shut up!" she commanded, holding her hand against

his gag. The man yelped louder, and she heard heavy footsteps above, moving toward the basement stairs. *No time for a phone call. I gotta get ready!* she thought, and ripped the place apart for anything useful. Shedding her coat, she grabbed the ballistic vest that covered the laptops and put it on, even though it was two sizes too large. Next, she found night-vision goggles in a foot locker and slipped them over her head. The dim room became bright gray with good three-dimensionality. The muffled footsteps above grew louder, as did the Russian expletives. Lin resumed her mad search.

"That'll do nicely," she said, discovering a steel box of hand grenades secured in cut-out foam. She grabbed four and stuffed them into her vest pockets, praying no bullets hit them. Not smart, she knew, but in her mind grenades were like condoms: better to have them and not need them than need them and not have them. And when it came to crazed Russians, she preferred grenades over condoms.

The basement door slammed open above her, and footsteps started down the stairs. The hacker screamed louder.

"Faster!" she told herself, opening a wall locker and finding MP5s leaning upright. "Good," she said, picking one up and cycling the charging handle. Then she dropped the MP5, spotting her weapon of choice.

"Sweetness," she whispered, picking up the Saiga-12 fully automatic shotgun with folding stock and collimator sight. Next to it were six banana clips, each holding twelve rounds of twelve-gauge shells, enough to obliterate a flock of ducks. Lin had only heard of this mythical weapon from her mafia informants. The thing looked like a black and bloated AK-47, and it was the wet dream of every Russian mobster to possess one. However, only Spetsnaz had the military-grade version, and now so did Lin. "Sweetness," she repeated.

Lin heard the man on the other side of the wall, and she fumbled to get the clip into the Saiga. The bound hacker began shouting ecstatically. The deadbolt inside the door released and a man heaved it against the wall, swinging it open. Lin's hands shook, and she couldn't get the ammo clip to sit properly in the weapon. She crouched in a corner, behind a footlocker, so she was not visible to the gigantic Russian across the room.

Slow is smooth, and smooth is fast, she reminded herself again, focusing on the clip and ignoring the man across the room. It clicked into place, and the man spun around. Lin charged the bolt and they both heard the round slide into the chamber. He raised his pistol and she the Saiga, followed by a pistol shot and an explosion of shotgun rounds. The man blew backward off his feet, and the hacker shit himself.

Lin turned off the lights and used her night vision as she prowled through the basement, covering her corners as she moved. The Russian voices above her were fre-netic now, and two heavy men came charging down the stairs. Lin was waiting and pulled the trigger, full auto. A *ruuurrrppp* sound shook the room, as the weapon walked upward and knocked her back. Gunsmoke clung to the air and two dead men lay facedown on the stairs, their bodies shredded by the wall of lead pellets. Hun-dreds of small holes peppered the dry wall in the stair-well, except for where the men had stood.

Lin loaded a fresh magazine and leapt up the stairs to the main hallway on the ground floor. No use sneak-ing around at this point. To the left was the kitchen and back door, but the passageway had two blind corners. When she worked on the FBI Special Weapons and Tactics (SWAT) teams, the shoot house taught her never to trust blind corners, especially when heavily armed Russians were lurking about. Lin glanced right, seeing the open atrium and front door. It was her best chance, even though she could take fire from the second-floor balcony.

All footsteps stopped and the house fell silent. *Bad sign,* she thought, not knowing where the enemy was. Slowly, she crept toward the atrium until she got to a bend in the hallway. Using a compact mirror, she peered around the corner. Nothing. She leapt up and the space around her exploded in automatic gunfire. Lin screamed involuntarily as she dove under a narrow hallway table, its marble top adding the minimum of protection.

"Come out and we won't hurt you!" yelled a man in bad English.

"Fuck off, dickless!" she yelled back, in Russian. One thing her time on the Slavic mafia beat taught her: *never* trust a Rusky with a gun. Another burst of rounds blew into the tabletop, splintering wood and marble around her. She was trapped.

"No need for such foul talk, little lady," said the man gently from around a corner. "Put down the gun and I promise not to hurt you."

Lin heard stealthy footsteps coming from the living room. Two pairs. *He's distracting me while his buddies flank me,* she realized. *I can play at that too.* "Who are you? Spetsnaz?"

The man laughed. "No, little lady. We eat Spetsnaz for happy hour."

"Then who are you?"

"OK, I will tell you since you ask nicely. We are Wagner Group."

"Russian mercenaries?!" exclaimed Lin, knowing he would only admit this if he intended to kill her.

"*Da,* little lady. Now come out, and I won't hurt you. I promise. I'm sure it's a misunderstanding, and no more people need to die tonight."

The two men in the living room were closing in and would soon block her exit to the front door. But she needed more information. "Wagner only works for the GRU. You're nothing but Spetsnaz little green men," she said.

The man laughed. "Is that what they think here? No, we do not always work for Moscow and, no, we are not all Russian or Spetsnaz. We are what Spetsnaz should be." Then his tone got sterner. "We work for ourselves."

Lin heard the footsteps sneaking around the atrium's far corner, near the front door. It was down the hall about twenty feet, and they would annihilate her in a cross fire if she tried to escape.

All of this truly scared Lin. The Wagner Group did the Kremlin's nasty work around the globe: Ukraine, Syria, Venezuela, central Africa, and now the United States. They were potent and almost wiped out Delta Force and Rangers in eastern Syria in 2018. When Russia wanted to fight a shadow war, they deployed the Wagner Group. When the Kremlin wanted to assassinate a leader, like the president, they used the Wagner Group because it offered maximum effectiveness and plausible deniability. Mercenaries operated without constraint, even compared to Spetsnaz. Lin's pulse raced.

I must warn the FBI, she thought. *But first I need to get out of here.* She breathed deeply to focus her spirit, as her father taught her at Golden Gate Park while they practiced tai chi. Trust your training, he would counsel, and let the Tao flow through you like water going downhill. You will survive. A lifetime of training came down to moments like this. *Focuuuuus*, she thought and exhaled.

"Little lady, are you OK? Please come out."

She heard the men around the corner. "How do I know I can trust you?" she asked in a high-pitched whine, feigning panic.

"Please, I won't harm you. Just lay down your weapon and slide it forward, so I can see it."

Lin shoved the Saiga in front of her, but still within reach.

"Good," said the voice. "Now, come on out slowly."

"Is it only you?" she whimpered while she pulled out two grenades.

"Yes, it's just me. You killed my friends, but I promise I won't hurt you. I know you are scared. Come out."

"OK, OK. I think I'm ready to come out, if you put your gun down too," she said, pulling the grenades' pins but keeping their spring levers depressed.

"Here's my gun," said the man, sliding an MP5 into the hallway. She still couldn't see him, which meant he couldn't see her, either.

"Just give me a few seconds. I'm scared," she said with frailty as she let fly the two grenades' spring levers. *One-one thousand,* she counted.

"Take your time," he said.

Two-one thousand.

"I'm scared," she pleaded.

Three-one thousand. She shot the first grenade like a

pool ball across the wooden atrium floor, banking it off a wall and into the living room.

Four-one thousand. Lin tossed the second grenade toward the voice, bouncing it off the back wall and into the voice. Then she ducked, plugging her ears.

The explosions concussed the room, shattering windows. Men screamed. Lin picked up the Saiga and moved toward the voice's corner. There wasn't much left of the man, and the hallway was blown out and on fire. Without stopping, she moved around the corner through the living room's back entry and saw two bodies at the far end, near the front door. As she approached, muzzle first, it was clear they were actually dead and not faking it. The living room was on fire, too.

Lin heard sirens in the distance. *I can't be caught here,* she realized. There would be too many questions, and it would end badly. She needed to find whoever was behind this, and she couldn't do it locked inside an FBI holding cell.

One more thing! Lin thought, and sprinted back into the burning house. Minutes later, she emerged with a laptop. When the fire trucks arrived, she was gone. The firefighters found two survivors in flex-cuffs, six bodies, and a secret room full of Russian spy gear and heavy weapons. First responders scattered as live ammunition popped off in the fire, which consumed the house and most of the useful intelligence. Then the news trucks showed up.

CHAPTER 36

Six black Suburbans snaked through the sparse night traffic, only feet from one another's bumpers despite their high speed. They shuffled their order as they passed through tunnels, and aggressively blocked other vehicles that got too close. Above them flew the four black Sikorsky S-97 helicopters, escorting them in stealth mode. The roads were generally clear at this hour, and the air-land convoy drove in a wide circling pattern, as Winters awaited a phone call. They stuck to the Virginia side of the river, where the roads were wider, allowing them more freedom to maneuver should a problem occur. Still, Winters didn't like traveling in the open. It wasn't the govvies he worried about; it was Apollo Outcomes. He was at war with them, and they both stalked the night. Operating in the open made him a target.

"Give me a secure line to the national security advisor," commanded Winters from the backseat of one of the armored Suburbans.

"Yes sir," said the aide. Moments later he handed Winters a handset. "It's secure."

"It's me. I have Locke, tied and trussed," said Winters.

"Excellent. I knew you would come through for me,"

said Jackson on the other end. "I think we can solve many problems with this guy."

"Wait, I'm not done, Jackson. If you want to use Locke as your fall guy, you must do something for me first."

"What?" answered Jackson, angry.

"Kill the president."

Silence. Then, "Say again?"

"Kill the president, Jackson."

"Are you mad?! Have you lost all sanity, Winters? What did they do to you in that prison cell?"

Winters did not react to the swipe but checked his watch, then interrupted Jackson's tirade. "Kill the president, per our original agreement."

"We're well beyond that, Winters."

"You know it's the only way. He will eventually find out that you had a hand in everything. When he does, he will come for you. It's cleaner this way, George. You know it is, and it will solve my problems too."

More silence. Winters could feel Jackson thinking it over. Both men knew they were in a standoff: Jackson could link all the terrorist events to Winters, and Winters could help enlighten the president to Jackson's treason. Both men also knew the standoff served no one's interests, and they needed a way forward. Winters was offering a path.

"Jackson, this is a onetime offer. I give you Locke right now, and your men kill the president. You can blame Locke for everything. We will both achieve our goals. Take the deal."

Jackson said nothing, still mulling it over, so Winters continued the assault. "When it's over, you can 'catch' Locke, link him to the Russians, and take full credit. I will even help you, if you wish. Think about it, George. The country is galvanized once more and hardened. Isn't that want you wanted? To do a little evil in order to achieve a greater good? To inoculate America against national security threats and unite the country? To awaken the sleepwalkers, as you put it?"

"Yes, but—"

"Then make a choice," interrupted Winters. "We don't have much time. It's a onetime offer, and the best you will get. You must finish what you started, and that means POTUS. If you refuse, then I will find a new partner. Remember our last conversation; you're expendable."

Winters could hear Jackson breathing into the phone, no doubt furious, but the man had to learn his place. There were authorities greater than the White House, and they weren't divine.

"OK, fine," whispered Jackson.

"Speak up. I didn't hear that."

"I'll do it. I'll make the arrangements for POTUS. But we have to use your men."

"Done. We will stage another terrorist attack, but you need to line him up. No mistakes this time, and it will be harder now," said Winters. President Anderson had disappeared since the first terrorist attack and attempt on his life. The Secret Service kept the man essentially under house arrest for his own safety, and few knew where. Not even Winters.

"President Anderson is at Camp David," said Jackson quietly. "The place has been turned into a fortress. You're going to have trouble getting in there."

"No, I won't," assured Winters. "Just tell me where he is, exactly, and I will take care of the rest." Jackson didn't respond, perhaps regretting his decision. "I knew you would come through for me, George. This is the right thing to do, and you know it."

"Brad, there must be another way. Killing the president of the United States. Well, it's—"

"Don't soften on me now, Jackson!" interrupted Winters, angry. "There is only one way this ends. You know it; I know it. As long as POTUS is alive, we're both at risk."

Jackson knew it was true but didn't want to admit it to himself. The plan seemed simple enough but killing the president—regardless of who sat in the chair—was twisting his soul in unexpected ways. It would harm the country and embolden enemies. Ultimately, all he could muster was: "I'm a patriot, Brad."

"Then uphold your end of the bargain, George," said Winters, detecting Jackson's wavering resolve. "I'll be watching your moves closely, and if I sense you might double-cross me . . . don't. I have three nukes in three American cities. Call my bluff, and watch one incinerate."

"No need to get nasty, Winters," said Jackson, steel back in his voice. "I said I would take care of it, and I will. Deliver Locke to me directly. Meet me in the same garage as before. Give me fifteen minutes."

"Don't be late," said Winters, and Jackson hung up.

CHAPTER 37

Lin's hands were still shaking as she drove down the George Washington Memorial Parkway. Adrenaline still raged through her veins, and she was driving to calm down. She didn't know where she was going nor cared; she just needed to drive. In the front seat sat her Saiga automatic shotgun, next to a bag of grenades and ammo. It would be impossible to explain if she got pulled over, but her mind wasn't there.

Should I have stayed at the scene? she kept asking herself, but there was no right answer. If she stayed, she would have been arrested, and who knew if the FBI would have believed her. Probably not. But running made her look guilty. Running always does.

The FBI will think I'm a criminal now, she thought, tears of frustration welling up in her eyes. She wiped her eyes with her sleeve, then her nose. *But I'm a good agent! I know I am.*

"Crap, crap, crap!" she yelled at the windshield, pounding the steering wheel. She pulled over into one of the scenic overlooks on the Potomac River, and got out of the car. Then screamed. No one was around, so she screamed again. Cars whizzed by and took no notice. She slumped on the hood, gazing at the lights of Georgetown across the river. In the distance were the bell towers of the National Cathedral, with a blinking red warning light on one for aircraft. The only sound was the occasional passing car and airliners on approach to the airport.

Lin fetched the Russian hacker's laptop from the car and sat down at a picnic table. Maybe it would reveal a clue. She opened it and tried several random passwords, in Russian, but it was no use. The thing was locked. She had contemplated kidnapping the hacker but had no time. Fire trucks were pulling into the burning house's driveway when she was still downstairs in the hidden armory, stuffing grenades into a rucksack. She had to leave immediately.

Another dead end, she thought, holding her head in her hands. She wanted to talk to someone but didn't know whom to call. All her friends were in the FBI, and she wasn't on speaking terms with her dad, even though she wanted to talk to him most. He would know what to do, but she couldn't face his judgment. She took out her phone and called the only person she could.

"Hello, Lin? Is that you?" asked Jason, waking up from sleep.

"Jason," she said, her voice breaking.

"What's the matter?"

"I can't . . ." She stopped and resisted the urge to sob, especially to Jason.

"Just slow down. Breathe," he said, and Lin took multiple deep breaths. "I'm guessing you went out to the safe house and found something?"

"Yeah," she said, getting control of herself. It was all she could say.

"Well, what?"

Lin put a hand over her eyes and looked down at the ground to help focus. *Get it together, girl,* she kept telling herself. *Don't let Jason hear you like this.*

"Lin? Are you there?"

"Yeah."

"What did you find?" asked Jason, and Lin told him. "Holy shit" was all he could say when she finished. "Holy. Fucking. Shit."

Neither spoke for several minutes.

"What's the Wagner Group doing running around Washington, DC?" asked Jason at last.

"I think they're the ones who are behind the bridge attack," said Lin. "But the guy said they weren't working for Moscow."

"Then who hired them?"

"I don't know. I don't even know if he's even telling a half truth."

"Well, it makes more sense than any other theory I've heard so far at headquarters," said Jason. They sat in silence, mulling over the implications. No one would believe them. Finally, he asked the only question that mattered: "What are you going to do now?"

"I need to find out what's going on. I need to finish my investigation. If not me, then who?" She paused, waiting for an encouraging response, but Jason said nothing. "Also, it's the only way to clear my name." His silence confirmed her suspicions that it was too late for that. *I don't care,* she thought and then spoke with fire. "What do I have to lose at this point?"

"Be careful what you wish for," said Jason, and Lin balled up a fist. It was exactly the kind of irritating thing her father would say.

"Are you going to help me or not, Jason?"

"Yes," he said, voice wavering. He would hang now, too. "Although I don't know why, Jen."

"Because you want to do the right thing."

"Yes, I suppose," he said unconvincingly.

"Because you like me?"

"Yes, that too."

"You're the only friend I have right now, Jason," said Lin, her vulnerable tone surprising them both.

After another pause, Jason changed the subject. "I talked to Dan in counterintelligence again. We went out for drinks and he got a little tipsy. He's super stressed. It turns out that safe house was under some sort of surveillance embargo."

"Surveillance embargo? I've never heard of such a thing."

"Neither had his boss, who ignored it. Seems like you're not the only rebel in the Bureau."

Lin chuckled, her mood lifting.

"It turns out the men in the safe house would frequently make late-evening runs."

"Yeah, they came home late tonight too. Did Dan say what they were doing?"

"This is when drunk Dan got all weird on me. He said the Russians would meet up with another party. At first, they thought it was CIA Ground Division because they were all huge dudes that dressed like Secret Service agents, drove black SUVs, and met with scumbags late at night in strange locations."

"But that's illegal. The CIA is not allowed to operate domestically."

"Yeah, agreed, which is why his boss ran it by some friends at Langley, totally deep background, but they told him it wasn't their guys. It's not us either."

"Then who was it? DIA? DOD? DHS? Who?"

"None of the above. You'll never guess, Jen. They were meeting with a company."

"A company?" asked Lin incredulously. "Like Booz Allen?"

Jason laughed. "Nope. Ever heard of Apollo Outcomes?"

"Who are they?"

"Heavy hitters. They run paramilitary ops for the government, strictly off the books. It's like the CIA and JSOC combined, but Apollo Outcomes can do things those guys can't. That's why they're hired."

"*American* mercenaries? Like Wagner Group, but working for us?" said Lin, not believing it, but cognitive dissonance had become the theme of her evening.

"Yeah, but even more hardcore."

"Let me guess. When you say Apollo Outcomes can do things the CIA and DOD can't, you're talking about domestic missions," she said. The CIA and DOD were absolutely forbidden from working inside the United States. From the Posse Comitatus Act of 1878 to the Church Committee of 1976, the one thing every intelligence, military, and law enforcement officer learns is no domestic spying or military operations. Not only was it illegal, it was considered a threat to democracy. However, outsourcing it to a private company would neatly circumnavigate the issue.

"Exactly. Dan's boss feared these guys were running some sort of modern COINTELPRO operation, so he started watching them too."

Lin stiffened when she heard COINTELPRO, the Bureau's low point. Starting in the late '50s, FBI director J. Edgar Hoover ran a covert and illegal program aimed at surveilling, infiltrating, discrediting, and disrupting left-wing political organizations. He thought the USSR was behind the antiwar riots and cultural war that seized America, and he took Machiavellian steps to stem the imagined threat. Some even blamed COINTELPRO for the assassinations of Martin Luther King Jr. and Malcolm X. The CIA launched its own domestic espionage project in 1967 called Operation CHAOS. All recruits at the FBI Academy were made to learn it so they would know what sin looked like.

"And is Apollo running a private sector COINTELPRO with Wagner Group's help?" asked Lin with anxiety. "It sounds like we have American mercenaries working with Russian ones to assassinate U.S. political leadership and frame terrorists. If so, we don't know who hired them, or why."

Jason let out a stressed sigh. "We may never know. The next day, Dan's boss was transferred to the Omaha office, and everyone was forbidden to communicate with him. They shut down the operation and were told never to speak about it again, or have their security clearance yanked. It's why Dan got so cagey before."

"Geez."

"Yeah. I had no idea. Nobody does. I didn't know the FBI could keep secrets like that."

Lin was thinking. As if he could hear her think, Jason said, "Wait, stop, Lin! Just stop. You're in enough trouble as it is. Whatever you're thinking, do not do it! Every time you do this, things get worse for both of us!"

"Where can I find these Apollo Outcomes guys?" she asked, starting up the car.

"Jen, don't even think about it. They're heavy hitters and work for pay grades way above ours."

"But you just told me they're doing some COINTEL-PRO thing, are collaborating with the Wagner Group, and the FBI is prohibited from investigating it. It's treason, pure and simple. If we don't stop them, who will? It's obviously an inside job, Jason, and the insider has the Bureau tail-chasing on purpose."

"And that's why you need to quit, right now," pleaded Jason. "It's too dangerous. Leak it to the *Times* or *Post*, I don't care. Just stop chasing leads!"

She scoffed and buckled up. "You know me. You know I can't do that."

"Yes, I do." He sighed. "I wish I wasn't in love with you."

Lin didn't know how to respond. She had not heard anyone tell her that in a long time, and she preferred it that way. All her past boyfriend experiences were humiliating catastrophes, and now this, and at this moment. She needed to focus, but Jason's impromptu admission jolted her.

Focus, she thought. *Compartmentalize.* "Give me a location, and I don't mean Apollo's corporate headquarters. I want the CEO's house or something like that."

Jason sighed again, and she could hear him work a keyboard. "I got one better. Something major just went down in South East DC. I would bet my monthly salary it's Apollo. Your best bet is to follow them."

"There's no time to follow. It's time to intercept."

"It's my ass if this goes badly. And it will." He gave her the convoy's last coordinates, captured by a traffic camera minutes earlier. She left tread marks at the scenic overlook and sped toward the capital, passing cars as if they were standing still. Lin no longer cared about police.

"Thank you, Jason. Really," she said over a headset as she swerved around traffic. "As a thank-you gift, I saved one of the Russian hacker's laptops for you. It's the only one that survived."

"Sweetness! I've always wanted one of those," he joked, knowing it would catapult their unofficial investigation and his career, if he found a way to "discover" it as evidence and get it unlocked. He would.

She told him the location of the scenic overlook. "It's sitting on a picnic table, so you should get there before it rains, or people show up."

"Thanks, Jen."

"And one more thing," said Lin. "When this is all over, dinner's on me."

CHAPTER 38

Jackson hung up the phone with Winters and poured himself a tall scotch, neat. It was nearly 2 A.M. and he stood in a silken bathrobe with his initials, GJJ, inscribed on its left breast pocket. His private study looked like old Beacon Hill, Boston. It was adorned in dark oak and brass fittings, with hunter green walls. A small marble fireplace with two leather chesterfield chairs sitting on an ornate Persian carpet with a tree-of-life motif. By the window, on a side table, stood an exquisite model of the clipper ship *Cutty Sark*, its rigging lovingly tied by tweezer. An authentic Tiffany desk lamp was the only light in the room, casting a multicolor glow on the room.

Jackson leaned back and put his pajamaed legs on the desktop, sipping the single malt with exquisite care. One does not gulp twenty-five-year-old Macallan. Pictures of his children and grandchildren crowded his desk. One showed a hoard of laughing grandkids piling on him at Ridgely's Retreat, their mansion off the Chesapeake. It was the best day he could remember in ten years, and he wanted more like it.

Winters had been working him over from the beginning, and Jackson had let him. He had a country to secure and did not have time for Winters's puerile mind games. The man was more conniving than Iago and more foolish than Oedipus. But that time was drawing to a close, and Winters had finally earned Jackson's full attention. Winters would regret it.

Kill the president? Impossible. Laughable, he thought, rubbing his head. It was clear now: Winters had gone insane in his Saudi prison cell. He was not the same man he used to know. Even if Jackson could orchestrate the president's death, he wouldn't dare. He now deplored his partnership with Winters and needed to make repair.

Christ. Henry and Martha are dead, he thought. They were family friends long before Henry became vice president, and they vacationed together on Martha's Vineyard one summer. It was divine. *I'm sorry, old friends,* he thought and took another sip of scotch.

Jackson leaned back, weighing his options. He understood predators like Winters, and what to do about them. He had been dealing with them his entire career. They mistook his niceness for weakness, and learned too late of their errors. Jackson had left a trail of gutted rivals as he climbed his way into the White House. Winters was no different.

"Damn Winters," Jackson muttered, angry that he had to expend power—real power—on the idiot. But he knew it was necessary: the man required a firm reminder of who was the alpha in their partnership. He had to bring the man to heel.

I have no choice. He's pushed me too far. Jackson picked up his secure government phone. Being the national security advisor afforded him great power.

"Give me Joint Task Force National Capital Region, special operations division."

The operator put him through.

"This is National Security Advisor George Jackson.

This is a Code One NSC emergency. Terrorist attack in progress. Activate Sierra Mike Uniform One Niner."

"Copy all. Authentication?" replied an alert military voice.

"Authentication code is . . ." Jackson authenticated.

"Authentication is confirmed."

"Target is linked to the following mobile phone," Jackson added, giving Winters's last used number. Winters thought he was calling from a concealed number, but Jackson had the NSA crack it long ago. The NSA had cracked all his known phones, which helped Jackson keep abreast of the man's many nefarious intentions.

"Copy."

"One more thing," added Jackson. "Capture, do not kill. I want the leader alive, but I don't care about the rest."

"Roger."

It's done, Jackson thought, hanging up the phone. Perhaps it was extreme, but breaking Winters required extreme measures.

CHAPTER 39

Helicopter rotors began turning at Andrews Air Force Base, just south of Washington, DC. Special Mission Unit 19 had been scrambled, and men in black tactical gear ran to the choppers sitting on the tarmac. SMU 19 was the government's secret counterterrorism assault force for the capital region, and comparable to SEAL Team 6 and Delta Force. Their mission: defeat terrorists who threaten the nation's capital. Their motto: "Life, Liberty, and the Pursuit of Anyone Who Threatens It."

"Go, go, go!" shouted the team leader, as shooters climbed aboard two MH-60M Black Hawks. These birds were unlike normal Black Hawks, and were customized for special operations forces. Next to them, two AH-6 Little Birds were already hovering, each equipped with Hellfire and Stinger missiles, and two multibarrel mini-guns that shot six thousand rounds per minute—accuracy by volume. Seconds later the helicopters lifted off in blackout flight. Four up-armored SUVs dashed out the base's main gate, sirens raging.

CHAPTER 40

Winters checked his watch again, and then looked up. His body swerved with the SUV, as they made turns at twice the speed limit. Traffic was light at this hour, as the tourists were still asleep in their hotels. Winters's convoy was a black flash in a dark night: six armored Chevy Suburbans escorted by four Sikorsky S-97 helicopters, all black and traveling in blackout mode. The police, if they could catch them, were the least of Winters's worries.

That snake Jackson better not double-cross me, thought Winters. He was taking a risk, but one worth taking. However, he had contingencies for Jackson, should he betray his trust. Winters always had such plans.

"ETA seven minutes, sir," said the convoy commander from the front seat. Winters nodded. They turned onto Memorial Bridge and headed for the Lincoln Memorial, which was lit up in splendor. If all went according to plan, it would be the last time he would ever meet with Jackson. The truth was, he didn't need Jackson to kill the president; he could do that anytime. Rather, he agreed to it just to torment the moron, with his morality of convenience and hypocrisy of necessity.

Men like Jackson were lice, and Washington suffered an infestation.

Seven minutes until I'm rid of this troublesome office seeker, thought Winters with satisfaction.

The hood and gag were suffocating, and I felt nauseous as the vehicle veered and lurched around traffic. I estimated we were traveling around 90 mph but I had no idea where we were going; I assumed Winters's lair. My hands and feet were each flex-cuffed, and I was belted into the backseat, stuffed between two brawny men. Their elbows jabbed my ribs every time we took a turn. I worked at the wrist cuffs, but they weren't budging. I was stuck.

I could only imagine what horror show Winters had ready for me at his makeshift Apollo dungeon. He had changed, no doubt. Torture does that to a man. Knowing Winters, he would exact his revenge on me, one torture instrument at a time, each with expert precision and medieval tenacity. I would become his new hobby, and he would nurse me along for months just so he could see me scream again. Winters was always a twisted person, but torture unleashed his inner Lucifer. And I would pay.

I had been physically tortured before, once by a warlord in the Congo and another time by police in West Africa. They were equally awful. Everything they teach you about endurance at SERE School is mostly worthless. There is no mental "happy place" to go to when someone is electrocuting your junk. You could pray, but God doesn't answer men like me, and why should he? Ultimately, it's just a long night. I had many long nights ahead of me.

The four helicopters of Special Mission Unit 19 skimmed the Potomac so fast they left a wake. They were locked onto the digital signature of Winters's phone, and Memorial Bridge was in the distance. The plan was standard operating procedure: the aviation would draw first blood and hold down the terrorists until the ground units caught up, who would go in for the capture and kill. They had practiced this endlessly, but this was their first live mission.

"Joker One, this is Joker Three," said a Little Bird pilot to the lead Black Hawk and pilot in command. "Are you seeing this?"

"Affirmative, Joker Three. I see four rotary-wing bogies, flying dark and moving east with the target over the bridge toward the Mall. Control, confirm?"

"Negative, Joker. We see nothing. Scopes are clean," replied Mission Control.

Terrorists with their own stealth rotary-wing escorts? thought Joker 1 with concern. No one had ever heard of such a thing. It was a clear and present danger, which meant there was only one course of action.

"Control, permission to engage?" asked Joker 1.

There was a pause on the radio net, as the mission commander sweated. The consequences of being wrong were extreme, but he was trained for this. In moments of extreme decision, always choose prudence.

"Joker, you are weapons free," said Control.

"Copy. We are weapons free. Engage," commanded Joker 1. The Little Birds fanned out.

"Arming Stingers. Acquiring targets," said Jokers 3 and 4, the Little Bird pilots. An *EEEEEEEEEEE* sounded over their headsets as the stingers locked onto the heat signatures of the enemy choppers. "Got tone. Firing."

Four missiles launched from pods on the side of the AH-6s and flew toward the Memorial Bridge. The same instant, the four Sikorsky S-97s scattered and dropped flares. The bridge shimmered in the twilight glow of burning magnesium, creating a surreal scene.

"Negative hits," said Joker 3.

Who are these guys? thought Joker 1.

"Incoming! Incoming!" squawked the command net. Winters peered out the window and saw his Sikorsky S-97s jerk left and right while dropping flares. They looked like starlit snowflakes as they drove through them. Cars swerved to avoid the descending goblets of white fire, not knowing what they were, and hit other vehicles. The convoy deftly maneuvered through the debris field as the Stingers rocketed overhead.

"Those were Stingers! Who's got eyes on? Where's the bogie?" shouted the convoy commander into the radio. Winters looked out over the river but saw nothing. *Jackson, is that you?* he thought.

"This is Bandit," said the pilot in command. "We got four bogies in our FLIR, south of the bridge six klicks and closing fast."

"Annihilate them," ordered Winters, sitting back again.

"Weapons free," ordered the convoy commander.

"Copy."

Above them, they heard the launch of heavier rockets designed to kill aircraft and tanks. The enemy choppers down river immediately dumped flares, lighting up the river near the National Airport. A 737 airliner on approach banked upward in an emergency procedure and accelerated back into the sky. Winters smiled. *Take that, Jackson.*

"Go to guns," commanded Bandit. "Engage." The attack helicopters flew past the convoy, heading toward the oncoming bogies. They were too close for missiles and would have to fight in an air duel of skill and nerve.

"Give 'em hell, boys," said Winters. Jackson had betrayed him, but he would leave a stinking turd on the White House's front lawn for him to clean up in the morning. "No prisoners."

"Holy crap!" said Lin, skidding around a three-car accident on the Memorial Bridge as flares dropped all around them. The white light lit up the sky and what she glimpsed made her heart stop. Meters above the bridge, four black helicopters flew in tight formation. She had never seen anything like them: dual rotor, one on top of the other, and a rear pusher propeller. Missiles were launched off side pylons and they headed south, toward the airport.

Then her eye caught the convoy that Jason told her about. Six black, armored Chevy Suburbans weaved through the wreckage on the bridge, driving almost bumper to bumper. They drove like NASCAR.

There goes my lead! she thought as she floored the accelerator to catch up and slalomed through the traffic. *I've come too far to lose them now.*

"Incoming! Incoming!" shouted Joker 1 as a warning alarm squawked in the cockpit. He yanked the cyclic and stick, and the Black Hawk banked hard right, its rotor almost splashing the water. The shooters inside held on as loose stuff in the cabin flew everywhere. The Black Hawk's flares showered the river but extinguished in the water before the incoming missiles could lock onto them.

Shit, thought Joker 1, watching all his flares go out. They were exposed.

The other Black Hawk exploded in an orange fireball that illuminated the early-morning sky. The impact was so intense that a million pieces rained down, making little splashes in the water several hundred meters in diameter. There was nothing left of the chopper, or the ten souls on board.

"Joker Two is down! Repeat, Joker Two is down!" It was the nightmare scenario they had drilled for over and over, but the reality was no less shocking.

"Copy, Joker Two down. Scrambling the Falcons," said Mission Control, referring to the F-16s of the 121st Fighter Squadron at Andrews Air Force Base. However, the firefight would be over by the time the F-16s arrived on station, something Joker 1 and Mission Control knew.

"Signal now moving down Independence Avenue. Jokers, give me covering fire. I'm tracking the signal," said Joker 1 to the Little Birds. Even secure phones emitted electrical signals, and they could be tracked with the right equipment.

There was a pause as they moved into position, then Joker 4 said, "I spot six black SUVs in blackout drive moving at high speed." The vehicles were traveling fast down the broad lanes of Independence Avenue, which lined the National Mall. They were in the open and vulnerable to fire, but not for long. In a minute they would come upon buildings, making a clean hit with a Hellfire missile risky.

"Signal is coming from either the lead vehicle or the second," said Mission Control. "Mission requires capture the leader and eliminate the rest."

"Take out the rear four vehicles," ordered Joker 1.

"Roger, switching to Hellfires," said Jokers 3 and 4. "Got tone."

"Take the shot!" said Mission Control.

Hellfire missiles launched off the rails of the Little Birds toward the convoy.

Winters turned around as he heard the explosions. The trailing three Suburbans were hit and a civilian car disintegrated, probably killed by a Hellfire missile. There would be no survivors. "Leave them. Continue mission," he said.

"Roger," said the convoy commander, and then ordered "Charlie Mike," for "continue mission," over the radio.

"Was Locke in one of those vehicles?" asked Winters.

"Yes sir," said the convoy commander. "The rear one."

Damn you, Jackson! thought Winters. *You will pay for denying me my vengeance.*

I sensed the explosion before I felt it. The air pressure quadrupled in the cabin as the armored Suburban lifted

off the ground and spun through space, flat like a fris-
bee. I felt the g-force pull my face away from my skull.
The noise was deafening, like being inside a lightning
strike. Actually, it felt like I was a shell being fired out
of a howitzer. We impacted a second later, bounced
twice, and rolled violently for what seemed a minute.
I heard the heads of the men next to me smash repeat-
edly against the bulletproof windows, and I stiffened
my neck to avoid whiplash. When the vehicle stopped, I
hung upside down, suspended in place by my seat belt.

Whatever hit us had struck our ass and ripped off the
rear end of the vehicle. Armored SUVs have blast glass
and bulletproof steel between the passenger compart-
ment and the trunk area. That, and being sandwiched
between thick guys, was the only reason I was alive.
And from the sound of it, I was the lone survivor.

The vehicle was on fire, and I struggled against my
flex-cuffs, but no joy. I was trapped, dangling upside
down in a lit gas can. My fun meter was pegged.

Lin followed the black SUV convoy as it circled around
the Lincoln Memorial and blew through red lights. Independence Avenue was a tree-lined boulevard, and
the SUVs accelerated to 100 mph on the straightaway,
with no headlights or lights of any kind. Lin struggled
to keep up, dodging cars. They were approaching the
bridge over the Tidal Basin when three Suburbans and a
car blew sideways off the road and into the trees. They
vanished like a golf ball hit by a driver. The concussive
wave hit her car.

"Holy crap!" screamed Lin, as she skidded sideways
and bounced off the median's curb, spinning uncontrol-

lably to a complete stop. Cars screeched behind her, also stopping, and she could hear the crunch of steel and glass as vehicles collided. Lin looked up and saw the surviving Suburbans speed away.

Dammit! she thought, as she watched them vanish into the dark night. She turned to the Mall and saw the three burning hulks that were once armored SUVs, now blown hundreds of feet off the road. *All may not be lost.*

Lin grabbed the Saiga shotgun and backpack full of grenades and jumped out of the car. Victims of the car pile-up behind her were tending to one another, and she could hear the sirens of emergency vehicles in the distance. She didn't have much time to scour the wrecks for clues.

There was nothing left of the civilian car, save a burning chassis blown two hundred meters away. It looked like a Toyota Camry, judging by the body parts in the trees, sixty feet up. One of the SUV wrecks exploded, causing her to jump. A millisecond later, she felt the hot, forceful wave impact her face. She ran to the second SUV, also on fire. No survivors. Lin had to turn back, so intense was the heat from the fire, and it would yield no clues. The last SUV's rear was blown clean off, and lay upside down among the trees.

There could be survivors, she thought, and approached with caution. Crouching as she walked, she could see people inside, hanging upside down, and lifeless. Then she heard a muffled scream.

"Anyone there?" she yelled and heard the mumbling increase with urgency. The vehicle was on fire, and she knew she should leave immediately. However, she couldn't. She needed information and this was her one chance, before the police showed up and locked the place down.

This is insane, she thought. *No piece of information is worth my life.* Nonetheless, she tried one of the doors but it was jammed. The explosion and rolling had bent the vehicle's frame, and the door was wedged shut. She tried two more doors, but they were stuck, too. The last one opened, and a man's body rolled out, clutching a Heckler and Koch SDMR assault rifle. Lin stepped over the body and looked inside. A man hung upside down in the darkness with a hood over his head and hands tied. He rocked back and forth, trying to free himself.

"Are you OK?" she asked, knowing full well the answer: the vehicle was on fire and could explode at any moment. He scream-mumbled in assent.

Lin reached in and released the hanged man's seat belt, and he plopped to the ceiling and crawled out. She pulled a combat knife from the dead man's equipment vest and cut his flex-cuffs. The man quickly yanked off the hood, removed the gag, and took deep breaths. Then he looked up and said, calmly, "Thank you. Now we should get out of here before the police arrive."

"Let's go," she said, turning to escape. She looked back but the man was not following her, as expected. Instead he was stripping the dead guy's weapons and ammo.

"What are you doing? The truck's going to blow! Get out of there!" she shouted from a distance, and the man sprinted toward her. They took cover behind a forgotten granite memorial in the trees and expected the SUV to explode, but it didn't. It just burned. The howl of fire trucks grew louder.

The strange man smelled faintly of wet dog and rubbed his sore wrists. He looked like one of them but was their prisoner. *Odd,* she thought. Hopefully it meant he would cooperate with her. Either that, or he might try to kill her.

"Thank you," he said again, then perked up when he saw what she was carrying. "Nice Saiga. Is that the 040 Taktika model? Only Spetsnaz has those. You're not Spetsnaz, are you?"

"Do I look like Spetsnaz?" she replied in a defiant tone.

"No, I don't suppose you do," he said, cycling the bolt of the H&K. "Do you have a car? We need to get out of here."

"Follow me."

"Three KIA, and one collateral," said Joker 3.

"Roger, BDA is three tango ground vehicles and one civilian," said Mission Control. *BDA* referred to "battle damage assessment."

"Keep the bogies off me. I'm tracking the remaining vehicles until ground support arrives," said Joker 1. "What's their ETA?"

"Joker One, this is Zebra One. ETA three mikes," responded the ground convoy commander.

"Roger, Zebra One. I'll keep him lit, you box him in," said Joker 1, skimming the Tidal Basin. The shooters' legs dangled over the side and the crew sat behind six-barrel rotary-door guns. They were operating in urban terrain, which was a high risk for collateral damage. However, their orders were clear: prevent another terrorist attack at all costs, especially since they reportedly had WMD.

"There! Eleven o'clock," said the copilot. The remaining three SUVs sprinted across the Tidal Basin bridge in complete darkness.

"Gotcha," said Joker 1.

"Light them up?" asked one of the door gunners.

"Negative," replied Joker 1. "Orders are capture the leader, and we don't know which vehicle is emitting the leader's digital signature. It could be any one of the three."

"We could disable all three vehicles," said the door gunner.

"Negative. Can't risk killing the leader."

The Black Hawk settled low behind the vehicles, captured in its powerful spotlight. All Zebra had to do was follow the light, and it would be checkmate.

No escaping now, thought Joker 1.

"Aauurgh!!" yelled Winters's driver as the Black Hawk's spotlight lit them up. He ripped off his night vision goggles and blinked several times, adjusting to the brightness. "Switching to headlights," he said.

The convoy commander was nervous, too. They would be trapped if ground vehicles caught them. Their only chance was for the Sikorsky S-97s to take out the Black Hawk and Little Birds before the ground vehicles arrived. *It's inevitable, but will it happen in time?* he wondered. *I have to lose the spotlight.*

"Take Maine Avenue, here," ordered the convoy commander, pointing right, and the Suburbans turned hard right. They sped under interstate and railroad bridges and through a nest of power lines, but still the spotlight would not go away. They raced down side streets and

a main road, lined with eight-story buildings. Yet the
Black Hawk skillfully followed them, flying expertly
between the buildings and leaping over seemingly invisible power lines.

"He's good," said the driver.

"We should have hired him," replied Winters.

"Hard left on South Capitol Street," said the convoy commander, tracking their movements on a dash-
mounted screen.

"Hard left," repeated the driver, and attacked the
turn at 60 mph. The rear end drifted and the lateral
g-force pulled them all to the right. Winters sat calmly,
hands on his cane. The two other Suburbans followed,
and civilian cars scurried out of the way.

"Catch I-395 and make the tunnel. It has multiple exits
and is our best chance of losing the Black Hawk before
ground units arrive," said the convoy commander.

"Copy," said the driver. The three vehicles sped
around cars at 90 mph as they entered the highway.
Traffic was thin at o-dark-thirty. They took the first exit
and descended into a tunnel that goes underneath the
National Mall. No more spotlight.

"Good. Now pull onto the shoulder, and back out in
blackout drive," said the commander. Using the side of
the road, the three SUVs reversed at full speed until
they reached I-395 again. The spotlight was elsewhere.
When they made the highway, they disappeared.

The two Little Birds took up ambush positions on the
Mall, waiting for their prey. Joker 3 hovered at the center of the World War II monument, its massive granite
colonnade providing some concealment against the

Sikorsky S-97s' infrared thermal sights, which could target pigeons in the dark a thousand feet out. Joker 4 hovered behind the Washington Monument, halfway up. It would remain invisible to the bogies, but no less deadly. The two Little Birds shared a collective targeting system; what one could see, the other could shoot.

"Joker Three, in position."

"Joker Four, in position. Stingers ready."

"Nothing on our scopes," said Mission Control.

Wait for it. Waaaait for it, thought Joker 3, monitoring his FLIR. He'd done tours in Iraq, Afghanistan, and Syria, but he'd never faced an equal. It was what he'd trained for his entire life, and it was intoxicating and terrifying.

Biiiing, sounded an alarm. "Bogey's got tone on me! Bogey's got tone!" shouted Joker 3, as he jerked the stick and cyclic. The nimble Little Bird darted between the Stonehenge-like slabs of the monument, breaking the line of sight of the enemy's laser targeting system.

"I have eyes on," said Joker 4 calmly. "Two bogies, due southwest, hovering low in the trees. Switching to Hellfires. Got tone. Firing." Two Hellfires screamed toward the tree line, and the Sikorsky S-97s jumped, dropping flares. The first made a clean break, and the missile obliterated an ancient oak. The second's rotor clipped a branch, causing it to shudder. In that instant, the Hellfire found its target and blew the chopper into the ground, making a crater.

Biiiing. Joker 4 heard the alarm and immediately spiral-dove around the Washington Monument, trying to elude the missile's guidance system. Then there was an orange flash and thunderclap, and the Little Bird vanished.

Motherfucker, thought Joker 3, as he skimmed the tree line. "Control, Joker Four is down."

"Copy, Joker Three. Falcons' ETA four mikes. Stand fast. Repeat, stand fast."

Joker 3 heard nothing. Three bogeys were hunting him and he was blind. He would be dead in four minutes unless he took charge of the situation. Taking a chance, he zoomed across the National Mall, flying so low he had to pull up to cross the Reflecting Pool. He made a copse of trees near Constitution Avenue, expertly gauging the diameter of his rotors. Only a few pilots in the world had the skill to fly their choppers through trees.

"Where are you?" he whispered, looking out the canopy through his FLIR. He'd grown up in the woods of northern Georgia, and his hunting instincts told him this was the spot to ambush his quarry. He had large fields of fire, and the trees offered some cover and concealment. Plus, the car traffic at his tail would create hash for the enemy's FLIR.

"There you are!" he said, as a shadow dashed through the World War II monument, his previous position. Missiles proved futile against these bogies because their reflexes were too fast. He would need to get close.

"Switching to guns," he said, and picked up the shadow in his FLIR as it banked toward him, unwittingly. "Gotcha!" He flew out of the trees and rolled to optimize the angle of attack. The Little Bird rocked as his mini-gun sent three thousand rounds of lead into the bogey. The Sikorsky S-97 turned left then right, trying to get away as it bled black smoke.

No escape for you, he thought as he matched his prey's every feint until it crashed on the Mall.

Biiiiing, sounded the alarm, and his reflexes sprung

to action. He ducked around the Smithsonian Castle, and then over and into the Hirshhorn Museum's donut hole. The alarm went quiet. The art museum was shaped like a gigantic "O," making its center a perfect helicopter foxhole.

"Falcons' ETA two mikes," said Mission Control. Joker ignored it, knowing the enemy would soon discover him.

Move or die, he thought, and cautiously hovered out of the Hirshhorn. He peeped over the roof and saw empty skies. The flashing lights of ground emergency vehicles were distracting and interfered with his FLIR, but it would do the same to his enemy. Fine by him. He had been flying attack helicopters for twenty-three years, and he was one of the best pilots in Task Force 160 SOAR, the Army's special operations aviation regiment, also known as the Night Stalkers. Any environmental challenge would harm the enemy more than him.

Joker 3 nearly flew on the sidewalk and then floated up to a position behind the Smithsonian's 1870s tower, using it as cover. When it comes to helicopter battles, whoever sees the other first survives.

"Where are you?" he muttered again. He scanned the Mall, its trees, the museums that lined it. His instincts knew where a chopper would hide, would avoid, would stand ground. Then he saw it: a Sikorsky S-97 stalking through trees across from him, near the Smithsonian American History Museum. The pilot was hunting him, but Joker 3 was better.

You're mine, he thought, and pitched forward to line up the shot when his peripheral vision caught the other Sikorsky S-97, one hundred meters to his left. It hovered in perfect ambush, waiting for him at the far end of the

Smithsonian Castle's roof. Muzzle flashes burst from its twenty-millimeter chain gun, shredding the Little Bird.

"Where did they go?!" asked Joker 1 after the convoy entered the tunnel but did not exit. "Anyone have eyes on?"

"Negative," replied the shooters who sat on the edge of the open doorway.

"Control, we lost them. Last seen vicinity of the Third Street tunnel," said Joker 1, as they searched the area.

"Roger, Joker One. Zebra One on site, and we have alerted local law enforcement. Falcons on station," said Mission Control.

"Copy all," replied Joker 1. "Status Joker Three, Joker Four?"

Silence.

"How copy Joker Three, Joker Four?"

"Joker Three and Four presumed KIA," said Mission Control. "Return to base. Falcons will handle the bogies."

Joker 1's hands squeezed the controls in silent fury, his face contorting with rage. Then, in a placid tone, he said. "Roger, returning to base."

Beneath the Black Hawk, an orchestra of sirens and flashing lights converged on the National Mall in the predawn light. The F-16s screeched above, waking up the city, but found no targets.

CHAPTER 41

"Who the hell are they?!" Lin shouted as she sped away from the firefight. "And who the hell are you?!"

The man didn't answer. Instead, he rolled down the window and stuck out his head, scanning the skies. He held the Heckler and Koch SDMR like a pro.

"Hey, I'm talking to you!" she yelled, and the man turned to face her.

"My name is Tom. Pleasure to meet you," he said with a smile. "What's your name?"

"Not important right now."

"Agreed," he said, and stuck his head back out the window, looking for helicopters. Two explosions shocked the night air, and a plume of fire shot up from the Mall. Lin could see the orange glare in her rear-view mirror.

"They must have taken out a chopper, but I wonder whose," he shouted over the wind.

"Who's 'they'?" asked Lin.

"I'll tell you when we're safe. Can you go faster?"

"We're going seventy," she said, tires squealing around turns. Rock Creek Parkway runs alongside the Potomac and follows its curves. Ahead was the Kennedy Center for the Arts, an all-in-one performance palace that looked like a giant Kleenex box.

"They're doing *Traviata* later this month. I was really hoping to catch a performance," said Locke, slumping back into his seat with the H&K muzzle pointing out the window.

"What?"

"It's an opera. You'd love it. It features a noble heroine," he said.

"Don't make me punch you."

She slowed down as multiple police cars sped by in the opposite direction. Their flashing lights temporarily blinded them, and Locke reflexively closed his shooting eye to preserve his night vision.

"Hey, dumbass. Hide the weapon," she said, and Locke quickly lowered the H&K as the last police cruiser passed in a flash of blue. In the background, the buzz of a mini-gun echoed through the city, accompanied by sirens in every direction.

Locke whistled in amazement. "They've really done it this time."

"*Who's* done *what* this time?" demanded Lin, frustrated by his lack of specificity. She needed answers.

"Get us out of here, and I'll tell you."

"Tell me now."

"It's not safe on the roads. They're looking for me."

She glanced at him. It was dark, but he looked vaguely familiar.

"Fine," she decided, and violently jerked the car left, cut across oncoming traffic, and made a hairpin turn onto an exit intended for the opposite lane. It dumped them underneath an elevated freeway in Georgetown that ran a mile. There was no traffic, just parked cars and massive steel girders and highway above. Lin floored it, and Locke braced himself.

"What's the matter? Scared I'm going too fast?" she said with a smirk.

"Nope. We're all good here," he lied, reaching for the seat belt.

Where have I seen him before? she thought as they topped 100 mph. The road narrowed and got dark, until it came to an abrupt end. Lin stomped the breaks and Locke braced himself as the Mini Cooper screeched sideways to a stop.

They were under an enormous stone trestle bridge, the type constructed by the great works programs of the 1930s. Above was a multilane highway that spanned the river and connected Georgetown to Interstate 66. Lin cut the engine. No one was down here at this hour, and the huge trestle hid them from helicopters and street cameras.

"Nice spot," said Locke, impressed, getting out of the car.

"Hey! Stay in the car!" shouted Lin, but he walked into the darkness. "Where are you going? Get back in here!" Locke continued to ignore her. *Damn him!* she thought, unbuckling and grabbing her Saiga. When she stepped out, he was gone. She looked back at the car and saw his H&K had disappeared, too. She had chosen this spot because of its seclusion. It never occurred to her that it was also the perfect place for a psycho to murder her.

This is bad, she thought. The only sound was highway traffic above, and the stranger had disappeared. He was her last, best clue. *I've come too far to turn around now,* she thought, furtively moving into the boatyard. *He could be anywhere, watching me.* Her heart raced, and she paused to breathe and calm down. Her father used to say: *If you face just one opponent, and you doubt yourself, you're out-numbered.*

You got this, girl, she told herself as she breathed through her fear. Ahead stood the boathouse, a green barn with white trim. Beyond was the river. Lin snuck forward, maximizing the shadows.

"Over here," came a whisper from around the corner, on the dock. It was Tom, but she didn't want to answer and give away her position. It could be a trap.

"Over here," he whispered again. Lin froze and listened, trying to discern his exact location, but heard nothing.

"Hey! Are you coming?" he shouted. Lin wheeled around the boathouse's corner, Saiga at the ready. Before her was a wooden dock the size of a small parking lot. It was painted red with a big white star in the middle. There stood Locke, the H&K dangling by his side as he stared across the river.

"What are you doing?" she asked, lowering the Saiga slightly.

"I missed this. Seeing this. Smelling the air. America."

Where have I seen him before? The thought nagged her. She scrutinized his figure, but it was dark out. "Who are you?"

"I told you. My name is Tom—"

"That's not what I meant," she interrupted.

"Ah. Well." He paused. "That's more complicated."

"There was a helicopter battle on the National Mall, a whole bunch of SUVs got blown away by missiles, and I find you bound and gagged upside down in one of them. Who were they? Why was there combat on the National Mall? How is that even possible?! Answers, now!" she demanded.

Locke sighed and walked over to the edge of the water. Lin followed cautiously, Saiga up.

Suddenly Lin realized where she had seen him before, and felt faint. His face was all over the news. He was the one everyone was looking for, the mastermind behind the death of the vice president and 230 Americans. He was extremely dangerous.

"Stop! Don't move. You're the nuclear terrorist, Tom Locke," she said, stepping rearward and aiming the Saiga at his back, but the muzzle shook nervously.

"Don't believe everything in the news," he said quietly.

"Lose the weapon. *Lose it!*" she commanded, and he let it slip off his shoulder and clank to the ground. "Kick it into the water!" He only kicked it four feet down the dock.

Damn him, she thought, knowing it was out of reach yet too close. However, she dared not interrupt the cuffing procedure. It was the most dangerous part of an arrest, and mistakes get cops killed.

"Get your hands up! Higher!" she said as he slowly raised both hands. "Get on one knee!" He did. "Now the other. Place both hands on the ground! Now lie down, on your stomach, and cross your ankles!"

Locke complied, still looking at the far shoreline.

Lin felt giddy inside. If she bagged Tom Locke, the FBI would have to reinstate her. She couldn't believe her luck. "Put your arms out to the side, and face right." He did, laying prone in a T position. Cautiously she moved around to his left side, where he could not see her, pointing her weapon.

"You have the right to remain silent," she began while pulling out the handcuffs. "Anything you say can and will be used against you in a court of law." She knelt down by his left arm and slung the Saiga over her back. "You have the right to an attorney." She grabbed his wrist and twisted it in a joint lock, making him grunt in pain. "If you cannot afford an attorney, one will be provided for you."

Lin knelt on his scapula while moving his wrist behind his back with both hands, the Saiga slung across her back. As soon as the metal touched Locke's skin, his body snapped into a crescent moon on his right side like a sprung trap. The force threw Lin backward, and the cuffs slipped from her hands and bounced into the river.

Crap! she thought, then spotted the H&K assault rifle a few feet from him. *CRAP! He's going for it!* But he didn't. As she pulled the Saiga over her head and into a firing position, Locke stepped forward, grabbed her arm, spun around her front, and catapulted her into a rack of life preservers. The Saiga flew through the air, landing in the middle of the dock not far from the H&K. Lin was buried in a mound of orange, gasping for breath.

You like to play rough. So do I. Lin rocked on her back, then kicked forward, landing on her feet. Locke was moving for the weapons. She grabbed a paddle and threw it like a javelin, hitting him in the head.

"Ow!" he yelped, staggering sideways while clasping his skull. She sprinted toward him and executed a perfect flying kick, five feet above the ground, and impacted his chest. Locke hurtled backward into a rack of upright metal canoes, which then collapsed on him.

"*OW!*" she heard from beneath the mound of metal. Lin smiled. The canoes started rustling, and Locke emerged both angry and bewildered.

"You want to dance? Let's dance," he sputtered, clambering to his feet and assuming a fight stance.

"I doubt you have the skills to be my dance partner," she taunted back, settling into her own stance. "I expect your moves won't satisfy me."

"They will take your breath away, guaranteed," he said, as they circled around the weapons in the middle of the dock.

Lin attacked first and fast, landing critical hits despite his blocks. Locke tried to keep up, but she was a tornado of speed, anticipating his every reaction. In a four-move combo, she delivered a devastating reverse roundhouse kick to his torso, taking him by surprise and flipping him on his ass.

Coughing, Locke stumbled up as she stood, arms crossed, smiling. "OK, that was a pretty good move," he admitted. "But I got stamina."

Locke launched into her, using elbows and knees like a prison fighter. Locke and Lin were a blur of limbs and grunts. She was quick but he was solid, absorbing massive damage and recovering quickly. He landed fewer blows, but each one made her body whither. Locke was slowly driving her to the water's edge.

Crap, he's good, she realized. *Time to end this before I get wet.* In a fiery combo, she blocked a punch and threw a palm heel to his nose. But Locke was quick, ducking her hand and smashing his left forearm into her abdomen, buckling her, and did a double leg takedown. They landed with a mutual gasp inches from the dock's edge, her long hair in the water and Locke on top between her legs, inches from her face.

Locke smiled. She grimaced. Both were breathing

heavily. Lin looked like she might kiss him but head-butted him instead, then rolled on top of him as he cringed in pain. Sitting back on his abdomen, she smiled with triumph.

"Ow!" he muttered, rubbing his nose. "That hurt."

"Had enough?" she gasped between breaths, still sitting on him. They were spent.

"We could go on like this all night, nonstop," said Locke hoarsely, in between gulps of air.

Lin's pulse was still racing, and she struggled to slow her breathing. She tried to speak but could only manage: "Uh-huh."

Moments later, he said, "That was . . . incredible."

"Uh-huh."

"You're really amazing, you know that?"

"Uh-huh." A few seconds passed. "You're not bad yourself, Tom Locke."

He smiled. "I told you I had moves."

"Yeah, I bet you would make a good dance partner," she said and they both chuckled awkwardly as she slid off of him. She wanted to arrest him, but she was too exhausted and had lost her handcuffs in the river. She would have to figure out another way.

"What's your name?" he asked.

"Jennifer Lin. People call me Jen."

Locke turned his head to see her. Lin's body lay still, except her breasts, which moved up and down with each breath. Even in the dark, her profile was undeniably alluring, even though she had kicked his ass.

Locke eyed the H&K and Saiga, somehow untouched during the fight. "You're not going to arrest me now, are you?" he asked half-jokingly.

"Not sure yet," she replied half-seriously.

Locke rolled on his side to face her and was taken aback by her physical splendor. She lay with her arms and legs sprawled out, and her long black hair cast to the right, as if blown. Her face was luminous against the night environs and her dark clothes. She was a Rembrandt.

"Are you gawking at me?" she asked.

"Only a little."

She rolled to face him and smiled.

CHAPTER 42

Jackson sat in his office, hands clasped under his nose as he watched the news. The TV was muted to block the news anchor's ravings, but the pictures were devastating. A Little Bird burned in front of the Vietnam Memorial, like an apocalyptic shrine. Another lay at the foot of the Smithsonian Castle. A Sikorsky S-97 helicopter was in an impact crater near the Reflecting Pool. The carcasses of three armored SUVs with armed men— "Terrorists," as the press dubbed them—were scattered in the tree line off the Mall, and shreds of a civilian car hung in the trees. The body count was twenty-four and rising. Jackson also knew a Blackhawk full of Tier One operators was missing and presumably at the bottom of the Potomac.

"What a clusterfuck," uttered Jackson, his hands trembling. It was beyond an official Charlie Foxtrot; it was worst case. Hysteria had set in, and I-95 was backed up as people fled the city for fear of follow-on terrorist attacks. Black smoke wafted through downtown Washington like a warzone.

The news dubbed it the "Battle on the Mall" and compared it to the 1812 British invasion, except the enemy was nuclear terrorists. At least the media was framing it as a win for America: the military had foiled the biggest terrorist attack in American history. But the world still lay in shock and disbelief. If this could happen to the U.S.'s capital, then where was safe?

Christ, Jackson thought. *What the hell happened?* It was a simple show of force. Winters wasn't supposed to fight back. Now what? Jackson was still processing the implications. He got the call from the Situation Room around 2 A.M., when the battle was taking place. At first, he didn't believe it, and then rushed to the White House. Things got worse from there.

How can I use this disaster for good? he thought, crossing his arms and legs. *Think, think, THINK!* If this attack galvanized the American people against its enemies, it could be harnessed for good. But it would have to start with the president. *I need to make him think it's his idea.* He imagined the president giving the Churchillian speech of his career, something akin to Sir Winston's rousing "We Shall Fight on the Beaches" address, which he'd given to the House of Commons at the outbreak of World War II.

Yes, it could work, he thought, sitting back with a partial smile. America focuses on external threats rather than internal bickering, the president sets his legacy, and Jackson shepherds the United States into a new era of vigilance.

But there was still one big problem. At the moment, no one knew of Apollo Outcomes' involvement, but they would. When they did, the trail might lead to him. Jackson turned pale and felt woozy. Clever people would figure it out in hours, if not sooner. The dead Sikorsky S-97 guaranteed that. Where did Winters get one of those? Jackson didn't know the helicopter was in production, much less illegally sold to a corporation.

Deal with that later, he thought. In the meantime, he needed to find a way to distance himself from Apollo Outcomes and tie Winters to all the terrorist attacks, present one included.

All is not lost. I can still salvage the situation, he mused. He could downplay his connections to everything. After all, he had taken extraordinary care not to ever be seen with the man, and everything Winters might accuse him of could be denied.

What did the old CIA used to say? thought Jackson with a grin. Admit nothing, deny everything, and make counteraccusations.

Winters, you are going down.

Jackson resolved to blame it all on Winters, and why not? For if there was anyone to blame, it was that perfidious cretin. The evidence was overwhelming, but it needed marshaling for investigators to reach the appropriate conclusions. Manipulating bureaucratic agendas was Jackson's forte.

Smiling, Jackson picked up his phone. "Give me the FBI Director."

"Yes sir," said the voice on the other end, as he was placed on hold.

I'll turn this misfortune into a fortune, he thought. The original scheme of framing terrorists for the bridge assassination was unraveling, as the FBI began questioning the ability of any group to organize such a sophisticated attack. Worse, someone in the FBI was leaking this conclusion to the press, and now everyone was focusing on Russia. Jackson now needed everyone's attention to shift one last time to Winters. The evidence would be overwhelming were it nudged into the light.

I need a new fall guy, and Winters is perfect, thought

Jackson. The solution had both elegance and rectitude, giving Winters what he opulently deserved. And it would be easy. In the Japanese martial art of aikido, you use the enemy's weight against him. Jackson would aikido Winters. He would put the FBI on the scent of the Sikorsky S-97, and that would lead them to Apollo and then, ultimately, Winters. If the Bureau veered down the wrong path, Jackson would lay breadcrumbs to get them back on the trail, and burn any investigator who got too close to him. *Child's play,* he thought.

"Where's the FBI director?" asked Jackson.

"Still waiting."

"Try his other numbers."

"I'm doing that, sir."

Jackson's mind drifted back to his escape plan. After the call, he would initiate a whisper campaign against Winters. A few leaked fake documents and accompanying deep background conversations with key journalists should do the trick. He would "accidentally" let slip something about a rogue mercenary company that attempted a shadow coup d'etat in the United States, and how he'd squashed it in the night. Unthinkable! Outrageous! Shocking! It was just the sort of claptrap the press ate up. Told enough times, it would eventually become reality in the minds of many.

But will it be enough to convince the president? thought Jackson with a frown. His own role with Winters was complicated, even though he'd covered his tracks expertly. Still, there were tracks. Jackson exhaled a worried sigh. POTUS possessed the worst sort of mind to influence—stubborn—and the man had a legendary temper that got in the way of, well, everything. Much of Jackson's job was anger management.

"Sir, I've located the FBI director."

"Excellent. Patch him through," said Jackson with a grin. He was going to get ahead of the problem.

"Sir, he's in the Oval," said the assistant over the phone. Jackson's smile disintegrated. "And the president wants to see you, too. He's angry."

CHAPTER 43

"Hey buddy, get up!"

Pain in my ribs woke me from a deep sleep. I was disoriented, having no idea where I was.

"Get up and get out of here. Now!"

Opening my eyes, I saw wooden rafters on the ceiling above, and smelled timber and varnish. Crew shells were stacked from floor to ceiling in steel frames, and small day sailers sat on trailers in the back. My back ached, as if I had slept on rope. A sail was my blanket, covering me from head to toe. The sun was high, and I must have fallen asleep in the boat house.

Pain shot through my ribs again, as another pain stabbed me in the side. "Ow," I muttered for compliance's sake.

"You and your girlfriend need to leave. I called the police. This isn't a motel," said a guy holding a canoe paddle. He was in his twenties and built like a lacrosse player but looked like a stoner.

Where's Lin?! I thought, panicked. I turned my face into a mound of black hair. Lin was asleep next to me, also under the sail. I had no recollection of entering the boathouse, making a bed, or falling asleep. Exhaustion must have overtaken us.

"Hey, are you listening to me? You need to leave. The

police are coming," said the man, jabbing at my side with the paddle again, but I blocked him. I wanted to whip out my H&K assault rifle and stick it under the jerk's chin to see if he would soil his preppy boxers, but I knew better. I couldn't attract any attention during a nationwide manhunt for me, so instead I played the fool. Hopefully the guy was an NPR listener.

"Sorry, dude. So sorry. Chill. We're moving," I said, trying to act the wimp. I needed to convince him that I was a nobody with a no-one girlfriend.

"Hurry up. Out."

"Come on, my honeysuckle," I said softly to Lin, keeping up the act. Cautiously, my hands traveled beneath the sail-blanket and found her side. I held my breath, fearing she might awake disoriented, panic, and blow my head off. Yet I had to play the nobody for the canoe tyrant. Slowly, my hands made contact with her side; she was warm and firm.

"Come on, darling," I whispered as I gently shook her awake, ready to defend myself. "Come on, my tulip, time to go."

"Get on with it! I don't have all day," he said, waving the canoe paddle menacingly.

"Come on, love," I said tenderly as the guy stood over my shoulder. Lin's eyes opened and then her hand shot up for my throat. Anticipating it, I grabbed her wrist and tried to make it look normal, but it just looked weird. I glanced back at the guy with a smile, hoping it would defuse the situation, but he looked horrified and curious, like a rubbernecker slowing down to view a gruesome traffic accident.

"She always does this when I wake her up unexpectedly," I whispered as Lin expertly broke my grip and grabbed my larynx with a Krav Maga hold. My whole body stiffened in pain, and both my hands clung to her wrist. "Easy, my darling," I rasped, and tried to smile though the pain. She looked pissed.

"You two are a pair of sex freaks. Is that what you've been doing in my boathouse? Heavy bondage and S&M? Let me guess. She's the dominatrix and you're the slave?"

Lin looked at him in revulsion and let go of me, blushing. I lay rubbing my throat and whispered hoarsely, "Y-y-yes." The pain was enormous, but I could not drop the act. Under no circumstances could I let him become suspicious. It was far better to be thought of as perverts than terrorists.

"I never understood the whole S&M thing," he said, folding his arms in disapproval. The man turned to Lin and said, "Take your gimp and get out of my boathouse."

Lin grinned slightly. "Come on, gimp. Up with you!"

"We're leaving," I said, sounding like a frog. Then I realized we couldn't stand up with the guy watching since our weapons were hidden beneath the sail. If paddle boy saw our artillery, he would flip out. Lin saw the problem, too.

"Could you, uh . . ." she said, pulling the sail up to her chin and spinning an index finger in the air, indicating she wanted him to turn around. "We're not decent and I need to get dressed."

The man dutifully turned his back, and we stood up, fully clothed. Our weapons lay at our sides, and we looked at each other, trying to figure out how to carry them away without the man glimpsing them.

"Um, do you have a spare beach towel or something lying around?" coaxed Lin.

"What do you need a beach towel for?" he asked suspiciously, and Lin looked at me for help.

Before I could say anything, he said, "Don't tell me. I'd rather not know. You'll find a pile of towels we lend to customers on the shelf by the door."

"Thanks," she said and walked across the boathouse, fetching towels. Minutes later, our weapons were wrapped in aquamarine blue. The guy eyed the odd package curiously.

"Like you said, you don't want to know," said Lin, then she added in a malevolent whisper: "Not unless you want to feel the whip and chain."

He involuntarily cringed, and she blew him a kiss. Then he began squinting at me. "Hey, aren't you—"

"Aren't I what?" I interrupted, a little too defiantly.

"You look like the guy on TV. The guy everyone is looking for. The guy who . . ." His voice trailed off in fright and recognition.

Lin stepped in. "Do you really think the world's number one terrorist mastermind would spend last night *here*?" She laughed. "I had him tied up four ways to Friday last night on your davenports. He's just a slave, trust me." She giggled and slapped my ass hard. It stung.

The guy looked at me, then her, then me again. "Just get out of here."

We walked to the car holding hands, keeping up the act, and it felt good. It had been a long time since I felt a woman's touch, and I missed it. I liked her. It was always my fate to find the right woman at the wrong place and worse time.

"You were pretty convincing back there," I said as we got in the car, and she flashed a knowing smile but said nothing. She started the Mini Cooper as I put the weapons in the tiny backseat, ensuring the towels covered them. As we drove away, a police cruiser passed us, heading to the boathouse.

"Honeysuckle?" She giggled. "Did you actually call me honeysuckle?"

CHAPTER 44

The Kremlin's smaller press room was adorned in eighteenth-century artifice. Pillars painted to look like precious green chrysocolla stone stood beside deep red walls. White wainscoting and crown molding with gold leaf trim gave the room a wedding-cake feel. On the walls hung menacing oil paintings of uniformed leaders from past centuries staring down at the gathered journalists. A single podium sat at the front of the room, on a dais. The low rumble of conversation gave way to silence as Russia's president, Vladimir Putin, took the tiny stage and greeted the room with a politician's smile. After pleasantries, Putin got to his message.

"Everyone knows the United States is being attacked by terrorists. We strongly condemn this brutal and cynical crime against civilians. What has happened once again emphasizes the need for the global community to join efforts to fight against the forces of terror. Russia stands ready to help the United States," said Putin with a grin.

Hands shot up around the press pool. Most were state-owned media, but some international outlets were present. Putin nodded at the front row and a reporter from Russia 24, a domestic network, spoke up. "Mr. President, America's media is reporting that Russian agents and not terrorists are behind the assassination of their vice president. I know you have denied all involvement, but why do you think Americans continue to blame us?"

"Russia has no involvement in the United States' problems. None. Some in America think they can blame others for their problems, but this is wrong. Terrorism in America's homeland is the result of their actions abroad. They have inflamed the Middle East and are now surprised they are on fire too. Sometimes it's easier to blame others than face the truth."

Hands went up again. Putin paused and then called on a Western reporter.

"I'm with Bloomberg News," said a young man in Russian. "You say Russia is not involved in the terror attacks. However, sources tell us that the FBI raided a Russian safe house outside of Washington last night and found evidence pointing to Russian collusion in the vice president's . . . death." The reporter was careful not to use the word "assassination."

"The FBI did not raid a Russian safe house last night. Check your facts."

"But sir—" said the Bloomberg reporter.

"Check your facts," interrupted Putin. "Next question."

"I'm Niles with the *Guardian*. Mr. Putin, it's well known that Moscow tries to interfere in the internal affairs of other countries. Examples include Ukraine, American elections, and the Brexit vote. Do you really expect the world to believe you when you say Russia is not involved with the chaos in Washington right now?"

"Yes. Russia has nothing to do with it. For twenty-five years, the United States has antagonized the world with its wars, and now it has come back to America's motherland," Putin said, and leaned forward casually, putting an elbow on the lectern while gesticulating with the other hand. "It's strange, even amazing. It's a typical mistake of any empire, when people think that nothing will have any effect. They think they're so sustainable, there can be no negative consequences, but those come sooner or later."

"Just to be clear," said the reporter, "you are saying Russia has absolutely no involvement in anything going on inside Washington right now?"

"That's what I said," replied Putin with condescension. "Did you know last night there was a helicopter battle in front of the White House? Yes, in front of the *White House.* Such a thing would never happen at the Kremlin." He chuckled.

"Yes. The entire world knows."

"Do you know what kind of helicopters they were?" asked Putin.

The reporter looked stunned, not expecting the president of Russia to interview him on live TV. "Uh, no."

"They were all U.S. military aircraft. Not Russian. Not any other country. *All* were American," said Putin, enjoying himself.

"What are you saying?" asked a reporter from a different Kremlin-owned media outlet.

Putin smiled and shrugged.

"I'm with the BBC," said another reporter. "Mr. Putin, could you please elaborate on your last point? If true, it doesn't sound like terrorism. What do you believe is actually happening in Washington?"

The Russian president looked down and smirked as he composed his answer. "It's the curse of empire. When a country gets the sense of impunity, that it can do anything, then it will turn inward and destroy itself. History shows this to be true. This has arisen from a dangerous American monopoly on power, from a unipolar world. Soon it will come to an end and we will all be safer."

"Do you think the U.S. is fighting some sort of civil war?" continued the BBC reporter, barely able to contain his skepticism.

"Who can say?" said Putin unconvincingly. "But thank God this situation of a unipolar world, of a monopoly, is coming to an end. It's practically already over."

The BBC man was about to ask a third question when he was cut off.

"Will Russia's policy toward the U.S. change now?" asked another state-owned reporter.

"Russia is prepared to assist America in its troubled times," said Putin. "We understand. After the collapse of the Soviet Union—the worst calamity of the last century—chaos ensued. Russia became a lawless and tyrannical country, on its way down. It was not until 1999, when I was first elected president, that we reversed course. Now we are a great power once again. Russia is prepared to help the United States in its moment of need, even though the U.S. did not help us."

"This is CNN. What kind of assistance are you offering? What does 'help' mean?"

"Building up tension and hysteria is not our way. We are not creating problems for anyone," Putin said. "I hope we can build dialogue."

One of Putin's staffers gave a subtle nod, and Putin stepped away from the podium. Everyone waited quietly as he walked toward the exit. Then suddenly he turned around to face the room again.

"I just want to help," said Putin with a big smile and open arms. Then he disappeared.

CHAPTER 45

"Listen, you need me. We want the same thing. We should work together, combine forces," I said as Jen drove. She had told me about her fall from the FBI, and how I could be her ticket back inside.

But she had yet to arrest me.

"Why shouldn't I haul your ass into the Hoover Building right now?" she asked, steel in her voice.

"Because you need me. You're alone and the FBI is hunting you, along with everyone else. You walk us into the Hoover Building and we *both* get arrested. It only helps the bad guys."

"Aren't *you* the bad guy?"

Somehow it hurt, coming from her. "Maybe you should slow down," I said gently as she took another turn too fast.

"Driving helps me think."

"Speeding gets us noticed, and that would burn us both."

Jen let the car coast until we resumed the speed limit. It was rush hour, but the inner city was almost deserted as everyone had either left town or shuddered themselves at home. The radio said highways to Baltimore and Richmond were a crawl and I-66 was stopped up. The last time I had seen the city this empty was September 11, 2001. Police had enforced an armed curfew, but no one wanted to be outside anyway. At the time, I was staying at the Army Navy Club on Farragut Square, and vets sat around the bar talking about Pearl Harbor while getting drunk before noon. It was a horrible Tuesday.

"What's the plan?" I asked, concealing my impatience. There was an international manhunt for me, and we were driving to nowhere. I had risked everything coming back to stop Apollo Outcomes—Winters, really—from conducting another terrorist attack on American soil for profit. But so far, my mission was a complete bust, and time was running out before the next attack.

And they have a nuke, maybe more than one, I shuddered to think. *I must find Winters and take him down.*

"I'm still thinking," she said, unconsciously speeding up again. Her interrogation of me started shortly after we got in the car. I figured I owed her, and she was the only potential ally I had left, so I gave her a little background. However, the more I shared the less she believed. Now she was in full denial and speeding.

"Do you have a plan?" I repeated. "Because—"

"I don't believe you," she interrupted. "There's no way a company could do what happened last night. Take out an elite special forces unit on the Mall? No way. Russia could *maybe* do it, but wouldn't dare. And you're telling me a corporation did? One that normally works for the government?! I don't buy it."

"Mercenary companies like Apollo Outcomes, Wagner Group, and others are how dirty foreign policy is done today. When you need something absolutely, positively, done in a shadow war, you outsource it. That way Washington or Moscow has maximum plausible deniability, and in the information age that's worth more than firepower."

Jen shot me a skeptical look. "Yeah, that's why we have the CIA and SEALs, for that kind of wet work."

"We are *all* former SEALs, Delta, CIA, and more. Where do you think Apollo recruits? Washington secretly likes mercs because if things go badly—and they do—then the client disavows the whole thing. The White House cannot abandon SEALs or CIA in the field, but mercenaries are expendable."

"But isn't that their job?"

"Sort of," I said, uncomfortably. "Also, mercenaries can do things special operations forces and the CIA cannot."

"Like what?"

"Like break the law: domestic military operations, spying on citizens, shaping operations abroad, political assassinations . . . lethality without the red tape. In the industry, we call it 'Zero Footprint' operations because mercenaries operate like ghosts."

"Bullshit. I'm an FBI agent and I've never heard of it. You think I would have," she said with sarcasm.

I sighed. "Apollo works above the FBI. You just don't know it because it happens waaaay above your pay grade. For example, the safe house you blew up last night. You said the FBI put it under a surveillance embargo. Ever heard of that before?"

"No, never," she admitted uncomfortably.

"That's what I'm talking about. Someone at Apollo called it into the FBI."

"How is that even a thing?"

"Not how, but why. 'Why' is the only question that matters," I said, and Jen took a hard left in anger, lifting the car up on two wheels. I clung to the armrest. Jen slowed down as she spotted a police cruiser around the corner. We exhaled as soon as it was out of sight.

"OK, smart guy, let me ask you a question. Washington uses Apollo for its dirty work and Moscow uses Wagner. Washington and Moscow are enemies. Then why are Apollo and Wagner working together? Wouldn't their big clients disapprove?"

"I don't know," I said, disturbed. The question was the supernova that blew my mind apart, and my fixation since she first brought up the Wagner Group.

Jen laughed. "It's obvious. They are in business together to overthrow the United States government!"

"Now wait a minute, Jen. Apollo would never—"

She cut me off. "Don't be an idiot. You're the operator but I'm the detective. You said ask only the 'why' question, and now you're afraid of the answer."

Maybe I was, I realized. My mission was failing. Since arriving, I discovered more questions than answers and I was nearly killed twice in twenty-four hours. If I were smart, I would leave while I still could. But I'm not smart that way. I never was.

"Tom, who is Apollo's real client?" asked Jen, using my name for the first time. I wanted to scream *Brad Winters,* but up till now I had omitted his name and the civil war within Apollo. It was dangerous information. Yet her tone was confident, as if she knew the answer. Did she know something I did not? *Unlikely,* I thought, so I gave the stock answer.

"Apollo works for the U.S. government. Sometimes they work for an ally or an American company sanctioned by the White House, usually in the extractives or financial services industries," I said. It was true, aside from Winters's rebellion.

Jen giggled. "You might be a top-tier knuckle dragger, but you make a lousy detective."

"Then tell me, Ms. Detective, who is Apollo really working for?"

"Russia."

My mind staggered. The National Security Council hired Apollo to wage shadow wars against Russia in Ukraine, Syria, the Baltics, Libya, and central Africa. I lost my team in Ukraine to Russian special forces and the Wagner Group. Only one word came to mind: "Impossible."

"Impossible? Think about it. Why else would Apollo be working with Wagner?"

I knew the answer was somehow connected to Winters, but I couldn't tell her. Not yet, at least. Then the bomb hit me: *Could Winters be working for Russia?*

"Well?" she pressed, speeding down an ally strewn with litter.

It made sense but it was too frightening to contemplate. My mind felt like a satellite spinning out of orbit and heading for earth. She was more right than she knew: The Kremlin must have bought Winters. If true, we were all screwed.

"Well?!"

I gave her the honest truth. "I don't know. Why?"

"Not to service safe houses. There's only one reason why anyone would hire Apollo Outcomes: to do their dirty work. You said it yourself. Things that no FSB agent or mafioso or Spetsnaz could do."

"And what dirty work, exactly?"

"To stage a palace coup inside the White House."

I guffawed, not ready to accept the implications. "Unlikely. It's the White House that keeps Apollo in business."

"Not if they cut a better deal with Moscow. They're

mercenaries, Tom," said Jen with a twinge of stigma she extended to me.

"In a former life, maybe," I said defensively. "I'm a patriot, Jen, first and foremost. I came back to stop Apollo and I'm risking everything doing it. That's what our country means to me."

Jen nodded. "Well, your former employer ain't. If Russia wanted to leverage the U.S., how would they do it? During the Cold War they threatened us with nuclear annihilation. Now they hire Russian mobsters to smuggle in nukes and employ mercenaries to bury them in American cities. Moscow could secretly blackmail whoever sat in the White House because no politician would ever break the bad news to the American people. Who cares about threatening World War III when you can turn the president into your own sock puppet?"

She could be right, I thought with a chill. My obsession with Winters had gotten in the way of my judgment. Earlier I assumed Apollo staged the terrorist attack to extort the government into more ten-figure contracts. It never occurred to me that they would go full-on traitor, Winters or not.

But the facts lined up. Could killing the president be part of the plan, if only a small part? Blaming terrorists was the ruse to distract law enforcement from the bigger mission of smuggling in the nukes and pre-positioning them around the country. There would be no one better than Apollo, with Wagner providing on-the-ground oversight for the Kremlin.

"America would be fucked," I concluded with a whisper.

"Correct, which is why we need to get inside Apollo headquarters and find some evidence. It's the only way we can turn the FBI and the rest of the country around before it's too late."

"So, then . . . you're not arresting me? We're working together?" I asked.

She paused. "Yes."

We both sat back, realizing the gravity of her decision. She wanted to save the country, even if it destroyed her career and labeled her a forever terrorist. I liked her.

"You're doing the right thing," I said, but she turned away in anguish. It's not easy walking away from family, career, a life.

"Let's go get the motherfuckers," she said softly, her voice cracking and her eyes moist.

"Oh, we'll get them. We will damn them to the inferno," I said. *I'm coming for you, Winters!*

"We need information. How do we get inside Apollo HQ?"

It made good sense, but there was a catch. "It would be easier to break into the CIA than Apollo HQ."

"Figure it out, Apollo boy," she said with a teasing smile. "Isn't that what you said their motto was?"

"Unofficial motto."

"What is their actual motto?"

"No clue."

We drove for a while in silence, both of us thinking. Traffic came to a standstill by the colossal National Basilica, the largest Catholic church in North America. People were praying.

"Well, we have one advantage," I said at last.

"What's that?"

"Everyone thinks I'm dead. Again."

"Time for a resurrection," said Jen with a smile.

CHAPTER 46

"I just fired the national security advisor," said the president, seated at the center of the large table in the Cabinet Room inside the West Wing. Sitting around the table were the principals of the National Security Council and select cabinet members. "I spent last night in a tiny safe room beneath the White House, holed up by the Secret Service. You know why?"

The room was quiet.

"Because there was a *battle* a few hundred yards from my bedroom last night." The president paused to let the silence do its work. "*A battle!*" Silence. "And Jackson was *surprised*! Ignorant advisors have no purpose, and things that have no purpose are replaced." Silence again. "So, I'm asking you. What happened?"

They all looked down, avoiding the president's gaze as he scanned the room.

"I want answers *now*!!" shouted the president, pounding the table with both fists, making a few cabinet members wince. "Who did this?!"

More silence.

"CIA, who did this?" President Anderson shouted, turning to CIA Director Nancy Holt. She faintly shook her head, knowing better than to engage the president during a rant. "How about FBI, any clue? Homeland

Security? DOD? Secret Service? Does anyone have a *freakin'* clue?!"

Finally, an aide in the back spoke up. "Uh, sir. We have no idea who did this."

President Anderson's eyes widened, and his mouth pursed as he balled his hands into fists. Holt reflexively looked away, the same way one looks away when a dog is about to run through an airplane propeller. The president unloaded a verbal barrage with spittle flying from his mouth, and the aide withered with each wave of invective. When it was done, the man stood there but his soul had departed.

"Does anyone else have wisdom to proffer?" asked the president, oozing derision.

"Yes sir, I do," Holt said, leaning forward in her chair. Her voice was firm, and this alone got the president's attention. "The downed enemy chopper . . . I know where it was made and who bought it."

"You do?"

"Yes sir. We haven't run all the details to ground yet, so it's premature to conjecture—"

"Out with it!" demanded the president.

"Apollo Outcomes," she blurted. Whispers crescendoed around the table as people reacted.

"The private military company?" asked the president, not believing it, either. "*Our* private military company?! We use them in the Middle East, Africa, Asia. Everywhere. If this is true, then why would they bite the hand that feeds them?"

"I'm not surprised," huffed Secretary of State Novak. "Apollo is not a private military company—they're mercenaries on the scale of a big global corporation. And this is what happens when you hire mercenaries, as we have increasingly done for the past quarter century. They got greedy, stupid, and dangerous."

Some nodded in agreement while others remained placid. President Anderson turned back to Holt and gestured for her to continue.

"We don't have all the details yet," said Holt, "and we need to be careful about drawing early conclusions."

"Concur. Let's follow the facts and then make decisions," said FBI director Romero.

"We're at war and don't have time for a committee," said the president. "We need to make decisions today. What do we know right now?"

"We know that one of the burning helo wrecks out there is not ours," said Holt. "It's an S-97, a next-generation attack helicopter made by Sikorsky in Stratford, Connecticut."

"Made in America?" asked the president, his voice high-pitched with incredulity. "You're telling me our military aviation was shot down by an American-made helicopter?"

"I didn't believe it either, until I saw the wreckage," said General Butler. "The S-97 is not even in production. How could a company buy one? And right under our nose?"

"Not one. *Four*," said Holt. More whispers as people turned to one another in astonishment.

"Four?" asked the president. "Explain."

"Multiple reports from witnesses," said Holt. "We're still running it to ground, as I said, and the CIA and FBI are working jointly on the investigation."

"We will find the answers. It's only a matter of time," added Romero.

"Good, good," muttered the president.

The room fell silent again, in a group ponder.

"What I don't understand," said General Butler, breaking the quiet, "is how Apollo obtained four S-97s without us knowing. The national security implications are severe."

"It's not wise to speculate—" cautioned Holt.

"Speculate!" interrupted the president. "No more wishy-washiness. I need to know. How did a corporation buy the most advanced attack helicopters in the world before we could, even though we commissioned them? And then use them to blow our helicopters out of the sky a few hundred yards from the White House?"

"Uh, sir. Well . . ." fumbled Holt, hesitant to offer a hypothesis that might prejudice the investigation. They needed to be careful because it was possible a foreign power was manipulating them, causing the U.S. to go to war against itself. Their best weapon at the moment was information, and this depended on a deliberative investigation.

"It's possible the S-97s are off-the-books copies made by the manufacturer. Sikorsky is double-dipping," said one of the president's political pollsters, who had no background in national security. *She shouldn't even be in the room,* thought Holt, except she was a presidential favorite. Holt glared at her, and the woman turned away.

"Unlikely," said Romero. "The U.S. government is Sikorsky's major client, and Sikorsky is owned by Lockheed Martin, one of the biggest defense contractors in the country. I doubt either would risk alienating their primary customer, no matter how much money Apollo shovels at them. No one is richer than the United States of America or buys more military aviation."

"Then how?" asked the president, leaning back in his chair.

"We have agents at Sikorsky and Lockheed right now," said Romero, holding up his phone. "Their executives are as shocked as we are and deny selling S-97s to anyone. In fact, according to my agents, the executives also didn't know S-97s were in the field."

"Maybe Apollo stole them?" asked the deputy national security advisor.

"A good question," replied Romero. "However, our agents confirmed all known S-97s are accounted for and in their hangars. All of them."

People all started speaking at once, offering theories. However, Holt sat very still. President Anderson noticed her silence and gestured for the room to quiet down.

"Nancy, what do you think?" asked the president.

"It's possible Apollo stole the plans and sold them to a hostile foreign power, who then fabricated the aircraft for Apollo offshore," said Holt. "They probably modified them to outperform our best aviation. Maybe they even anticipated battling Task Force 160." The Special Mission Unit helicopters last night were part of Task Force 160.

The room was quiet again. The more everyone thought, the worse the implications became. Finally, General Butler broke the spell. "I might be a dumb old grunt at the end of the day, but there are only two things I want to know. Why the hell is Apollo Outcomes killin' our boys? And when can I take them out?" He leaned over to the president. "It'll all be over by COB, I promise. Just give the word."

The president nodded, his expression darkening. Others in the room nodded too.

The attorney general raised his hand and spoke. "Sir, I would counsel holding off on the military option until the investigation is complete. Apollo Outcomes is a U.S. company and undoubtedly has citizens in it. Killing them without a trial would be illegal. Remember the siege at Waco, Texas, in 1993. We must observe their rights."

President Anderson's hands formed fists again, and the General's expression looked like he had smelled something rancid.

"The people at Apollo Outcomes forfeited their rights when they declared *war* on the United States of America," said the president, suppressing his rage. "I swore an oath to protect the Constitution, and that means against enemies foreign and *domestic*. I will do what is required to uphold my oath. Do you understand me?"

"Sir, you are considering the extrajudicial killing of American citizens. Even if they are domestic terrorists, we must respect their rights because we are a rule-of-law society," said the attorney general with delicacy.

"What do you want me to do? Sit back and let them get away with war as they tie everything up in court for years, all to be dismissed on some technicality? Is this what our society has come to: endless legal proceedings while corporations murder our troops and get away with it? You think Americans will stand for it? You think I will?" President Anderson leaned forward so he could look the attorney general in the eye, and spoke in a hiss. "Understand me. I will risk impeachment before I let our country travel down that perverse road."

General Butler nodded, and so did Novak. Romero looked pale.

"It's called 'lawfare,'" said Holt. "Enemies both foreign and domestic attempt to tie us up in our own legal system while they exploit us. Russia and China do it. So do many others."

"So might Apollo Outcomes," said Butler. He looked angry, not only because he had lost troops but because they were killed by a Frankenstein corporation that the Pentagon helped create.

"Sometimes you got to break the law to achieve justice," said the president.

"Breaking the law to enforce the law is not justice, Mr. President. It's tyranny. The time for military action has not yet come," argued the attorney general. President Anderson's eyes grew wide with impatience, and General Butler looked like he wanted to stuff the lawyer into the room's fireplace and light a match.

"There is another reason to slow-go the military response," intervened Holt. President Anderson whipped around to face her, surprised. "We don't know how deep this goes yet, sir. We don't know if Apollo is holding some sort of bargaining collateral—"

"'Bargaining collateral'?" interrupted the president. "What's that mean exactly?"

"Blackmail," said Romero. "They could have something locked away so that if they are attacked, we get hurt. If they had the gumption to attack our choppers on the Mall last night, then they were probably prepared for the blowback."

The president leaned forward, both elbows on the table, and looked vexed.

"What could they possibly do?" asked General Butler. "I mean, really, we are a superpower and they are just a corporation. We can squash them like an Alabama fire ant."

"They could dump classified information on the internet, like WikiLeaks. Or release politically compromising footage like sex tapes to foment a debilitating scandal. They may have a trove of government secrets that they can sell to our enemies. Goodness knows we read them into enough secrets," said Romero.

"Don't forget, General, we used them to do our dirtiest work for years. What they know and could release to the worldwide media . . ." Holt sucked in a breath. "Well, let's just say that not all weapons fire bullets."

"It would be goddamned devasting!" said the president, pounding the table with his fist. A few cabinet members jumped. Some began wondering if Apollo had dirt on POTUS.

"It's a negotiation insurance policy, in case we come after them," concluded Romero.

The general laughed. "Who cares? We are the U-S of A. Ultimately, what's a corporation going to do to us? File a lawsuit?" He turned toward the attorney general with a mocking grin. "We're at war. Who. Cares."

"We should," said Romero.

"And why is that?" said the general.

President Anderson was watching the conversation like a tennis match.

"Because they may have nukes," said Holt, chilling the room. "A few days ago, we received intelligence about loose nukes on U.S. soil and we assumed it was a phony or a terrorist group. We're still chasing down leads, but the trail is suspiciously well concealed."

"It's true," said Romero. "It might not be a terrorist group after all, but a false flag operation run by someone very sophisticated, we think Apollo. If so, those nukes are probably hidden in several U.S. cities by now. That would give Apollo substantial bargaining collateral."

The general's nostrils flared. "What are you implying?" he asked, leaning forward in his chair. "That Apollo also tried to assassinate the president and got the vice president instead? That they're prepared to nuke American cities? Connect the dots for me."

"Yes, be specific," said the president. His earlier bravado had transformed into genuine concern.

Holt cleared her throat. "All I'm saying is this: We move against them, then they could move against us, and it could involve mushroom clouds. We need to get smart about Apollo first, and then make our move. If my theory is correct, Apollo has spent a great deal of time planning this and has anticipated our responses. Few outsiders know our systems and playbooks better than Apollo. Hell, we've all hired them. This makes us extremely vulnerable, and it's not the time to shoot from the hip. Instead, we need to take careful aim, like a sniper. One shot, one kill."

The general nodded. Everyone else in the room was frozen.

President Anderson turned to Holt. "Out with it, Nancy. I know that look. You're holding something back." All eyes turned to her.

"There is an additional possibility, Mr. President, and one we cannot ignore," she said. "Apollo may have a new client."

"Who?" asked Romero.

"Russia."

The room let out a collective gasp.

"The Russians?" exclaimed the general, shifting in his seat uncomfortably.

"Follow the facts," said Holt. "Radiological teams have confirmed trace amounts of weapons-grade material were smuggled through New York Container Terminal on Staten Island. The Russian mafia facilitated the smuggling. Last night, someone hit a safe house used by the Wagner Group, a Russian mercenary company, in McLean, Virginia."

"But we used to hire Apollo to kill Wagner in Ukraine and Syria," said the general, perplexed.

"They're mercenaries, general. They'll work for anyone," said Novak with disdain.

"We cannot ignore the possibility that Apollo, Wagner, and the Russian mob may have all been hired by the Kremlin to pre-position WMD in our major cities."

President Anderson turned white. No one spoke.

"That's why we need to proceed with care, Mr. President," said Holt.

"Buuuuuullshit!" said the general, nearly leaping out of his chair. "We need to move against Apollo now, before the situation gets worse. What are the Russians going to do to us if we take out an American company? Declare war?" He scoffed. "No, of course not. And let's take out Wagner, while we're at it. Russian mercenaries operating on American soil? In the nation's capital?!" The general calmed himself down and spoke slowly in his Southern drawl. "Mr. President, this is a clear and present danger, if there ever was one."

All eyes turned toward the president, awaiting a decision. The man slumped forward, his eyes narrowed, then looked up at Holt.

"I'm declaring a national emergency. I want to know everything earthly possible about Apollo Outcomes and the Wagner Group. Everyone connected to them, where they operate, their financials. *Everything.* Treat it as a counterterrorism operation, and not a legal case." President Anderson turned to the attorney general, who remained stoic. "Make arrests, disregard civil rights—I don't care, just find those nukes. When they're all accounted for, we move against Apollo and Wagner. Moscow be damned! You have seventy-two hours," he said to Holt, and then turned to General Butler. "And I want options. One shot, one kill."

Holt nodded, and Butler smiled.

CHAPTER 47

Three black Chevy Suburbans sped around the outer rim road that encircled Dulles Airport. A rusty chain-link fence was the only thing separating the potholed road from the runways where 747s took off. There was no traffic since only utility vehicles used the road, and rarely even then.

Inside the middle vehicle, Winters checked his watch and frowned. Every second on the ground was a second too long. The battle last night left clues that would lead to his identity, and at some point this morning, he expected all of American law enforcement to crash down upon his head. Even he could not escape that nightmare. He was surprised they were not on him already.

I need to be in the air, thought Winters, *before it's too late.*

"Driver, how much longer?" he asked, leaning forward from the backseat.

"Five minutes, sir."

Winters slumped back and twirled his antique cane. The morning sun spread warmth across the yellowed grass patches in between the runways. Winters scowled at the sun for being so bright. It was irritating.

Your move, Jackson, he thought. Last night was a surprise. He did not expect Jackson to make the mistake of attacking him in the open. For that, Jackson was punished. The Apollo forces had done devastating work. However, it left Winters exposed, and that was nearly as bad. Apollo had won the battle but muddled the war. Now he had to flee the country and manage his clients, who would soon ask difficult questions.

What will I tell them? thought Winters. His clients were even less patient than he was. *How can I turn this fiasco into a win?* Nervously, Winters checked his watch again.

"Driver, how long?"

"Less than two minutes."

Too long, he thought, twirling his cane faster. The small convoy came to a stop in front of a gate in the chain-link fence. A man from the lead vehicle got out with a large pair of bolt cutters and snipped the padlock, then swung open the gates. The convoy passed through. Normally they would have driven through the front gate to Dulles's corporate executive jet terminal, but these were not normal times. Precautions were vital.

"Sir, the pilots say they are ready to go."

"Excellent," mumbled Winters absentmindedly. His thoughts shifted from managing his clients' expectations to exploiting the situation. Unexpected turns of events always produced opportunities, but he could not see any good ones now. The battle on the Mall would surely expose him.

I'll frame the other half of Apollo for the battle, he thought with satisfaction. A few phone calls with media executives should do the trick, but he knew it would not be enough. The spotlight of the federal government would fall on all of Apollo, including him, and it was the last place he wanted to be. Like all creatures of the dark, Winters abhorred the light.

Damn you, Jackson! he thought bitterly. He reviled

being cornered, especially on the cusp of his plan's fulmination. Now everything was in jeopardy. *What a fool Jackson is. Or was.* There was a good chance the man would be cashiered. However, Winters preferred dealing with the devil he knew rather than what could follow.

Maybe, if I'm lucky, the president will appoint an academic to replace Jackson. They were the easiest to fool since they thought they knew everything but, in reality, comprehended nothing. Winters smiled at the prospect.

"We're almost there, sir."

"Good. Confirm with the crew that the package is already on the plane," said Winters. The driver radioed the plane.

"The crew confirms the package is on the plane."

Excellent, thought Winters. *It will be my day of days yet!* But first, he had to get airborne and out of the country. It was his most vulnerable moment of the operation, and it made him neurotic.

The convoy raced down the tarmac, passing lines of parked private jets, and pulled up to one sitting alone. It wore Apollo's corporate colors: black underbelly and gray top. It had no other markings. Winters had commandeered one of Apollo's Gulfstream Vs and a faithful crew; he found money went a long way toward inspiring loyalty.

"Sir, we're arriving," said the driver as he stopped in front of the aircraft's stairs. A man rushed to the passenger door and pulled it open with a grunt. It was laden with several hundred pounds of bulletproof armor. Winters carefully extracted himself from the vehicle and hobbled his way up the stairs. In the distance, a car with flashing blue lights accelerated toward them.

"Take care of it," said Winters as he climbed the stairs. The convoy commander nodded and gave a sharp whistle to his men. They jumped back into the SUVs and sped off to intercept the airport security vehicle. Winters smirked, knowing how it would end. The aircraft stairs retracted the moment Winters was inside the fuselage, as he was its only passenger.

"Care for coffee or tea, sir?" asked the steward.

"Show me the package," demanded Winters. The steward pulled out an aluminum briefcase. It was slightly bigger and thicker than a standard case, and it was badly scuffed and dented, in contrast to the faultless interior of the Gulfstream jet. Winters smiled.

"Good. Now give it to me, and get us off the ground," he said, as he belted himself into the nearest seat.

The steward turned and gestured to the pilots, and tucked the case next to Winters's feet. The turbines roared and the plane lurched forward, making the steward stumble. Winters could hear the airport radio chatter emerge from the cockpit, which still had its door open, and watched as they taxied for the runway. Out the window, he saw the three large SUVs block in the airport security vehicle and his men get out. They were not armed, a smart move. However, Winters had no doubt they would get the job done.

Good men are hard to find, he thought. The plane swung onto the runway without slowing and immediately went full throttle. As it nosed up, he could see his men get back into their vehicles and drive away. The jet climbed at a steep angle and hit some turbulence passing through a cloud bank. The blue sky shimmered in the beyond, and they banked east, toward the Atlantic and international airspace.

Free at last, thought Winters, his hand affixed to the aluminum briefcase.

CHAPTER 48

"It's mission impossible," I declared, and tossed my pen at the pad. "There's absolutely no way we can get inside Apollo's headquarters. No way!"

Jen was taking a shower. "What?" She insisted on leaving the bathroom door open so we could converse, but so far it wasn't working well. And it was distracting. Very, very distracting. I tried to be a gentleman and not look. A Fort Benning obstacle course would have been easier.

"I said: no way in!" I repeated, louder. Her shower was going on ten minutes, and steam perforated the minuscule hotel room. Even my pad of paper felt damp.

"Not a winner's attitude," she scolded. I peeked around the door and saw her feline silhouette moving behind the shower curtain, her long black hair falling to one side. She made shadows and vinyl curtains sexy.

We rented a cheap room off Highway 50 on the out-skirts of DC. It was all we could afford with our shared cash on hand. When we checked in, the Indian guy at the counter asked if we wanted the room by the hour. Jen blushed and I said no. The place was a fleabag brothel, but it eschewed surveillance cameras and cops, making it a perfect safe house for one night.

The water turned off, replaced by a *drip-drip*. Next

came the rustling of towels, not the fluffy, gigantic ones at the Four Seasons but the skimpy, puny ones.

Focus, Locke. Focus! I know I shouldn't have, but I did. I could see her vague reflection in a fogged-up wall mirror attached to the bathroom door, the kind that's four feet tall. Long, jet-black hair tumbled down her naked back as she dried off. Fog could not conceal her toned body. Jen could have been a swimsuit model.

"Tom? Did you hear me?"

I snapped out of my trance, not knowing what I missed. "Uh, yeah, sure."

Jen emerged wearing nothing but two towels: one for the hair, and the other for everything else. In street clothes, she was attractive; now she was molten hot. However, she was also inscrutable. I was always awkward around women I was truly attracted to, and I was never sure how to proceed. To be a gentleman in this day and age is a quandary. If she was interested, she would let me know. At least I hoped that was how it worked.

She grinned slightly. "Everything OK with you, Tom?"

"Oh, yeah, yeah. No problem."

She discarded the towel around her head, and wet hair billowed out. Strands fell to her waistline. I tried not to gaze at her glistening legs or anything higher. It was frustrating.

"You seem . . . off," she said.

"No, I'm fine. Just frustrated."

"Frustrated?" she asked coquettishly, as she sat next to me on the bed's edge, crossing her legs. She was still wet, and the remaining towel was waterlogged and semitransparent.

"*Very* frustrated," I muttered, staring at her naked thighs. *Focus, Locke! Snap to.* I looked away, and collected my thoughts. "I can't figure out a weak point in Apollo's defenses. It's *very* frustrating."

Jen giggled. "Oh, is *that* what's bothering you?"

"Yes," I lied. I thought she could tell.

"Maybe there's something I can do to help?" she smiled devilishly. Jen reached across me and I leaned back to make room. Her towel slackened as she stretched over my lap for the pad of paper, her wet hair cascading on my legs. I wanted to rip off the thin towel, but couldn't. *Look away!* I told myself. Once she grabbed the pad, she sat back up, leaving my pulse sprinting.

"Tell me what you know," she said professionally, preparing to take notes as she saddled up next to me, hip to hip. The towel was meagre, like a miniskirt.

"Uh, OK," I said, trying not to seem distracted.

"From the top."

"All right." I told her what I knew. In a past life, I had spent countless hours at Apollo's corporate headquarters at Tysons Corner in northern Virginia. It looked like any other banal people warehouse, but inside it was an electronic and physical fortress. Its security was tighter than the CIA. I ended with: "I don't see a way in."

Jen stared at the floor layouts I had sketched out, to the best of my memory. "Could we pose as building inspectors or something? I still have one friend at the FBI who might be able to arrange a legal reason for us to be there."

"Don't bet on it. Apollo's lawyer will meet us at the front door. Then they will recognize me, and nab us both." I groaned. "I'm telling you, the place is worse than Fort Meade meets Terre Haute."

Somewhere in the background, a headboard was banging furiously, which we tried to ignore.

"There's always a way in, Tom, we're just not seeing it," she sighed, tossing aside the pen and paper. She leaned back on her arms. "I need you to help me clear my head."

"Sure," I mumbled.

Holding the remaining towel with one hand, she slunk across the bed. There wasn't much towel to go around as she maneuvered herself against the headboard. It was revealing. She patted the spot next to her, and I lay back, too.

The headboard banging got louder.

"Real classy place you found us," she said coyly, poking a toe into my calf.

"They don't ask questions at establishments like this," I replied, fixated on her toe. "Or have cameras. Drives off business . . ." My sentence trailed off as she squirmed to get into a more comfortable position, her towel relaxing along the way. It seemed to shrink across her body.

The headboard banging stopped. Someone must have gotten their money's worth. Jen and I looked at each other; her expression exuded raw power, like during a dock fight. My body tensed reflexively, but she ran her fingers through my hair tenderly. Then she kissed me, a peck at first and then vigorously. I reached around her waist and ejected the towel, my enemy. My hands traced up and down her smooth body as we kissed.

Jen was as passionate a lover as she was a fighter, and as physical, too. An hour later, we lay together entwined. She was perfectly asleep on me, while I felt I had gained a bruise or two. Best bruises of my life. I lay in reverie with Jen's naked body against my side, her head on my shoulder and my hand on her ass.

Riiinnnggggg. Riiinnnggggg. The hotel telephone jolted us awake. *Riiinnnggggg. Riiinnnggggg.* Under a pillow on the floor lay a decades-old phone with push buttons and annoyingly loud bells.

I felt Jen's body tighten and her hands grip my sides with each ring. "Should we answer it?" she whispered.

"No one knows we're here. Wrong number," I said, reaching down and hanging up.

Jen started giggling and nuzzled her face into my shoulder. "Gosh, I can't believe how jittery I am!"

"I know a cure for that," I offered, but she was already on top of me. I felt her thighs wrap around my waist, as she reached down.

Riiinnnggggg. Riiinnnggggg.

Argh!! I thought, scanning the room for a club, bat, bazooka, or anything else that would silence the phone.

"Hello?" It was Jen, the phone's receiver to her ear as she lay flat on my chest.

What are you doing?! I thought.

"It's for you," she said in a stunned tone. I shook my head no, while she nodded yes. Then she put the receiver to my ear, and started kissing the other. It was very persuasive.

"Hello," I said. Lin's kissing swelled in intensity and her hot breath in my ear hijacked my brain. The enchantress was distracting me for her pleasure.

"Dr. Locke?" said a garbled voice on the other end, its sound digitally altered to conceal someone's identity. My hand grabbed her hips to cease their mischievous wiggling, but she put my hand in a joint lock, paralyzing me while still kissing.

"Aaahhh!" I cried in pain.

"Is this Tom Locke?" asked the voice again.

"Who is this?" I managed in a hoarse whisper.

"We wish to meet with you."

"Who *is* this?"

"We have much to discuss—"

Jen surprised me, and I gasped.

"—much in common."

With focused concentration, I mustered: "W-w-why should I?"

"All will be revealed when you arrive."

It could be a trap. Must ask one more question, I commanded myself as Jen became electrified. I summoned all my strength to form the words: "How can I trust you?"

There was silence. "You cannot. But we want Winters, too, and we know where he is. Do you want a piece of him?"

Jen collapsed on me, her hair covering my face and the phone. She lay motionless, and I could feel her heartbeat race against mine. But my next words took no effort. "Absolutely."

CHAPTER 49

Jackson sat in his living room, watching the news unfold in his bathrobe and drinking twenty-five-year-old scotch from the bottle. It was 10 A.M., he was drunk, and it felt good. His plan to enmesh the president in his cover-up had failed spectacularly. Now he watched the news with a vacuous expression, like a German soldier after D-Day. He gulped another swig of whiskey.

News choppers circled the Mall, showing the burning wrecks of aircraft and vehicles. It was Yemen with a reflecting pool. The news anchor was recalling what was known: the bridge explosion, the unsolved VP assassination, the mysterious battle on the Mall, a White House in pandemonium, loose nukes, and a country under attack. He stopped talking midsentence, listening to something coming in through his earpiece.

"We have breaking news," it began, but the news banner said it all: NATIONAL SECURITY ADVISOR FIRED! B-roll footage of Jackson took over the screen.

"Ah, come *on*!" yelled Jackson and switched channels.

". . . sources say National Security Advisor George Jackson was fired . . ." said another newscaster.

"Shut up!" said Jackson, changing the channel again.

". . . breaking news, the president has fired Jackson . . ."

"No, no, no!" screamed Jackson as he flipped through the news channels.

". . . Jackson fired . . ."

". . . fired . . ."

". . . terminated . . ."

". . . blamed . . ."

". . . his fault . . ."

". . . treason?"

"No, no, no, no, no-o-o-o!" yelled Jackson. He stood up on the couch and threw a cushion at the monitor.

Then the news changed again, under a different BREAKING NEWS banner. It showed a SWAT truck and police cars pulling up to an elegant Georgetown mansion. The truck's back doors swung open and SWAT poured out, turtled up in paramilitary gear. The cameraman shook the lens as he tailed the SWAT team toward the house's front door. A trailing SWAT member turned around and waved for him to stop following, which the cameraman did.

Jackson froze and stared at the screen in a drunken haze. That house. It was—

"No, no, no, no, no, no, no, no, no, no!!!!" Jackson screamed and tripped off the couch and smashed his head into the coffee table, scotch spilling everywhere. A crash of wood and steel came through his front door.

"FBI! FBI! HANDS UP! GET ON THE FLOOR!"

The SWAT team surrounded him, some aiming tasers while others held MP5 submachine guns. Jackson held up trembling hands and blood trickled down his forehead, where he hit the coffee table. Jackson's eyes darted around the room like a caged animal, and he began hyperventilating.

"You are under arrest!" shouted a policeman, then read him his Miranda rights as two other men roughly threw him face-first on the coffee table and cuffed him.

"Wa-wait! There must be some mistake," pleaded Jackson. The anger, scotch, head injury, and arrest had him drowning in cognitive dissonance.

"No mistake," said the arresting officer in a commanding tone. The two other SWAT lifted him to his feet but he could not stand.

"What am I being charged with?" Jackson said in a wispy voice.

"Treason."

Jackson let out an involuntary whimper as the men dragged him down his grand hallway, his bare feet dragging on the floor. The great room with twin wraparound staircases was lined with pictures of him meeting world leaders, advising presidents, international awards, American flags—all meant to impress and even intimidate guests. Blood dripped from Jackson's head, smearing a trail on the polished oak floor.

"There must be a mistake, there must be a mistake. I'm George Jackson, the national security advisor. There must be a mistake," he kept repeating softly.

The blast of winter air through his bathrobe coupled with the dozen cameras sobered him up as the FBI hauled him across the lawn. Jackson stared blankly at the news cameras, seeing the reporters' mouths move but hearing nothing.

In a brief moment of self-awareness, he knew. His legacy could have been ending terrorism in America, negotiating a peace in the Middle East, putting China in its place. He was destined for greatness, something he had known since childhood. But it was not to be. This

moment, on his front lawn, was to be his everlasting
legacy: a scotch-soaked drunk in a bathrobe with blood
running down his face, being perp-walked by the FBI
for treason. Jackson wanted to float away but was instead thrown into the back of a SWAT vehicle.

CHAPTER 50

The Mercedes-Maybach made its way up the steep country road that was barely two cars wide. Dusk's shadows darkened the forest, giving it a haunted feel, and Winters half expected Hansel and Gretel to emerge. Like the car, the forest seemed prolifically manicured. But that was Austria: cleanliness, order, and child-eating witches.

The aluminum briefcase sat next to Winters, and he kept a hand planted on it at all times. He checked his watch out of nervousness now rather than necessity. Winters disliked meeting his client, but especially since the operation had drifted so far off track.

What went wrong? he thought as the car took a tight turn. He had turned it over in his mind ever since boarding the jet in Dulles. Winters gazed out the window and twirled his cane in annoyance. The sun was disappearing, and the forest shadows grew opaque and creepy. How did it happen?

Locke, he thought with malice. He was the X factor, the independent variable, the free radical. Everything went awry when he appeared, an absolute surprise. No one could have foreseen it. *You should have stayed dead!* Winters did not even have the privilege of revenge. Jackson also took that away from him, and Winters squeezed the cane's ivory monkey head in silent rage. *Eternal shame is too good for you, Jackson,* he thought as they rounded the last turn on the switchback. *Crucifixion is better.*

The car reached the top of the ridgeline, where a medieval castle stood, dominating the valley below. The lights of Vienna twinkled in the distance, and the Danube River meandered through the far plain. For most, it would have been an idyllic sight, but Winters was inured to its glory, unless it came with raw power.

The castle was lit up and well maintained, rare for an eight-hundred-year-old building. Like all citadels of the Middle Ages, it was not large compared to those of later centuries. But unlike eighteenth-century palaces, it was a true stronghold and not just a symbol. A central keep with banqueting hall was surrounded by high walls, each with a mixture of square and circular towers. Walls ten feet thick protected those inside, and battlements lined the ramparts that overlooked a dry moat. Perhaps it once had a drawbridge, too, but the Mercedes-Maybach drove up a ramp and fixed bridge. Immense wooden doors opened to swallow the vehicle, and the gate's raised portcullis looked like teeth. After the Mercedes-Maybach passed, the portcullis came down.

Winters stiffened as the car came to a halt on the cobblestoned inner courtyard. Staff dressed as if they were plucked from a Habsburgian docudrama opened the car door and assisted Winters out. He shook them off, hating being touched. A valet reached in and retrieved the beat-up aluminum briefcase.

"Be careful with that," snapped Winters, startling the man. Winters was far too jet-lagged and strained for pleasantries. "Take me to the master of the house."

"He awaits you in the library," said the head butler. Winters followed him into the keep, as did the valet carrying the steel case. The interior was fully updated with modern amenities yet retained its old-world personality: racks of antlers lined the plastered walls, suits of armor and weapons adorned the passages, and hefty wood furniture filled each chamber, along with rich tapestries and silks. With the exception of the lights, nothing looked younger than three hundred years old.

Looks like the goddamned Wizard of Oz *in here,* thought Winters. He didn't care for the Old World. A man like him would have been hindered in the ancien régime owing to his low birth station while ingrate nobles raped the people, generation after generation. *God bless America,* he thought while passing through a hall of shields, each with an aristocratic coat of arms. Winters had always identified with Robespierre—a misunderstood revolutionary, in his mind.

"Herr Winters, the library," said the manservant while heaving open large double doors. Winters hobbled in without acknowledging the butler. The medieval library was a three-story atrium lined with bookcases from floor to ceiling. Narrow steel balconies lined the walls, affording access to its leather-bound tomes, some dating back to the Gutenberg press. On the ceiling was a magnificent rococo mural depicting the heavens above, with an eight-pointed star at its zenith. Reading tables stacked with oversize books made the place look almost scholarly.

Winters walked into the middle of the library and

heard the door clink shut behind him. At the far end
of the room sat a gargantuan marble fireplace, ten feet
wide, with an intricate carving of a forgotten battle, and
an eight-pointed star at the center. Leather wingback
chairs were arrayed around the blazing fire, all facing
away from Winters and the entrance. Four Rottweilers
lay sleeping at the blaze's edge, weighing about 170
pounds each. A hand extended from one of the wing-
backs and placed an empty cordial glass on the side
table, next to a silver platter of raw meat.

*All the money and connections in the world and the
fool shuts himself up in a library. What a failure of
imagination,* thought Winters with disdain as he limped
over the oriental carpets. The four dogs lifted their heads
in unison as he approached, and he froze. Winters hated
dogs, especially these four.

"Mr. Winters, thank you for coming before I had to
beckon you," came an old man's voice from the wingback, facing away from Winters. He was the library's
only occupant besides the dogs. His gravelly baritone
spoke in Queen's English with no trace of his Germanic
heritage.

"You would never need to beckon me, Chevalier. A
good servant always knows when he is needed before
his master does," coaxed Winters, flipping his bitterness
into delighted sycophancy. Winters waited. After a
pause, a hand emerged from the wingback and waved
him forward. Winters tottered forth and the Rottweilers
put their heads down.

"Are you here to deliver good news or the other
type?" asked the man, still staring at the fire. He was in
his eighties and had a long face, square jaw, puffiness
under his eyes, and a receding line of formerly blond

hair. The wrinkles on his face made him look rugged rather than old. On each hand he wore a large ring as old as the castle, one a family signet and the other an eight-pointed star.

"Good news," responded Winters with a smile, standing in front of a man he knew only as the Chevalier, or "knight" in French, which puzzled him because the man was Austrian. In fact, he was more than Austrian; he was a true Habsburg, one of the last.

"Are you certain?"

His skepticism was an affront to Winters. "Absolutely. We have achieved all of our objectives. Per your commission, I have sewn seeds of chaos and distrust at the highest levels of the U.S. government. I have generated paranoia among the American people against terrorists. Some think Russia is behind it, but they are a small minority." Winters coughed nervously, hoping it would not upset his patron. "The United States overwhelmingly believes terrorists are behind everything, and not Moscow."

"And what of the instrument?"

The library's double doors swung open and the valet carrying the aluminum briefcase appeared, as if summoned. The valet carefully laid down the case on an ottoman next to the Chevalier's feet, and promptly disappeared. The old man looked slightly pleased to see the battered metal case.

"Voilà," said Winters, beaming with pride. "A nuclear briefcase. The fate of three cities and whoever sits in the Oval Office rests at your feet."

"Open it," commanded the Chevalier, leaning forward with anticipation. Winters entered a combination in the ten-digit tumbler lock, which unlocked the side latches. Flipping them up revealed two small fingerprint readers. Simultaneously, he pressed both index fingers on the pads and heard an internal click. Winters opened the case and rotated it to face his client. The internal workings looked like a customized laptop with a handset, biometric authentication, and more buttons.

"Turn it on," ordered the Chevalier.

"I can send for a technician—"

"Turn it on," interrupted the old man.

Winters paused.

"Activate it, Mr. Winters," repeated the Chevalier. "I must have absolute confidence in the genuineness of the instrument before I deliver it to the people I represent."

Was the medieval fossil going to nuke a city? thought Winters, then wondered whether he would be horrified or impressed. "May I please sit to do this?" The Chevalier always made his servants stand. Only peers were allowed to sit.

How I loathe this antiquated turd, thought Winters behind his amicable smile.

The man nodded. Winters sat down in a wingback and pulled the ottoman closer so he could work the nuclear trigger. He fished out a necklace from inside his shirt and removed the control key from its end. It resembled a thumb drive, but only fit this unique nuclear briefcase. Winters inserted the key into the control panel, and the laptop lit up. It scanned his face, iris, all fingerprints, and accepted a pass-code sentence that Winters typed. The screen changed from sky blue to a world map. A few keystrokes later, three bombs with eleven-digit numbers appeared on the map.

Winters smiled and spun the metal briefcase to face the Chevalier. "There you are. New York City, Los Angeles, and Washington, DC. Their fate is in your hands. You can blackmail presidents, auction off a mushroom cloud, or blow up one just to create mayhem."

"I want proof of concept."

"Excuse me?"

"You heard me, Mr. Winters. I want proof of concept. Destroy a city."

Winters was speechless. You don't shoot hostages just to prove they can die, otherwise you lose your leverage. "Did you have a particular city in mind?"

"No. Any one will do."

Winters's throat went dry and he could feel his palms get sweaty. Despite what some believed, he was a businessman and not a mass murderer. Yet his client demanded it, and the client was always right. Winters looked at the map with the nukes. Which city would he end today? Los Angeles was smug and always took national security for granted, making them an ideal candidate. Or maybe New York, where he was mugged once as a kid. Nuking Washington would eliminate a few personal enemies, a nice perk.

"How about DC?" offered Winters.

"Fine."

Winters worked the keyboard, and the Chevalier leaned closer to observe. Using the track pad, Winters selected the bomb located in Washington and clicked it. The screen zoomed to a satellite image of Sixteenth and O Streets, just five blocks from the White House. Winters had his teams hide all three nuclear weapons; he knew the noisome inhabitants of this building, and he grinned.

Gotcha, he thought with contentment. Winters right-clicked the target indicator on the map, and a menu appeared. He scrolled down to "Detonate." Click. A safety screen appeared:

Do you wish to detonate K-class weapon 0124?
Latitude: 38.909140 Longitude: -77.037150
Confirm   ***Cancel***

"Sir?" asked Winters, turning to the Chevalier, who continued to stare at the screen. The "Cancel" button was blinking but the cursor stood over "Confirm."

"Remarkable," said the Chevalier at last.

"Would you like me to confirm?" asked Winters, holding his finger over the "Enter" key.

"No, no, not necessary, Mr. Winters. I am satisfied," said the Chevalier as he leaned back into his seat once more. "Shut it down."

Winters exhaled more loudly than he wished as he pressed "Cancel" and shut down the system. The valet appeared again, as if summoned, to take the aluminum case away.

"My client will be pleased," said the Chevalier, who was a cutout for an end client. They never spoke of it, but Winters knew it was the Kremlin.

"You will need a technician to reset the pass codes so your client can operate the controller," said Winters, watching his greatest achievement disappear into a side room of crossbows.

"We already have such a technician on-site," said the Chevalier. "He will inspect the equipment now."

You were testing me, you bastard! thought Winters with spite.

"You have done well, Mr. Winters," said the Chevalier, and Winters nodded sagaciously. "Everything went nearly according to plan. *Nearly.*"

Winters looked up, confused. "I delivered on all your objectives, did I not?"

The Chevalier shook his head. "All except the most important of all: anonymity. We cannot abide the battle on the Mall last evening. It was too public. Secrecy is our safety and strength, and you have exposed us," said the Chevalier, using the royal *we*. "As they say in medicine: 'Doctor, the operation was a success, but the patient is dead.' You delivered our objectives but made a pig's breakfast of the entire affair."

"With respect, Chevalier, let me explain—"

The Chevalier interrupted him before Winters could continue. "No. Your actions speak for you." The man's voice was firm, and one of the dogs lifted his head in concern. "You disappoint me, Winters."

"I can assure you, Chevalier, none of this will blow back on you or your client," soothed Winters. "Terrorists and their collaborators will ultimately take the blame, as you instructed. I've fabricated an 'insider threat' terrorist scenario within Washington circles, so that everything will fall on the heads of two individuals. The first is George Jackson, the national security advisor who regrettably went insane. The second is Tom Locke, a lowlife mercenary turned nuclear terrorist. The evidence trail will lead to them; I have arranged it."

"And where are they now?"

Winters smiled, feeling the Chevalier coming around. "Jackson has been arrested for treason, and I will manufacture the necessary proof to see him convicted. Locke was killed last night." Winters shifted uneasily, as his men had yet to find Locke's body. However, how could he survive a direct hit from a Hellfire missile? Locke had to be dead. "It's easy to blame a dead man with a suspicious past."

"Dead?" asked the Chevalier in a tone that unsettled Winters. "Are you certain?"

"Absolutely, my Chevalier," said Winters, concealing alarm that the Chevalier might know something he did not. "Locke was killed by missile fire on the Mall, and a good thing too. He was in a convoy leading a group of renegade mercenaries. They were hired by a rich Middle Eastern monarchy, or at least that is how it will play out. Thankfully, the American military learned of Locke's plans and took him out on the Mall last night. That was the true impetus for the battle: to stop Locke and his terrorist plot."

"Is that so?" asked the Chevalier in mild surprise.

Winters grinned internally, believing he had successfully circumnavigated the Locke affair. Now to seize the initiative.

"Who do you think tipped off the Americans? It was *me*," said Winters. "It was the only reason they caught Locke so quickly. I saved you too, Chevalier. Locke was a dangerous man. He was a greater threat to you than you realize. It was worth the risk."

The Chevalier's expression soured. "I will judge threats and risks, not you. Do you understand me, Winters? I can use capable men regardless if they are good or evil. All men are governable, for those with the acumen to do it. My family has been doing it for a very long time. Now, which do you think you are, Mr. Winters: governor or governed?"

The geriatric reprobate! thought Winters, and was tempted to withdraw the hidden sword inside his cane and slice the dunce's throat open. Then he eyed the sleeping Rottweilers. *Time for that later,* he thought.

"Your quiet is confirmation enough," continued the Chevalier, and Winters's hand tightened around the ivory monkey head. "We have doubts about you, Mr. Winters. We even question whether you comprehend the task we commissioned you to perform. Your brusque methods may have imperiled us." The Chevalier paused, allowing the implications to fester in Winters's mind. The Rottweilers lifted their heads, as if on cue, to glare at Winters. "That is unforgivable."

"Sir, I think there may be a misunderstanding," said Winters coolly.

"Locke is alive!" bellowed the octogenarian, the dogs looking up in alarm.

"Alive?" stammered Winters, his face pale. "Impossible!"

"What is impossible is your dim grasp of reality, Mr. Winters." The old man flung a piece of meat at one of the Rottweilers. It ripped the meat with its mandibles before swallowing it with an audible gulp. Winters stood and unconsciously took a step backward.

"No. Locke has to be dead," muttered Winters.

"You have disappointed me for the last time, Mr. Winters," said the old man, his tone imperious. "Locke undid your fragile work in four nights. You are an incompetent."

Winters scowled. "But Chevalier—"

The old man cut him off. "You will return to the United States and make repair. You will finish what I commissioned you to start." He tossed three more hunks of meat at the dogs, who swallowed them without chewing.

"But I—"

"And eliminate Locke this time," interrupted the Chevalier again. "Everywhere he goes, calamity follows. No more mistakes, Mr. Winters." He paused to throw a handful of meat, and the animals inhaled it midair. The old man threw larger, boned morsels. "On pain of death."

Winters's jaw went slack as he watched the Rottweilers rip apart their food. The valet mysteriously appeared again, followed by two armed men in body armor wielding cattle prods.

The Chevalier faced Winters at last. "Never forget Mr. Winters; you're expendable."

Winters's face went ashen as the valet and guards escorted him out.

CHAPTER 51

Putin sat in Stalin's old office in the Kremlin, cradling a gilded teacup. The room was smaller and less ornate than his official chambers, but he felt the great man's presence here. The Soviet Union began its slow decline after the Man of Steel's death in 1953. The fall of the Soviet Union remained a personal injury for Putin. If he could restore just an iota of the glory that Stalin had imbued in the USSR, then his reign would be a success. Working in the great man's office reminded him of his charge.

Putin sat behind Stalin's smallish wooden desk, over-looking a large U-shape of chairs rimming an oriental rug before him, a court audience before a throne. The walls were deep red fabric with oil paintings of the great man on all sides, peering down on the occupants. Be-side the desk sat the old couch where Uncle Joe would sleep during World War II. Putin tried it once but it was absurdly lumpy and he got no sleep.

However, today Putin and his aides were doing some-thing Stalin never did: watching TV. All the international news networks streamed live coverage of America's turmoil. An aerial view of the smoking National Mall was shocking, even to the Kremlin apparatchiks, who smiled. Next came the pundits who agreed loose nukes may be covertly hidden in American cities by unknown foes, although many suspected Russia was behind it. The apparatchiks' smiles grew. Lastly, live footage of National Security Advisor George Jackson being dragged out of his home wearing only a bathrobe and handcuffs and arrested for treason. The apparatchiks beamed.

"What an idiot!" laughed one of the aides, and the rest joined in the ridicule chorus.

"And to think," said Putin while stirring his tea, "I barely lifted a finger."

Everyone chuckled in smug glee, a stark reversal from a few hours ago. Operation Zapad-20 (West-20) was launched in 2016 to sow chaos in America's capital, but declared a failure earlier this morning after one of their safe houses was mysteriously taken out. Everyone assumed it was a CIA hit, but their sources in the Agency denied it. Putin didn't care much because it was only mercenary casualties. The Wagner Group served many purposes, including dying.

But now this? thought Putin as he sipped his tea, smiling. The chaos yield surpassed even his optimal hopes. This was no accident; it was the work of a master.

"I wonder who did this," said one of the aides.

"Who knows. Who cares. How did Shakespeare put it?" said Putin, then spoke in heavily accented English. "'All's vell that ends vell.'"

Everyone chuckled.

CHAPTER 52

"Who was that?" asked Lin after I hung up. Only her mouth moved. The rest of her lay immobile on top of me.

"Dunno," I replied, equally spent. *How did they track me?* I wondered. "We should leave."

After a pause, she said, "Yeah."

Neither of us moved.

"We need to bounce," I said in a tender whisper. With a sigh, she rolled off and I sat up, ruing our predicament. My head was puzzling through the mysterious call.

"What did they want?" she asked, as I put on my pants and checked the time. It was 1900.

"They said they know where Winters is, and invited me to the party," I said from the bathroom.

"It's a trap," she offered.

"I know," I agreed, lacing up my boots. "That's why we need to scoot."

"Crap," she uttered, putting the back of a hand over her eyes. Neither of us wanted to go; instead we wanted to make the evening last all night. Now we were on the run again, from people we did not know. Real life was intruding once more. "Crap," she repeated.

Jen got vertical and started putting on her pantsuit.

"We need to find you something more practical to wear," I said.

"Practical to wear?" she guffawed.

"Yeah. You can't go running backstreets in a pant-suit," I said. At least she wore tasteful running shoes; presumably her heels were still under her desk at work.

"What?!" she retorted, offended. "As an FBI agent, I chased and arrested Russian mobsters all over New York City dressed in Ferragamo. Turns out Italian wool works just fine for roundhouse kicks and judo throws." Her eyes bore into me. "What do you know about women's clothes, anyway? When I want your fashion advice, I'll give it to you."

Yikes! I thought, chastised, while doing a functions check on my H&K. Then I did her Saiga and handed it to her.

"Thanks," she said coolly, taking the weapon while brushing knots out of her hair.

Catching myself in the mirror, I realized it was me who needed civilian clothes. I looked like a lost SWAT team member.

Knocking at the door.

We both froze, looked at each other, and then at the door. The knocking continued. Thinking the same thing, we swapped weapons. She took up a protected position from the bathroom, aiming the H&K at the door. The Saiga's wide shot pattern would have obliterated the enemy and me.

The rapping got louder. I stood with my back to the wall that was flush with the door, Saiga pointed at whoever walked through it. Jen nodded at me and I nodded back.

"Who is it?" I asked in a normal voice. The knock's rhythm changed to something out of a Bugs Bunny cartoon. Jen and I exchanged quizzical looks, and then fixed on the door again.

"Who *is* it?" I repeated in a stern voice.

"Open up," said the voice, exasperated.

Tye?! I thought. *How is that possible?*

"Let me in, lover boy," whispered Tye. Jen looked revolted, as I waved an all-clear sign, and opened the door. There was Tye, dressed in sport hiking clothes. The guy probably never wore a tie in his life.

"Tye!" I said in shock after the door closed. He bear-hugged me and, I think, cracked a rib. Jen looked bewildered, lowering her weapon.

"Introduce me to your lady," said Tye before I could ask a single question.

"Tye, Jen," I said, motioning one to the other. "Jen, Tye."

Jen looked equal parts polite and appalled.

"Nice weapon, Jen," he said admiringly. "Sounds like you're C4 in the sack, too. A real *heat* round," he joked.

Jen's face turned crimson, and she unconsciously pointed the H&K at Tye's chest.

"Whoa, whoa, whoa!" I said, lowering the assault weapon with my hand. "Tye's a friend."

"You know this jerkwad?" she asked me, astonished.

"Yeah. He's a battle buddy," I replied.

Her expression read: *Are you serious?* My expression replied: *Hells yeah.*

"Come on, lovebirds, we gotta go, now!" said Tye. "If we can track you, so can they."

"Wait," I interrupted, my head spinning. "How did

you find us? I thought you were captured. How are you here?"

"I'll explain in the van. We need to evac now," he said. Hastily we wrapped our weapons in bedsheets and followed Tye down the hall. Clients were busy behind the thin walls, and Jen avoided touching surfaces, door-knobs, everything.

We exited down a second-story fire escape with a defunct alarm. In the alley, a beat-up white van idled ready. I noticed it had new high-performance tires and was probably not your average plumber's ride, despite appearances. Tye opened the rear doors and gestured for us to enter as if he were a butler. Jen shook her head at his puerile behavior despite the gravity of the situation, while I grinned. We clambered inside and sat on a few wooden crates that probably concealed weapons and ammo.

"Let's go," Tye told the driver, and we sped out.

My mind reeled in confusion, I had so many questions. *Is he saving or abducting us?* That Apollo was divided was clear; however, which side Tye and Lava fought for was not. Maybe they worked for Winters? My mind didn't want to accept it, but I could not ignore it.

"Where are we going?" I asked.

"Someplace safe," said Tye, watching the road ahead. Jen looked concerned.

Exhaling deeply, I sat back. Tye was right about one thing: if he could find us, others could, too. The hotel was not safe. Probably no place was, except maybe with Tye and Lava. They were our least bad option. I regret-ted dragging Jen into Apollo's civil war, and needed to find out more.

"How did you find us so quickly?" I asked.

"You never were lost, buddy. Remember when Lava came to your safe house and he gave you a thermos of special energy drink?"

"Yeah, it tasted like fruit punch. I'm guessing now it had some sort of tracing agent."

"Correct, it was laced with nanotech. It lasts for a few days, and we've been tracking your every move."

I wondered who else could track me. The thought chilled me, but I needed to move on to the next question. "Tye, how is it possible you are here? I saw you and Lava get captured next to me on a rooftop by Winters's men." Then I realized the truth. "Have you both turned? Are you working for Winters now?"

Tye laughed, as did the driver. "No, Tom. It was a setup. Winters's men captured us, but not everyone on his team is working for him. We have guys on the inside feeding us intel and releasing captives, including Lava and me. We escaped. It was all part of the plan, and you were the bait."

"The bait?" asked Jen, shocked.

"Correct. I'm sorry, Tom, but we had no choice," said Tye, turning to face me with sincerity in his voice.

"No choice?!" responded Jen defensively. She seemed more irate than me.

"The public doesn't know it, but there's a secret war going on in the United States and the stakes are existential, just like during the Cold War," said Tye. "Our client wants Winters's foreign client identified and neutralized, 'off the books' in ways the CIA can't do anymore. That's our contract. We've been running a mole hunt to smoke Winters out, but he doesn't make mistakes. Our mission in New York was to hack Elektra and reveal

Winters's client, but the mission failed. They now have nuclear weapons on U.S. soil, waiting to detonate." Tye turned to me. "We are *losing* and need an edge. That edge is you."

I heard but did not comprehend. "Say again?"

"We needed to flush out Winters but we didn't know how, then you came back from the dead. We used you as bait, Tom, knowing you were the only thing that could lure Winters out of the shadows. But to set Winters in play, we had to get you captured, and fake our own capture. Then it was simply following the body trail, which led us here."

"Where is 'here'?" asked Jen.

"'Here' is the imminent demise of Brad Winters and his mysterious client," said Tye, turning to face us again. "Are you still fit to fight, Locke?"

"Always."

"How about your girlfriend?" he asked, looking at Jen.

"Always," she said, with less enthusiasm.

"Good. Because we're going to need every swinging muzzle we can find for this one."

"One what, exactly?" asked Jen distrustfully.

"For this operation," said Tye with resolve. "We are going to take down Winters once and for all. And we need your help. Both of you."

CHAPTER 53

Winters slumped in the leather chair as the plane hit turbulence. His steak went untouched; it reminded him of the Rottweilers. He sat alone in the corporate jet, save the steward, who avoided him, and checked his watch again.

Eight hours, he thought. He had eight hours to formulate a new plan, because that was when the plane would land outside of Washington. So far, his plan was rudimentary: kill Locke. Everything else was already in place: the nukes, the controller, and the extortion. Why could the old man not see his victory? But Winters knew the answer.

"Inbred nitwit," he muttered. Generations of intermarriage had dimmed aristocratic IQs over the centuries the same way a fine oil painting fades when left in sunlight. The old man was timid, like a serf. But the Chevalier's treating him like a dog was unforgivable.

"When I am done with Locke, I am coming for you, Chevalier," he swore under his breath. Settling scores gave him purpose. Only now did Winters comprehend that he always possessed the tools he needed and had never required the Chevalier's assistance. Experience is something you get only after you need it.

It's now my *time,* he thought. Once Locke and the

Chevalier were disappeared, Winters would locate and reclaim the nuclear briefcase. Then he would bring the U.S. and Russia to the brink of war, exploiting the ensuing chaos for wealth and power. Iago was his favorite Shakespeare character, and Winters never understood why Iago was vilified rather than admired.

Yes, it would be easy enough, he mused, inspired by the Chevalier's near detonation of Washington, DC. Two crazed countries with a history of enmity; simply vaporize an American city and frame Russia. The rest would take care of itself. He didn't give a damn about either anymore. The Americans were hunting him, owing to his connection to Jackson, and the Russians soon would be. The Chevalier would undoubtedly tip off Moscow once Winters had outlived his usefulness.

Faithless black knight, Winters thought as his hand squeezed his cane. He was happy to see them all burn. Revenge is justice in an unjust world, he believed. But first, there was a personal matter begging his attention.

"Locke, Locke, Locke," hissed Winters. "Where are you?" Locke was a bad-luck charm that needed killing. Until he was off the gameboard, nothing was certain. More important, watching Locke tortured to death slowly would give Winters peace. After all, it was Locke who'd set him up in Saudi Arabia, where he spent a year in a torture gulag awaiting beheading. He escaped, but his larynx was crushed and his right knee smashed. Locke owed him, and he intended to collect with payday-loan interest.

"Now that you have earned my full attention, Locke, there is no place you can slither to this time," said Winters with the zeal of a trophy hunter. He had already activated every stringer at his disposal to search for the miscreant, although it would be instantaneous if Elektra was still online. *What a waste,* he thought with pity.

Winters flipped through the news channels to get his mind off of Locke. They all replayed footage of Jackson being hauled out of his house drunk, in a bathrobe at ten that morning. Winters belly-laughed, and it made him feel better. *Old fool. I warned you, didn't I?*

The news prattled on about stock market jitters, politicians blaming one another, urban flight, domestic terrorism, Brad Winters.

What?! Winters lurched out of his seat. There was a picture of him on the TV, an older photo taken from before his Riyadh internment. Winters turned up the volume.

"Brad Winters . . . conspiracy . . . Winters . . . domestic terrorism . . ." The newscaster was remarkably well informed about Winters's background. No journalist knew this much about his life.

Impossible! he thought, feeling lightheaded and sweaty. Flipping channels, he saw every major news outlet carried a similar story. A foreign-language news crawl even had his name: BRAD WINTERS. In a panic, he checked internet news sites; his name, picture, and biography were plastered everywhere.

"Shit!" exclaimed Winters as he shut off the monitor, cringing. "Shit, shit!" Winters was always five steps ahead of everyone else, and ten ahead of his foes. How had he been so spectacularly blindsided? It was a bullet in the head for a man like Winters.

Who did this to me? His mind raced. Maybe it was the Chevalier? *No, he has too much to lose by exposing me now.* Jackson? *No, I dusted my trail. All Jackson's raving will lead the FBI in circles.* Locke? *No, the media would not find him a credible source.* Apollo? *No, they would never risk the blowback.* A foreign power? Terrorists? Others? No. He had many enemies but none with this level of information.

Whoever leaked my identity to the press has power, real power. The kind that Winters sought, and that was what scared him. It had been a long time since he tasted fear. Even in the Riyadh prison cell, he somehow knew he would negotiate a way out. But now, who would he bargain with?

Damn you, whoever you are! he thought with venom. With shaky hands, he picked up a water glass and drank. *I will outlast this, find you, and kill you.*

"I'll need a new plan," said Winters to himself. "Bold. Creative. Unexpected." His fingers absentmindedly tapped the burl wood table. Gazing out the window, his brow furled in concentration as he puzzled out the angles. He considered turning the plane around to seek safe harbor; he had multiple secret bank accounts and a private island halfway around the world just for such a day. But he shook his head.

"Nothing changes, except the timeline," he concluded. "The sooner I control the WMD, the sooner I become a superpower, and then game on." There would be no shortcuts. He still had to start with Locke, then the Chevalier, then the nuclear briefcase. All within days. Then find and fix whoever leaked his identity to the media. It was mission impossible for most, but not Winters.

"I will survive this," he resolved. He sat immobile with a grave expression, his fingers interlaced under his nose. Ten minutes passed. Twenty. Thirty. At last he smiled, then laughed. *It was so obvious!* he thought.

"Hammersmith Hall," murmured Winters with a proud grin. It was the Chevalier's estate on Long Island's Gold Coast, managed under layers of shell companies, and where he first met the Chevalier. No one would think to look for him there. Even better, it was defendable. The 1904 mansion sat on a private peninsula, surrounded by water and hundreds of acres of patrolled land with an Israeli-style border fence. Nothing got in or out without the guards' knowledge. It was an ideal location to regroup and prepare for an attack he knew would be coming.

"Overkill is underrated," he said, picking up the phone. Within ten minutes, all his key assets were mobilizing for Hammersmith Hall, and most would arrive before he did. He instructed the estate to receive his visitors, but neglected to say they would be extremely armed and dangerous. Once his Apollo teams locked down the estate, they would prepare for the next phase: attack. Later, Winters would solicit the Chevalier's forgiveness, after his victory. *In fact, that meeting could be the perfect opportunity to capture the Chevalier,* Winters thought with a grin.

"Pilots, divert to Westchester, New York, and lay on a chopper. A fast one."

"Yes sir," said the voice over the intercom.

Just one more call to make, the most important one of all, he thought as the plane banked slightly right. After he was finished, he placed the phone back in its holder and stared at the dark clouds below. *Not only will I kill Locke, I will destroy all my enemies in a single blow.*

"The die is cast," he declared, reminded of Julius Caesar crossing the Rubicon to invade Rome.

CHAPTER 54

After driving an hour on country roads, we pulled into a community airport in The Middle of Nowhere, Virginia. The tarmac's residents were single-engine planes, two crop dusters, and one Stearman biplane. At the end was an uncharacteristically large hangar, our destination. The massive doors shut behind the van as we coasted to a stop.

"We're here," said Tye, stepping out. We were not alone. The place was teeming with people and vehicles of all types. Crammed in the hanger was a Bombardier corporate jet and four turboprop, twin-engine cargo planes, like the aircraft Lava used over Manhattan. A work crew was heaving a space-age hunk of machinery up the tailgate of the nearest one.

"Is that a drone?" asked Jen as we passed. It looked like an armed rotary-wing drone with its boom and blades folded up. Attached was a cargo chute.

"Yes," I said, thinking that would have been handy in Manhattan. Mechanics were sliding air-to-air missiles on the rails of two fixed-wing jet drones, presumably our escorts. They were twenty feet of black sleekness, and looked like half-size fighter jets rather than the wide-wing variants used by the U.S. government.

"What are those?" asked Jen, amazed. She was pointing to the two fighter jet drones.

"Apollo proprietary tech," said one of the mechanics, overhearing her. "We call them Hunters because they can search and destroy targets autonomously. No humans in the kill loop."

"But isn't that dangerous?" she asked, as I tried to pull her along. We had a lot to do. The mechanic looked confused, as if saying, *All war is dangerous.*

"She's new here," I told him as we left.

"Hey, Locke, grab gear. You'll know it when you see it," shouted Tye over the din as he walked away. Parked against the wall was a box van of HALO equipment and oxygen bottles. Another was loaded with body armor and weapons. A third was filled with ammunition and demo. An assembly line of technicians equipped male and female warriors. Apollo was getting ready for battle; except I had never seen a full-court press before.

"What is this place?" asked Jen as we ducked under the wing of the corporate jet. People shuffled around us, moving with a purpose, but there was a jitteriness in the air. Several were wheeling matte-black dirt bikes onto one cargo plane. Jen cocked her head in surprise, noticing they had no license plates, lights of any kind, or mufflers. They were unique.

"Apollo Outcomes, my old company," I said. *Or what's left of it,* I thought. Apollo's civil war had taken a toll, and the hangar had a Rebel-Alliance-on-planet-Hoth vibe.

"What are we doing here?" whispered Jen, troubled.

"It's not your fight, Jen. You don't need to be here," I said, hoping she would say it was her fight, too. But she said nothing. "Let's find Lava, my old commander. We both have questions and he has answers."

Two people passed us wearing head-to-toe battle armor that made them look like black cyborgs, and with futuristic assault rifles slung over their shoulders. Jen stood still, gaping.

"What is that?" she asked, pointing to their weapons.

"Precision-guided firearms. One shot, one kill, guaranteed by AI. Shoots around corners, from choppers, and through Kevlar like margarine, even when sprinting. Standard issue at Apollo."

"Holy crap," she murmured.

"Our military could have the same equipment if the government's procurement system wasn't so FUBAR."

"I'm starting to understand what you were saying about Apollo. I just didn't . . . believe it," she said.

"Few do. I didn't either, until I was recruited. They don't hire; they only recruit," I said, scanning the hangar for Lava, but no luck. Along the back wall were four thirty-foot satellite trucks, like the kind TV networks use, except these were different: NSA-level command and control nodes with cyber warriors and drone pilots for mobile operations. In the past, one truck would support a high-intensity mission. I had never seen four deployed simultaneously. In fact, I had never seen four at all.

It looks like a final stand, I thought.

"Tom, who's that?" asked Jen. In a corner, a burly tall man surrounded by people waved at us.

"That's Lava," I said. "Let's go."

We clasped forearms and he pounded my back in greeting. "Nice to see you back, Tom. We need your gun on this one. It's big. It's everything."

"Lava, about using me to get Winters . . ." I said with anger, but he cut me off.

"And who is this?" he asked warmly, extending a hand to Jen.

"Um," Jen looked at me, wondering if she should give her real name.

"You must be Ms. Jennifer P. Lin, former FBI agent," said Lava. "You know the Bureau has issued an arrest warrant for you." Jen's face went white. "Makes no difference to us, of course. We're outside the law."

"Jen's one of the good guys . . . er, gals," I said.

"So I've heard," said Lava with genuine admiration. "Good work last night, taking down one of Wagner's safe houses, and solo no less. I'm impressed." Her mouth dropped. "Even Tye was impressed, and that's rare." Lava chuckled. "I don't know what you did this morning, but he called you a thermonuclear tigress." Lava gave me a knowing smile.

Jen's expression transformed from astonishment to wrath, and her fists balled up.

"More later. But first . . ." Lava clambered onto the top of a truck so all could see him. "Gather around, everyone! Gather around!" People dropped what they were doing and assembled in front of Lava. They numbered about seventy in all, the last of Apollo Outcomes. It was once six hundred.

"It's been a long campaign. We've all lost friends, but the time has come to strike back and end this war in a single, decisive attack. Our client leaked Winters's identity to the media, hoping it would force him to make a mistake we can exploit. It did."

The group murmured in speculation, and Lava continued.

"We have actionable intelligence on where and when Winters *and his entire team* will be in three hours. We must hit them *now,* while they are regrouping and not when they have regrouped. Surprise is on our side, making this our one, best, and last chance to eliminate the threat. If we fail, Winters and his foreign enemy client may destroy three American cities and dictate terms to the White House. We can never allow that to happen."

Murmurs of alarm in a variety of languages escalated. Lava then gave the mission brief, making an impromptu "sand table" on the hangar floor using airplane chocks as buildings, rope for terrain features, and coffee cups as units, both friendly and enemy. He walked around with a broomstick, pointing at units as he explained the plan.

"This is crazy!" whispered Jen in my ear as the plan became evident.

"We specialize in crazy," I replied with no irony. She grabbed my hand, perhaps unconsciously, but her expression remained impassive for the rest of the brief. At the end, the team let out a battle cry, and everyone hurried back to their tasks. Wheels up in three-zero mikes.

"We need to talk," said Jen in her business voice. I followed her into a tool cage toward the back of the maintenance annex.

"Who are you fighting?" she asked.

"Wagner Group mercenaries and Apollo renegades," I answered, and explained Winters. She absorbed it.

"Let me get this straight," she said. "Your old boss, Winters, finds a foreign client. In exchange for power, money, whatever, he recovers three nuclear bombs that he previously stole from Pakistan—"

"I tried to stop him in Iraq and Syria," I added.

"—then he goes into business with the Wagner Group, Russian mercenaries—"

"They wiped out my team in Ukraine. Winters sold me out," I interrupted again, bitter.

Jen ignored me. "—and Wagner hires the Shulaya mafia to smuggle nukes into New Jersey. At the same time, Winters returns to Apollo and creates a schism within the company, hijacking half of it. They bury the three nukes in American cities, and give the trigger to a foreign, unknown client. Is that correct?"

I nodded.

"You have some fucked-up colleagues," she opined.

I nodded again. "No longer colleagues, and about to become extinct. Winters's whole team is massing as we speak, and we can take them out in one assault. It's gutsy, but Lava is right. It's our one and only chance."

"And who is your client?" Jen asked, ever the investigator. I honestly did not know, and she shook her head in disapproval.

"I trust Lava," I blurted, surprising myself. But my gut knew him to be true.

Jen glared at me. "Are you really dumb enough to do this, Tom?"

I was taken aback. "Yes. Absolutely. Why do you think I came out of hiding from halfway around the world? If we don't stop this here and now, we might as well auction off the Oval Office to any foreign power willing to pay third parties."

Jen crossed her arms and shot me a look of enraged disappointment, as I stood resolute.

"Hey!" It was Tye's voice, as he poked his head into the tool cage. "I've been looking for you everywhere.

We got fifteen minutes before wheels up. You need to suit up, Locke." Then he noticed our body language. "Lovers' quarrel?"

Jen spun around and scowled at him. I had never seen Tye slink away so fast. I grabbed her hands and we hugged, then kissed. I could taste her salty tears. Curiously, I never thought about death before an operation, no matter how risky. Death is what happens to other people, I irrationally believed.

"You don't need to do this. It's not your fight," I said again.

"Yes, it is. You came out of hiding and I left the FBI for the same reason. We've risked everything for this opportunity." We kissed again.

"Let's go, yous!" bellowed Tye's voice from the hangar. A minute later, we emerged. The hangar was frantic, and the main doors were open. Vehicles were departing and ground crews were towing out the aircraft. The night air refreshed the hangar.

"Locke, you're on me again. We're on bird alpha," said Tye, pointing to one of the cargo aircraft. "You know the drill."

"Roger," I said, looking at the tech assembly line by the three box vans. They were waving to me to hurry up.

Then Tye turned to Jen. "Are you in the fight?"

Jen paused and looked at me then the aircraft. One of the turboprops spun to life, followed by others. She nodded.

"Is that a yes?" asked Tye with care.

"Yes, yes. Count me in. I speak Russian. It might come in handy."

"I know it will," said Tye. "Everyone is glad you're on the team." He pointed to the corporate jet being towed onto the tarmac. "You're riding in that. When it lands, you will be on the ground team. Jinx will brief you in-flight. Locke can help with your equipment." He slapped me on the shoulder twice, put on his black helmet, and jogged over to our cargo plane.

Jen and I suited up at the vans, and I taught her how to operate the tactical cuff with its AI. She opted to keep her Saiga automatic shotgun and grabbed four more grenades, "for old times' sake," she said nervously.

"Hey Locke, hurry your ass up!" I heard Tye yell from the aircraft. The hunter drones taxied to the air-strip and screeched into the sky. One of the cargo planes started rolling. It was time.

"Come back to me," I said.

"Kick ass, my darling," she whispered in my ear, then slapped my butt and sauntered to the Bombardier jet, her long hair billowing in the prop blast.

I smiled, locking the image of her in my memory, then double-timed to the lead cargo plane. Minutes later, we were all airborne and flying north.

CHAPTER 55

The business helicopter touched down on the manicured lawn after dark, the rotor wash blowing leaves and dirt into the empty marble swimming pool. The backdrop was a faux Normandy castle, complete with ivy-covered turrets and hypergothic architecture, like Neuschwanstein's baby cousin.

Staff members rushed out to greet the chopper; some wore butler black tie while others looked like SWAT. Winters lumbered out of the aircraft, his overcoat flapping in the down wash. As soon as the door closed, the engines whined as the pilots pulled pitch, sending the Sikorski S-76 up in a graceful swoop toward Long Island Sound.

"Where are the commanders?" yelped Winters to no one in particular. "I want a sitrep ASAP!"

A man dressed in black body armor with a bullpup assault rifle nodded to the others, who returned to the mansion.

"Who are you?" demanded Winters.

"I've been assigned as your aide-de-camp for this phase of the operation, sir," said the commando, clearly not a job he volunteered for. "The commanders are assembling in the library, waiting for you, sir."

Winters's chin bobbed, a faint nod of approval.

Hammersmith House sat on its own peninsula, which

jutted out into the sound. It was built during the Gilded Age by a robber baron of industry, its stones meant to rival the nobility of Blenheim Palace in England. Exquisite gardens sloped downward from the grand portico to the shoreline and offered superlative views of Connecticut on the horizon. The surrounding grounds were mostly wooded, lending a pastoral beauty at odds with the asphalt of Manhattan, thirty miles away. However, Winters took no notice of it.

"What are our troop levels?" asked Winters as he walked across the lawn to the mansion. He moved with vigor, despite his infirmity. The scent of battle animated him, giving him inexplicable strength. Whatever monster he had mutated into, he began as a soldier at West Point, and he was a good one, too.

"About ninety percent assembled, sir. We expect stragglers over the next twenty-four hours."

Winters shook his head and the aide felt the scorn. "Show me the rest of the defenses," he said as he marched forward.

Heavily armed men dressed in black scurried about, turning the Gold Coast mansion into an Afghanistan firebase. The estate's staff scampered about, mortified. The decorative eighteenth-century porcelain collections were a particular worry, and a footman sprawled his body across a display case as two paramilitaries eyed the hand-painted figurines with curiosity.

Winters and the aide reached the expansive stone patio facing the sound. It was built for outdoor parties of four hundred during the Gatsby era, but now it entertained missile launchers and auto-turrets, covering every conceivable avenue of approach.

Winters surveyed the battleground: a one-thousand-foot lawn and garden from the mansion to the sea. Men were laying antipersonnel mines, and two Boston Whaler speedboats were pressed into service patrolling the banks with machine guns and automatic grenade launchers. Then he looked skyward.

"Where's the air defenses? I ordered this kitsch shrine transformed into a fortress. Nothing in or out. And that means the goddamn heavens too!" he shouted, jabbing his cane at the stars.

The aide gestured to the roof. Winters leaned back and squinted into the moonless sky. "Give me those," he said, removing the aide's night vision. Donning it, he could see men patrolling the imitation battlements. Some were snipers while others had surface-to-air missiles on their shoulders. "Where is our radar? What kind of early warning do we have?"

"We have tapped all ground radar from local airports," said the aide. "It's not Patriot missile quality, but it should work."

"Not good enough," Winters grumped. "Drones. Show me."

"Follow me, sir," replied the aide.

They entered the mansion, a temple of antiques and art. They passed a squad of Russian-speaking mercenaries, then Spanish speakers. Then a group of English speakers unpacking crates of Claymore mines and blasting caps. The only things they all had in common were heavy weapons and a penchant for black.

It's like the Tower of Babel in here, thought Winters. There were two command languages, Russian and English, increasing the chances of fratricide. To date, the Wagner Group and Apollo mercenaries had never fought together, only against each other.

Winters hobbled across the harlequin tile of the grand foyer, commandos stepping out of his way in respect. He walked like MacArthur returning to the Philippines. The aide gestured toward the front door, a monstrosity of wood and iron. Beyond it, on the other great lawn, were rows of armed rotary and fixed-wing drones.

"The fixed wings are capable of vertical takeoff. Another six are patrolling the skies right now. What you see is the airborne quick reaction force that can deploy within twenty seconds. Main armaments include 7.62 mini-guns, Hellfires, and Stingers," said the aide like a salesman.

"OK," mumbled Winters, and the aide smiled. It was as close to a compliment as anyone would receive from the boss.

"Do you want me to show you the forward firing positions?" asked the aide. "We have minefields, mortars, and obstacles to channel a ground assault into an ambush kill zone. We requisitioned"—meaning *stole*—"and outfitted speedboats. Two are patrolling the shoreline as we speak, using acoustic detection for a waterborne assault. The Russians made improvised depth charges."

"What about an air assault?" asked Winters, listening closely as they walked the grounds.

"The Wagner Group has next-generation Verba surface-to-air missiles scanning the sky, better than the ones the Russian army uses. They are positioned across the peninsula, giving us defense in depth and interlocking fires. Anyone foolish enough to attack us by land, sea, or air will be sent to their maker, and fast."

Winters liked the man's spirit, and paused to consider if he would be his next protégé or cannon fodder. He judged the latter, and hobbled away. Both men snaked

HIGH TREASON · 359

through the firing line, as mercenaries filled sandbags and converted marbled architecture into fighting positions. The library reminded Winters of the Chevalier, with his exquisite carpets, the smell of old leather books, and eight-pointed stars on the ceiling.

"Atten-HUN!" yelled a former Marine as Winters entered the spacious room. Everyone stood at attention, their battle dress a collage of origin and technology. Winters took the seat at the head of a long oaken table. The magnificent library now served as a tactical operations center, with map boards, laptops, and large monitors. The background noise was a polyglot of radio chatter.

The staff was bifurcated. At Winters's right sat English-speaking ex-Apollo warriors with next-generation battle gear. On his left were the Russian commanders of the Wagner Group. What they lacked in tech they made up for in attitude. There was neither enmity nor love between them, just a common mission.

"Skip the brief. I just walked the line, and do you know what I saw?" said Winters, pausing for an answer from the group. None came. "Weak defenses. We're not ready."

"Sir, with all due respect," said one of the ex-Apollo commanders. "We've only been on the ground a few hours and have secured the AO. Give us a day and it will be Fort Knox."

"We don't have a day," rasped Winters. "Make no mistake about it. What's left of Apollo is a desperate, cornered wild animal. They will attack tonight. *Tonight!*" Winters grasped his throat in pain, as alarm was expressed in numerous languages.

"But how is that possible?" asked a Wagner Group

commander with a heavy Russian accent. "Even we didn't know where we would be eight hours ago."

"Because *I* leaked them our position," responded Winters coolly.

Silence. Then the Russian spoke again, with care, voicing what everyone was thinking. "But why would you do such a thing? Why not wait a day? In twenty-four hours we will be at one hundred percent strength and dug in."

"Because it's a trap. Waiting a day would not bait them because they know we have numerical superiority. It must be tonight! If they thought we were still collecting our forces and vulnerable—and they had the element of surprise—they would attack us with everything they have. When they do attack, we will obliterate them in a single battle!" Winters leaned forward, fist clenched and spittle flying from his mouth.

The commanders pumped their fists in the air, whooping their support in a babel of tongues. Winters continued, and they quieted down.

"We have more troops, more firepower, and the advantage of a prepared defensive position. They think we are weak and regrouping, but that is a ruse. Their attack will be our opportunity to wipe them out cleanly, once and for all!"

Cheers resounded and butt stocks banged on antique tables.

"And when the last of old Apollo is gone, there will be nothing to stop us. Our moment of victory is at hand!"

Multicultural battle cries filled the library in a roar of warfare. Winters sat back, pleased. With any luck, Locke would come, too—and when he did, Winters would have a special surprise waiting for him.

CHAPTER 56

The cargo airplane's rear ramp lowered, and night air blasted us. The lights of Manhattan were far below, and two more cargo planes flew behind us. Somewhere beyond were the Hunters escorting us. The Bombardier corporate jet and the other cargo airplane had flown ahead and were already on the ground. Jen would be among them, but doing what I didn't know.

"Five minutes," came the pilot's voice over my headset. The door light flicked on to red, meaning it was not time to jump. We were not the only thing HALOing in; two rotary-wing drones were packaged up and ready to free-fall. The loadmaster came aft to triple-check their cargo chutes as we inspected our own. With a voice command, my HUD came alive.

"OK, team, this it," came Lava's voice over the command net.

Tye turned to me. "You a go?"

I nodded, and he slapped the side of my arm in support.

"Check equipment!" shouted Lava, and we all sounded off. I was slinging the newest precision-guided firearm with tag-and-shoot technology. It looked like a regular 7.62 mm assault rifle with a built-in sound suppressor, except it had a larger scope with a convex bug-eye. No need to zero it, either; its onboard computer did everything. The weapon also produced enough chamber pressure to shoot through any kind of body armor. Strapped to my thigh was a tactical bullpup shotgun less than two feet long that held nine shells. Good for tight firefights.

"Ground team on the move," said Lava, and we cheered. Lava was the mission commander and monitored all Apollo command nets, while I heard just my team's. Like horse blinders, sometimes it's better to focus on what's in front of you rather than the whole world.

"One minute," said the pilot. The loadmaster made a final adjustment to the drones' rigs and then scooched forward, away from the tail ramp.

"I want a nice, clean exit," said Lava, standing on the edge of the ramp with the ground thirty-five thousand feet below. Lava always led by example.

"Ten seconds," said the pilot.

"Clear the deck," commanded Lava, and we all got behind the drones, ready to push.

"Five, four, three, two, one." The light switched to green, and the two drones were sucked out the fuselage by a drogue chute, making an audible *zing*. We followed, diving en masse off the ramp headfirst. The other two planes zoomed overhead, and I felt their prop blast.

Looking around, I saw thirty-five jumpers and six drones hurtling to Earth. Each drone was packaged up in a ball of aluminum and firepower. In the southwest, the lights of Manhattan contrasted to the inkiness of the sound to the north and Connecticut in the distance. At this altitude, our planes were out of range of all but the best surface-to-air missiles and in any case would be profiled like commercial flights. In the distance, my HUD tracked the two Hunters circling us protectively, but they were invisible to most radar and the naked eye in the moonless night. We were also mostly invisible. Skydivers are difficult to spot on radar, making HALO a good ingress for covert missions.

"Chase the drones!" commanded Lava, and we all dove ahead. My HUD lit up one of the drones in green, five hundred feet below; the machine's small drogue parachute slowed and stabilized it as it fell. Its twin side rotors and tail boom were folded in, making it more streamlined. I assumed the flat-track position in my wingsuit and sped toward it.

"Locke, give me a hand," said Tye, who had already met the drone and was now kneeling on top of it and working a loose cargo strap. But I was coming in too fast. "Watch your speed! Watch your speed!" he said as I nearly collided into him.

"Quit screwing around, Locke," he jibed as I circled around for another pass. His armed reach out and snagged me, pulling me in, while his other was anchored to the drone.

"Thanks, man," I said. Because he was my designated battle buddy, we could communicate directly without anyone hearing us.

"Don't mention it."

"Positions," commanded Tye as four more jumpers arrived. We gathered on one side of the drone. "Control it! Control it! It's rotating clockwise!" said Tye, floating above us. With precision, he dropped and rammed against the direction of spin. We all fought it, gaining control.

"Now fly it!" shouted Tye. The drone had no wingsuit, like us. To get it over the drop zone required "flying" it, but that was an understatement. Lining up on the same side, we spread our legs in the delta position, pushing the drone toward the estate twenty-four thousand feet below.

"That's it! Keep it up," said Tye.

The Bombardier and the other cargo plane touched down at a community airport about twenty miles from the objective. The ground commander, call sign Jinx, went over the mission inflight. Lin couldn't believe what she was hearing. It was suicide. Even crazier than the time her FBI SWAT team was ambushed by two dozen mafia foot soldiers in a Brooklyn warehouse. She took a bullet that day, saved by her body armor. But it felt like a truck hit her.

No one else on the plane seemed too concerned about the plan's insanity quotient, so she kept her mouth shut. The last seventy-two hours had been a string of life-stunning events, so why question things now?

The Apollo tactical armor felt strange, almost flimsy. As soon as she deplaned, she did a series of high kicks on the tarmac that landed in a split. Incredibly, the armor moved with her like a leotard. While still in a split, she held up her armored hands and waved them around in the dark, her HUD revealing colors, allies, objective, her vitals, everything. *Unbelievable,* she thought.

"Hey Princess, gonna stop playing with yourself and get back in the war?" It was her assigned battle buddy. She went by the name Valkyrie and was one of the few women to serve in Delta before jumping the fence for

Apollo. Lin did not care for her, and the feeling was obviously mutual.

"On me, Princess," said Valkyrie as they double-timed to the cargo plane, where the rest of the team was wheeling out motorbikes. Only the field surgeon remained in the Bombardier. Lin followed Valkyrie into the cargo plane and helped unstrap a large dirt bike. Before Valkyrie could walk it out, Lin blocked her.

"Listen, Valkyrie, if you want this night to go well, stop calling me Princess. Do you understand?" said Lin in her command voice.

"Anything you say, Tinkerbell. Now help or get out of the way."

Lin let her pass. Now was not the time to pick a fight. Valkyrie started the bike in perfect silence; it was electric.

"Come on, get on," said Valkyrie. Lin swung her leg over the back and mounted. "Strap in, Dimples." Lin's fists balled up, and she fantasized about twisting this jackass's neck.

Be cool, Jen. Be cool, she thought, calming herself down. She looked around for a strap or seat belt but saw none. Valkyrie twisted around and reached down, extracting two thin nylon straps from each side of the seat.

"Clip these to your belt," said Valkyrie. Lin snapped them to the body armor's D-ring belt buckle. Conveniently, they had quick-release levers in case she needed to ditch.

What the crap am I getting into? she thought.

"Keep that Saiga up. Don't shoot until I tell you. And do not blow our surprise," cautioned Valkyrie in a tone suggesting she disdained babysitting newbies.

"Got it," said Lin.

The crew wheeled out an armed rotary-wing drone from the cargo plane, and unfolded its dual, traverse rotors. It looked like a miniature V-22 Osprey with a rotorless tail boom. Its chin was a mini-gun turret, and missile pods were its flanks. A minute later it was hovering, controlled by remote pilots.

"Our guardian angel," said Valkyrie over the headset.

The municipal airport was closed after dark, but it did not stop a beat-up, compact car from speeding toward them, an amber strobe pulsing on top.

"Ye gads, local airport security. Pathetic," spat Valkyrie. The two aircraft powered up and started taxiing toward the runway.

"Let's ride!" yelled Jinx, a woman. Apollo's ranks had a lot of female warriors, Lin realized. She liked it.

The drone vanished into the darkness, scouting the route ahead. Sixteen riders mounted twelve bikes. None of the vehicles had lights because the HUD showed everything like daytime. Lin found it a little freaky.

"Keep the Saiga pointed forward, but do not shoot my arm, baby doll," said Valkyrie. She accelerated so hard that Lin almost dropped her weapon. The only thing that held her in place were the safety straps.

Crap! thought Lin as she struggled to right herself. The shadow bike gang swooshed around the security vehicle in black silence, making it skid sideways as the driver panicked. Then they ghosted into the night.

"Sir, we've got activity. Looks like you were right," said the aide, although it was unnecessary.

Of course I was right, thought Winters. The library-cum–tactical operations center had been buzzing since they'd electronically eavesdropped on a call to the police. The local airport security guard reported seeing a corporate jet and military cargo plane land and its crew start unloading motorcycles. The police thought nothing of it, but Winters knew it was Apollo.

"High alert," commanded Winters as he stirred a cup of tea. Like Napoleon, he liked to fast before battles. It honed his strategic thinking.

"*High alert!*" yelled the battle captain, and a siren blared outside. Men ran to position. The battle captain had the body of an operator and the face of a cowboy. In a past life, he commanded at every level in U.S. Army Special Forces, up to general. Now he quarterbacked operations for Winters and was exceedingly good at it.

"Get the fixed wings in the air. Find them. Kill them," said Winters calmly. All was going as planned. *They are easy to bait because they are stupid*, he thought as he sipped his tea.

The battle captain gave a nod, and pilots in the library wearing virtual reality goggles worked joysticks. In the background, the jet drones whirred to life. A second later they were gone.

"Fixed-wing drones deployed," confirmed the battle captain. Silence, save the background radio chatter. The long, oak library table was crowded with specialists wearing headphones and working laptops. Monitors displayed what the drones saw, which was nothing out of the ordinary as they skimmed the roads and trees, scanning for prey.

Winters checked the time and estimated they had four minutes before the Apollo motorcycles would cross the estate fence. Plenty of time to kill them, he knew.

"How many tangos?" he asked. "Do we have an estimate?"

"Ground surveillance radar?" said the battle captain.

"Scopes are clean," replied a technician.

Something nagged at Winters. With a corporate jet and cargo plane, he calculated a motorcycle ground attack could range from ten to sixteen riders, and probably a drone. A threat, if they had the element of surprise, but they didn't. But could this small force really be Apollo's main effort? It didn't completely scan, yet all the other sensors showed zero activity.

"Chatter on local 5G spectrum in ops box," said a tech. "Could be something."

"What are they saying?" asked the battle captain, who walked up behind him and looked over his shoulder.

"Uh . . . hard to discern. One guy is telling another he thinks he just witnessed wild horses running in the night. Other guy thinks he's high again."

"That's them," said Winters.

"But sir, it could be anything," said the battle captain with caution. He did not want to tie up precious assets chasing down every hunch. They had one minute to find the threat.

"That's them," repeated Winters. "Deploy the drone QRF."

The battle captain nodded, and the rest of the drones took off.

"Annihilate them," said Winters, sipping tea. Main effort or not, he saw no reason why they needed to live.

"Incoming!" yelled Jinx over the radio net, and Lin's heart jumped. Four red dots blinked on her HUD, indicating the enemy drones. A missile arced across the sky and blew up their drone, sending it crashing into the trees where it exploded.

"Follow me," said Jinx, and the lead bike peeled off the back road and into the wood line.

Did she just drive into the trees? thought Lin in horror. Then all the bikes raced into the woods, going for cover. Trees and speed afforded some protection against missiles.

"Hang on!" yelled Valkyrie, as they bounced through the woods at 40 mph. It was a mature forest with minimal underbrush, making it dangerous but navigable. Missiles exploded tree trunks around them, blowing shards of wood everywhere. Lin was too stunned to be scared, as Valkyrie dodged trees.

"Contact! Request backup," radioed Jinx. "Backup twenty seconds," Jinx relayed to the team.

"Jinx, you have three more fast movers inbound," warned Mission Control, and Lin's HUD showed two additional red dots in the distance, although she could see nothing.

"Ah shit," said Valkyrie.

Before Lin understood why, she felt her weight press into the seat as they raced up a sharp slope and became airborne, jumping thirty feet in the air. They were exposed.

Eeeeeeeeeeeeee! sounded an alarm in Lin's earpiece.

"Tone!" yelled Valkyrie as they flew through branches. Missiles burst trees around them as they fell back to earth. They landed hard and Valkyrie fought for control, showing great skill as they recovered.

Three drone jets screamed over them, skimming the treetops. Then they exploded; Lin felt the concussion

370 ·

wave as they fireballed through the night sky. A second later, one of Apollo's larger Hunter drones shrieked above.

"Yeah!!" shouted Valkyrie.

"We just lost three drones," said the battle captain in shock. "What happened? Surface-to-air missiles?"

"Negative. The thermal trails came from the air, and low altitude," said a tech, monitoring a laptop.

"An enemy drone?" said the battle captain, contemplating the implications. If true, it was new stealth technology and could tip the battle.

We're not prepared for this, thought Winters.

"We lost two more!" shouted the tech.

"Where is it? Somebody get me a bead on the enemy drone!" commanded the battle captain. "We can't kill what we can't see."

Hunter drones, thought Winters uneasily. They were next generation, and he realized they possessed no radar that would see them. Apollo had only two prototypes, but he had assumed them defunct due to technological challenges. Apparently not. He wondered if one or both were flying.

Both, he reasoned. *But no matter.* He had numbers on his side.

"Approaching phase line Zulu at speed," said Jinx, referring to the estate's border fence. "Requesting zero one, cleared hot."

"Roger. Stand by, Jinx," said Control.

Lin heard a jet engine rev up somewhere behind her,

then felt the noise as a Hunter screeched overhead at high decibels. Moments later the ground shook and the sky was on fire. A hundred-foot-high wall of fire and white phosphorus shot up into the night, cutting a highway of flame through the perimeter's double steel fence and antitank ditch.

"I love the smell of napalm in the evening!" shouted Valkyrie.

Holy crap! thought Lin. They were the only two words her mind could conjure as the motorcycles drove into flame highway.

"Good hit, Control," said Jinx.

"Hang on, Princess," said Valkyrie. "YEEEEEEEE-HAAAAAW!!!" she screamed as they hit the ditch hard and flew up the backside, making a twenty-foot jump over the remains of the security fence.

"We're in," confirmed Jinx to Mission Control.

"They're in, all of them," radioed Lava, and the HALO team whooped.

"Looks like I lost a case of scotch, Locke!" teased Tye over our closed battle buddy net. "I bet Jinx your honeypot wouldn't make it to the fence."

"Tye, don't be jealous. I still have feelings for you too," I jabbed back. Six packaged drones were being pushed by six warriors each, in free fall. Below us I could see the dark outline of woods and the paler loam of meadow, despite the moonless night. Far below was the mansion, and somewhere was Jen.

Focus, Tom, I told myself. Thinking about Jen now would get me killed.

"Prep drones," ordered Lava. We had less than two

minutes to unfold our drone and make it operational, otherwise it would crater into the earth. Unfolded, the drone looked more like a miniature Osprey tilt-rotor aircraft than a standard helicopter. It had two arms, each with a rotor that could swivel for steering, and a tail boom with stabilizer fins. For armaments, it had two side pods that held four missiles each, capable of destroying air or ground targets, and a chin turret with a six-barrel 5.56 mm mini-gun. The pilot was in a mobile command truck driving someplace in Virginia. The drone would be our close air support on the ground, but unfolding it in freefall required aerial ballet.

"Let's do it!" said Tye, our fire team leader. Tye pulled a quick-release strap, and the cargo netting and aluminum pallet flew away. Next, in a choreography of precision, we simultaneously unfolded the drone's left and right rotor booms, then the tail boom. The machine began to wobble dangerously.

"Careful, careful!" said Tye as we frantically sought to steady it. Once stabilized, we worked like a floating pit crew, fastening bolts on the rotor booms and locking them in place. Tye rechecked the drone's parachute straddled across its back, in between the rotors. A ring-like blade guard surrounded the propellers, preventing them from accidentally slicing the parachute chords.

"Five thousand feet," said Lava. Tye crawled around the drone upside down, inspecting our work. When done, he said: "Drone Six, ready."

"Copy. Systems check," said the pilot over the network.

"Three thousand feet," said Lava.

"All systems green. Ready for chute deployment," reported the pilot. "Thanks, guys."

"Happy hunting," said Tye. "And cover our asses."

"Wilco," said the pilot, ground-pounder-speak for *Understand and will comply*. At 750 feet above ground level, the pilot would deploy the parachute and start the rotors. At one hundred feet, the drone would drop free of the parachute and fly on its own, and kill something.

"Fifteen hundred feet. Positions!" said Lava. We banked away from the drone and toward the lit-up mansion among dark woods, a superlative drop zone. Below, I could see paramilitaries on the grounds. There were significantly more than Lava briefed. It felt like a trap.

"Tye, there's a lot of tangos down there," I said, speaking just to him.

A second later, he replied: "Roger, things are going to get sporty."

"One thousand feet," said Lava. "Check your DZ."

My HUD lit up a blue patch of gabled roof on one of the east wings. We each had a patch. I steered with my body, adjusting my heading.

Lava switched to a countdown. "Five."

The roof came alive like a Christmas tree, as my HUD identified all the enemies in red.

"Four."

"Marking targets," said Control. Apollo's computer system conducted collective targeting that racked and stacked threats, assigning each of us multiple targets. Three red dots blinked on the roof: my prey.

"Three."

I was speeding at 140 mph, and the ground was coming up uncomfortably fast. Timing would be everything.

"Two."

I breathed deeply, readying my body for what followed.

"One."

My parachute deployed automatically, and my body jerked upright. The HUD displayed a negative-three-second countdown clock. When it got to zero, we would all shoot simultaneously in perfect ambush.

So it begins, I told myself as I unzipped my arm wings and pulled out my weapon. The precision-guided rifle locked onto my three targets; all I needed to do was aim, pull the trigger, and the computer would fire at the optimal time. Other black parachutes descended on my sides. We surrounded the entire mansion.

Three, two, one, I counted as I aimed and squeezed. The weapon fired three shots, its built-in sound suppressor muffling the noise. It sounded like three taps on a door. One of the targets fell over the side. The three blinking red dots turned gray: targets down. The whole roof went gray, as I reached up for the toggles and steered for a landing.

"All targets down," confirmed Mission Control. "Congratulations."

My boots skidded across the steeply angled gable roof, then I was jerked backward, hard.

What the—? I thought, looking up. My parachute was snagged on an ornamental roof spike. Decorative iron spikes lined the roof's spine, and I was caught. I yanked my riser's quick-releases, and I slid down the slate roof, crashing into a dead mercenary with a .50-cal sniper rifle. My bullet had penetrated his steel-plated body armor, center of mass.

Six stories below me, men in black combat gear patrolled the estate's grounds. There seemed to be hundreds, but we were undetected. Surprise and stealth were still ours.

"Phase one complete," said Lava. "Move to phase two."

"They're in, sir," reported one of the intel techs. The battle captain watched the monitors in alarm as the dozen motorcycles penetrated the perimeter fence and sped through the woods toward the mansion. They were effectively skirting all his defenses, avoiding roads and security checkpoints. His plan to channel a ground assault into an ambush zone was now defunct, since it assumed the enemy would use roads and not motorcycle through woods.

"This can't be happening," muttered the battle captain.

Winters was also concerned, although he dared not reveal it. Twelve loose Apollo operatives on the grounds was bad. Twelve plus two Hunters was a disaster. But Winters knew how to even the odds.

"Deploy everything," said Winters.

"Deploy everything," instructed the battle captain over the command net.

"Ground teams," said Winters. "Annihilate them."

The Wagner Group commander smiled and gave orders in Russian. He looked like a bodybuilder in fatigues who only shaved twice a month. People called him Colonel Yuri, but that was not his real name. At his disposal were 120 high-end mercenaries drawn from around the world, and all were lethal. Outside, men scurried into vehicles, shouting in different languages. Twelve armored SUVs sped to confront the intruders, with a ten-to-one advantage in terms of combatants.

"Battle Captain, make sure the ground team also has air support," instructed Winters, and the other man nodded. Winters wanted the battle over fast. *If it's a fair fight, you're not trying hard enough*, he thought.

"Two more drones downed by the enemy," said one of the techs.

"We still can't see their UAV," said another.

"Somebody ID that enemy drone!" shouted the battle captain. The Hunters were picking apart their air force, gaining air supremacy. The threat was mounting.

"We can't. It's invisible to our sensors," said an aggravated tech.

The battle captain turned to one of the Russians. "I want your snipers on the roof to stop looking at the ground and start looking at the sky. Do you understand me? We need eyeballs in the sky looking for the enemy drone!"

The Russian nodded and worked his radios, then gave a puzzled look as if something were wrong. He tried again, and his expression transformed to terror.

"Sir, sir," he said in a thick Russian accent, trying to flag the battle captain's attention, but he was interrupted.

"I'm tracking the lead motorcycle!" shouted one of the drone pilots.

"On screen," commanded the battle captain, and one of the large monitors showed the infrared profile of a dirt biker speeding through the trees. "Take him out."

"Firing," said the pilot and automatic gunfire sounded outside, in the distance.

"Missed," said the battle captain, disappointed. The speed of the bike and tree branches prevented a clean shot.

"Flush them toward this area," said Yuri, pointing to a spot on the map.

"What's there?" asked the battle captain, examining the spot on the topographical map.

"Our ambush zone. We're already in position. *All* of us," he said. "Just have your drones flush them toward us. The terrain features will channel them into the ambush zone. Then we will destroy them."

The battle captain nodded, and ordered the drones to drive the enemy toward Yuri's grid coordinate.

Winter was impressed. "Excellent plan, Colonel Yuri," he said. "But what happens when they don't go through your ambush zone?"

The Russians shrugged. "Then we will run them down and kill them. As Stalin said, there is a quality about quantity."

Winters smiled approval and decided he liked Yuri.

"Sir, sir!" It was the Russian radio operator. Yuri and the battle captain turned to face him, and then heard a loud thud outside, as if someone dropped a bag of cement mix. Then another.

"What's that?" asked the battle captain.

"Check it out," ordered Winters, and two fighters ran out of the room.

"That's what I've been trying to tell you," said the Russian. "Parachutes! A lot of them!"

A second later, one of the fighters radioed in. "Two bodies," he said in an Armenian accent. "Both snipers, probably from the roof."

"The roof!" said the battle captain. The Russian tech looked worried. "Shooters to the roof, now!"

"Pull back everything!" shouted Winters. *"The motorcycles are a ruse!"*

Sirens blasted around the mansion followed by shouting in Russian over outside speakers. Last time I heard something like it, I was in Ukraine being ambushed by Russian Spetsnaz special forces, and it did not end well. My HUD showed the sky dotted with red enemy drones speeding toward us. Men below started shooting at the roof.

"We're compromised, proceed to Phase Three. Seize the objectives!" said Lava as a stream of bullets erupted the slate roof around me. I dove behind the faux battlements as an enemy drone stalked me. A dead Wagner mercenary lay twenty-five feet in front of me with an SA-18 surface-to-air missile by his side.

Go for it! I told myself, sprinting for the weapon. The roof blew up around me again in a stream of mini-gun fire, and my back felt like I was being pounded by a jackhammer. I was knocked off my feet as bullets hit my body armor. Coughing, I willed myself to roll over despite the pain.

The enemy rotary-wing drone swerved to a hover, its mini-gun trained on me. I raised my rifle at it and heard the buzz of the mini-gun, then watched it explode. Its flaming body crashed into a battlement and tipped over the side. Behind it was Drone 6, its mini-gun whirring to a stop. I mustered a thumbs-up, and it flew away, in search of new prey.

God, I hate getting shot, I thought as I sat up. The Apollo tactical suit stopped the three bullets, but it still hurt like hell.

"Locke, where are you?" It was Tye. "Stop your lolly-gagging and get down here, we need an assist!" My HUD registered three green dots in the floor beneath me; the dots were blinking, indicating request for backup.

"Copy," I wheezed and got to my feet. Bullets zinged through the air as a full-on drone dogfight was occurring before me. A black streak screeched overhead, and an enemy drone was blown to pieces. My HUD tracked the Hunter do a six-G turn and return to smoke another enemy UAV. Two kills in four seconds.

"Glad that thing is on our side," I muttered as it screeched by.

"Locke, say again?" said Tye. "Get down here!"

"Good copy," I said, and hopped across dormers. Below I saw multiple black armored SUVs crash out of the woods and plow through the baroque gardens, then fishtail to a stop at the base of the mansion directly beneath me. About forty heavily armed men in combat armor got out and ran into the mansion.

"Uh, Valhalla," I said, using Lava's call sign. "Spot report: thirty tangos just entered the building, south side, first floor."

"Good copy," replied Mission Control. Valhalla must have been busy.

"Locke, where are you?" asked Tye, angry.

I turned to run and saw Jinx fly out of the wood line, followed by more Apollo bikes. But not all of them. Chasing them was a fleet of enemy SUVs, armed dune buggies, and dirt bikes. It was a running firefight, and two of the Apollo fighters were hit; one of the passengers was slumped over, shot.

"*Jen!*" I screamed. They were driving into a death trap. Gauging the ground six stories below, I took out my 550 parachute cord. *I can repel down, if I double up the strand,* I thought. Not ideal, but I would land without breaking my legs.

"Get in here, Locke! We're pinned down and about to get wasted!" shouted Tye. I had never heard him panic, ever. It was an evil choice: Tye versus Jen.

"Control, we're getting chewed up. We need backup!" yelled Jinx as she sped through the woods. Their plan worked, sort of. They drew the enemy out of the mansion long enough for the main effort to HALO safely to the roof. But it failed because there were ten times more enemy than expected. Winters had laid a trap to lure them in and kill them.

"Control?" she repeated.

"Deploying a Hunter your way," said Control. Automatic gunfire ripped through them and she saw one of her teammates fall.

NO! thought Jinx. *They will pay,* she promised, as she twisted around and returned fire. She was down to nine riders. Then she noticed her own bike losing power. She looked down; it had somehow taken a hit and was grinding metal.

"Control, my bike has taken damage and slowing. If I fall, Valkyrie is my second. Confirm," she said.

"Confirmed," said Valkyrie.

"Confirmed," said Control. "You are four hundred meters from the objective. Make it!"

The Hunter shrieked overhead, then four seconds later passed above again. Two enemy drones dropped out of the sky on fire. Jinx dodged one as it smashed into the ground and rolled toward her.

"Jinx, heads up!" warned Control.

But it was too late. Jinx's bike shot into the air as the sloping downhill turned into a twenty-foot drop, sending her across the great lawn of the estate. The whole team was airborne as they followed her blindly over the edge, and she heard Valkyrie's trademark *yee-haw!* The team landed rough, but not as hard as the enemy. The bikes made it, like Jinx, but the armed speed buggies and SUV flipped end over end. One exploded. It was hard to imagine anyone survived.

"Jinx, get to mansion ASAP and assist Valhalla," ordered control. "Urgent!"

Bullets sprayed everywhere as they were caught in the open, and one hit her in the back, pitching her forward. She fought through the pain to keep control. An enemy bike was on her tail, and no matter what she did, it was getting closer.

I need to kill my tail fast, or it will kill me, she realized.

Jinx hammered the back brake, locking the wheel up. The enemy bike zoomed past. As her bike started to slide, Jinx laid it down on its left side, pulling up her left leg so it didn't get crushed. She let go. The bike continued to skid as she lifted up her precision-guided rifle, locked onto the enemy rider, and squeezed the trigger. He went down.

Jinx slid to a stop, her body armor making the ride feel like snow. Other vehicles swerved around her, shooting at each other, but Jinx ignored them. She pushed the rider's immobile body over with her foot, put the muzzle at his neck where the body armor was weakest. The man jerked up a concealed 9 mm pistol, and she fired. He died.

"Jinx, how copy, over?" said Control.

Jinx looked up and saw five SUVs barreling down on her. They had no shooters sticking out of the windows because bulletproof glass does not lower, so the drivers intended to run her down.

Move! she thought and sprinted for the fallen rider's bike, mounted it, and accelerated forward, kicking up dirt.

"Jinx?" asked Control.

"Negative, Control," she said. "We need an assist. Outnumbered."

The SUVs fanned out across the gigantic lawn, running over antipersonnel mines while trying to catch and crush her between two vehicles. Jinx scanned the terrain. There was nowhere to run.

"Roger," said Control after a pause. "We have no reinforcements."

Ahead, Jinx saw the last of her bikes disappear into an eight-foot-high hedgerow. *Where did they go?* she wondered, and opened the throttle. The SUVs followed.

"Copy, Control," she said, speeding for the hedge row, and saw the entrance. Then she understood; it was a garden maze, the kind made of hedges that occupied an entire acre. She entered the maze and skid-turned around the corners. The lead SUV followed and crashed into the ancient hedges, stuck. Jinx smiled.

"Valkyrie, status over?" said Jinx, muscling the bike around ninety-degree turns. She heard shooting a few hedges over.

"We're eight, I think. Lost in this goddamned maze with the enemy!"

"Me too."

The library was a hive of intensity as techs worked their stations. Outside was a hurricane of explosions and automatic gunfire, with the occasional shriek of a Hunter drone. The mansion's interior had become a battle zone, and more of Winters's reinforcements streamed in by the minute.

"Everyone, to the mansion!" ordered Winters, smiling. It was a war of attrition now, guaranteeing his victory. The battle captain nodded in affirmation while speaking into two different headsets. Yuri was last seen slinging his AKM rifle and GP-25 grenade launcher over his shoulder and leaving the room with two other Wagner mercenaries. The battle got louder, and closer.

Yuri's got a point, thought Winters, admiring the Russian's leadership. *Time to get in the fight.* Pulling out an ampule, he stuck it up his nose and snorted the Mr. Hyde Dust. Instantly his body tensed up, and his cane dropped to the ground. His heart pounded in pain, like it might burst, but he ignored it. He exhaled loudly but no one noticed in the fervor of battle.

"Yeeessss!" he roared, standing up. The ache in his leg faded as he limped over to a large weapons case in the corner. He flipped open the lid and removed a precision-guided grenade launcher. It looked like a revolver for 40 mm grenades, and it could sniper-fire six of them in five seconds. Winters held it, admiring its weight as he aimed through the reflex sight. Next to it sat a field bag of medium-velocity, high-explosive rounds. He slung the whole bag over his shoulder.

"Tom Locke," he said, lumbering out of the room.

"Tye, where are you?" I panted, bounding down the stone stairs two at a time. Jen would be OK, I reasoned, because she was . . . Jen. Also, Valkyrie was her battle buddy, who I only knew by reputation: she was bulletproof.

"Here! Over here," said Tye, and a green dot blinked on my HUD. The stairs dumped into a vaulted hall that overlooked an elegant four-story atrium with multiple rooms off balconied hallways. Four large chandeliers hung from the coffered ceiling, with bullets zooming through them. Wagner and Apollo were in a three-dimensional firefight, shooting across the atrium from different levels.

"Incoming!" shouted Tye.

I reflexively hit the floor. An RPG rocketed over my head, blowing out a wall at the far end of the hall.

"Are you OK?"

"Roger," I said, spotting Tye pinned down in a vestibule closet. Enemy were swarming the opposite side, and several IR laser dots danced around the vestibule entrance, ready to kill whatever stepped out. But that wasn't the biggest problem.

"Take out the RPG!" said Tye.

I high-crawled to the marble railing and used my weapon's scope to scan for the RPG. I saw two Wagner mercenaries running across the ground floor and get whacked by an Apollo sniper in the rafters. I scanned right and spotted a Wagner fire team assault into a room, blowing it up.

No one could survive that, I thought sadly. Then I located Lava one floor below. He was firing his pistol into a room, until it ran dry. He threw it at the target, and ran inside, knife drawn.

It's Stalingrad down there, I realized, *except there's a lot more of them than us.* I continued to scan. On the third floor, I spotted two Wagner commandos running from room to room; one carried an RPG.

That's my target, I thought, as I picked up and

sprinted toward a staircase, using speed as my cover. Bullets ricocheted around me as I skidded across the marble floor and down the stairwell, my weapon facing forward.

Turning the corner, I ran down the third-floor balcony hallway, bullets everywhere, and slid to a stop by the door where I last saw the RPG. Holding my rifle parallel to my chest, I stuck it into the room and saw one of the Wagner troops in my HUD. I locked on and fired; he fell. The other spun and shot at me. I tossed in a grenade, and took cover. Where there was once a room was now a pile of bricks covering antique furniture and two Wagner bodies.

"Thanks, Locke," said Tye.

"Hold fast. I'm coming to you."

"Negative. I can take care of myself. Find Lava, he needs backup," said Tye. I could hear him shoot and move as we talked.

"Copy," I said, sneaking around the atrium perimeter with my weapon at the ready. I slipped into the room I saw Lava enter, but it was empty. There were signs of an intense firefight: bullet holes, spent cartridges, bodies. I followed the blood trail through a Versailles-like bedroom and down an interior hallway.

"Lava?" I asked. "Find Lava," I commanded my HUD, and it enlarged a green dot next to two red ones. He was in close combat. I ran down the hall, rounded a corner of another palatial bedroom, and then felt myself picked up and thrown through a standing mirror.

What . . . ?! My mind raced as my body got to its feet and raised my rifle. Powerful hands yanked it away and threw it across the room, then slammed me into the floor so hard my helmet busted through the plaster. Looking up, I saw a colossus of a Russian with a week-old beard and gray peppered hair.

"My mercenaries have killed many of you," he said in a thick Russian accent. "You will die, like your friends."

"Not today," I said, pulling my knife. But the Russian colossus anticipated it, grabbed my forearm, and tossed me across the room and into an armoire.

Ow, I thought, writhing on my back. Heavy footsteps approached, and the man appeared above me, brandishing a fire poker like an iron stake.

"Wagner better than Apollo. Let me show you," he said, raising it to impale me. Another hulking figure tackled him, and both crashed through a Chippendale letter desk. I got to my feet and recovered my weapon as Lava picked the Russian up and rammed him through the bathroom door.

"Lava, stand back!" I cried, aiming my rifle at the Russian behind him.

"No, Yuri's mine!" he commanded. "Blood debt. Now go!" He waved at an open door that blended into the wall. It was the secret passage he'd entered through. "Find Winters. Kill him!"

The Russian howled and tackled Lava from behind, but Lava tossed Yuri with a judo throw. Last I saw, both colossuses were punching it out as I disappeared down the secret passage to find Winters.

Lin fired her Saiga from the back of the dirt bike like a rear turret gunner, as Valkyrie bounced around corners. They had been playing deadly hide-and-seek for five eternal minutes, and ammo was getting low.

"He's still on us," cried Valkyrie as they sped toward a dead end.

"I know," replied Lin, slamming the last magazine in the Saiga.

The enemy dirt bike made the corner as Valkyrie slammed the brakes. Like so much of the garden maze, the dead end revealed a 180-degree turn, and she skidded around it, planting her right foot like a pivot. Dirt and stone kicked up as she accelerated down the opposite side of the hedge wall.

Lin was ready with her Saiga, and she aimed it at the hedges. As soon as the enemy passed the other side, she squeezed, and automatic shotgun fire blew a lateral gash through the hedge wall. Then came the thud of a body hitting dirt.

"Nice job, Princess," said Valkyrie. It was their fourth kill in five minutes. To Lin's amazement, they made a good team.

"Thanks," said Lin.

"Now to get out of this infernal maze," she said, zooming up and down the corridors. The hedges were impossible to walk through, their little branches deceptively strong.

"Valkyrie, this is Jinx. How copy?"

"Charlie miking," she said. All was OK.

"Get to the mansion. They need help badly."

"Good copy," said Valkyrie. By now the mansion was burning, casting a red glow in the sky. No fire trucks could save it because Winters had sealed the estate.

"Head toward the glow," said Lin.

Valkyrie nodded. "Seems your boyfriend needs saving."

"Don't they all?" joked Lin, and they both chuckled.

Minutes later they were out. The fight had left the great lawn and moved to the mansion's interior. Only the occasional burning hulks of ex-drones littered the otherwise pristine grounds. The building fire was impressive in a terrifying way. The century-old structure made of wood and stone was engulfed in flame.

Valkyrie drove through the garden and up the stairs, to the wedding-size patio overlooking the sound, and skidded to a stop. Lin leapt off.

"Hey, wait!" shouted Valkyrie. "Where are you going?! The building is falling down."

"No time. Boyfriend needs saving."

"Locke! Locke! *Locke!*" It was Winters, his voice wafting through the secret passage, as if he knew where to find me. "Locke, I know you are nearby. I see you on my monitor."

I froze, realizing he must have locked onto the nano-tech streaming through my veins just as Tye did when he found me at the hotel. *I hate technology,* I thought.

"What's the matter Locke, scared? Show yourself!" taunted Winters.

I continued to move. Winters wasn't the only one craving this moment; I had come out of hiding and risked everything for it. I followed the voice's echo through the secret passages, despite the ongoing noise of battle.

Dead end.

"Locke, I know you are close by," shouted Winters from the other side of the wall. Examining the passage, I noticed a faint breeze emanating from the corners. On the floor were century-old scuff marks.

Another secret door, I realized. Searching around, I discovered a handle and pulled at the door. It opened onto a covered wooden balcony at the rear of a magnificent banqueting hall, the kind you might see at Oxford, except it was lined with suits of medieval armor, part of the estate's gilded charm.

"Locke, where are you?" shouted Winters from below, louder. I crept forward onto the balcony, probably where the musicians played for the lord's dining delight. Using the rifle's scope, I peered over the balcony's edge. The three-story walls were blanketed in colorful murals of kings, knights, princesses, cities, battles, and Jerusalem. Every mural contained eight-pointed stars, some overt and others hidden. Even the coffered ceiling was covered in eight-pointed star ornamentations.

At the far end of the hall was a hearth the size of a horse with a roaring bonfire casting shadows around the great hall. Above it was a painting of an enthroned king in full eight-star regalia, holding court over all who dined in the hall. To his left and right were murals of full-size jousters, also in star regalia, tilting their lances toward each other.

"Locke, don't be a coward!" goaded Winters.

Then I spotted him pacing atop the massive banquet table, almost inviting a headshot. He wore advanced tactical goggles and carried a weapon that looked like a cross between a grenade launcher and a .45 revolver.

Finally, I can end this nightmare, I thought as I lay on my back and held my weapon up to get a target lock on his torso. *Steady,* I told myself, as the site picture jiggled as I zoomed. It was like shooting around a corner, and I could not get a clean target lock.

"Locke?" asked Winters, stopping but not facing

me. "Locke, is that you?" He placed the weapon on his shoulder, rocked it back toward me, and fired.

Incoming! My mind panicked as I rolled sideways, and the balcony was blown to smithereens. The concussion threw me down the servants' narrow stairwell to the first floor. Looking up dazed, I saw an eight-pointed star painted on the ceiling. I was in the banquet hall's antechamber on the floor below, but hidden from Winters.

"I know you're still here," cried Winters.

I heard a *thunk* and rolled for cover. The banquet hall's main doors exploded into wooden shards, and the blast wave concussed me. The body armor offered protection, but I would not survive a direct hit.

"Locke, come out and fight. You were a fool, but never a coward."

Pointing my weapon around the corner, I saw Winters scanning for me. He wore no visible body armor, just a Jermyn Street bespoke suit, Hermes tie, and grenade launcher. Classic Winters.

Thunk. I spun away from the wall but too late. The grenade impacted the other side of the stone wall, throwing it and me to the other side of the antechamber. I bounced off the back wall, breathing through the pain. Through the new hole, I saw Winters and he saw me.

"Locke!" he said, aiming the grenade launcher at me. But I was quicker. I snapped off a round and he fell backward, off his feet and onto the floor. *Thunk.* His weapon fired up as he fell, and the ceiling exploded. Chunks of concrete, brick, and timber crashed into the hall.

Warily, I got up, ignoring the pain, and approached the pile of rubble where Winters once stood, weapon pointed forward. *Dead, finally!* I thought with a smile.

Thunk. I dropped and felt the *zing* of a round pass above my head and explode the wall behind me. Then coughing from under the rubble.

Winters is still alive! Impossible, I thought, not understanding. He must have had some new reactive chest armor under his shirt. The coughing came from under the oak banquet table, shielding him from the ceiling's demise.

"Come on Locke, show yourself. Tell me the gods have been merciful and granted me revenge," he said in a rational tone.

"Revenge is mine, old man," I said.

"Lo-o-o-o-o-ocke," hissed Winters. I heard bricks move, and suddenly Winters was standing ten feet before me, aiming his grenade launcher at me. I leapt sideways as I heard the *thunk.* Another portion of the wall blew out, and the roof timbers began to creek as the structure weakened. Flames licked the hall's wooden paneling.

"You're out of ammo, old man," I said, noting the grenade launcher's six-shell cylinder.

"No matter, Locke," he said, tossing it away and holding up his fists. "Why should a guy like you be afraid of an old man like me?"

My weapon was trained on his chest. *Do it,* I told myself. *Do it!* But I couldn't. Winters did not deserve a clean death, not after killing 230 Americans, assassinating the vice president, and threatening to nuke three U.S. cities. It was why I came back.

"You stand guilty of high treason," I said, taking off my helmet. "A bullet in the head would be too good for you." I dropped my rifle. "I have returned to render justice." I tossed my mini-shotgun. "My way."

Winters smiled as I took up a fighting stance. We circled. The banquet hall was on fire and coming down around us, giving a hellish appearance, but neither of us noticed.

He jabbed with shocking speed, and sucker-punched my throat, followed by a cross elbow to the jaw, knocking me sideways and off my feet. *Where did that come from?* I thought, surprised and seeing stars. Winters grunted as he kicked me hard in the stomach. I felt it through the body armor, paralyzing my diaphragm so I could not breathe. Turning red, I rolled over and sipped air.

Winters snorted as he bent down and picked up my shotgun. "You were my biggest disappointment, Locke," he said, aiming the shotgun at my face. "So much wasted potential."

I raised my forearms to my face, arms clasped tightly together, as I heard the shot. The pellets deflected off my body armor, pushing my forearms into my head. Winters unloaded the shotgun, pumping its action in rapid succession. Each shot was a body blow, but none of the pellets penetrated the armor.

"Damn you, Locke!" he screamed, throwing the shotgun at me as I stood up.

"I condemn you to death for high treason," I said, walking slowly toward him. With every step I took, he limped backward one, bumping into wood-hewn chairs and a drinks cart. Finally, he stopped, sandwiched between me and the massive stone hearth, its fires blazing. He turned to face it, then me. He was cornered.

Winters's expression softened. "There is no honor in killing an old man, Tom. Take me into custody. Let the law decide. It's the honorable thing to do."

"We are past honor," I said, and roundhouse-kicked him into the fire. The man screamed and thrashed as the inferno consumed him. I grabbed a dusty bottle of brandy off the drinks cart and sprayed it on him; it caught fire midair, like unholy water. Flames shot up from his clothes and face, blinding him. Hoping to escape hell but unable to see, he bolted into the back wall of the ten-foot fireplace and smacked his skull on the stone, then fell backward onto the fire again. The shrieks were gruesome.

Only now did I feel pity for the man who tried to murder me three times. I walked to a suit of armor and jerked away a large Zweihänder sword, leaving the suit to collapse in a jarring clang as I walked back to the screaming fire, where the burning man tried to stand. Stepping halfway into the flames, I thrust the sword through Winters's chest, pinning him to the back wall. A moment later, I withdrew it and his body collapsed onto the fire. I watched it burn, ignoring the stench.

The hall started collapsing around me, on fire itself. However, I could not break my gaze; I needed proof the flames would claim this devil. The body lay motionless, consumed by flame. Satisfied, I walked through the burning hall, as timber beams groaned above, having suffered too much destruction. Picking up my helmet and rifle, I walked out of the great hall, down a passage, and into the library. It had been converted into a tactical operations center, but its occupants had fled. The battle must be over. I paused to admire the temple to books before it perished. Flames were already licking at the bottom rows.

"Locke!" cried Jen. "Tom, what are you doing? We got to get out of here, now!"

"No, wait. Let's take a second to admire this, before it's gone. All of it," I said, sadness in my voice. It was an Armageddon of books, knowledge, culture.

"Seriously?!" Bits of flaming ceiling rained down.

"Yeah."

She gut-punched me, and I gasped. Then she picked me up and took me in a fireman's carry to the window, which her Saiga obliterated. Then she tossed me out headfirst. Next, she landed on me.

"Ow!" I said as she rolled off.

"Serves you right, you dunderhead," she said, grabbing my arm and yanking me to my feet. The entire mansion was ablaze with no firefighters because all roads to the estate were blocked. We ran into the baroque garden and flopped in a concealed flower bed. There we lay on our backs, staring at the moonless sky and its soft, flame-red glow. Automatic gunfire occasionally echoed in the distance, as did the wail of sirens. Soon the police would arrive and we would need to vanish again.

"I need a vacation," she said.

"Me too."

CHAPTER 57

The Chevalier descended the narrow spiral stairs to the castle vault. The medieval stairway was encased in rough-hewn stone and was barely a man's width, allowing a single defender to hold off a group of invaders. The air was moist and stank of mildew as he approached the bottom. Once a mighty athlete, the Chevalier was still nimble despite his age.

To think that Winters believed I served the Russians, he thought. Earlier, he had downgraded Winters from "useful idiot" to "brazen knave," a more dangerous species of moron. Now he was demoted to full dead, an improvement but not without costs to the organization.

At the bottom of the stairs, he felt around and found the light switch. Dim fluorescent lights flickered to life, and he continued through tunnels dating back to the castle's founding in the thirteenth century, if not earlier. Before it was a stone castle, it had been a wooden fortress. No one knew how old the passages were, and some speculated they dated back to the Roman era.

At last the Chevalier came to a heavy wooden door with black iron rivets and an ornate hinge that looked like ivy covering the door. He pulled out a key made of titanium, inserted it in a secret hole hidden in the metal ivy, and opened the door. Beyond was the vault. Lights automatically turned on. The air was climate controlled and fresh.

The space was cavernous and two stories tall, with no windows. The vaulted ceiling was painted night blue with eight-pointed stars crafted in silver leaf. Inscribed around the rim of the ceiling was: *Monstrant regibus astra viam* ("The stars show the way to kings"). The walls and columns were painted red with gold leaf trim. As a boy, he remembered how the secret room would shimmer under torchlight. Now it looked comatose with modern electrical lighting.

Not everything new is better, he lamented as he entered. Lining the walls were treasures that the Louvre would salivate over. But his greatest prize was the tomb of Sir Geoffroy de Charny, who fell defending the king of France at the disastrous Battle of Poitiers in 1356. De Charny was one of Europe's most admired chevaliers during his lifetime, a true and perfect knight. Now he rested here, in the family vault, after centuries of aristocratic intermarriage that took his remains across Europe.

"How are you today, old friend?" asked the Chevalier, patting the sarcophagus.

De Charny and the French king founded the Order of the Star in 1351, and the group went underground after the battle, where it had remained and thrived ever since. Once a secret society dedicated to good, it had devolved into a for-profit conglomerate controlled by a dozen intermarried families.

Mon Dieu! How we have fallen, he thought. Only he took the Order's original vows seriously, and was hence dubbed "Chevalier" by his cousins. It was not a compliment.

"I wonder what counsel you would give us now. It is a desperate hour," he said to the sarcophagus. With a sigh, he approached a mammoth wooden desk with stars carved into it, and took a seat. A bank of large-screen monitors lit up and looked wholly out of place in the ancient vault. Eleven faces stared back at him, some old and others merely middle-aged.

Oh dear, I'm late again, he thought.

"The Order of the Star is now convened," an elderly woman said, her voice sharp and alert.

"Let us not waste time. Chevalier, please provide us with an update," said a man in his forties on a private jet. Its ceiling was a light corporate gray with a subtle pattern of eight-pointed stars.

"It is a setback, cousins. Our headquarters in Manhattan and Long Island estate were destroyed in one week. Elektra was demolished, as you know, and our agent is dead—"

"Are we exposed?" interrupted a man, about as old as the Chevalier. A few others nodded their mutual concern. The rules of the Order did not permit interruption, but these were exceptional times.

"No, cousin. As of now, we are not exposed," replied the Chevalier. "I am working to contain the problem. There is no link between us and our field agent, Winters. Ultimately, others shall be blamed, and we will remain anonymous, as always."

"Blowback could destroy the Order," spoke a woman in her fifties. "It's not 1351 anymore. News travels fast now." The Chevalier dismissed her swipe.

Another member spoke up. "As I said from the beginning, it was madness to stoke an arms race between the U.S. and Russia for profit's sake. Even with our substantial holdings in the cyber, aerospace, and defense sectors, such a scheme was hubris."

"Not so," countered the Chevalier. "Our predecessors did well in the 1930s, backing Franco and the Communists."

"But it midwifed World War II and the Holocaust," said the youngish woman.

"We did not create Hitler—" said the Chevalier.

"Nor did we stop him," she interrupted.

The Chevalier nodded acquiescence. "Not our finest hour, cousins. But let us not be hypocritical. We have always done well by war. The Order's vast wealth was not made in the cool forges of agriculture but in the furnace of conflict."

"Perhaps, but you risk too much," added a hoary voice. "For 670 years our families have worked together to achieve greatness, and now we gamble everything?"

"We are great *because* they gambled," said the Chevalier, pounding his fist on the medieval table. "We plan our enterprises cautiously and carry them out boldly. It has been our way since Chevalier Geoffroy, but we have grown flaccid in our success and decadence."

The Council erupted in raucous argument.

"Silence! Silence!" gaveled the elderly woman who convened the meeting. Everyone fell quiet.

"All is not lost, brothers and sisters. We still have this," said the Chevalier, pulling out the aluminum briefcase. "Inside is the fate of three American cities. Shall we proceed with a new plan?"

Heads nodded and knuckles rapped.

CHAPTER 58

President Hugh Anderson sat behind the Resolute Desk, his forehead resting in his hands as if he were praying. He was alone. The situation was far worse than most knew.

Lord, you know I've never been much of a church-goer. But if you're listening, I could sure use some help, he prayed. He glanced around the empty Oval and saw oil paintings of dead presidents staring down at him. Judging him.

"Yeah, and what would you do?" he asked defiantly, but Washington, Jefferson, Jackson, Lincoln, and Teddy Roosevelt remained mute. "Didn't think so."

Anderson sighed and looked out the window at the Rose Garden. It was just shrubbery and the yellow grass of March. Dozens of pictures were displayed on the small credenza behind his chair, and he grabbed the one of the vice president, himself, and their wives deep-sea-fishing off Key West ten years ago. He had caught an eight-foot-long sailfish, and all four of them sat at the back of the boat, holding it on their laps for the camera with big grins. He could still smell the engine fumes, fish guts, and salt spray. *Happier times,* he thought with a smile, and his eyes glistened.

"I'm sorry, Henry and Martha. Please forgive me,

wherever you are," he said, and a tear streamed down his face as he delicately put the picture back in its spot. *Good grief, I haven't cried in forty years,* he thought as he struggled to hold it in.

Henry and Martha were not supposed to die. *What was I supposed to do?* he thought, choking back tears. *Don't blame yourself. Blame Brad Winters.*

"Winters," he whispered with loathing, prolonging the name like a curse. Somehow Winters had corrupted George, another old friend. He picked up a second picture, this one of Jackson and himself at a rodeo in Dallas while on the campaign trail. They were both holding plastic mugs of cheap beer and wearing cowboy hats. Ever the Boston Brahmin, Jackson looked uncomfortably out of place in a button-down oxford shirt and blue blazer amid cows.

"You old codger," he said. Anderson wanted to give his friend a pardon but knew he couldn't. Treason is treason, and his was high treason. "We all make our choices."

And I made mine, he thought. Forty-five years paddling around the DC swamp bestowed a sixth, seventh, and eighth sense for bullshit. He smelled the reek of feces from Jackson and Winters shortly after his inaugural address, two years ago. But how to rein them in? Both men were powerful and shrewd, and they could manipulate the system for their protection just as easily as he could order their arrest.

That was when he had turned to Apollo Outcomes. Sometimes you needed an outside-the-system solution to fix an inside-the-system problem. In this case, he needed someone to bring Jackson and Winters to heel—by any means necessary—while keeping his name out of it. Apollo did its job perfectly.

Thirty minutes earlier, Apollo had confirmed that all three nuclear weapons in the three cities were recovered and disarmed. Jackson was contained, Winters had disappeared, and the Wagner Group was destroyed, at least on American soil. None of it would make the news.

Only Winters's client remained a mystery, but Apollo was on their scent now. Soon they would be neutralized, one way or another. Unlike the CIA, Apollo could liquidate America's enemies where they hid. The company was not constrained by Executive Order 12333, which prohibited assassination. All it took was a phone call and a phrase—"Search and destroy"—and it would be done, off the books of course. National security without the red tape.

A knock on the door. "Mr. President? Are you ready, Mr. President? We're running late," came a woman's voice on the other side. It was his press secretary.

"Give me another minute, please," he replied, as he removed a handkerchief and dried his eyes. Then he straightened himself and checked his looks in a vanity mirror kept in the top drawer.

Focus. Insight. Hope, he thought. He closed his eyes and took three deep breaths. Holding in the last breath, he opened his eyes and gave a long exhale. Refreshed, he said, "Send them in."

The door swung open and journalists streamed in, crowding the Oval. People murmured in anticipation. Half an hour ago, the White House press office shocked the media world and announced the president would deliver a speech. In it, he would explain who was be-

hind the VP's assassination, the terrorist attack on the
bridge, and the battle on the Mall. All would be made
clear. The press release simply said "new evidence had
come to light" and the "responsible party will surprise
you." Lastly, "these incidences prove the world is facing
a new breed of threat."

The global news cycle went berserk.

All his life, the president wanted to deliver a speech
that would change the destiny of the world. As a boy, he
kept a copy of *100 Greatest Speeches in History* on his
nightstand, and would pen overwrought monologues the
way artists doodled on scraps of paper. Such is the legacy of every great statesman, from Pericles to Churchill,
and *his* moment had finally arrived. But he was about to
do something previously unthinkable: ad lib it. Not even
an outline. Somehow it felt true.

Anderson beamed as everyone got situated, with the
staccato of camera shutters punctuating the air. Under
the desk and against his legs were a dozen blown-up
photographs. Each photo was a secret shot of Winters
meeting Jackson: deep in a garage, in a pew of an empty
church, lunch at an elite members-only club, parked at
the end of a runway, and other obscure venues. Each
photo would make a dramatically timed appearance
during his speech, and all were courtesy of Apollo Outcomes, which would go unnamed.

Once the reporters were packed in, the president
opened his mouth and delivered his perfect Churchillian speech.

EPILOGUE

We lay together under the cabin roof, our minds and bodies contented. A warm ocean breeze gently blew chimes made of seashells, making a peaceful clacking sound. The surf sang us a lullaby. Our cabin sat on a rocky outcrop with its own deck and pool overlooking the aquamarine Pacific, with a petite stairway to the sand. The bungalow had no walls because it had no neighbors, other than sea turtles that occasionally dug nests in the beach below. Polynesia is where you go to escape the world.

"Are you awake, my darling?" cooed Jen, stirring slightly. We had been doing this for two weeks or more, and it had become our new lifestyle.

"Barely," I murmured, pressing her naked body into mine. She giggled.

"What do you want to do this afternoon?"

We had spent our days talking about life's mysteries, hiking the volcanic ridgeline, sparring on the beach, scuba diving the atoll, and playing in our bungalow. Of our list, we favored playing the most.

"I have an idea," I whispered, as she inhaled sharply and closed her eyes.

Before we left, Lava and Tye were heading for Austria. New mission, they said, inviting us along. But

we demurred. In the course of one week, our individual lives exploded and then miraculously reassembled
as one. We wanted to explore it together, away from the
din of the world.

"No one deserves a break more than you," Lava
had said, nodding. "I've asked our client to clear your
names, so you can travel normally again. Your names
have been purged from every government watchlist and
Interpol database. Think of it as a parting thank-you."

"Wait, how's that possible? Who's your client?!"
asked Jen, ever the FBI agent. But I knew better than
to ask such things, and I also had a hunch.

"When you get bored—and you will—call me," said
Lava. "We need quality people. Also . . ." He pulled out
two slim phones slightly larger than a credit card. "If
you ever need our help, give us a call."

"For anything," added Tye.

"We take care of our own," said Lava, putting his
hands on our shoulders. We exchanged man hugs and
departed.

That was more than two weeks ago.

Now, Jen crumpled on me, breathless. We were both
sweaty.

Bzzzzz. Bzzzzz.

"What's that?" asked Jen, alarmed. We'd packed no
electronics.

Bzzzzz. Bzzzzz.

I got up, trying to locate the source of the electronic
noise.

Bzzzzz. Bzzzzz.

Jen reached into her backpack and started rummaging around.

"I think it's coming from here," I said, digging through my backpack.

"No, I'm pretty sure it's here," she said, holding up a travel purse.

I held up my passport pouch, also buzzing, and we exchanged quizzical glances. Opening them, we pulled out the slim phones Lava had given us. We had forgotten they were there.

"Hello?" "Hello?" we answered simultaneously, hearing each other as if we were on a conference call.

"Voice match indicates Tom Locke and Jennifer Lin," said a serious voice.

Jen paused, thinking about whether to respond. Not me.

"Affirmative," I said.

Jen shot me a glance saying: *What the heck are you doing?*

My expression read: *Hey, Lava gave us this phone. It's probably OK.* But she shook her head in dumbfounded amazement.

"This is a secure line," said the voice. "Lava, Tye, and their entire team went missing outside of Vienna twenty-six hours ago. We need help investigating what happened, and a possible rescue mission. We are critically low on available personnel right now. Are you available to assist? It's urgent."

Jen's face screamed: *Wait! Let's think this through like rational adults and arrive at consensual decision.*

"Absolutely! When can you extract us?" I blurted.

Jen glowered at me, her expression saying: *You are totally untrainable, Locke.*

"We already have a seaplane inbound to your location, ETA ninety minutes. It will take you to Fakarava airport, where a jet is on standby."

"Roger," I said, and the phone went dead.

"Tom Locke, don't make me punch you," said Jen, joking. I think.

"Look, honeysuckle, we're built for action and Lava needs our help. He'd do it for us," I added. "Besides, he was right. We'll soon get bored here, all this paradise. Yuck!" I teased. Jen punched me.

"Ow!" I said, although she didn't hit hard. Then she pounced.

"We only have ninety minutes," she said.